The Dwarves of Rahm:
Omens of War

By: Michael K. Falciani

Three Ravens Publishing
Chickamauga, GA USA

The Dwarves of Rahm: Omens of War By Michael K. Falciani
Published by Three Ravens Publishing
threeravenspublishing@gmail.com
P O Box 851, Chickamauga, Ga 30707
https://www.threeravenspublishing.com
Copyright © 2022 by Michael K. Falciani

Credits:
The Dwarves of Rahm: Omens of War By Michael K. Falciani
Cover art by J. F. Posthumus
The Dwarves of Rahm: Omens of War By Michael K. Falciani
/Three Ravens Publishing – 1st edition, 2022

Mass Market Paperback ISBN: 978-1-951768-68-3
Trade Paperback ISBN: 978-1-951768-67-6
Hardback ISBN: 978-1-951768-66-9
Ebook ISBN: 978-1-951768-65-2

Contents

Dedication

This book is dedicated to my daughter Shea, the strongest person I know.

Acknowledgements

My thanks to my editor Laura and my test reader Andy, who continues to give me good advice whether I want to hear it or not. To Jenny R., the first at Three Ravens Publishing to give it a go, and Jennie P. for her wonderful cover art.

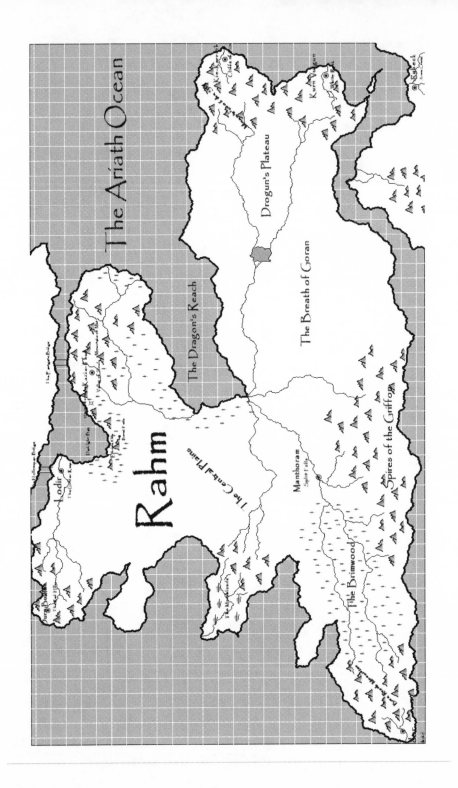

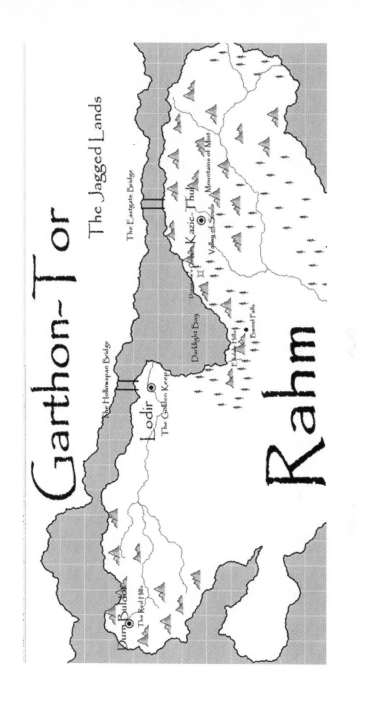

Michael K. Falciani

The Dwarves of Rahm:
Omens of War

Part I
The Stonebreaker's Son

Chapter 1: Monchakka

One month ago

Stonebreakers.

That's what they call us.

We're the bulwark, the best of the best in the dwarven army. We stand on the front lines taking the hardest shots our enemies can dish out, come hell or highwater.

That's our family's heritage.

My father, Arik Ironhenge, is a Stonebreaker to his core. He serves as Supreme General to the dwarven king of Kazic-Thul.

In our clan, it's his way, or no way at all.

Don't get me wrong, father's no fool; he knows other dwarves have their uses. The Ragers are valued because of their unquenchable lust for blood. The War Priests are venerated based on their fighting prowess and their skill with wounds. Hell, even the Bolters are given a grudging respect, knowing they can be counted upon when needed.

Then, we have the Engineers.

My father barely acknowledges their existence—and when he does, it's only to deride them.

'Bunch of lily-livered cowards,' he'd fume. *'Any dwarf that's afraid to go toe-to-toe with the enemy is no kin of mine!'*

As Arik's only son, there has been only one choice for me. I've been trained from birth to be a Stonebreaker.

There's just one problem.

I'm terrible at it.

On the whole, dwarves are a stocky race, built much like the rocks we mine; solid, tough and thoroughly unforgiving. Me? Well, I'm something of an enigma. Taller and leaner than my kinfolk, I stand out for all the wrong reasons. While not a complete weakling, I lack the compact strength of my brethren, especially when it comes to holding the front lines in battle.

It isn't all bad, at least, I don't think so. Lanky as I am, I'm one of the swiftest dwarves in the kingdom. With these long legs, I can outrun anyone in our clan. Furthermore, our battle strategists tell me that I've shown a keen mind for tactics—a real student of war.

My father, being the way he is, heard none of it.

"You don't get respect running about delivering messages," he'd growl. "It's earned in battle!"

For me, it was Stonebreaker or nothing.

In the spring of my nineteenth year, everything changed.

My father was leading a division of dwarves, some eight hundred strong, to the Grimdale Mines.

That's when the raging horde attacked.

Boiling out of the mountains, several thousand wildly screaming orcs and goblins swarmed my father's force.

Seeing how precarious his position was, the general set up was a hasty defense and called for his fastest runner to carry a message to the king.

Ironically, that meant me.

"Tell King Helfer we are besieged," he said grimly. "We'll hold on as long as we can, however, without reinforcements…," he didn't finish his sentence. Even a soldier as inexperienced as I was could see the division was doomed.

"Yes, General," I answered, pressing my lips together somberly.

"Go," he snapped, "and hurry back lad. When the fighting begins, I want you on the front line, right at my side. Honor will be ours!"

I nodded once and turned away. I didn't give a damn about his honor. I just wanted my father and his company to live. I knew getting aid to the division was of paramount importance. I blitzed my way past the horde's advance scouts just as they closed their trap on my father's division.

Chancing a look back, I saw how dire his position was. Surrounded on three sides by the sallowskins, my father was backed into a corner with nowhere to run. There were some natural fortifications at the base of the cliffs where a few boulders had fallen through the years; but those, I knew, wouldn't be enough.

It was only a matter of time.

I turned and ran, focusing my efforts on returning to the garrison as quickly as possible, some twelve miles distant.

Two hours before dusk, I staggered into the keep and made my report to the king.

Sadly, it was not the only piece of bad news he received.

Our enemies had had a busy winter. The yellow skinned vermin were attacking dwarves up and down our lands. Third company, over by Dunhill, had been decimated on their way to the fortress at Snowpeak. They returned with fewer than fifty survivors. A shipment of wheat from the winter fields had been set upon by yet another horde, with nearly a third of its defenders slain. One by one, runners came in, each with a disaster to report.

With the kingdom in a state of pandemonium, his majesty couldn't muster enough forces to save everyone.

"The General is no mean soldier," he said to me, when I asked what message I should carry upon my return. "I cannot risk more lives to save him. If he can hold out for a week, I may be able to dispatch aid. As things stand now, I'm calling all available warriors to gather here and help those we can."

I felt my chest go cold. Father didn't have a week. He'd be lucky to last a day.

"I understand sire," I responded, numb at the finality of his decision.

"You don't have to go back," the king said, not unkindly. "One soldier won't sway the balance in his favor. I've no wish to see you die in vain. The General would understand."

"No sire, he wouldn't," I disagreed, my heart dropping into my boots. Bowing swiftly, I left the war hall in a daze, stunned at the king's words.

That was the day I discovered destiny has a funny way of sneaking up on you. There I was, tromping down the corridor, uncertain of what I should do, when destiny chose that exact moment to intervene.

"You Arik's lad?" a voice asked from off to my left.

I looked over and spotted a dwarf, trim like me, standing a finger's width shorter than I did. He was leaning against a carved statue of the dwarven Highgod, Goran, standing in the full light of the setting sun. Though the dwarf carried at least twice my years, his green eyes sparked with the vitality of youth.

"Aye," I grunted, wondering who he was. "I'm Monchakka Ironhenge."

The dwarf reached under his leather jerkin and pulled out a white, clay pipe. "Ashten Raine," he said, in a manner of introduction. "Captain of the Gray Company."

Despite the concern I had for my father, I cocked one of my eyebrows in surprise.

The Gray Company was...*legendary,* that wasn't the right word. More like...*infamous.* A group of mercenaries who worked for the highest bidder. Professional, yes, but loyal only unto themselves. Thirty of the roughest bunch of dwarves you ever laid eyes on.

Every one of them, an Engineer.

I nodded in acknowledgement, curious as to why I'd captured his attention.

Ashten withdrew a small pouch from his pocket. "The finest leaf this side of the Arendell River," he said, expertly packing his pipe.

"Can I...help you with something?" I asked, irritated at the delay.

If I'd upset him with my tone, he hid it well. Instead, he smiled through his thick brown beard and lit his pipe using a magnifying glass to capture the light of the sun. "No, lad," he said, as the embers flared. "I was thinking I might try saving the general."

My face must have betrayed the confusion I felt, because Ashten's smile broadened. "Dozens of times in the past the general has risked his arse to save dwarven lives. I'd be a poor excuse for a kinsman if I missed this opportunity to return the favor."

My heart leapt at his words. This was the last thing I'd expected. A smile sprang to life on my face but died a quick death moments later.

"The king has ordered every dwarf available to gather and await his directive," I frowned. "He'll not risk you for the general's division."

Ashten laughed in genuine humor, stroking the brown braids of his beard. "I don't take orders from the crown," he answered, with a hint of sarcasm. "Helfer hoards his gold like a maiden protects her virtue. Till he starts paying, the company and I go where we please. In this case, we have a mind to save the general."

My chest swelled with hope, until another thought hit me like a kick to the stomach. "You work for pay?"

"I do," he replied, blowing smoke through his smile.

My face hardened with determination. "I don't have much; but, whatever the cost—I'll pay it."

"Will you now?" he asked, his smile fading. "It's unwise to bargain without first knowing the terms."

"I meant what I said," I snapped firmly. "Whatever the cost, I'll pay it!"

Ashten puffed thoughtfully on the stem of his pipe and exhaled slowly.

"All right," he said affably. "We'll discuss the price after the deed's done, so long as you agree to deliver. For now, we'd best prepare."

"We?" I blinked in surprise.

He gave a snort. "Aye! Did you not think you'd be invited? You've firsthand knowledge of the terrain and you've escaped once from the sallowskins already. A lone runner, racing through hostile country, living by your wits—why wouldn't I ask you to join us? I want you to scout and, if the need arises, to fight alongside my company."

"But…I'm trained as a Stonebreaker," I protested.

Ashten smiled. "Nobody's perfect."

Within the hour I had exchanged my heavy suit of banded armor for a cuirass of boiled leather. It was a shade loose around the waist and sported scorch marks along the backside, but otherwise seemed serviceable. Next, I handed over my pitted battle-axe and reinforced iron shield. In return, I was given a sturdy knife, its curved blade ten inches in length, along with a black hafted hammer—more a tool than a weapon.

Finally, I was handed a rifle. Measuring some three-and-a-half feet long, it fit my hands perfectly. This wasn't some ceremonial piece made for hanging over the mantle, but a true instrument of war. As I studied the weapon, one of the Gray Company, a grizzled veteran wearing a patch over her left eye, paused, and watched me closely.

"Here." She unslung a worn leather bandolier from over her shoulder. "Since you're taking my place tomorrow—thirty shots of lead, laddie. Make 'em count."

I noticed her left leg was wrapped in blood stained bandages.

"Damn Sallie ambush," she explained, seeing my look. "Goblin Archer got off a lucky shot before I could lay him low. Haven't had time to see a priest yet."

"My thanks," I answered, with a quick nod of appreciation. Taking the bandoleer, I dropped it over my shoulder.

The elder she-dwarf nodded and limped away.

"Wait," I called out. "What's your name?"

She tossed me a wink over her shoulder. "I'll tell you when next we meet."

The she-dwarf turned the corner and limped out of sight.

At that moment, Captain Raine strode up to me, accompanied by a fierce looking female. "This is Ghost." He nodded at the newcomer. Her dark eyes were mirrors of my own. "She's my second in command. You two will be walking point together when we depart. I've asked her to give you a few tips about your new gear. I know there's little time, but I thought it best you learn something about that rifle. We don't want you accidentally blowing your hand off tomorrow on the road."

I couldn't tell if he was joking or not.

I spent the following hour debriefing Ashten and his other two lieutenants.

The first was an older dwarf, tall like me, with a face so wrinkled, it appeared dried by too many days in the sun. His name was Badderson Sarl, but everyone called him Bad. He was missing the pinky finger on his left hand and had a tiny barrel of whiskey the size of my fist tucked inside his graying beard, just under the chin. Armed with a sour disposition, Bad knew more about explosive concoctions than anyone else in the company. He peered at me from beneath a pair of thick goggles, but said nothing, other than to ask the captain an occasional question.

The second lieutenant was so small, I nearly mistook him for a child. I was never told his proper name, but Ashten referred to him as Ratchet. Nearly as young as I, Ratchet had a forked blonde beard and any number of tools hanging from the belt around his waist. He wore an overly large conical helmet with a wrench latched in place above his right ear. Young as he was, Ratchet was one of the finest tinkers in the entire kingdom. He oversaw maintenance on the mechanical turrets the company employed, along with the other technological gadgets his squad utilized. Ratchet had a nervous habit of twitching his nose every few minutes, but he listened quietly, watching with steady blue eyes.

Ghost was away on some errand, while the four of us pored over a map highlighting the area where my father's division was trapped. Ashten was meticulous in his questions, asking me things Arik would have considered trivial. What terrain covered each part of the valley? Was it made up of grass, dirt, trees or other types of foliage? I endured at least an hour of questioning before he was satisfied.

Long after sunset I was dismissed. I thought I'd get a bite to eat and then grab some shut eye, as the company was set to leave before dawn the next day. However, Ghost hunted me down and spent over an hour instructing me on the use of the rifle. Her lesson included how to load and reload the weapon, along with teaching me its basic care and maintenance. The dark eyed dwarf grudgingly let me squeeze off a few rounds, all the while tutoring me on the fundamentals of riflery.

She spent a handful of minutes going over the various types of grenades the company utilized and under what circumstances to use them.

At the end of our time together, she looked at me and snorted to herself. "Maybe, just maybe, you'll be an asset tomorrow."

She handed me two metallic spheres—shrapnel grenades she'd called them—and walked away.

"Wait!" I called out, holding the cold iron orbs like they were live vipers. "When do I use these?"

"When things go to bloody hell," she called back, ominously.

Not exactly the confidence builder I was hoping for.

Staring at the grenades, I attached them carefully to my weapon belt, praying they wouldn't explode in my face.

Needless to say, I didn't sleep very well that night.

It was at least four hours till dawn when Ghost jostled me awake. Eyes sandy with exhaustion, I climbed out of the uncomfortable cot and set about gathering my things. I secured the weapons first, triple checking the grenades to make sure their pins were in place. My backpack was laden with enough food for two days. Someone had placed a coil of rope and three flasks of oil in the pack, along with a full canteen, a telescope, extra ammunition, and a watertight box containing flint and steel. Hardly standard issue for a Stonebreaker, but common enough, I guessed, for an Engineer.

After strapping the bandolier in place, I threw on the smoky gray cloak Ghost had given me the night before. Lastly, I hauled the backpack over my shoulders and took a moment to study my companions.

Say what you will about Engineers, but those of the Gray Company were steely eyed and ready. Most carried more gear than I did. In addition to their packs, they shouldered turrets and tech equipment of every shape and description. Each bristled with weaponry in the form of knives, pistols, hammers, and rifles. Only Ghost was as lightly burdened as I. Slight as she was, I wasn't surprised. She *did*, however, carry a four-foot rifle slung over her back—the longest such weapon I'd seen.

Once they'd finished packing, the thirty of us exited the barracks in an orderly fashion and rolled out the front gate. The four guards stationed there, Stonebreakers all, shook their heads and turned away.

So much for the fellowship of dwarves.

That's how we began our trek under the stars, on a mission to save the general.

"Stay close and move quietly," I heard Ghost mutter in my ear from near the front of the column. "As sure as the sun rises in the east, the sallowbacked sons-a-bitches will have a scouting force out looking for easy meat. It's our job to find *them* before they find *us.*"

I smiled despite the situation. Something I noted about Ghost; she didn't mince words with anyone, not even the captain.

For two hours we moved as quietly as thirty heavily laden dwarves could. Quickly at first, our pace slowed after the first hour. Ghost and I were up front, fifty yards ahead of the rest of the company. As luck would have it, it fell on me to discover a group of our enemies.

The sallow-skinned species make for a motley crew of hardy opponents. Tough as nails and as nasty as they come, the orc race is all savage strength and power. Goblins, on the other hand, are infused with equal parts magic and mischief. Crafty bastards, they numbered in the tens—if not the hundreds—of thousands. Both races have contested with my people for centuries and, working together, form a fearsome enemy.

They make for terrible scouts though.

I could hear a band of them some thirty paces away, arguing amongst themselves, oblivious to my presence. Out of nowhere, Ghost rose up from the ground next to me, her eyes fixed on the sounds in front of us.

"What's your call, Stonebreaker?" she asked quietly.

I paused, caught by surprise. "You're asking me?"

"Aye," she nodded. "Let's see what Arik taught you."

I blinked once, considering the alternatives. "How many are there?" I asked.

"No more than fifty," she replied. "It's an advance force, sent to waylay a unit like ours and warn the main army ahead."

We could have gone around the group and left them behind with no one the wiser. This held momentary appeal, as tackling an advance party of sallowskins was not our primary objective. However, leaving them alive would mean they could fall on the next company of dwarves that came this way. There was also the issue of being caught between this group and the main force that had trapped my father. If we wanted to beat a hasty retreat, we'd need to have a clear path back to the garrison.

"We eliminate them," I said, more to myself than to Ghost.

The corner of her mouth curled in a smile.

"My sentiments exactly."

I discovered some interesting things about my comrades during that skirmish.

For a bunch of lightly armed and armored warriors that usually deal death from a distance, I was amazed at how well the Engineers fared in hand-to-hand combat.

Captain Raine gave the order for a silent attack. That meant no rifles, pistols, grenades, or turrets.

"And absolutely no explosions," he raised an eyebrow, with a long look toward Bad.

The old grenadier's shoulders drooped in resignation as he yanked out the largest spanner he owned.

Ghost led her squad of sharpshooters past our enemies, making certain not to alert the sallowskins to our presence. I was left with Ashten and the main force, who would strike from the front and drive any survivors toward Ghost and her dozen.

Our attack commenced as the pale light of the moon crept from behind a ghostly cloud, bathing us momentarily in silver. We moved quickly, with less noise than a dandelion's pappus billowing in the wind.

Our adversaries didn't know what hit them.

Using knives and hammers, the only sounds that broke the silence in those first few seconds were the meaty smacks of metal striking flesh. More than a half score of the enemy died in our initial attack.

One of them, a huge orc warrior wielding an iron warclub, took Ratchet's knife in the stomach and let out a roar of pain. The sound alerted the rest of the camp that something was amiss. Drawing my knife from the chest of a goblin, I took careful aim and hurled my hammer toward the wounded creature's temple. I heard an audible crack of dwarven steel striking bone. I watched in grim satisfaction as the orc's head snapped backward, his neck broken.

Despite the warning cry from the orc, it was already too late. Like wraiths rising from a graveyard, the Gray Company raced through the enemy camp killing without mercy. A handful of sallowskins that were out of our reach had enough sense to make a mad dash for safety. They were summarily impaled and bludgeoned by Ghost and her crew.

Before I could catch my breath, the battle was over. The attack had been executed perfectly. Not a single dwarf had suffered so much as a scratch.

I couldn't help but wonder at the efficiency of this company. Thirty Engineers, a group as ragged as any I'd encountered, had wiped out nearly forty of the enemy in less than a minute with nary a sound. As I looked around in wonder, I caught Ghost staring at me. She picked something up from the ground and sidled her way over.

"Nice throw," she said, brushing a wisp of dark hair from her eyes. She handed me my hammer and turned away.

A memory, long buried, stirred. For just a moment, when she'd brushed her hair away from her face, I felt as though I'd met her before.

"We've a few miles to go, lad," Ashten said from behind me, interrupting my reverie. "Get back up there with Ghost and keep your wits about you. This may not be the only group we have to contend with."

Chapter 2: Reckoning

Whether it was luck, or overconfidence on our enemy's part, we covered the rest of the distance without mishap. It was more than an hour until dawn when we arrived at the Grimdale Cliffs. The valley was covered in shadows, save for the dancing lights of distant campfires. I could see thousands of orcs and goblins surrounding the knot of dwarves trapped at the base of the escarpment. On the northernmost flank I could make out several machines of war in the light of a waning bonfire. I counted a half-dozen catapults and one rudimentary trebuchet. The horde must have rolled them out of the mountains last evening, else they would have already pounded my father's division to dust.

Ashten pulled Ghost and me aside, waving for his lieutenants to join us.

"All right, we've gotten this far," he began, "Let's see if our luck holds. Bad," he continued, looking at the wrinkled dwarf. "Take six of your squad and set up some fireworks along the northern flank. I want those war machines reduced to ash before our primary attack. That should cause the distraction we need. Wear the clothing we took off the Sallies, but for the love of Andovar, keep to the shadows. None of you are ugly enough to pass for a goblin—not even you!"

Bad snorted softly with laughter.

"Tell Kyrin to prepare the field in front of us in case we need to leave in a hurry," Ashten leaned in, getting back to business. "Have Sterns and Higgs gather the extra oil and assist her."

"You want them seared, blackened, or charred?" Bad asked, rubbing his hands together.

"You decide," the captain answered with a grunt, "but keep your squad's noise to a whisper. All it takes is one dropped wrench and we're cooked."

Bad nodded and shuffled off.

"Ratchet, you and yours get those turrets ready," Ashten said to his tinker. "If it comes to any kind of drawn-out fight, their operation will mean the difference between life and death."

"You want them in front of Kyrin's field or where we stand now?" Ratchet asked, swinging his head toward the field in question.

"Put the majority behind it, but leave four or five of the more mobile ones in front to support Ghost's group—and we better have Donia make a keg of her brew. I want it up there," he said, pointing at a group of boulders nearby. "That'll be our fallback position if things turn against us."

"She'll be cutting it close," Ratchet's voice rose in pitch, his nose twitching rapidly. "Donia needs at least two hours to prepare it properly."

"Then tell her straight away," Ashten replied. "Stix can help, if you can spare her."

Ratchet put a knuckle to his forehead and slipped away without another word.

"As for you," he said, turning to Ghost and me. "You two have the most difficult task."

He sat down on a rock and took out a piece of parchment from inside his jerkin. Using a flat, metallic plate drawn from his pack, Ashten began scrawling on the parchment with a quill dipped in ink that appeared from some hidden pocket on his person.

"You need to sneak past the enemy and deliver this to the General," he stated without looking up.

I frowned in confusion. "We should be able to accomplish that without difficulty—most of the sallowskins are asleep."

Next to me, Ghost snorted and shook her head. "Getting in isn't the hard part," she said without humor. "It's convincing the general our plan is a good one that will prove difficult. He's the cog that needs grease in this little operation, else the whole thing falls apart."

We made our way past the sleeping horde with relative ease; the few that were awake weren't watching for anyone moving closer to the dwarves, only those trying to escape. Our disguises stood up under any cursory looks we may have received, and before I knew it, we were through the enemy encampment.

As I walked past, I could see that dozens of dwarves had been slain since I'd left. Most had been hauled back to the edge of the dwarven defenses, though a few were still laying out in the open where they'd fallen in battle. Hundreds of enemy corpses littered the ground— more than three times the number of our dead. With their numerical superiority, the blackbloods could afford those losses.

We could not.

I took off my helmet upon our arrival, nodding my way past the dwarven guards. Ghost hung back from me a bit, keeping herself out of sight. It didn't take long for my father to make his presence known.

"What, in the name of Goran, are you wearing?" he cursed, stomping over to me. "An Engineer's rig? Take that off and put on your armor! Where the hell are my reinforcements?"

"Father, please," I said quietly, leaning my rifle against a large stone. "I bring word from the king. Dwarves have been attacked all over the realm. He could not send aid, not with our forces scattered as they are."

My father's eyes dropped to the ground. "I feared as much," he muttered under his breath. Raising his gaze, he flashed me a look of pride.

"Then we will die a hero's death," he said proudly, a grim resolve in his voice. "Come lad, find a suit of mail from one of our fallen brethren. We'll show this piss-colored rabble the might of Clan Ironhenge."

With those words, he began to walk away.

I knew I couldn't let him.

"No," I said simply.

He stopped and turned, looking at me coldly. "What did you say?"

I stepped forward. "I said no, General. We don't have to die here today. The king could not send aid—but others have volunteered in his stead."

I watched as my father's eyes darkened in the torchlight. "Who?" he hissed.

Knowing what his reaction would be, I braced myself.

"The Gray Company you hard headed dolt!" I heard Ghost snap, as she stormed past me.

The expression in my father's eyes changed from dark anger to a blazing fury as he advanced forward, stopping only inches from her face. "What in the *hell* are you doing here?" he demanded. "Are you the reason Monchakka is dressed in these coward's clothing?"

"Shut your bleating mouth!" she snarled back, giving as good as she got. "If you had half a brain in that cavity you call a head, you'd not be in this predicament."

"What's that supposed to mean?" he barked at her, ready to explode.

"It means, if you'd had an Engineer to scout, you could have avoided this ambush!" she shouted back. "Instead, you're too arrogant to think anyone but your precious Stonebreakers are worthy enough to fight at your side."

I saw him clench his fists and knew they would come to blows. Ghost did not shrink back—instead, she raised her chin, daring him to strike.

"That's enough, both of you," I snapped, stepping between them. "We've no time for this!"

Reaching under my cuirass, I pulled forth a folded parchment.

"This is a plan concocted by Ashten Raine, the leader of the Gray Company," I said, looking at my father. "Follow it, and we can all escape from here with minimal losses. Otherwise, the crows will be picking over our corpses by mid-morning. The kingdom is under attack, it needs its General. If you and your division are lost here, our people will die with you. We need you father—don't throw away your life because of your pride. I only ask that you follow Ashten's plan."

It was the first time in my life I'd ever stood up to anybody. I think the shock of it gave the General pause. He stared at me for a long moment, before snatching the parchment out of my hands.

"When this is over *lad*, you and I will have a reckoning," he hissed, without looking at the parchment. "And you, Aurora," he snapped at Ghost, "will leave Kazic-Thule forever."

"I don't take orders from you anymore, Arik," she spat defiantly. "I'd just as soon leave you to die here along with your stupidity, but the lad here wants you to live. Lucky for you, he's worth a battalion of your soldiers, else I'd leave you here to rot!"

Turning around, Ghost strode back the way she'd come, leaving me gaping in astonishment. "Follow the plan you hard-headed jackass," she called out behind her, "else you're all dead in the valley."

Looking at me, the general spoke, his voice shaking in rage. "Come Monchakka, else you'll *never* be a Stonebreaker," he growled, crumpling the parchment in his fist.

"No," I answered quietly.

"What did you say to me?" he hissed.

I turned to him; my mind made up.

"I said no," I repeated.

He made to speak again, but a raised hand from me stopped him.

"Do you know why Ashten volunteered to come for you?" I asked. "He said, 'Dozens of times in the past, the General has risked his arse to save dwarven lives. I'd be a poor excuse for a kinsman if I missed this opportunity to return the favor.'"

I paused, letting those words sink in. "He and his company respect you, father, that's why they've come. They wouldn't let you die here in this valley, not if they could stop it from happening. You are worth more than that."

I reached up and put my hand on his broad shoulder.

"I'm proud of you father," I continued, giving him a smile. "Proud to be your son, because Ashten is right. You always give of yourself."

For the first time since I'd known him, he was listening, truly listening to what I had to say.

"I know you don't care for Engineers. They're not what you consider, 'true dwarves,' to be. While I've spent less than a day in their company, and I can tell you this; they are brave, strong, and as loyal to the dwarven cause as you or I. You've always taught me that actions speak louder than words—well, look around. Your friend, the king, didn't dispatch a single soldier to come to your aid. He tried to dissuade *me* from returning. No one else is here—only the Gray Company. Their actions speak volumes as to who they are—just as you taught me."

I reached out and took the crumpled parchment from his hand, smoothing it out as best I could. "Look at Ashten's plan," I urged him. "He's certain it will work."

My father's eyes flicked down at the parchment, and then came to rest back on me.

"What of you?" he asked quietly, still smoldering. "Will you not stay and fight by my side?"

With a sigh, I picked up the rifle I'd been given. "I cannot stay. I'm sorry father, but the company needs me more than you do."

"You think these *Engineers* can be trusted?" he scoffed with a sneer.

I shrugged, "All I know is if you don't act, none of us will leave this valley alive. Ghost told me that you and your division are the most important cog in this machine. We can't do it without you. Give them a chance—they may well surprise us all. It's your choice father, but I trust them as much as I trust you."

With that, I ran after Ghost, catching up to her in moments.

"Aurora?" I asked.

"Not anymore," she fumed. "That was my clan name before my brother banished me."

I paused, stunned at this new information.

"Your brother?" I asked, grabbing her by the wrist.

"Yes," she answered, ripping her arm out of my hand. "That idiot general is my elder brother, Arik. I was once his sister, Aurora Ironhenge. He wouldn't let me near you as a child. Heaven forbid you follow in *my* footsteps."

She placed the orc helm she carried back on her head as we approached the enemy lines. "We need to get back," she snapped.

My mind raced. Only a deep rift between the siblings could have caused Aurora's exile, as clan members were notoriously loyal. Despite her anger, it was clear she still cared for him.

I ceased my musings in the face of the upcoming danger. Our family's drama could wait.

I put my orc helmet on and strode after the only person I'd ever seen defy my father's command.

Upon our return, Ghost made her report to Ashten while I waited with her squad of sharpshooters. They were a close-knit group and spoke quietly to one another, ignoring my presence completely. That suited me fine, as my mind was still reeling from the morning's revelations.

Sunrise was but a quarter hour away. Already, I could see light beginning to glow beneath the horizon. Most of the horde was still asleep, though a few camps were beginning to stir.

When Ghost returned, she took her squad to the southwestern side of the enemy encampment using the boulders and underbrush as cover. She left us in strategic positions a few paces apart from one another. I was the first one placed, along with a young sniper named Kora. She had black hair, a pretty face, and seemed none too pleased about being saddled with me.

From our position in the underbrush I could make out hundreds of enemy tents in the pre-dawn gloom. Each was made from neatly sewn animal hides. The closest was less than forty yards away. There was no movement from the inside the tents, but I kept my eyes open for any sign of trouble.

"You should close your left eye," Kora whispered to me.

"What?" I asked, startled at her voice.

"Your left eye," she said again. "Keep it closed, Stony."

"Why?" I asked, glancing over at her.

"It helps maintain night vision," she explained, looking at me like I was the biggest lummox in the kingdom.

I pressed my lips together in a grimace but said nothing.

'Stony,' she'd called me, short for Stonebreaker. I let out a sigh. No matter where I went, it seemed I struggled to fit in.

"It shouldn't be long now," she muttered, craning her head around the boulder in front of her.

"What are we waiting for?" I dared to ask.

She shook her head and frowned. "What do you think?" she scoffed. "We're waiting for Bad's distraction."

"How was I supposed to know that?" I snipped back, feeling a touch of embarrassment.

She paused and turned back to the tent. "I thought the captain informed you when you spoke with him earlier," she explained with a sniff.

"He didn't tell me any specifics," I replied, a bit shortly. "I don't even know what we are doing out here."

I could *feel* her eyes rolling in the darkness next to me.

"I always have to break in the newcomers," she murmured under her breath.

"What?" I asked, getting annoyed.

"Nothing," she mumbled, scanning the encampment with her open eye. "When Bad's distraction goes off, things will get busy here in a hurry. Whatever you do, don't shoot. Wait for the Sallies to rush away. The last thing we want is the horde looking for us here in the open. Once a large number have committed to the northern camp, we'll open fire."

I waited a few moments, digesting her words. "How will I know when to attack?" I asked cautiously.

She sniffed again.

"You won't; wait for Ghost. When you hear the report of her sniper rifle, you'll know."

I had another question, but I didn't want to sound more ignorant than I already felt.

"Spit it out," Kora snapped.

"What?" I asked, wondering if she'd read my mind.

"I know you have more questions," she answered, "and I hate waiting. Besides, poking fun at you helps pass the time."

I knew she was teasing me, but I asked my question anyway. "Are there any of the enemies I should target in particular? Or should I just blast away?"

I saw the beginnings of a smile work its way across her face.

"I'm charged with finding goblin Shamans," she answered quietly. "Though our squad tries to focus on any caster we see…Archers as well. You're new. If you hit *anything* with sallow skin, I'll be impressed."

That was enough information for me, and I really didn't feel like talking to her anymore.

Dawn arrived and the enemy encampment rose with it. Quickly I checked my weapons and ammunition. The grenades Ghost had given me were still hanging from my belt, along with the knife and hammer. I saw Kora place several bullets at the ready on the boulder in front of her. I mimicked her actions, earning a satisfactory nod.

Now all we had to…

A deafening explosion rocked the northernmost encampment, waking everyone in both armies. One of the catapults nearly disintegrated under that destructive force. A massive plume of fire and smoke billowed into the sky, briefly illuminating the entire valley.

Seconds later, five successive detonations went off, each louder than the last. The wood and metal of the remaining catapults were torn to pieces. The trebuchet collapsed, reduced to nothing more than burning embers. To say the horde was taken by surprise would be an understatement. Fires flared up at the edge of the northern encampment, as dozens of smaller explosions went off, burning both tents and flesh alike. Screams of pain and rage echoed through the valley, sure evidence that Bad and his crew had commenced with their attack.

I glanced at Kora, who was smiling, shaking her head in wonder. I realized at that moment, standing under the glow of dwarven pyrotechnics, that she was an exceptionally beautiful female.

"What does he put in his gunpowder?" she mused to herself, still smiling. She caught me staring at her like a moon-eyed calf and cuffed me on the side of the head.

"Stay focused," she hissed, as the smile ran away from her face. "Bad and his squad are pulling the army to them. We need to weaken the forces here so your big bad daddy can ram through."

I nodded sheepishly and turned back toward the encampment in front of us.

Our enemy's response was faster than I'd expected, though highly disorganized. Hundreds of orcs and goblins ran streaming from the camp located on the southwest side of the valley. Scores of creatures scurried past, some passing only a few yards in front of us.

As the seconds turned to minutes, a massive orc, a black iron chain wrapped tightly around his chest, emerged from a large tent to our right. I saw him gaze north, and then turn toward the boulders we were crouched behind.

A single rifle shot cracked through the crisp morning air.

The orc staggered back a step and dropped to his knees before falling bodily upon his face.

Ghost had entered the fray.

A rapid staccato of gunfire could be heard off to my right as other members of her squad let loose. Next to me, Kora snapped off a shot and I saw a goblin archer drop instantly.

"That's one," she muttered in satisfaction.

At the same moment, a second goblin, this one dressed in ritualistic garb, exited the tent and stared at Kora's hiding place.

A Shaman.

"Bloody hell," I heard Kora curse, as she frantically reloaded her weapon.

The Shaman lowered its staff and moved its hands rhythmically, gathering its mystic power.

There was no time to lose.

I shouldered my rifle, hearing the echo of Ghost's words from the previous evening. Take aim and exhale; pause halfway through. Easy on the trigger. Too hard and your shot will go wide. Squeeze it slowly, and your bullet will fly true. Once you're ready, fire away.

I fired away.

A high-pitched burst of gunfire reverberated in my ear. It was immediately followed by a jolt of the rifle's recoil against my shoulder. I watched as the lead bullet tore through the throat of the shaman, spraying dark blood in a fine mist, killing it where it stood.

Dazed, I glanced over at Kora who looked at me, stunned.

"Reload, dummy!" she barked, aiming, taking out another target. "One lucky shot doesn't make you a ruddy marksman!"

For the next few minutes, the squad fought, killing scores of the black-blooded creatures, while ducking, bobbing and weaving behind whatever cover they could find. Ghost had taken out their squad commander, leaving the sallowskins in our vicinity with no immediate leadership. Finally, one of the orcs got savvy to our game and led an entire company toward our position. Seconds later, Ghost appeared next to us along with the rest of her squad, the enemy hot on their heels.

"Fall back!" she screamed, as a handful of arrows sliced through the air over our heads. "Get to the turrets and we'll re-engage!"

I grabbed the pack I'd set on the ground, turned and ran. Retreat was not something a Stonebreaker would do so readily, but under the circumstances, it made perfect sense to me.

I chanced a look back toward my father's encampment hoping to see his forces advancing.

My heart sank.

There was no sign of movement.

We sprinted nearly one hundred yards through the underbrush until I saw five turrets set up in front of us.

"Two by two flanks," Ghost barked, breathing heavily, reloading her rifle. "Ratchet!" she yelled, looking for the tinker.

"I'm here," he said, popping up from behind one of the turrets, wrench in hand.

"What have you got in store?" she asked, wiping sweat from her brow.

"I've got a tri-foil accelerator hidden in the brush ahead," he answered, excitedly. "I had an issue with charging it initially, but the primary discharge valve...,"

"I don't need a technology lesson!" she snapped, shaking her head. "Just make sure it works!"

Kora grabbed me by the collar and shoved me toward the end of the line. "Reload and get ready for more," she ordered, panting next to me. "Don't do anything stupid, Stony. It's a wonder you're still alive the way you fight with your head sticking out all over the place."

She pulled out her water skin and drank from it deeply. "Damn Sallies never quit," she muttered, looking in the direction from which we'd just run. "By the Trine, here they come."

The turrets, each manned by a tinker from Ratchet's squad, started booming away as the swiftest of our enemies came within range.

"Save your ammo," Ghost yelled, her voice steady. "Let the turrets do their work. Ratchet, be ready," she snapped, her eyes never leaving the approaching sallowskins.

A handful of goblins fell to the repeated sound of dwarven technology. A pair of archers stood outside the range of the turrets, but a quick salvo from our marksmen ended the threat in a hurry. More and more of the blackbloods charged forward, until over fifty orcs and goblins were in range. The turrets fired nonstop, smoke streaming out of their exhaust ports. Undeterred, the enemy continued their advance.

"Now, Ratchet!" thundered Ghost, shooting a leather clad Orc Ravager at point blank range. The creature fell backward onto one of its fellows, bellowing in agony.

The tinker hopped behind a boulder and threw his switch with a maniacal laugh. "Die, blackbloods, die!" he screamed. A massive surge of energy hummed across the field.

And nothing happened.

"Goddammit Ratchet!" Ghost screamed, as scores of the enemy raced forward, now only a few yards away. "All hell's breaking loose! Switch that thing on!"

Suddenly, I knew what I needed to do.

I reached down to my belt and ripped both grenades free. Pulling their pins, I whispered a prayer to Goran and let fly.

The grenades bounced off a gigantic orc's hastily raised shield and I saw the creature's face twist in confusion some fifteen yards away.

"You crazy son-of-a…everybody, get down!" Kora screamed, dragging me to the ground.

That's when my grenades went off.

A metallic burst shot outward in all directions killing, maiming and wounding anything that moved in a thirty-foot radius. Yelps of pain and surprise could be heard from the enemy, located only a few feet away. When the dust settled, there was a foot deep crater where the grenades had exploded.

"Are you *insane?*" Kora screamed in my ear, looking up in the aftermath. "By the gods, you could have killed us all! I said don't do anything stupid, you idiot, meat headed Stonebreaker!"

In retrospect, I could see her point. The grenades were deadly projectiles and could have injured our fellow dwarves. However, they *had* managed to stem the tide, and that's what we needed in the moment.

Not that anyone thanked me.

"Got it!" Ratchet cried in glee, as he flipped the switch again.

A low hum emanated from the underbrush in front of us, and this time, blue bolts of lightning shot outward in every direction.

If my grenades had slowed them, then Ratchets tri…whatever accelerators, stopped our enemies in their tracks. Dozens of sallowskins were electrocuted, while the survivors bolted for safer ground.

"Sorry about the delay," Ratchet apologized, looking over the crisped corpses, smoke rising from each. "One of the binary cortex wires came loose…"

"Save it," barked Ghost, her eyes turning to me.

"You said all hell had broken loose," I explained with a shrug, brushing dirt from my leggings. "What did you expect me to do, stand here and let everyone die? Besides, it worked, didn't it?"

Ghost just shook her head and started muttering under her breath, something about greenhorns.

"Next phase," she said, regaining her focus. "Fall back to Kyrin's field. Stick to the outskirts unless you want to roast with the Sallies. Ratchet, you and your squad get the turrets moved. We're going to need everything we've got."

Again, we retreated, leaving more than a hundred dead in our wake. I looked back toward my father's encampment.

There was still no sign of him.

I cast my eyes downward, my spirits falling.

"Buck up Stony," I heard Kora say. "It's not over yet, unless, of course, Bad lets you near the flamethrower."

I smiled despite my concern. I wasn't sure how I could both *like* Kora and want to kick her at the same time.

We regrouped at the east end of Kyrin's field, taking care to walk along the edge. I don't know what Kyrin had done to it, but it smelled of tar and naphtha.

Ashten was there, along with Bad and his crew. I noted Bad's cuirass was scorched in the exact same spot as mine, making me wonder if he'd been my armor's previous owner.

So far, we'd been lucky. I counted thirty dwarves still standing, though there were a smattering of wounds to go round. I spotted the dark haired she-dwarf named Donia clambering atop a pile of boulders near the entrance of the valley. Finishing her task, she sprinted over and joined the rest of us.

"Brew's a mite underripe, captain," she huffed, "but it'll do."

Ashten nodded curtly and addressed us all. "Anyone see movement from Arik's camp?" he asked, his face like stone. There was soot along his neck, and blood ran from a cut on his cheek.

"I've checked, sir," I answered, not quite able to look him in the eye. "They haven't marched...at least, not that I could see."

Ashten swore under his breath. "We're going to have the entire horde on this little patch of dirt in a few minutes! What the hell is he waiting for?"

I looked at Ghost, who shook her head slightly. I knew she didn't think he'd come.

"You should go," I said, casting my eyes at the entire company. "We won't survive without his help, and I don't know if he'll show in time."

I glanced at Kora, who was staring at me without expression.

"I know the field is soaked with some kind of flammable substance," I continued, swinging my eyes to Ashten. "I'll stay behind and fire it—hold them off—so you and your company can escape. There's no reason any of you should die here. You've fought unbelievably well against incredible odds. I'll stay and buy you time."

I stepped forward and saluted Ashten who was watching me closely. "Thank you for trying, Captain. You and your company are the bravest dwarves I've ever met."

"They're approaching," Ghost reported, licking her lips.

"Go, while you still have time!" I shouted, turning around, running back to the field.

I halted at the line of turrets and slammed a bullet home, surprised to see my hands were steady. Rifle loaded, I yanked the flint and steel out of my pack as the enemy continued their approach from across the field. Striking the flint against my knife, I frantically tried to catch a spark, knowing I was about to die.

"Idiot Stonebreaker," said a voice from behind me.

There was Kora, a frown on her face. "That's not how an Engineer lights a fire," she continued, loading her rifle.

"What are you doing?" I stammered in surprise.

"We're not about to leave you behind," I heard Ghost say from the other side of where I was standing.

At that moment, hundreds of the enemy came pouring onto the field, screaming for dwarven blood.

"*This* is how Engineers light a fire," Ashten muttered, falling in line next to Ghost. He took a red canister from his belt and pulled the pin.

Up and down the line, every member of the Gray Company had come forward, each preparing for battle.

"What are you doing?" I shouted. "You need to save yourselves!"

"No lad," Ghost said, smiling at me. "You're the one worth saving."

She looked at Ashten and her smile turned fierce. "Light it up!" she roared.

Stepping forward, Captain Raine threw his canister into the middle of the field, one chock full of Sallies. A blast of red-hot flame burst from the inside of the canister and the ground underneath the sallowskins erupted.

Scores of the enemy were incinerated in moments as the naphtha drenched area exploded in a blazing inferno. Orcs and goblins howled in agony as they tried vainly to escape the flames.

One minute passed, and the flames continued, roasting everything inside it. Sallowskins were climbing all over one another trying to escape. A couple even ran toward us, yellow flesh burning, the naphtha clinging to their skin. I watched as the dwarfess, Donia, brained one as calmly as if she were striking a tent peg with a mallet.

Another minute passed by, and the flames began to dim. By the end of the third minute, the flames had been reduced to a smolder.

"Get ready," Ashten muttered, palming his last grenade.

Up and down the line, rifles were shouldered, and the turrets set to auto fire; the company had no tricks left to play.

On the other side of the field, hundreds of orcs and goblins, infuriated at the death of so many of their number, prepared to rush our position.

"Aim," the captain shouted, his voice as cool as a mountain spring.

"Good to have known you, Stony," Kora said quietly, touching my shoulder with her hand.

The last of the flames died out, and the enemy surged forward.

"Fire!" Ashten roared, throwing a grenade into the midst of the onrushing horde.

Every turret boomed, and every dwarf shot at the incoming mass. It didn't matter.

I have to give it to the Sallies. Twisted and evil they might be, they fought like they were possessed. I saw one massive orc known as a Chain, take five bullets to the chest and still, he came forward. Hundreds of goblins rushed the field, one already littered with their dead, without batting an eye.

We had no choice but to run.

"Fall back," Ghost shouted as she hauled Ashten to his feet. The captain had taken an arrow to the shoulder, spinning him to the ground.

"Come on Stony!" Kora screamed, letting off one more volley, then sprinted for the rocks behind us.

En masse, the Gray Company ran for their lives, scrambling atop the boulders that would serve as our final defensive position.

I watched as the sallowskins fought their way to the hated turrets, ripping them apart in frustration and anger. Ratchet stood next to me, tears streaming down his face at the wanton destruction of his machinery.

"Push it through," Ashten growled, his teeth clenched in pain.

"Bite down on this love," Ghost replied, placing a wooden branch in Ashten's mouth.

He nodded, as she drove the arrow through his shoulder and out the other side in a burst of warm blood.

"Get me close," Ashten said, his face white with agony.

I noticed a keg of dark ale sitting in a hollow atop the boulders. Several members of the company had gathered around it. Each had been wounded in some way, but now, by some miracle, were healing.

"Donia's brew," Kora explained, sweat dripping down her face.

"You drink it?" I panted, winded from the run.

She shook her head. "Drinking it without distillation will tear your insides apart. The healing is in the fumes."

"I had no idea," I said, impressed once again.

Despite our circumstances, Kora gave me a wicked smile. "Even if we die, the Sallies will be sure to quench their thirst. We'll take a few more before the day is done."

Ghost dragged Ashten over to the keg and he breathed deeply, letting the healing vapors do their work.

"The turrets are destroyed," Bad reported from over his shoulder, watching the horde with a sneer. "Orders Cap'n?"

"We fight," Ashten answered with a grimace, rising to his feet. He yanked a pistol from his belt, stepping forward once more.

"I'm out of bullets," I said quietly to Kora, as I drew my knife and hammer.

She nodded once and loaded her rifle. "I'll cover you Stony."

Smiling ferociously, Bad ripped the tiny barrel from under his beard and guzzled a huge gulp in his mouth. Taking up a fiery brand, he held it in front of his lips, ready to immolate anyone of the enemy who got too close in flames borne of whiskey.

The last of the turrets were destroyed and the Sallies eyed us for a moment, knowing we could not escape. Like a dam bursting, they ran forward, howling in rage.

"BAZAD ARRUM!" echoed through the valley, checking the horde's advance.

"What's that?" Kora whispered, her eyes everywhere.

"BAZAD ARRUM!" sounded again, closer than before.

"That's the war cry of the Stonebreakers," I said incredulously, scanning the landscape.

At that moment, a fighting wedge of more than six hundred dwarves rolled around the corner and rammed into the horde.

At its head was Arik Ironhenge.

"BAZAD ARRUM!" thundered through the crisp morning air.

The Sallies might have been determined, but they weren't about to stand up to that armored churning mass of heavy infantry. As the tip of the wedge hit, it rolled over the orcs and goblins like an ocean wave pounding against the shore.

Our enemies died screaming in their hundreds.

Predictably, the survivors panicked and ran for their lives, retreating to the safety of the main vanguard of the horde.

Before I could blink twice, the battle was over.

When the chaos of the field cleared, my father strode forward, glaring up at the Gray Company, still standing at the ready upon the boulders.

"We've a reckoning, Monchakka," he spat at me, ice in his eyes.

Yep, that's my dad.

"If I may," the captain said, stepping forward. "Even with your forces, General, we're badly outnumbered. I think it best we return to the garrison at once.

"And who are you?" my father asked, narrowing his eyes against the glare of the sun, unable to make out the captain's face.

"Ashten Raine," the dark eyed dwarf answered proudly, "Captain of the Gray Company."

Arik snorted into his beard. "You have no authority here."

The captain smiled.

"Forgive me, General—perhaps you've forgotten—it's *Prince* Ashten Raine," he said, shocking me to the core. "Leader of the Gray Company and youngest brother to King Helfer, who caved in for the first time in his life and commissioned me for this rescue."

My father took a long, hard look at Ashten, who did not flinch under his gaze. "You haven't spoken to your brother in years. You expect me to believe that?" Arik barked.

In answer, a ball of flame shot from the boulder to my right. Bad was standing there breathing his mouthful of whiskey into a fiery sphere.

"I'll not be wasting anymore of my fine spirits on account of you General," he snarled, his mouth finally empty. "You two can have your pissing contest later. The Cap'n speaks sense. Let's be off!"

My father frowned but nodded in acquiescence. Turning to his division, he roared out an order in his stentorian voice.

"Stonebreakers, home!"

"BAZAD ARRUM!"

Hours later, we stood in the throne room giving our account to the king. Afterward, his majesty thanked us for our service and told us to await further instructions.

Captain Raine—or Prince Raine I suppose—took us to the nearest tavern for a few pints of well-earned ale. As the second round arrived, he raised his hands for silence.

"After an eventful twenty-four hours, there's a final matter that needs to be addressed," he began, looking directly at me. "A matter of payment. Monchakka, you promised recompense for our services, no matter the cost."

I looked at him and nodded once. "I did make such a promise, Captain," I said, rather grimly. "Name your price."

The dwarven prince smiled. "You Monchakka. You are the price. I request that you join my company as a full-fledged member, effective immediately."

A stunned smile crept onto my face, as cheers went up around me. Hands clapped me on the back and mugs were pounded upon tabletops.

"Well?" Ashten asked. "What do you say, son?"

I glanced at Kora, who raised an eyebrow and rolled her eyes.

"No!" boomed the voice of my father.

All eyes turned to the Supreme General of the dwarven armies. His face was a mask of controlled anger.

I knew our time of reckoning had come.

Slowly I stood, my oak chair scraping loudly against the tiled floor in the stillness of the tavern. Quietly, I stepped forward.

"There's a war coming," I began, looking him straight in the eye. "I would fight in that war father, the best way I can. Despite your finest intentions, it comes down to a choice—a choice I alone must make. Before you raise your voice in argument, I beg that you hear me out."

Arik nodded once, though his face did not change.

"Today, you saw a band of thirty Engineers overcome incredible odds to save your division of Stonebreakers. Yet, that same division saved the Engineers as well! The two forces needed one another. Working together, they accomplished something neither could affect on their own. Think of what more we could do, given the opportunity! That is how you and I should be, General—not in contention, but working as one."

Several heartbeats passed; not a sound could be heard. I could almost hear the gears whirring in his head. I knew, for the first time in his life, the General was considering my words.

All he needed was a little push.

"Before you answer, think on this," I continued, reaching out with a hand, placing it on his shoulder. "How many warriors would you have lost without the Gray Company? How many more dwarves might we save together? If the king approves of his brother as an Engineer, why can't you?"

Arik wet his lips, glancing over at Ashten.

I smiled at him. "Your sister, Aurora, has been right all along, Father. There is a place of honor for everyone in this clan, not just the Stonebreakers. If you wish for me to fight in this war beside you, I must do it under my terms. That means it will not be in the banded iron of a Stonebreaker, but in the leather rig of an Engineer."

I withdrew my hand from his shoulder and extended it toward him. "What say you General?"

Arik glanced at his sister, who was glaring at him, awaiting his decision.

A half-dozen heartbeats passed, as the entire room held its collective breath. Finally, the General reached forward and gripped my forearm, taking it in the warriors' handshake.

"If it's to be war, then we'll be needing the entire clan!" he boomed, grabbing Ghost, embracing her tightly. The exiled dwarfess burst into tears, squeezing him back.

The crowd roared, swarming all three of us in hearty approval.

Despite my exhaustion, I couldn't sleep—not yet anyway. I climbed up the stairs to the top of the battlements and looked out at the stars.

We were under the king's orders now, as he'd finally agreed to fully finance his brother's company.

Ashten Raine, I thought with a smile. *What a difference he'd made.*

After the General had retired for the night, I asked the captain why he'd picked me. What had I done to deserve a spot in his company?

His response was simple.

"A good dwarf, such as yourself, is worth more than a mountain of gold. You were willing to stay behind and sacrifice your life for the good of the company. Friendship, loyalty, doing what is right; our deeds are what will be remembered in this life. You have those qualities, Monchakka. Everyone in your family does. That's why I asked you to join my company—besides," he had stopped, giving me a warm smile, "like Ghost, you're a hell of a scrapper!"

I smiled at the memory. I was touched by his words; more so because I could see that he meant them.

I heard a step behind me and turned to see Kora come up the stairs. She'd pulled her dark hair back and was no longer geared for battle. She wore a simple white dress, cinched at the waist with a belt of black leather.

I smiled at her, and she shook her head in amusement.

"What are you grinning about, Stony?" she asked, her tone playful.

I shrugged offhandedly. "Nothing really, I just figured you came up here to thank me for saving your life today."

She furrowed her brow in a look of disbelief. "When did *you* save *me*?"

"From that goblin Shaman," I answered simply. "He was about to blast you with his magic, and I saved the day."

I don't know what had gotten into me. Usually I was shy around she-dwarves. Maybe I was succumbing to the effects of the alcohol, but for whatever reason, in that moment, I was feeling euphoric.

She scowled at me, mostly, I suspected, because she knew that I was right. "Psssht, you got off one lucky shot and I'm supposed to swoon in your arms?" she scoffed. "Is that what you think, Stony?"

I smiled, ignoring her question. "You know what the best part of my day was?"

"When I saved *you* from those grenades you threw?" she asked, somewhat archly.

"No," I said, laughing at the memory. "It was when I ran out of bullets and you said you'd cover me," I answered. "I knew you liked me then."

She tried—Goran knows she tried—but she couldn't keep a smile from her face. "I do not like you, but—I suppose you aren't a *complete* waste of my time."

Stepping forward she slipped her hand in mine. "You are, however, an idiot. You know that, don't you?"

I leaned in and kissed her lips. They were soft and warm.

"I know," I answered. "I'm an idiot Engineer."

"Don't do anything stupid," she said, teasing me with her eyes.

"Oh, I plan to," I said, kissing her again.

Michael K. Falciani

The Dwarves of Rahm:
Omens of War

Part II
A Dreg's Honor

Chapter 3: Blackmailed

Present time

The thing you have to understand about me is, I'm a lover, not a fighter. Don't get me wrong, I *can* fight. I just prefer not to, not unless there is no other option.

Of course, *because* of my propensity for the aforementioned lovemaking, it tends to *lead* to fights. Fathers, uncles, brothers, cousins, and yes, the occasional husband—all want to thrash me at one point or another. It's not *my* fault I make those of the fairer sex feel wanted and desirable.

However, because of this proclivity for loving and fighting, I often find myself on the run.

That's why I'm surprised to be in the middle of my latest debacle, running for my life once again. For once it's not to escape from a slew of jealous lovers, but to save them—and before you ask, yes, it's because of a female, though not one I would have picked in a million years. She is the haughtiest, most condescending dwarf maiden I've ever encountered.

How did this happen? Well, like so many of my stories, it all started with a smile.

"Play one more," pleaded the patrons of the Wishing Well tavern.

I tipped a frothy mug of ale to my lips and drank it down in one pull, wiping the foam from my mouth with the dark blue sleeve of my frayed and weathered tunic. I held up my free hand and waved it at the crowd.

"I'm off for the night," I cried, grinning at the audience.

"That's what you said a half-dozen songs ago," a spice merchant replied, raising his mug in my direction.

I could have kept playing if I'd wanted to. My fingers weren't sore from plucking at my lute, and my jack had been consistently filled between songs. However, something more pressing had captured my attention.

A buxom dwarf lass, a twinkle in her striking blue eyes, had danced a jig three songs in a row, easing her way closer to the stage each time. She'd smiled at me on my last song, flashing me with the kind of smile that held the promise of a warm bed and soft flesh. Spinning on her heels, with a braid of long blonde hair whirling behind her, she'd blown me a kiss and headed for the door.

I knew it was time to go.

I collected my wide brimmed hat from the front of the stage, dumping the coins collected into my money pouch. I doffed my hat to the crowd and bowed to the raucous sound of cheers and applause. Carefully I made my way to the front of the inn and paid my fee to the proprietor, a surly eyed dwarf by the name of Pyrs.

"I've a meal set aside for you when you're ready. . . if you bother to come back tonight, that is."

"I wouldn't wait up," I answered, giving him a wink.

Pyrs frowned at me and shook his head. "One of these days Omens, you're going to dip your wick into the wrong wax."

I laughed aloud. "Maybe I will barkeep, but not tonight."

I spun a silver coin on the counter in front of Pyrs and left, trailing after those blue eyes.

"All rise," a stern-faced bailiff said the next morning. More than a dozen dwarves stood in court at the bailiff's command. I know this because I was one of them.

Mine was the first case of the day.

I stood, clapped in irons, staring up at the disapproving gaze of the city magistrate.

"You again?" the wrinkled face of the old dwarf complained, adjusting the spectacles on his face from atop his raised wooden desk.

"Nice to see you, Magistrate Baeron," I quipped, flashing him with a friendly smile.

"How many times is this now?" he groused at me.

"Appearances in your court?" I mused. "Four, no five times…without a single conviction."

Baeron leaned forward, tiny flecks of food clinging to his scraggly gray beard. "That's because your… *conquests,* refuse to press charges."

I shrugged and gave him my most innocent look. "What can I say? I have been blessed with a—silver tongue, so to speak."

"So, I've heard," Baeron grunted. "Remind me, what was that last charge you managed to beat?"

"I don't see the need to bring up past transgressions, your honor. Those are ancient history."

"Come now, what was it?" he insisted. "Something to do with the constable's sister, as I recall."

I grinned at the memory. "Oh yes, though it was his eldest niece the first time, and his youngest sister the second—to which were you referring?"

The magistrate shook his head. "Don't you ever tire of living like this Omens? Always in trouble? Constantly on the run?"

I shook my head in good humor. "Not in the least."

He frowned down at me from his desk. "Remind me how you convinced those lasses not to throw you in a cell."

"Well, I explained it to them," I answered with a smirk. "It came down to a simple question of inheritance."

"Excuse me?" Baeron questioned.

I shuffled close to the desk. "I pointed out the similarity in the...*assets* they'd inherited through common bloodlines," I explained with a wink.

The magistrate crossed his arms in front of his chest. "What, pray tell, *assets* were those?"

"Their bosoms sir," I answered, fighting to suppress a smile.

The crowd behind me tittered.

"My hand to Andovar," I continued, raising my palm to the sky. "That family is blessed with the most magnificent breasts in the eight kingdoms—believe me magistrate, I've looked."

The courtroom behind me burst into laughter.

"Quiet down," Baeron barked, quelling the noise. "This is a court of law, not some dust filled taproom."

"Well, you did ask," I reminded him.

The magistrate leaned forward, glaring at me in disgust. "Why, in the name of Goran, did they buy into that load of tripe?"

I shrugged. "Why wouldn't they? It's true—such perfection in size and symmetry is rare. As a humble male, I told them I stood helpless in the face of such majestic splendor. They agreed with me and convinced their patriarch to drop the charges."

"Hmmph," he snorted, glancing down at the parchment in front of him.

"What of this latest incident?" Baeron asked. "How would you explain that?"

"That's one I don't understand," I replied, giving him a bewildered look. "I didn't do anything wrong."

The Magistrate shot me a skeptical glance. "I've heard that before," he sniffed. "Why don't you explain your side of things."

Scratching absently at the three day growth on my face, I described to him what happened.

"I accepted an invitation last night from a comely lass who asked me to accompany her to the palace. Being the gracious fellow that I am, I accepted. Once we arrived, well, one thing led to another and during the course of our…interactions, we disturbed the guards."

"How did you disturb the guards?" Baeron asked.

I gave him the most innocent look I could. "The female in question, Rhosyn by name–well, she rather enjoyed the…administrations I was giving her."

"And?" he pressed, looking down at me, past his spectacles.

I leaned in close and answered in a loud whisper. "She made enough noise to where the guards thought she was being attacked."

The crowd laughed again, banging on the wooden railing with approval.

"Settle down!" the magistrate barked, slamming his hand on the top of his desk.

As the crown quieted, I gave the magistrate a beaming smile.

"Happily, the guards arrived *after* the culmination of our time together, if you get my meaning," I finished.

"You had to add that, didn't you?" Baeron growled at me, shaking his head in disgust. "Is there anything else?"

I gave him a shrug.

"The guards hustled me out of there before you could say, 'fish on a skite,'" I continued, rather annoyed. "I'd even go so far to say if there was a crime committed last evening, it was against *me*. I had to spend the rest of my night in an uncomfortable cell instead of in the arms of that beautiful maiden. I'm sure if I can confront my accuser, this can all be put to rest in a matter of minutes."

That is when the magistrate did something I had never seen him do.

He smiled.

Baeron nodded to the bailiff, who strode purposely to the door at the back of the room and opened it.

In walked a haughty looking female—strikingly attractive; with full lips, flaming red hair and a pair of brilliant green eyes. She was quite ravishing really—with all the makings of one of my conquests. In retrospect, I should have studied her *manner* more closely than her *figure*. I found out too late that flattery wasn't always the best course of action.

As she walked close to me, I spoke to her in my most contrite tone.

"My lady, I'm not sure what I've done to upset a beautiful maiden such as yourself—if you give me but a moment of your time…"

She spun around and struck me, hard across the face with a slap I never saw coming.

The explosion of pain on my cheek dazed me momentarily. I blinked several times, trying to clear my head of the blow.

"What the hell was that fo…" I managed to stammer out, before she cracked me again.

"Shut your bleating mouth, dreg!" she snarled.

I have to admit, her blows hurt more than the insult, though not by much. That second slap was delivered with enough force to set my head ringing.

Dreg.

It was the name given to those that lived among dwarven society without a clan.

By the time I'd recovered my senses, the magistrate was in the middle of listening to the plaintiff's testimony, a rather smug look of satisfaction on his face.

"…broke into my royal bedchamber and seduced my handmaiden, Rhosyn," the she-dwarf was saying. "I can't have some filthy dreg taking advantage…"

"I beg your pardon magistrate," I interrupted, raising my hand in protest as my head cleared, "but that's not accurate. I was *invited* by Rhosyn. I didn't seduce her, and I certainly didn't take advantage of…"

"You took her in *my* room!" the girl thundered. "My handmaiden is not pressing charges against you dreg, I am!"

"You are pressing charges?" I asked in confusion. "What for?"

If the red haired she-dwarf had been a volcano, she would have erupted. "What for? WHAT FOR?" she shrieked. "For rutting in my bed as if it were your own personal whorehouse, you disgusting dreg! By Goran, a goblin Fang has better manners than you!"

"Wait a second," I said, my anger stirring. "I'm under arrest because I used your bed? You can be upset, certainly, but that's hardly a criminal act."

"I'm appalled that a creature like you is even allowed in dwarven society," she railed, continuing her tirade. "A dreg skald, without name or clan. You are a public menace and a disgrace to dwarves everywhere—as are all of your foul kind."

I could feel the heat of anger burgeon in my chest. For the first time in months, I allowed my temper to get the best of me.

Eye's smoldering, I retaliated.

"It's better than being a highborn *slag* who spends her days bored to death in the palace," I spat. "You're not fooling anyone with this charade, *Highness*. You aren't upset that I used your bed. You're angry because you weren't in it. You're naught but a selfish harridan, that no male in his right mind would bother with—and every dwarf with half a brain in the city knows it!"

"What did you say to me?" she shouted in fury, her head snapping forward.

"Omens, stop," the magistrate warned.

"You think I don't know who you are?" I raged, ignoring his warning. "Princess Merin, last remaining child of the *putrid* King Orius. A dwarfess with no friends, scorned by all—with a tongue so sharp, it can cut through mythic steel."

"Omens, enough!" the magistrate shouted, rising from his seat.

"The hell it is!" I fired back. "If I'm going to rot in some cell because of this bitch, then I'll speak my mind."

I'm not sure what would have happened next as the two of us stood there, glaring white hot daggers at one another, nor will we ever know. By the grace of the gods and their divine intervention, destiny chose that exact moment to change our fates forever.

The door to the room burst open and a squad of the king's guards entered the chamber.

"Princess," said the leader, a stout fellow wearing a suit of banded armor. "The city is under siege. Your father requests your presence immediately."

"Under siege?" Merin asked, choking back her anger. "How?"

"Reports just came in," the captain replied gruffly. "An army of sallowskins, some thirty-thousand strong, has crossed the Hollowspan bridge. They are less than a half-day's march from the front gates."

The whole room went silent.

Except for me.

"How did they get past the guards on the other side of the bridge?" I muttered, but no one heard me.

"Please, highness," the captain continued, "your father is waiting."

"Looks like you have other things to deal with Princess," I snorted, loud enough to capture her attention. "I'll just retrieve my belongings from your room and be on my way."

I held up the iron shackles to the bailiff, who looked sourly at the magistrate.

"Let him go," Baeron said, waving his hand at me in irritation. "You are all dismissed. Many of you have families to care for, and this attack takes precedence."

The fiery redhead glared at me in loathing. "Lieutenant Regan," she called, motioning to a burly dwarf with a dark brown beard. "Escort the dreg to my chambers, make sure he touches *nothing* but his own belongings," she snarled before stalking out. "Have the rest of my room cleansed of his filth."

I canted my head to the side. "It was nice meeting you," I called out loudly, my tone mocking her departure.

She slammed the door behind her in response.

"How do you put up with that pain in the ass?" I asked, nudging the burly guard next to me with my elbow. He refused to smile behind his sand-colored beard.

"By the gods I've seen executioners that are more pleasant," I continued, shrugging off his silence. "She'd thaw the ice off a mountain in the dead of winter."

The bailiff unlocked the shackles and removed them from my wrists.

"Now," I said, turning to the guards, each of whom had the marking of a hunting cat on the back of their wrist. "About that escort…could we swing by the stable at the Wishing Well Inn first? My pony is there, and I hate to leave Nel unfed."

That should have been the end of it—I'd gather my things and leave. It wasn't the first invasion the city of Lodir had faced, I doubted it would be the last. For the time being, I was content to take my leave. I was happy to conduct my business in other dwarven kingdoms, as none of them were currently under siege. As much as I enjoyed my time at the Golden Keep, I wasn't about to stay and die for it.

I was making my way out of the princess's chambers when Rhosyn waylaid me—again. We had been interrupted the night before and she *really* wanted me to, how to say this delicately—finish her off. Besides, I have a weakness for blondes—and brunettes—and redheads–and, well, dwarven maidens in general.

What can I say? I make no apologies—I like what I like.

Against my better judgment, I extended my visit to the palace an hour longer than I should have.

Totally worth it mind you, I'm not complaining. Rhosyn was *well* worth the time spent.

Sadly, such enjoyment always seems to come at a cost.

"Skald Omens?" came a voice from the corridor outside Rhosyn's room. "I need a moment of your time."

"I'm not a skald, I'm a bard," I muttered aloud, "and I'm leaving."

Turning around I came face to face with the dwarven king.

King Orius was the ruler of the Golden Keep. A no-nonsense type, he had led the city of Lodir for over fifty years. Many of the dwarves in his kingdom had known prosperity, despite their proximity to the northern continent of Gathron-Tor, home of our ancient enemies, the sallowskins. He had led his people through two wars in the past and was now readying for a third.

The fact that he was standing alone in the hallway with me as an army of sallowskins closed in was nothing short of remarkable. Knowing his reputation, it also made me uneasy.

"Majesty," I said, wary of his appearance. "To what do I owe the…honor?"

"Let us dispense with the pleasantries," he said, raising his hands dismissively. "I have enough subjects bowing and scraping as it is. I've no wish to listen to another, especially one that despises the sight of me."

"I see," I remarked quietly, my mind racing. "Well, I'm just on my way out, Sire. Best of luck with the invasion."

He furrowed his brow, and I knew I was in trouble.

"I thought you might do an old king a service," he said, turning away, walking down the corridor.

"I don't think I will," I replied, barely able to check my anger. "You may rule Lodir, but you are no king of mine."

"I think you will reconsider," he snorted over his shoulder.

Six of his royal guards, the same ones I'd seen in court, stepped into the hallway. I stared into the hard black eyes of the burly guard I'd heard Merin address earlier.

"You'd best keep a civil tongue, dreg, or I'll rip it out," hissed the one called Regan, his eyes glowing with anger.

I hesitated a moment, and swore under my breath, knowing I had no choice but to follow the king and do as he bid. I strode after him, shutting the door carefully behind us.

The room was draped in tapestries, each hanging from the top of the dusky sandstone walls to the bottom. Sewn in the colors of red and gold, they were masterfully crafted pieces of work.

"The horde that has come is far larger than its predecessors," Orius began, his voice rumbling like stones tumbling down a mountain. "I will need assistance to fend them off, else the Golden Keep will fall."

"You need someone to go for help?" I surmised, relaxing a bit. As long as I could leave the city, I'd do whatever he wanted.

"Partially, yes," he agreed, cupping water from a silver bowl located on his ebonwood desk. Carefully he splashed the water on his face, leaving it to drip from his graying beard. "However, you are one of the dregs, an outcast, living on the edge of dwarven society."

"I do my best," I replied, making no attempt to hide my anger.

He smiled at me, toweling off with a brown linen that lay next to the silver bowl.

"Despite your misgivings, I know the dregs are an important part of our culture. It bothers me that they have been looked down upon for so long. Many are decent, ethical dwarves. They work at jobs most clans folk would deign beneath them. The dregs walk a hard path lad, but many do so with honor."

He pushed open a doorway that led into his private chambers. I had to resist the urge to wrap my hands around his throat and choke him with his lies. His dislike of the dregs inside the Golden Keep was well documented.

"Despite my views on the matter," he continued, oblivious to my disgust, "another dwarven king won't come to my aid on the word of a dreg alone."

I froze, sensing where this conversation was heading.

"You want me to take someone to Kazic-Thul?" I guessed, in reference to Lodir's closest neighbor. My eyes narrowed. "Who?"

I watched as the king's smile morphed from friendly, to cruel.

"I believe you've met my daughter," he answered, waving his hand to the corner of the room.

"Hello dreg," Princess Merin spat, venom dripping from her tongue.

Son of a bitch.

Chapter 4: Warrior Fish

We struck a bargain, the king and me. I'd lead his despicable spawn of a child to the city of Kazic-Thul, and Orius promised I'd be given a place in Clan Wingfoot of Lodir. It was a lesser clan, but I'd have a surname, nonetheless. On most occasions, I'd have been thrilled. Even though I make the best of it, being a dreg isn't fun. Much of your time is spent at the edge of dwarven society, surviving off the scraps, just as King Orius had said.

In this case, however, I think I got the worse end of the deal. I did not believe for a second the black hearted Orius would live up to his end of the bargain. He was a bigot and a bully, who had gone back on his word numerous times in the past. Unfortunately, I wanted out of Lodir, and this was the quickest way of going about it. Young dwarven males of the city, who had little to no military training, were already being pressed into service. This lack of readiness more often than not led to these inexperienced troops dying in the first minutes of battle. I had no desire to be on the wrong end of an orc Sorcerer's staff while it executed some powerful sallowskin magic.

There were a few moments when I regretted the deal I'd made. I caught Merin glaring at me as we prepared our resources. I could hear her mumbling under her breath about me. She kept talking about the, "despicable scum," and the, "disease ridden filth," she was being forced to ride with…and those were the kindest things I heard.

I almost became envious of those staying behind to oppose the horde. It might be better to face the jagged blades of sallowback iron, than the viperous tongue of the princess.

There were, however, a few perks.

For once in my life, I had my pick of equipment. I already owned most of what I needed, but I took care to replenish my supplies. My backpack was loaded with the essentials. A deerskin shelter, treated with oil to resist the elements, was already rolled tightly behind my saddle. My backpack carried everything from flint and tinder to food and drink. In the way of weapons, I had an iron longsword hanging from my belt, along with a sturdy knife and a well-worn hatchet. On the outer part of my pack, a coil of rope was latched to a grappling hook, along with a trio of bronze pitons. I tucked my lute into one of my newly acquired saddlebags, wrapped in a water-proof blanket of wool. I also helped myself to a lantern, tucking it securely behind my saddle.

Merin was more lightly equipped, though she carried a longknife and a small hand-held crossbow, coupled with a quiver of thirty, eight-inch bolts.

We left at midday, before the sallowskin horde was in sight. Leaving from the southern gate, Merin and I turned southeast and rode as fast as our ponies could carry us on the old trade road. Made of hard packed dirt rather than stone, the hooves of our mounts thrummed along the path for the next few hours alternating between a steady walk and a mile eating canter.

This was a flat area of the southlands, with waist-high grass the color of gold stretching as far as the eye could see. Eventually the plains gave way to rougher ground near the eastern coast of the Saltwater Passage, the narrow file of water that separated the two great islands of Rahm and Garthon-Tor. Hills spotted with trees became the norm rather than the exception the further east we traveled.

The princess and I didn't speak much, partially because we were moving quickly, and partly because we hated each other.

An hour shy of sunset, that mutual abhorrence came to a head.

I pointed to a copse of trees a half mile distant located off to the side of the road.

"We'll make camp there," I said, nodding at the evergreens.

"We need to press forward, *dreg*," Merin argued. "My city needs aid. We cannot break for camp just because *you* stayed up all night carousing and are too fatigued to continue."

I looked over at her, swallowing the first words that came to mind. "Highness," I began. "While I understand your urgency, we both need rest. Our mounts have been on the move in the heat of the afternoon sun. They, too, need to be fed and watered."

"You're just lazy," she accused, her voice biting, "like all the dregs."

Something in me snapped. Princess or not, I wasn't going to put up with this bitch for the entire trip. It was time to set a few things straight.

I dismounted from my shaggy mare and walked over toward Merin.

"What are you doing?" she asked, angrily. "I said we need to press…"

I reached up and dragged the princess from her mount, dumping her unceremoniously to the ground. Sputtering with rage, Merin tried to get up, but I sat on top of her, pinning her arms to the ground.

"Let go of me you son-of-a-whore," she screamed, thrashing on the ground in an effort to break free.

"What kind of language is that?" I mocked, my voice mild. "What would your subjects think?"

"Get off of me, damn you!" she continued, trying to bite my hands.

"Not until you're ready to listen," I replied, spreading her arms wide.

She stopped struggling and glared up at me. "I'm not some daft female you can win over with some frilly words," she snarled. "You're like every male I've ever known—a selfish prick who will stop at nothing to get what he wants."

I frowned at her and shook my head.

"I don't know what you're talking about princess, but the person you are describing isn't me. It's true, I like the ladies, but I've never forced myself on any of them. They come to me, quite willingly, and enjoy themselves to the fullest."

I plucked her crossbow from the side of her belt and stood up, releasing my hold on her.

"We are going to have a talk, you and I. At the end of it, all I want to hear you say is, 'I understand.' Is that clear?"

She stood up, refusing to brush herself off, and continued to glare at me defiantly.

I pointed north in the direction of Lodir. "Back in the city you're a princess, beholden to none but your father. Out here, you are a spoiled child who will get herself killed if left to your own devices."

I scratched at the unkempt hair growing on my face and shook my head. "You can hate me all you want, Highness, but know this—I agreed to see you safely to Kazic-Thul, and I am a dwarf who keeps his word. However, I don't have time to run everything I do past you. Life moves fast out in the wild, where one mistake can cost you your life. If I make a decision you don't like or disagree with, that's too bad. I've spent much of my life on the move, and few are better at it than I. This is not a democracy where everyone gets a vote—it is a dictatorship, and I am in command. Now, Princess, do you understand what I am saying?"

She looked at me with hard green eyes. I could almost hear the internal debate she was having.

"I understand," she grated, staring at me in utter hatred.

"Good," I said, handing her the crossbow. "Now get on your mount and follow me. It's time we make camp."

We followed a nearly overgrown game trail that led into the trees in an effort to hide our presence. This was a rest area I had used many times in the past. Few knew of its existence and, to my knowledge, only I remembered where it was. Some thirty paces into the woods was a small clearing. It housed a dark pond, roughly thirty feet in diameter that was fed by a quick flowing stream that bubbled out of the hills.

I set about the mundane tasks of feeding Nel and rubbing her down. Afterwards, I tethered my pony to a tree near the pond so she could drink her fill at her leisure. Merin followed my lead, though I could tell she wasn't well versed in the care of her own mount. Once the ponies had been seen to, I set up my shelter and hollowed out an old fire pit using the broad side of my hatchet.

"Where's my shelter?" I heard the princess ask in her petulant voice.

I looked over at her saddle bags and realized she hadn't packed one.

"You can share mine," I suggested absently.

"Absolutely not," she snarled, outraged.

I wasn't in the mood to argue.

"That's fine princess, you can sleep out in the open if you like," I said agreeably. "There's nothing quite like spider mites burrowing into your ear to give you pleasant dreams."

"What?"

"Or perhaps you prefer the nocturnal insects that buzz around your face all night?" I continued blithely. "A friend of mine once had more than a hundred bites on his cheeks—had to soak his head in an ice-cold stream all morning to get the swelling to go down."

"You...you're not serious?" she gaped at me.

"I'm afraid I am, Princess," I answered. "Scorpions, snakes, carrion, skunks—we could run to anything out here. But, if you don't want to share my shelter, I won't make you."

I watched in quiet satisfaction as she unrolled her blanket and crawled into my deerskin tent.

It was still a half turn of the hourglass until sundown, so I set about trying to catch some fish to enhance my dinner. At the edge of the pond, I lifted a flat stone that concealed a fishing line I'd hidden a few weeks back. Seeing a pod of insects nearby, I caught one and pierced it with the hook attached to the line. I tied a pebble to the string and tossed the hook in, yawning absently as it sank to the bottom. I drew it back slowly, hoping for a strike.

I didn't have to wait long.

Five minutes later, a pair of speckled trout lay on the bank, each nearly eight inches in length.

"What are you doing?" I heard Merin ask from behind me, her tone surprisingly neutral.

"Supplementing my meal," I answered.

There was a moment of silence.

"Could I try?"

Glancing over my shoulder, I saw the princess looking at me earnestly, her usual contempt absent.

"Alright," I agreed, making room for her next to me.

"What do I do?"

"Take this," I said, handing her the hook and line. "Now, you see those insects over there?" I asked, pointing to the fat bodied creatures I'd used for bait.

"Yes," she replied, making a face.

"You need to catch one and put it on the hook," I explained.

"Catch one?" she asked, skeptically.

"Aye."

"How?"

Giving her a quizzical look, I snorted softly. "Are your fingers broken?"

"No," she answered, sounding annoyed.

"Well then, you've got everything you need, don't you?"

After a moment of reticence, the princess went to work. For a few seconds she stared at the black bellied creatures, trying to convince herself they would not bite. Her hand shot out, unsuccessfully trying to grab one of the insects. She missed, swore, and missed again. The third time was the charm as she managed to trap one of the cricket-like bugs between her thumb and forefinger.

"Now what?" she demanded, holding the wriggling thing as far away from her as she could.

"Put in on the hook."

"You do it."

"No, you have to do it yourself if you want to learn."

Making a choking sound from somewhere inside her throat, Merin managed to jab the insect onto the needle thin hook.

"Alright, I did it, now what?" she panted, like she had just finished a strenuous exercise.

I couldn't help but smile to myself as I watched her struggle with the simple task. "Now you throw it into the pond," I explained.

"Throw it in?"

"Yes, wait—no, by Goran—not the whole line," I cursed, seeing she had nearly chucked it all into the middle of the water. "Just the hook, bait and stone. Hold the rest of the line in your other hand."

Clumsily she threw the hook into the water where we watched it sink to the bottom.

"Good," I said encouragingly. "Now, pull it gently toward you, not too fast."

"Like this?" she asked, yanking at the line.

"Easy," I corrected, covering her hand with my own, showing her how it was done. She glanced up at me and I saw it, just a hint mind you, but it was there.

The inkling of a smile.

Her eyes widened in alarm.

"What was that?" she asked, looking out at the line. "I felt the string quiver."

"That's a fish going after the bait," I explained.

"What do I do?" she nearly screamed.

"Wait for a hard pull against you, like it's trying to swim away. When you feel that, yank it in."

"How will I know?"

I smiled at her ruefully. "You'll know."

A heartbeat later, the string went taut.

"I think…it's…yes, it's there! It's there! What do I do?" she yelled excitedly.

"Pull it in!"

Merin wrenched on the string harder than she needed too, jerking the fish clean out of the water to land on shore.

"I did it, I did it!" she yelped with joy, as she crouched down to observe the catch.

The trout went wild, flopping like mad, *quite* close to her feet.

"Oh! Oh! It's touching me," she shrieked, hopping away from the fish.

"Grab it! You have to get the hook out!"

"Are you *crazy*? I'm not touching that thing, it's all…slimy!"

"Well, I'm not doing it for you," I shouted back, trying not to laugh.

"Kill it, kill it!" Merin screamed, letting go of the line.

"It's going to fall back in the water," I warned, seeing it flop close to the edge.

I heard a clicking sound and the air hissed. Blinking quickly, I saw the fish, a speckled trout, no more than three inches in length, had been pinned to the ground with a black crossbow bolt.

I looked up at Merin who was pointing her weapon at the tiny fish. I gaped at her in question.

"Well, he wouldn't stay still," she said defensively, as though that explained everything.

"Nice shot," I replied, impressed.

"Is it dead?" she asked, nudging it with her toe.

"Oh, it's dead," I answered, fighting to suppress my laughter. "You certainly showed him."

I went ahead and cleaned the fish for her, thinking the princess had had quite enough excitement for one day.

I prepared our meal by skewering the trout on a stick sharpened with my knife. Merin refilled our water skins and cut several slices of bread and cheese from our provisions. Using an oval tin from my pack as a plate, we sat down to eat.

Rarely had I seen a person prouder of their accomplishments than Merin was, retelling me the story of her catch, as though I had not been there as a witness the entire time.

"I mean, did you see him fight when he was on shore?" she asked, seeming to have forgotten our rocky start.

"Oh yes," I replied, humoring her. "He was like a warrior."

Her eyes lit up. "Yes! That's exactly what he was—a warrior fish!"

Raising the blackened trout to her mouth, she smiled. "I will remember you always," she said to the dead fish, before biting into its charred flesh.

I couldn't hide my laughter.

"Are you mocking me?" she asked, her mouth full.

"A little," I answered honestly. "But it's a pleasant surprise to see you so…even tempered."

She stared at me, then shrugged her shoulders and went back to eating.

We finished our meal in silence, as the fire burned down to its embers. I washed the dirty tin in the pond and made certain to discard any trace of food far from our camp. While I knew this glade was safe, I didn't want to invite any predators to the area by mistake.

When I returned to the fire, Merin was seated on her blanket, enveloped in a reddish glow. I stopped short and took in the sight.

She truly was a beauty. When I had first seen her in court, her physical appearance had been tainted for me by her words and actions.

A couple of slaps to the face will do that to you.

Now, seeing her happy and content, she was stunning. Since our argument on the road, Merin had been a far more agreeable traveling companion. The episode with the fish had bonded us, more than I cared to admit.

Shaking my head, I came to my senses. Pretty or not, she was a dwarven princess, and I was nothing but a nameless dreg.

Steadying my nerves, I walked back to the fire and sat down across from her.

"There you are," she smiled, looking up at me. "I was just thinking…is this how you live? On the road all the time?"

"Sometimes," I poked at the fire with a dry branch.

"It must be nice," she sniffed, giving me an envious look.

I looked at her, puzzled. "Nice? It's living out of my backpack all the time, never knowing where I'll sleep one night to the next—or under what circumstances."

I threw the stick in the fire, watching it catch as orange sparks rose into the darkness.

"It seems nice to me," she put her feet up on a stone near the fire, oblivious to my irritation.

I snorted at her.

"At the moment, we are under clear skies with full bellies after a warm meal," I explained. "Believe me princess, that's not always the case. Should it start to rain, everything I own will be drenched. If we manage to get any sleep we will wake up, our possessions covered in mud. Should the winds pick up, this pleasant little glade will become uncomfortably cold, with little chance of a fire."

She shifted from her spot on the ground, looking at me intently.

"If it's so terrible, why do you live like this?" she asked quietly.

I rolled my eyes. "What would you have me do?" I asked. "I'm a dreg, remember? A pariah to dwarven society—with no name or clan. Worse, I'm a bard. An outcast, even among the dregs. Sure, folks like to hear me sing and tell stories. Afterwards they always look down on me, wishing the vagabond minstrel would go away. Most of the time I'm looking over my shoulder for those seeking revenge, or worse, to rob me."

"Maybe you should stop sleeping with every maiden that bats an eye at you!" she snapped.

I shook my head in wonder at her ignorance.

"If only it were that simple," I said, looking up into the night sky. "Do you know why I started my carousing ways? Believe me princess, it wasn't out of love, or some perverse desire like everyone thinks. I did it out of necessity—so I could sleep in a warm bed with a roof over my head at night. I started doing it so I could survive in the winter. Do you know how many dwarves freeze to death in Dregtown? Your people, living under the reign of King Orius, dying in the streets by the score, all because they weren't born into the right family."

A silence descended upon our campsite as Merin considered my words.

"I didn't know that," she said finally. "When we get back, I'll tell my father. He's a fair dwarf. Once he learns of the dreg's plight..."

"You think he doesn't know?" I asked, incredulous. "He has always known. Hell, he's part of the problem! Twenty years ago, during the last siege of the Golden Keep, he came to the poor quarter on the outskirts of Lodir. He made the dregs living there the same promise he made me today. 'Help defend the city and I'll adopt you and your families into a clan. 'He feasts upon what the dregs want most—the promise of a name and a better life. The dregs, ignorant as they are, bought into his assurances. My father died fighting for King Orius based on that pledge. He was killed defending..."

I stopped, knowing what I was about to say wouldn't endear the princess to me.

"Once the siege was over," I continued. "Orius spent a fortune in gold building a monument honoring the clans of Lodir—etching the names of the fallen in stone, forever remembering the sacrifice they made."

I stopped speaking, as the memory filled me with anger.

"The dregs got nothing for their efforts," I spat. "Not a copper coin, not a single word of thanks. All that gold, spent on some worthless, useless monument, while most of Dregtown was destroyed. Hundreds of the dregs begged the king to hold true to his promise. He assured them they had not been forgotten. As winter set in, he closed the gates to the inner city and left the dregs to rot in the ghettos and slums they call home. Many froze to death in the poor quarter that winter, including my mother."

I stopped, seeing the look on Merin's face. "I was naught but a wee lad princess, but I remember the king and his promises."

Her face had changed from a shocked silence to shame.

"Omens, I'm...I'm sorry, I didn't know."

"That is the way of the world princess. Those in power do what they want...the rest of us make our way the best we can. It has always been like that, and it always will be."

I stood up and strode to my saddle bags, angry at myself for getting drawn into that conversation. *Idiot bard!* I thought. *Did you think you'd get her to change anything?*

I rummaged through the bags, picking out my lute, and a thin pipe fashioned from a hollowed-out piece of bamboo. Satisfied, I walked back to the fire to see Merin looking at me strangely.

I sat back down and placed the lute on my lap. "I apologize princess, I should not have said anything. You'd best get some sleep, we'll have a long day tomorrow."

She leaned back against a rock, pursing her lips. "I'm glad you told me," she sighed. "No one at the palace ever gives me the truth. Everyone tells me things are, 'fine' or 'not to worry,' as though I am a child who needs protection. You, at least, are honest with me. I appreciate that, though I doubt I'll ever agree with you."

For once, I didn't know what to say. Instead, I plucked absently at the lute strings, checking to see if they were in tune.

"I have to ask," she said, looking at me thoughtfully. "If you know my father won't live up to his agreement with you, why take me to Kazic-Thul? Why not just dump me here in the wild and leave?"

I frowned at her and stopped my playing. "I told you, I'm a dwarf of my word. I needed to get out of Lodir and taking you to Kazic-Thul was the quickest way. I may despise your father and his policies, but I've no wish to see Lodir fall. It's my birthplace. My family has lived there for generations; my parents are buried there. I'm the last of my line, nameless as it is. I won't let the sallowskins take Lodir out of spite for the king. You may not think much of the dregs, highness, but we're just as honorable as any clan dwarf, oftentimes more so."

I picked up my lute and began plucking at the strings again.

"For a dwarf who professes to be a Skald, I have yet to hear you play," Merin remarked, giving me a little smile.

"I'm not a Skald," I retorted. "Skalds recite poetry and the like. I know only a few poems and recite even less."

"Then what are you? A troubadour?"

I shook my head. "I often wear the guise of a troubadour. They're known for the singing of folk songs and ballads—but that's not what I *am*."

"I ask again, what are you? An itinerant minstrel? A Jongleur? What?"

I sighed. "I am a bard. One who uses music to influence others. There is a magic to it, if you have the discipline to learn. Observe."

I placed the lute on the ground next to me and took up the bamboo flute. Placing it to my lips, I began to play a soft melody, gentle and slow. Within seconds, I faded from sight.

Merin sat up in shock.

"Omens?" she asked, sounding frightened. "Where are you?"

"I'm here," I answered, ceasing my melody. Immediately, I flickered back into view.

"H…how did you do that?" she stammered at me.

"I told you," I replied, setting the flute aside. "I used magic, bard magic."

"Incredible," she whispered in awe. "What else can you do?"

"Nothing more tonight," I answered shortly. "I think it best that we get some sleep. Tomorrow will be a long…"

I trailed off and canted my head to the side.

"What? What is it?" Merin asked, looking around.

"I thought I saw something between the trees in the distance," I answered. "A flash of light, from a fire perhaps."

"You think we are being followed?"

"Best not to take chances," I answered, motioning toward the shelter. "Get inside while I put out the fire. We leave tomorrow before dawn."

Chapter 5: Barrel Falls

When morning came it was cold and dark. I'd spent a restless night in the shelter, jumping out of my skin at every sound. Finally, I drifted off sometime after midnight, though I woke hardly feeling refreshed.

Merin, somewhat surprisingly, slept well, despite her reticence at being forced to share a tent with me.

Not wanting to risk a fire, we gathered our things by the light of the crescent moon above. I took Nel by the bit and led the princess and her mount out a different path from the one we had entered on. Call me overcautious, but I didn't want to risk anyone seeing us depart unless it was necessary. The light I'd seen last night had spooked me and I wanted to put some miles between myself and its source, whatever that may be.

Once back on the Old Trade Road, I nickered to Nel, and we rode at a trot. A quarter of an hour later we were almost half a league from our campsite before we eased our pace. I wanted to make good time this morning and try to get to a small town I knew of located a day's journey away.

Sallowskins were not known as cunning strategists. However, they had learned a few things from their past invasions. I knew they'd be occupying the roads leading to Lodir which is why Merin and I had made our escape before they could cut off our exit. King Orius had sent riders upon our departure the previous day. They moved both west and south along the great road to warn other kingdoms of the attack. That didn't mean the sallowskins wouldn't have groups out scouting, killing random dwarves, especially before word of the invasion had spread.

Lodir had enough of a military presence where they could hunker down and wait if they needed to. Those traveling the roads to the Golden Keep did so at a risk.

Like the previous day, we alternated riding our mounts between a canter and a walk, giving the ponies time to rest. It was mid-morning, with the temperature rising rapidly, when we encountered our first group of travelers. A half-dozen Bolters, each dressed in leather armor, armed with short swords and crossbows.

"Remember what I told you," I whispered to Merin, who rode a few steps behind me. "Keep your head down and let me do the talking. We don't need anyone knowing who you are or what this mission entails."

"They are clan dwarves," she argued. "I doubt they will accost us."

"They are dwarves of the Bronzefist clan," I countered. "They are exceedingly arrogant, especially toward dregs."

I pulled Nel to the side of the road some ten paces from the group.

"Honor to your clan, brothers," I said in the customary dwarven greeting, tilting my head downward in respect.

"You honor us," said the first, an older dwarf, with a graying blonde beard. "You've come recently from Lodir?"

"Aye," I replied, giving him a tight smile. "Ill news, I'm afraid. The city has come under attack. A horde of sallowskins numbering in the thousands crossed the Hollowspan Bridge yesterday morning."

We were met with a rumbling surprise as this was the first they had heard of it.

"That is ill news," the leader said, shaking his head.

"You've been on the run since?" snorted a second dwarf, younger, with a silver tassel in his chestnut colored beard.

I nodded at him. "Yes, we left at mid-day. You are the first travelers we've encountered since our departure."

"You're almost thirty miles from Lodir," the older dwarf scoffed, looking at me with suspicion. "You must have been moving fast."

"Just like a dreg to run with his tail between his legs," the younger dwarf barked harshly, turning to his fellows.

I furrowed my brow but turned to address the older dwarf.

"I've been retained to escort my companion to Kazic-Thule," I answered, motioning to the princess. "She has business there that cannot wait—and I can earn a bonus in silver if she arrives the day after tomorrow."

The leader frowned at me, his eyes sliding to Merin. The others took notice of her as well, and I realized quickly that I'd made a mistake. Cursing myself for a fool, I knew there would be trouble.

"Is what he says true?" the elder dwarf asked the princess, his hand sliding to the handle of his crossbow.

Merin, as good as her word, nodded, without speaking, and gave the leader a brief smile.

"What's your name, dreg?" the elder dwarf asked, turning his attention back to me.

"Omens, of the Golden Keep," I answered, keeping my tone neutral.

"I've heard of you," the dwarf with the silver tassel growled. "It's said you're a cuckold, without honor, who charms his way into the beds of dwarf maidens throughout the southlands."

The other dwarves laughed at his words. I relaxed my face and laughed along with them, seeing my way out of this predicament.

"Aye it's true," I agreed raffishly. "Though some clan maidens are harder to charm than others."

"Oye, what's that supposed to mean?" asked a third dwarf, sporting a fierce black beard.

"Nothing at all," I replied. "It's just that some clan females are more…*satisfied* than others—if you take my meaning. For example, the Mistwalker Clan of the Red Hills–those are some well-serviced females. Difficult to lure any of them away from their mates. Then we have the Clan Ironhenge of Kazic-Thule. I'd had more luck charming a goblin archer than an Ironhenge lass."

"What of Clan Bronzefist?" challenged the second dwarf, thrusting his chin out defiantly.

"Is that your clan?" I asked, feigning ignorance. "You're in luck. They're the best of them all. I've never been able to seduce a single maiden from your coterie. Too smart for me, and too gratified," I finished with a wink.

The Bolters relaxed at those words, appeased at my assessment. The older dwarf snorted in wry humor and the tension lifted.

"Be safe brothers," I warned, bowing again. "May the road rise swiftly in front of you."

"Hold your tongue," the black bearded dwarf snapped angrily. "We are not brothers to a dreg…especially an honorless skald of no name."

The dwarf with the silver tassel in his beard leaned close to Merin as his pony walked next to hers. "When you tire of that Skald prick, ask for Tanno, Bolter of Clan Bronzefist. I'll show you what a *real* dwarf is like."

Merin, still playing her part, flashed him a smile as the rest of the group filed past.

"Let's get out of here highness," I whispered, once they were beyond earshot.

"What a bunch of idiots," she muttered, patting the neck of her mount. "They cared more about their honor than the invasion. Is it always like that for you? Is every clan dwarf that rude and grating?"

"It's usually easier," I answered, guiding Nel back onto the middle of the road. "Their blood was up because you were with me."

Her forehead wrinkled with a frown. "What do you mean?"

I glanced back, making sure the Bolters were far away from us. "I have a well-earned reputation for getting on well with the fairer sex," I explained. "But I also know dwarf males. When a female is involved, the males tend to become belligerent—each thinking they are the cock of the walk."

I paused, glancing over at Merin. "Especially if the female is of exceptional beauty."

"You...you think I'm an exceptional beauty?" she stammered.

I laughed softly, looking over at her. "If there's one thing I pride myself on princess, it's my eye for beautiful things—be it a golden sunrise or a snow-capped mountain soaring above a green meadow. You, Merin, are like the first bloom of spring after a long, cold winter. Poems are written about maidens like you."

"Thank you," she managed to say, turning away from me.

"Anyway, had I not stroked those Bronzefist egos, there may well have been blood-shed, and we don't have the time for such nonsense."

"It's not right," she said, looking at me with concern. "You're risking your life on this venture, all for dwarves like them."

I raised my eyebrow in question. "Yesterday you treated me in much the same way, highness," I said. "Did you think the world around us has changed since then?"

"I never meant..."

A raised hand from me halted her words. "We can discuss the cultural issues in our society later," I quipped. "For now, we need to put some distance between ourselves and that Bolter, Tanno."

"Why is that?"

I smiled devilishly. "I lied to them. Bronzefist females are notoriously unhappy with their mates."

She gave me a hard look. "How do you know this?

My smile widened.

"Tanno's wife explained it to me three nights ago, after I'd made love to her four times."

We continued on for the rest of the day, our mounts eating up the miles between us and our destination. An hour past midday, it began to rain. It started as a drizzle for the first few minutes, until dark clouds rolled in. After that, we rode under a steady stream of precipitation for more than an hour. At its worst we took cover in a grove of trees near the road and crawled under the thick boughs of an ancient elm. While it did not keep us dry, we managed to escape the heaviest of the downpour.

The deluge lasted only a few minutes before going back to a steady rain. We took the opportunity to feed our mounts a few handfuls of hay, and I slipped each pony an apple from my pack.

"This is not what I had in mind when I agreed to go on this trip," Merin complained, wiping water from her face.

"Says the lass who slew the greatest fish warrior ever known," I answered, with a sideways grin. "The storm won't last forever princess—and you're tougher than you look."

Emboldened by my words, Merin nodded her head with resolve. She had some backbone in her, I'll give her that.

Back on the road, the rain sputtered to a stop a few minutes later. I caught sight of a bright rainbow streaking across the sky behind us as I glanced over my shoulder.

I felt my pulse begin to race.

Merin had shaken off her dark hood. Her thick red hair was drenched, and the bare skin of her face and arms glistened with a bright sheen of water in the sunlight. The sight of her face, coupled with the rainbow behind her, was enough to make my blood stir.

I hadn't lied earlier. I prided myself on enjoying beautiful things in life. At that moment, I'd never seen anything more spectacular than the sight of the princess in front of one of nature's most vibrant wonders. I am wise enough to know such things are rare in this world. They don't last forever, despite what the taletellers say. I captured the moment in my mind, knowing it would soon fade.

"What are you staring at?" she asked, running a hand through her hair.

I gave her a crooked grin.

"You Merin...you're a vision."

She gave me a slow smile and she became even more radiant.

"There's a rainbow behind you," I said, not wanting her to miss out.

She turned away from me and I forced myself to face front, eyes back on the road. I saw miles of yellow hills and dark skies ahead of me, but in my mind, I saw only green eyes and a brilliant smile.

Despite the weather, we encountered a few more travelers, though none were as unpleasant as the Bolters of Clan Bronzefist.

Two hours until dusk, we managed to make it to the dwarf town of Barrel Falls, a stopover for those traveling from Lodir to Kazic-Thule. I was tempted to continue onward for another hour, but our mounts, I knew, could use the rest. Truth be told, so could I. The princess too, looked done in. Unlike yesterday, she did not voice a complaint when I called for a stop. It had been a long day on the road, and we'd made good time, but that speed had come at a cost.

We made our way to a tavern I was familiar with, The Toad and Peach. They had fair rates and good food. Most importantly, they let me perform free of charge. I had a decent relationship with the proprietor and knew as long as I kept the patrons spending coins, I'd be welcome.

I paid the innkeeper for use of his stables and set about caring for the ponies. Nel was used to the road and had fared well. Merin's mare looked more tired than her rider, and that was saying something, as the princess damn near nodded off leaning on a rick of hay.

I led Merin to our shared room where the princess collapsed on the mattress, falling asleep before she'd taken off her boots. She lay there on the bed, one foot dangling off the side, breathing peacefully in slumber. I gently pushed her leg onto the mattress, covered her with a blanket, and left for the common room below. While I was tired from the journey, there was still much to be done.

Most of the talk in the common room was of the impending battle at Lodir. Word had spread ahead of us somehow, though no one seemed to know any details. Recognizing the information I carried might cause a panic, I ordered a bowl of hot beef stew, kept my mouth shut, and listened.

Of all the rumors I heard, one in particular stood out. It came from a powerfully built young dwarf wearing a flat cap of olive green. He was clean shaven, with icy blue eyes and sand colored hair. I had the odd feeling I'd seen him before but found I couldn't place him. He mentioned that fewer travelers than normal had come into town that day. Folks in the tavern knew there had been the storm to contend with, so that was given most of the blame.

I wasn't so sure. The rain had been unpleasant, but most traders were used to such conditions. I suspected something else was at play, though I could only guess at what. I would have to be wary.

I finished my meal and returned to the room to see Merin was still asleep. On a whim, I shaved off my goatee, using my knife and a bucket of water the innkeeper had provided. I took a moment to relieve myself in the chamber pot and shook off my damp clothes, spreading them out to dry. Taking stock of my belongings, I nodded to myself and climbed into bed. I'd spoken to the innkeeper, and we agreed I'd perform an hour after sundown. That gave me a good two turns of the hourglass to rest.

Suffice it to say my rest was cut short.

"By the Trine, who the hell are you?" a voice shrieked from beside me.

Sitting up quickly, I rolled out of bed and grabbed my knife and hatchet, ready to defend the princess. She was standing on the other side of the bed looking at me in horror, holding the blankets tightly to her chest.

"Who did you see?" I barked, looking everywhere.

"You, you bastard," she shrieked again. She threw the blankets on the bed and grabbed the bucket I'd used to shave with. Before I could blink, she tossed it at me, cold water and all. I knocked it aside the best I could, but the water splashed all over my clothes.

"Are you daft girl?" I sputtered, annoyed as hell. "I just got them dry!"

"Who are you? What do you want?" she yelled again. I saw her eyes drop to the chamber pot. Quickly, she lifted it up.

"Stop it right there," I warned, holding my hands out toward her. "I just pissed in that. There's no need for you to soak me twice. I've got to perform in an hour, and I don't think the patrons want the smell of fresh urine wafting over them all night. I've got nothing dry to wear now as it is."

"Omens?" she asked, looking at me quizzically.

"Well, who did you think it was? An Orc Witchdoctor?"

She lowered the pot a fraction. "I...I didn't recognize you. You've shaved off your beard."

"By Goran girl," I hissed, lowering my weapons, "just cut my throat while I sleep next time—save me the anguish of your company."

She frowned at me, placing the chamber pot back on the floor. "It's an honest mistake," she said. "You look nothing like you did."

"Why, because I'm clean?" I asked, picking up my trousers, now soaking wet.

"No," she answered, dropping her eyes to the floor. "You just look…different."

"Yes, well, I'm sorry about that princess, but I can't go on stage wearing naught but my britches."

"Don't you have other clothes?"

I ground my teeth in frustration. "Aye, lass. I have other clothes, but I don't have them *here*. This was supposed to be a simple escort mission, not an epic journey to find the fabled mythic steel weapons of the ancients."

I sat down on the bed and shook my head. "There's only one thing that can be done before I perform." I looked up at her, pointedly. "You'll have to go buy me some new clothes."

"But I don't have any money," she protested.

"Oh, of course you don't," I mocked, throwing my hands in the air, irritated. "Why would you? You're only a princess with access to the golden coffers of the royal vault! Why bother yourself with coins at all?"

She blinked at me, her eyes flashing dangerously. Then I heard her sigh. A moment later, she was throwing on her cloak.

"Fine, I caused this mess, so I'll fix it. I'll go get you some new clothes. I saw a shop on the way in, I'm sure I can work out something with the owner."

"No," I stood, walking around the bed, shaking my head. "You can't go telling everyone who you are. The more people who know, the more trouble it will cause."

I stepped over to my pack and pulled out a small leather satchel. I reached inside and took out five silver coins, each stamped with the face of her father.

"Take these," I said, handing her the coins. "Go to Prichard's. He's a fair dwarf, he won't cheat you too badly. Pay no more than you have to. What you've got there should be more than enough to buy me a new tunic and trousers."

Taking the coins, I saw her purse her lips sourly.

"I *am* sorry, you know," she said, somewhat angrily.

"It's alright lass," I replied with a sigh. "You scared me is all. I thought someone was attacking you."

"I'll make it up to you," she promised, looking determined.

"Nothing too fancy now," I warned her. "I don't have to look like a court popinjay—a nice black tunic and gray trousers will do. I expect a decent amount of that coin back."

"I won't let you down," she said, leaving me standing in my undergarments.

I sighed after she left, knowing I'd likely never see any of my money again.

Chapter 6: Bard Songs

Merin returned within the hour. In her hands were the aforementioned clothes she'd promised me. The tunic was a bit loose but would do for the night. When I asked her for what was left of the remaining silver, she sniffed and turned away, placing a large package she'd been carrying on her side of the bed. Deciding I'd had enough rows with her already, I left it alone for now.

I made my way downstairs, seeing a large crowd had gathered in the common room below. I suspected word had gotten out that a bard was performing and those travelers staying in town had come for some entertainment. A few were wayward merchants just passing through, while others I knew to be local folk that lived nearby. They all looked excited at the opportunity of hearing my performance.

There were a handful belonging to the military class as well. I saw a knot of Bolters near the front of the inn, their craft obvious, as each was dressed in leather armor while cache of light crossbows lay on the wall near their table. Adjacent to them were a pair of Stonebreakers. A male and a female with thick necks and broad shoulders, clear evidence of their military training. I scanned the rest of the crowd and took in the faces. One of them stood out to me. Making my way over, I gave the she-dwarf I'd spotted a wry smile.

"What's a well-respected Engineer doing in a place like this?" I asked, stopping in front of her table.

The she-dwarf looked up at me and shook her head in mock sympathy. "I didn't know they were letting *any* dwarf in," she sniped back. "I suppose even tale-tellers like you need a place to hang your hat for the evening."

My smile widened as she stood from her chair, taking my hand warmly.

"It's good to see you in one piece," I said, gently placing my head against hers in the ancient dwarven greeting. "How have you been, Ghost?"

"Never better," she responded lightly, taking her other hand, placing it behind my neck. Drawing back, my old friend cast her gaze behind me. "Are you on the run from a slew of jealous husbands again?" she teased. "Or just looking for new conquests to keep your bed warm tonight?"

I snorted and shook my head. "Just business tonight luv. I'm taking the stage in a few minutes."

"I heard that," Ghost smiled, sitting back down. "That's why we came in."

I glanced at her table, seeing a pair of young Engineers, a male and a female, looking at me closely.

"What about you? Did you get sick of putting up with Ashten?" I asked, looking around. "Where is the penny-pinching bastard?"

Ghost grunted and kicked a chair out from under the table, offering me a seat.

"Captain Raine took the rest of the company east, two days ago," she explained. "Left me here to collect money owed by the innkeeper. Fifty gold coins well earned. The innkeeper, Cherak, has assured me payment by the end of the night. In the meantime, Ashten made for the old outpost near Birch Hill."

"Draymore's old digs?" I asked, surprised. "How long's it been since it was inhabited?"

Ghost leaned forward and took a drink of her ale. "Going on twenty years now," she replied with a shrug. "King Helfer ordered it active once again ever since the incursion into our lands from the north."

I nodded, knowingly. "Cleaned up the horde, have you?" I asked, suspecting her answer.

"Aye, once General Ironhenge got organized, we pushed them out within a fortnight," she said, with a nod toward her companions. "This is his lad, and our newest recruit, Monchakka Ironhenge."

The young, dark-haired male seated across from me nodded in greeting.

"Monchakka, this is Omens," Ghost said, introducing me. "Next to him is Kora, the best young sharpshooter I've seen in a long time."

"Better than you?" I asked, raising an eyebrow in question.

"She's getting there," Ghost answered, winking at Kora.

"It's nice to meet you," Kora said, giving me a brief smile.

"I have heard of you," Monchakka said thoughtfully. "It's said you once traveled into the Jagged Lands."

I hesitated, flashing Ghost with a quick look.

"A dark time to be sure," the elder Engineer said, tossing Monchakka a warning glance.

The young dwarf raised his hands in apology. "I meant no offense. I'm cursed with an overabundance of curiosity, as my superior officers keep telling me."

It was at that moment I realized the two dwarves with Ghost were different than most I'd met. Neither had mentioned that I was a dreg, which nearly every clan dwarf in Rahm brought up within the first few seconds of meeting me. More surprisingly, the lad had apologized to me, a thing that had never happened in all my dealings with clan dwarves. Kora, too, had been polite and respectful. They were decidedly different from what I was used to.

"No apology needed," I said, brushing the matter off with a wave of my hand. "Did you say your clan name is Ironhenge? I didn't know they had Engineers."

Monchakka glanced over to Ghost, who positively beamed. "Two now," she said, happily. "My clan has taken me back."

That was some news.

"The General allowed you back in?" I asked in surprise.

"Aye," she said with a nod. "I'm Aurora Ironhenge again, though I still prefer Ghost."

I sat back in my chair, stunned. If a baked walnut like Arik Ironhenge could rescind his order and let his sister back into the clan, maybe there was hope for other dregs like me after all.

It dawned on me that Ghost was one of the few dwarves I might trust with news of the invasion. I was about to tell her, when I spotted the innkeeper, Cherak, waving at me to take the stage.

I stood from the chair and took hold of my lute. "I best be getting ready," I said, nodding at all three. "I'll meet you for a pint after if you like? I have much to tell you."

"Until then," Ghost said, raising her tankard in my direction.

There are those that will tell you performers just get up on stage, play their instruments, and sing. That is only partially true. There's an art to it that many are ignorant of. I like to get the crowd's attention right away and then mix up my shows a bit. Ballads and poems don't always have the effect you are looking for. It's alright to slow things down now and then, but you don't want folk bored. It's up to the performer to get them in the right mood. Yes, I want to entertain them, but it is also about making money. Oftentimes crowds can be stubborn, and you have to play the same songs over and over every night. Other times they want you to dazzle them with something new. It's hard finding the balance sometimes, but I do enjoy the challenge. Living on the edge like this, it makes a dwarf feel alive inside.

Lucky for me, I had played at the Toad and Peach many times in the past and knew the crowd quite well. I started off with a local favorite, an up-tempo piece that was sure to get the throng into a jovial mood right away.

Well, I saw a right fair maiden,
standing across the way.
With eyes as blue as an ancient sea,
and her hair as gold as hay.

The bard was playing an old fair jig,
and I knew this was my chance.
I strode across that fine inn floor
and I asked that maid to dance.

She said, "Ho, hey, hold your tongue,
Why should I dance with you, my son?
Ho, hey, the nights still young,
You best be on your way."

So, I sat down and drank my ale,

Omens of War

Bowing my head, dragging my tail,
Knowing the whole pub had seen me fail,
I'd best be on my way.

That's when this song, takes a turn,
for better or for worse.
For in came old lord Grengi's son,
like a low down dwarvish curse.

He walked to that fair maiden,
and said to her, "Let's go!"
She slapped his face and crushed his jewels,
With a knee down far below.

She said, "Ho, hey, hold your tongue,
Why should I dance with you, my son?
Ho, hey, the nights still young,
You best be on your way."

I saw him fall down to the ground,
his pain a fearsome sight,
and I knew that I'd been lucky,
I wouldn't ice my boys that night.

The lesson learned as I tell this tale,
is a lesson I know well.
Best save the lads and sleep alone,
Then risk a maiden's pit of hell!

I sang, "Ho, hey, I'll hold my tongue,

Why would we dance with her, my sons?
Ho, hey, the nights still young,
I best be on my way,
Oh, I best be on my way!"

That old chestnut did the trick.

Once I had their attention, I was off and running. I told a joke or two, to lighten the mood further and dazzled them afterwards with a few carefully selected pieces I knew would catch their fancy.

Maybe it's arrogant of me to say this but, standing in front of a common room filled with my kin always gave me an immense amount of joy. It wasn't that I could manipulate them like a master potter with a lump of fresh clay, though the thought *did* hold some appeal. It was the idea that I, a lowly dreg, could lift the spirits of the room with something as simple as a song. Truth be told, it was addicting. Not all nights were like that, because not all crowds were lighthearted—but when things went well, I had a power over them, a feeling I quite enjoyed. Some nights the feeling was strong enough where I would have played for free.

Not that I was about to admit that to any of the innkeepers.

More than that, for a brief time I felt as if I belonged, accepted by my kinfolk, and valued for my talents.

After the first hour I ended with a rousing song that had the crowd on their feet, twirling about the dance floor. Simple rule of barding, always leave them wanting more.

I stepped off the stage to heartfelt applause and collected my earnings, promising I'd return within the hour. Only minutes ago, I'd caught sight of a second troubadour who walked through the door and my spirits lifted further. It was an older bard, by the name of Corwin Braeven. He was affectionately known to all of us as Jax, because he was a Jack-of-all-trades when it came to barding. He was a virtuoso with nearly every instrument we dwarves had invented.

"They're letting in all kinds of riff raff these days, I see," he quipped at me, giving me a broad smile.

"Says the leader of the riff-raff," I grinned back, embracing him.

"I heard you were in Lodir, laddie. Have you come from the Golden Keep?" he asked, his smile fading.

"Aye, bad business there," I answered, looking around warily. "Best we discuss it in private."

"Fair enough," he grunted, looking back to the stage. "Are you done for the night?"

"No, but if you like, the next hour is free. They're all warmed up for you," I replied, my smile returning.

"Kind of you," he said, declining his head in thanks.

"Anytime for you, Jax," I said, and I meant it.

Bards are a loose knit lot, with no set rules of engagement. Should a second bard come in as Jax did, it is considered impolite to cut into the profits without asking first. It was Jax who taught me that, so, quite naturally, I gave way to the more experienced player. I needed a rest anyway, and Jax was a fine performer. I had learned much from him in the past, and, it turned out, I would learn more from him tonight.

I returned to Ghost's table, where all three Engineers were smiling up at me.

"You never cease to amaze," Ghost said, giving me a hearty clap on the back. "It's no wonder the ladies can't keep their hands off you. I'm spoken for, and I'd happily lavish you with attention if you played like that for me."

I laughed. "None of that now," I said with a shake of my head. "Ashten's a friend and I'd hate to have the Gray Company on my arse for dallying with the finest shot in the eight kingdoms."

"That was very well done," agreed the other female, Kora, clearly impressed.

"My thanks," I said simply, giving her a small smile.

"First class sir," Monchakka broke in, rising from his seat to shake my hand. "Magnificent playing! It makes me wonder if I could learn."

"You've just taken up Engineering," Kora said, frowning at him.

"I know, but—I'd still like to give it a try," he replied, waving the serving lass over. "Let me buy you a drink," Monchakka continued. "What's your pleasure?"

"An ale, for now," I answered happily, sitting down.

After Monchakka had ordered a round for everyone, I leaned closer to Ghost, glancing carefully at our surroundings.

"There's a few things I should bring you up to speed on," I said, eyeing the dwarves around us.

"What's that?" Ghost asked, taking a quaff of her drink.

I proceed to tell the trio of the events at Lodir that had inspired my impromptu journey.

"Two hordes in the last month?" Ghost questioned, raising her eyebrows. "One at Kazic-Thule and now Lodir? When's the last time that happened?"

I shrugged, leaning back in my chair when I saw Monchakka's eyes widen.

"Damn me, who is that?" he asked, somewhat breathless, looking at the staircase leading from the second floor.

I turned around and there was Merin, dressed in what I'm sure were the finest clothes Barrel Falls had to offer. I don't know why green always seems to look good on redheads, but the princess was no exception.

She wore a tight-fitting emerald tunic, stitched in white lace that left three inches of bared midriff and just enough of her bosom to where I caught myself staring a bit too hard. Around her waist was a belt of black leather fastened atop curve hugging pants. Someone, I guessed it wasn't her, had polished her black boots to an ebony shine. Her thick hair had been pulled behind her in a tight braid, while a finely etched brass clasp held the braid in place.

I sighed.

At least I knew what happened to my extra silver.

As good as she looked, I could not help but feel annoyed. I'd asked her to stay in the room and keep a low profile. This was the opposite of what I'd requested.

"I don't suppose you ever listen to anyone other than yourself?" I asked, tossing her a frown.

She sniffed at me and pulled up a chair. "Why should you have all the fun, while I'm cooped upstairs?"

Kora snorted with laughter. "I like her already."

"Give it a minute, you'll be running for your life," I muttered back, taking a long drink of ale.

I introduced the three Engineers and sat back in my chair watching Merin closely. She was laughing at something Kora had said, while Monchakka blushed furiously.

"What the hell is going on?" I heard Ghost say in my ear, leaning in close to me.

"What do you mean?" I asked, as innocently as I could.

She glared at me. "You think I don't know who she is? What the hell is the princess of the Golden Keep traipsing around with you for? Don't tell me you seduced her too."

"I told you," I tapped my chest, belching softly, "Lodir is under siege. No one in Kazic-Thul was going to launch a rescue operation on the word of a dreg. King Orius dispatched his daughter to carry the word, and I was chosen as her escort."

Before I finished, Ghost was shaking her head. "That makes no sense," she argued. "He could have sent a platoon of Stonebreakers if he wanted. Why only you—a low born bardic dreg? No offense mind you, I know your worth. I just don't understand what he was thinking."

I shrugged, quickly losing my good humor. "I don't know, and I don't care," I replied, now surly. "I just wanted to get out of Lodir before it became a butcher's yard."

Ghost was absently chewing on the inside of her cheek. "By the gods, I wish Ashten were here," she muttered. "He knows more about the nobles than I do. He mentioned Orius to me last week. Something about the political rumblings of Lodir, but I can't remember what it was."

"It's of no consequence now," I waved, turning my eyes to Jax, who was climbing on stage. "In two days' time, I'll drop her in court and be clear of it all."

Ghost gave me a long look and eased back in her chair, a worried expression on her face. "Is that Jax?" she asked, leaning forward.

"Aye," I grunted, sitting back in my seat, a feeling of unease building in the pit of my stomach. It didn't bother me that Ghost had called me a dreg. We had been boon companions once, and I believed her when she said she knew my worth. What irritated me was that I suspected she was right about the king. It *didn't* make sense. I'd been in such a hurry to get out of Lodir, I hadn't thought it through. King Orius could have sent a company of royal soldiers to summon aid. Hell, that's what he should have done. Why had he selected only Merin and me? The more I thought about it, the more anxious I grew.

I let out a deep breath and tried to relax. There wasn't much I could do about it now. I'd just have to live up to my word and deliver the princess. I allowed the others to draw me into their conversation, which consisted of Kora and Merin poking fun at Monchakka, who was proving to be an incredibly good sport about it. I could tell he liked Kora, though his eyes drifted to Merin from time to time.

Jax started to play an upbeat melody and Monchakka raised an eyebrow at his fellow Engineer, asking her to dance. Ghost wandered off to see about getting some food, which left the princess and me alone at the table.

"Are you going to ask me to dance?" she queried, giving me a hopeful smile.

"The princess, dance with a lowly dreg?" I mocked, my good humor returning.

"Yes, it will be the scandal of the year," she smiled back, rising from her seat, taking my hand.

I should have known she would be a good dancer. In my line of work it paid to know a few steps as a professional courtesy. Merin, however, was by far my superior. Together we pranced around the dance floor, her red braid twirling behind her. The princess wore a smile that I'd not seen before. It was the look of a dwarven lass who was letting loose for the first time in her life. As the melody grew faster, I watched as she was passed from partner to partner, until she came all the way back to me.

The fast-paced song was soon over, and we all clapped and shouted for more. Jax, seeing me on the dance floor, waved me up onto stage.

"Let's give them the ole, 'Cheeks a Glow,'" he said with a wink.

Michael K. Falciani

I nodded my head and flashed him a smile. There was a reason Jax was the best at this profession. He could read a crowd like a sage reads a book. I walked over to our table, swept up my lute and climbed on stage.

"You take the lead," Jax insisted, winking at me.

I nodded again and addressed the crowd.

"Well folks, it looks like you've a bit of luck tonight, as the gods have graced the inn with two bards this evening."

A raucous cheer went up and I raised my hand in acknowledgement.

"Since that seems to be the case, Jax and I are going to play an old favorite. Feel free to sing along if you are so inspired."

I sat down on my stool and looked over at Jax who had put away his lute and drums and taken out a handmade spike fiddle. He winked at me, and I began to play.

Well, I sat right down on an old inn stool,
on a day not long ago.
When a fair dwarf maid, with dark brown eyes
gave a smile, her cheeks a glow.

And I knew right then, what I had to say,
"I'm in love with you lass, don't you go away."
And she said to me, as she gave me a smile,
"Come and sit with me lad, won't you stay awhile?"

So, she took my hand, to an old inn room
on a day not long ago.
She lay on the bed, with her dark brown eyes,
And she smiled, her cheeks a glow.

And I knew right then, what I had to say,
"I'm in love with you girl, don't you run away."
And she said to me, as she gave me a smile,
"Come and lay with me boy, won't you stay awhile?"

When morning came, that maid was gone,
on a day not long ago.
That fair dwarf lass, with dark brown eyes
had left me all alone.

And I knew right then, what I had to say,
"I'm in love with the girl, but she ran away."
So, I've traveled the roads, to both here and there,
And I've never seen a maiden that was quite as fair.

I've searched the lands, both high and low,
And I'll keep on searching for those cheeks a glow.
When I find that maid, I'll give her a smile,
Cause I'm in love with the girl, and I'll stay awhile.

When the song came to a close, we heard the loudest cheer yet. Jax's hat was nearly overflowing with coins after such a performance of a crowd favorite. By the end there wasn't a dwarf in the building that wasn't singing the refrain at the top of their lungs.

I stood up and thanked Jax, giving my old mentor a hearty shake of the hand. "You truly are the best," I said to him, my voice rising above the din of the room.

"You improve every time I see you lad," he shouted back, clapping me on the shoulder. "Now, do an old dwarf a favor and go dance with that lovely lass you've been making eyes at all night."

I raised an eyebrow at him and stepped off the stage to find Merin smiling at me brightly.

"That was wonderful," she exclaimed. "I've never heard anyone play like that."

"Now you have," I replied. "It's a difficult piece to perform alone. With two bards it's more manageable, and Jax is the best."

My older counterpart, ever the showman, slowed things down and started to play a ballad, while tossing me a wink in the process. Many of the dwarves paired off and soon, were dancing rhythmically around the inn.

"I've never seen dancing like that before either," Merin said, blushing slightly, looking at the other dwarfs on the floor. Each couple was holding one another closely. "I fear I am not well versed in the world outside the palace."

I smiled at her. "It's as easy as walking on a well-worn path," I answered, holding out my hand.

She took it and placed her other hand on my shoulder, mimicking what the other she-dwarves had done. I held her firmly, placing the palm of my hand on the small of her back.

For the first few moments she held a look, caught somewhere between excitement and terror. I nearly laughed aloud.

"Try to relax," I said softly. "It's just a dance, it doesn't mean we're engaged to be married."

She smiled at me and instantly appeared more at ease. I glanced over at Monchakka and his partner. They looked very happy together, as he leaned close and whispered something in her ear.

Kora smiled brightly at his words and leaned forward, kissing him on the tip of his nose.

"I'm sorry I tried to douse you with water," Merin said, taking me by surprise.

"I'm just glad it wasn't the chamber pot," I replied, with a wry grin.

She gave me a tinkling laugh in return and my heart skipped a beat. I caught myself staring at her again, but this time I refused to look away.

"Begging your pardon lass," I said, staring into her emerald eyes, "but you truly are a sight to see."

"What do you mean?" she asked, wrinkling her nose.

By Goran, she even made a little nose-wrinkle look good.

"I mean that you are breathtakingly beautiful," I answered, honestly.

The corner of her mouth curled in a frown. "I know that I am not," she said, looking away from me. "You're mocking me again."

Gently I placed my index finger under her chin and guided her eyes back to mine.

"I'm not mocking you this time Merin," I said kindly. "I've been to all eight dwarven kingdoms and there are beauties aplenty—but not a single one is quite like you."

She looked back at me shyly and smiled.

"Why would you say that?' she asked. "You think I'll fall for a charming rogue like yourself just because you paid me a complement?"

"You think I'm charming?" I asked playfully, giving her a crooked smile. "The rogue part I understand—but charming? If I didn't know better, I'd say you were using your feminine wiles on *me*. It won't work. I've a heart of gold—I won't allow it to be sullied by the likes of you."

The more I talked, the more she laughed. Hearing the sound was like listening to the clear bubbling water of a mountain stream. Innocent and pure, she made me feel something I'd not felt in a long while. I drew her close to me and whispered in her ear.

"I…I was wrong about you," I admitted, stumbling a bit. "You're not friendless or a harridan. On the contrary, you're quite wonderful. Inside your chest beats the heart of a great soul. I feel privileged to have met you, Merin."

When I leaned back, I saw a change come over her. She wasn't just smiling at me. She was looking at me differently—with green eyes that held a longing that I knew all too well.

Normally that was the goal—seduce the female and move on to more… pleasurable activities. Tonight however, there was a problem.

I felt it too.

This was not the oncoming feeling of lust that I often experienced before lovemaking…no, this was different. I felt the heat of desire building in me yes, but—there was a feeling of warmth and caring that made everyone else in the room fade away.

As the song came to a close, I leaned in and kissed her, a kiss filled with the passion we both felt in the moment. I had never experienced anything so strongly before in my life. Her lips were soft and hungry, filled with a need only I could satiate. After a handful of rapid heartbeats, I drew away, looking at her face in wonder. I gave Merin a small smile and gently stroked the side of her face.

"Omens…I," she began, her voice husky.

I would have paid a barrel of gold to hear what was going to come out of her mouth next.

Sadly, at that exact moment, the inn came under attack.

Chapter 7: Battle at the Toad and Peach

A scream came from outside, followed by a war cry every dwarf in the northern cities knew all too well. If sallowskins had proven anything to us through the years, it was that most of them were bloodthirsty and savage. The door to the inn was smashed off its hinges as dozens of orcs and goblins rushed in.

There was a moment, just a moment, mind you, when almost everyone froze. The shock of seeing so many of our blood enemies in the Toad and Peach was a surprise, to say the least. Lucky for us, *almost* everyone froze.

Everyone except Ghost.

A large orc known among dwarves as a Chain, because of the black iron links wrapped tightly around their bodies, let out a bestial roar cowing the crowd of dwarves in front of him.

A rifle blast sounded from the back of the room.

A bullet cast in hot lead tore through the orc's chest, slamming into the creature's heart. The Chain fell backward, toppling to the ground, dead.

"Have at the piss-colored bastards!" Ghost screamed, reloading her weapon.

Her cry did the trick, as every dwarf in the building swept up whatever weapons were close and leapt into action.

I grabbed Merin by the hand and sprinted with her toward the stairs.

"Go!" I yelled, pointing up to our room. "Get inside and bolt the door, don't let anyone in!"

"What about you?" she asked, her eyes darting to the wild melee that had exploded in the common room in front of us. "You haven't got your sword."

"I'll be alright lass," I shouted back. "Now go!"

Not looking to see if she had followed my instructions, I ran over to the table where the Engineers were wreaking havoc with their rifles.

"Take this," Monchakka yelled, tossing me his longknife. Thankful to have some kind of weapon, I entered the fray.

A pair of goblins leapt in front of me. The first sallowskin I saw was a member of the goblin infantry known as a Stick. He was dressed in animal hide armor and held a wooden spear with a serrated blade of obsidian in front of him. The second was another of the goblin foot soldiers, referred to commonly as a Fang. He held a crude bronze hatchet already covered in dwarven blood. In his off hand was a warped wooden shield. They both looked at me, an unarmored bard holding nothing more than a knife, and smiled.

That was their first mistake.

Maybe your average, run-of-the-mill dwarf might have been in dire straits, but not me. The goblin's slip-up was in thinking all I had to fight with was a knife.

Wrong.

Like I said, bards have magic. We use our instruments for all kinds of things. However, the first instrument of battle we are taught to use isn't a lute or drum—hell it's not even a real weapon, like a knife.

It's our voice.

I stepped forward and let out a thunderous bellow that halted both goblins in their tracks.

"Dek'kar!"

A burst of sound shot from my mouth and stunned the pair of blackbloods in front of me. They became disoriented momentarily and that was all the time I needed. The hatchet-wielding goblin lowered his shield at my vocal attack and made for easy pickings. I dispatched him quickly with a swift thrust to the chest. The second managed to get his spear up, but the serving lass standing on his backside brained him with a crushing blow from a metal tankard to the head.

Despite my initial success, the room was close to being overwhelmed. The squad of Bolters that had been sitting at the front of the room were standing behind the two Stonebreakers, firing quarrels as fast as they could. The Stonebreakers, a male and a female, had only their shields to defend with. Neither wore their armor and both were being driven back by a raging trio of Chains.

I saw one of the Bolters go down, a goblin arrow lodged in her side. A fourth Chain, larger than his fellows, with several links of armor painted red, rushed at the pair of heavy dwarven infantry. The huge orc shoulder slammed their shields, bodily forcing them apart. The female recovered quickly, but the male was thrown aside, leaving him isolated and vulnerable.

"Cover me!" yelled Monchakka, racing forward, scooping up the wooden shield dropped by the goblin Fang I'd killed.

Kora snapped off a shot, spinning a more lightly armored Orc Ravager that rushed in front of Monchakka from its feet.

Inspired by the Engineer's courage, I ran forward blindly, determined to assist him. Shifting the knife from my right hand to my left, I grabbed the goblin spear that lay on the dance floor and charged in behind Monchakka.

By now, dozens of combatants on both sides were down. My kin had slain more of the sallowbacks, but we had fewer numbers remaining. The trio of Chains had broken off from the female Stonebreaker, fixated on killing her brother in arms.

The male Stonebreaker was close to his end, barely able to fend off a barrage of crushing blows from the Chains' warclubs. Monchakka had drawn his second weapon, a black hafted hammer and added his shield to the Stonebreakers defense in the nick of time. Blocking the next blow, the wooden shield splintered from the force of the Chain's attack. Monchakka responded in kind, swinging his hammer, connecting with a meaty *thwack* upon the orc's temple, crushing the skull.

Taken by surprise at the loss of one of their number, the other two Chains focused on this new threat.

They never saw me coming.

Taking aim, I drove the goblin spear toward the neck of a second Chain. I missed my mark and the spear slid off the orc's chest, snapping at the base of the spear head. Unable to stop my momentum, I continued forward, crashing into both of the remaining orcs, bearing all three of us to the ground. A wild melee ensued, where I lashed out blindly with my fists and knife, trying to keep myself alive long enough to regain my footing.

"Easy," I heard Monchakka say, breathing heavily from above me. Extending the bloody head of his hammer, I was able to grab hold and climb to my feet once more.

"What happened?" I asked, looking at my knife, slick with the dark blood of the enemy.

"It's not over yet," I heard Jax say grimly, holding what was left of his spike fiddle in his hands. I learned after that he had broken it over the head of a goblin archer who had taken aim at Ghost.

"I just crafted it too," he lamented, dropping the fiddle to the floor, shaking his head sadly.

Monchakka swept up the male Stonebreakers shield, as its owner was lying unconscious on the ground, and ran over to assist the female Stonebreaker, who was still contending with the remaining Orc Chain.

I glanced down at the Stonebreaker at our feet. He was still alive but had taken a terrible blow to the chest. Without the services of a priest, he would not be long for this world.

I did not want to leave the wounded fellow, but I knew my skills were needed elsewhere. I leapt forward and intercepted a yellow skinned goblin Fang who had taken off after Monchakka. Spinning, the goblin lunged at me with his sword, nearly lopping off my hand in the process. As it was, I suffered a shallow cut on the back of my wrist where the weapon grazed my arm. Raising my knife, I managed to block the Fang's back swing, while I lashed out with my fist, punching the goblin square in the jaw. The Fang dropped to the ground, and I stepped forward to finish him off.

The sneaky little bugger wasn't done yet though. He kicked out with his foot, striking the back of my knee, causing me to stumble to the ground again, my knife slipping from my grasp. Seizing his opportunity, the goblin rose above me and brought his sword down, intent on driving it through my chest. Desperately I brought my hands up, barely managing to halt the blow. We were locked in a life and death struggle for several seconds, neither of us able to gain the advantage.

A crossbow bolt slammed into the Fang's neck, killing him instantly. I pushed his dead weight off me and looked behind me to thank my savior.

There was Princess Merin, standing on the top of the balcony, her now empty crossbow in hand. Seeing me make eye contact, she hurled an object toward me. Stepping forward, I caught it and smiled.

My sword.

I'm not going to lie and say I'm the greatest swordmaster in the eight kingdoms. As I've said before, I'm a lover, not a fighter. However, with a sword I am *well* above average, more than a match for most sallowskins when I have my preferred weapon of choice. Now that I had my blade in hand, I was ready to avenge my fallen kin.

Armed with both sword and knife, I attacked and slew four more of the Stick and Fang brigade, along with an Orc Ravager. That Ravager put up a serious fight, wounding me on both my shoulder and arm. Behind me, Jax was making quick work of the enemy with his staff, while Ghost and Kora continued their deadly barrage.

Monchakka and the female Stonebreaker were still defending against the last Orc Chain. He alone was keeping the sallowskins in the fight.

His death, I knew, would break them.

Only a single Bolter was still standing behind Monchakka and the Stonebreaker, the other five having fallen in battle. The last was a dark-haired dwarf lad who looked even younger than my twenty-four years.

"Kora!" Monchakka yelled, blindly swiping at the orc with his hammer. "Shoot this bastard!"

"I don't have an angle!" she yelled back, ducking under the table as a goblin arrow flew past her head.

"Thin out those archers!" I heard Ghost scream, frantically reloading her rifle from her cover behind an oak chair.

Jax ran forward and let out a bellow of his own.

"Brak'dur!"

Older and more experienced, Jax's bellow was more effective than mine had been. The score of remaining sallowskins were stunned by its force. While only a half-dozen other dwarves were still on their feet, they were able to take advantage of the momentary lull in fighting. Led by Jax, they evened the odds considerably in a matter of seconds.

I ran forward and used a second bellow of my own. My vocal attack wasn't aimed at the goblins or the Ravagers, but at the huge Orc Chain still engaged with Monchakka and the Stonebreaker. I let loose, hoping to stun the monster as I had done to the goblins earlier in the fight.

"Dek'kar!"

It didn't work out like I'd planned.

The Chain, red links and all, roared back at me, completely unaffected by my vocal attack. Instead, the huge sallowskin swung his war club, forcing me to throw myself out of its range. I crashed to the floor, landing heavily on my shoulder. Monchakka, seeing his chance, lashed out with his hammer, smashing it into the orc's chest. The blow shot up sparks as it was repelled by the black iron chain wrapped around the orc's body.

The Chain looked at Monchakka with contempt and batted aside the Engineer's hastily raised shield with his club, knocking him backward. Off balance, Monchakka fell to the ground next to me, the shield spinning from his grasp. The female Stonebreaker, worn down already from the bludgeoning she had taken, valiantly rushed in front of Monchakka in an attempt to keep him from being killed.

"Not today, you blackblooded bullocks!" she screamed.

The Chain swept her aside with his war club, its crushing attack slamming the she-dwarf against the inn wall where she collapsed in a daze.

I knew at that moment, we were done. This was our end, or should have been, laying as we were, defenseless, facing a merciless enemy.

The last three goblin archers had pinned down Kora and Ghost. I, along with my other allies, were stunned or dead.

That's when I saw them. I could scarcely believe my own eyes. Standing in the back of the inn were two figures crouched in the kitchen doorway. The first was a dwarf, dressed in the yellow smock of a neophyte Mage. She whispered something under her breath and leveled a staff of holly at the knot of archers still shooting at the Engineers. A blast of fire shot from her staff, scattering the goblins, freeing Ghost and Kora from their barrage.

The second figure in the doorway was a Shaman—a *goblin* Shaman. I couldn't make out his face, as the hood of his ivy green cloak was draped over his head. I saw him place his staff on the ground and extend a hand. He, too, whispered words of magic. Before I could do anything, climb to my feet, or shout a warning, the snarling form of an ethereal wolf sprang from the goblin's staff, leapt past the dwarves and landed directly in front of the Chain. The orc, taken by surprise, hesitated and swung its war club at the wolf, causing the ghostly form to dissipate into the air.

"Stay down!" Ghost screamed, oblivious to the Shaman's appearance. Shouldering her weapon, the sharpshooter aimed and pulled the trigger. Her shot slammed under the ribs of the Chain, who took the hit prodigiously and puffed out his chest. A second shot from Kora glanced off the orc's thick armor as he raised his club to crush Monchakka.

Free of the Chain's attention, I ignored the pain in my shoulder, scrambled to my feet and launched myself off a chair that lay nearby. Leaping on the orc's broad back, I tried desperately to keep him from executing his attack. The large, muscular creature grabbed hold of me by the collar and hurled me aside like I was a small child. I crashed into the remaining Bolter, both of us toppling to the ground in a heap. The orc let out a roar, lifting his club high overhead, preparing to crush Monchakka's skull.

There was a steely snap of metal twine, as a hissing sound cut through the air. A black crossbow bolt, made from eight inches of dwarven steel, hit the orc in his open mouth, punching through the back of its throat, driving into the base of the creature's brain.

The huge Chain staggered backward, its eyes wide with shock, and toppled to the ground with a resounding crash.

I untangled myself from the Bolter and looked behind me.

There was Merin, her mouth open in shock, staring at the orc she'd killed.

Her perfect shot had saved us all.

I glanced back at the doorway searching for our rescuers.

Of the Mage and Shaman that saved us, there was no sign.

After the battle ended, there was still much to be done. Of the nearly seven hundred dwarves that lived in Barrel Falls, one hundred twenty five had been slain. Nearly twice that number had been wounded, many of whom lay close to death. The single priest that lived close by had saved a half-dozen already, including the male Stonebreaker at the Toad and Peach. Unfortunately she had exhausted herself in the process.

They would have lost more if it weren't for Jax and me. We spent the next two hours playing our lutes, working our bardic magic upon as many of the wounded as we could. Some were too far gone for our ministrations to have much effect. However, we did manage to save dozens of lives that otherwise would have slipped into the shadowy realm of death. Jax, in particular, was effective. His healing music worked wonders on anyone who heard it.

As I played, I noted the wounds on my hand and shoulder faded, and the bruised ribs I'd suffered lost much of the pain I'd felt after the battle. Monchakka's wheezing lungs returned to their normal state of breathing, as Kora helped him to their room.

Ghost was storming around town, determined to find out where the sallowskins had come from and discover the purpose of their attack. She returned after two hours and pulled me aside.

"We need to talk," she growled, looking at me pointedly.

I nodded and followed her into the corner where the table she had been sitting at earlier in the night had been turned into a medical supply area.

"What's wrong?" I asked, feeling a weariness settle upon me.

"Tell me again what you are doing with Princess Merin way the hell out here in Barrel Falls?"

"I told you," I answered tiredly. "The king sent me to lead her to Kazic-Thul on a mission to summon aid against the horde attacking the Golden Keep."

She looked hard at me, trying to determine whether or not I was keeping information from her.

"Stop eyeballing me like that," I snapped, raising my hand in irritation. "I'm too tired to lie, not that I would in an instance like this."

Her face relaxed a fraction. Ghost glanced over at Merin who was helping bandage the leg of one of the patrons I'd managed to bring back from death's doorstep.

"Do you think the princess would compromise your mission?" Ghost asked.

I looked at her in confusion. "Compromise? How?"

"Do you think she told anyone about this trip?" Ghost pressed.

"No, I don't believe so," I answered. "I was with her from the time King Orius spoke to us until we left."

Ghost pursed her lips, chewing over my intel. "Who else knew about your mission to Kazic-Thul?"

"As far as I know, no one," I replied. "Save the king, of course."

She studied my face, seeing no sign of deceit.

"Then how do you explain this?" she asked, taking a folded parchment out of her pocket.

Handing the paper to me, I opened the parchment and looked at it in shock.

It was a picture of Princess Merin, professionally drawn by someone who had seen her face and knew it well.

"Where did you get this?" I asked, feeling uneasy.

"That huge Orc Chain had it tucked inside the pocket of his breeches," she answered grimly.

I frowned at the parchment and looked up at Ghost.

"No orc hand drew this," I said, feeling like I'd been kicked in the stomach.

"No," she agreed. "It was drawn by a dwarf, someone who knew what they were doing."

I stared at Ghost, her implications obvious.

"It could be a renegade," I suggested, refusing to believe what my gut was telling me. "Another dwarf, angry at the princess?"

She frowned and shook her head. "You know it's worse than that Omens," she murmured, turning the paper over.

On the backside, written in bold hand, was a simple note.

To my beloved daughter.

Underneath it was a rough sketch of another dwarf, hastily drawn, but easily recognizable. With that handsome face and winsome smile, I blinked twice, dumbfounded at the sketch on the back of the parchment.

"By Andovar, what the hell is going on?" I swore under my breath. It was a picture of me.

Chapter 8: Battle Scars

The thought that Orius had commissioned the sallowskins to kill his last remaining child *and* me weighed heavily upon my mind. Neither Ghost nor I could be certain what was going on. It was possible the picture had been stolen by someone close to the king, but that was highly unlikely. Ghost advised we keep the information to ourselves until she could talk it over with Ashten. He was the younger brother to King Helfar and was likely to have a greater insight on the matter. In the meantime, Ghost had volunteered her services to help me get the princess safely to Kazic-Thul.

I trudged up the stairs an hour past midnight, beyond tired, followed closely by Merin. We entered the room, and I closed the door behind us. I placed a half-full bucket of warm water I'd carried up the stairs on the floor. The princess stopped, facing away from me, looking out the window into the darkness of the town. She had been quiet, withdrawn over the last half hour, saying next to nothing to me or anyone else.

"Omens?" she asked, a catch in her voice.

"Highness?" I answered, immediately concerned.

She turned around, with tears in her eyes. "What happened tonight?" she asked, breaking down, unable to hold back her emotions.

Imbecile, I thought to myself, as I moved forward to hold her. She was a princess, unused to violence and bloodshed. I had barely checked on her after the battle, having been preoccupied with healing the fallen. Merin, bless her soul, had been assisting with the wounded. Her clothes were covered in stains, with both the red blood of our kin and the black blood of the enemy. She had watched dwarves slip into death, her words, the last they would ever hear. I, her protector, the one dwarf responsible for her well-being, had done little to comfort her after this terrible ordeal.

Now, in the hours afterwards, the weight of the attack had set in. She reached out to me, the only dwarf nearby whom she felt she could trust.

I held her in my arms, comforting her as best as I could.

"I'm sorry lass," I said, rubbing her on the back as she wept against my shoulder. "You're safe now."

After a few minutes, her tears lessened, and she drew her head away from mine, looking at me closely.

"I'm sorry," she whispered, her voice filled with sorrow. "I know I'm supposed to be stronger, braver—but I've never been in a battle before. I've never seen death up close. That serving girl, the one who brought us our drinks–she died tonight. I held her hand as she passed. I didn't even know her name."

I sighed and touched her hair gently. "Aye, I heard she passed, and she's lucky to have had you there in her last moments."

I leaned in close, wiping the tears from Merin's face.

"Her name was Gia. She died trying to save her kin. I saw her brain a goblin I had stunned earlier. She hit it with a metal tankard. She did not show fear, nor remorse in the face of danger. Gia died, yes, but she died for us all. When she passed, she was looking up at a face she helped save. Remember her bravery tonight princess, and every night hence. That is what dwarves do for one another. Had I been killed tonight, I would have been proud to have fallen among such brave kin, which includes yourself."

Merin looked down at the floor. "I didn't do anything," she said harshly, her voice bitter. "I ran up here, into our room and I was afraid. I didn't want to go back down. I was scared that I would be killed."

"But you did come back," I said with a frown. "Even though I told you not to."

"What would you have me do?" she snapped, growing angry. "Monchakka was down there—so were Kora and Ghost. I couldn't just leave them to die!"

She pushed away from me, her face twisted in fury. "And you!" she snarled. "With no weapon, you still charged at the enemy. By the Trine, you're a dreg! Spit upon by society, living on the edge of civilization. You don't owe me anything, do you hear me? I didn't want you to die, not for me!"

She stepped forward and shoved me again.

"So, I picked up my crossbow and grabbed your sword," she huffed at me accusingly. "I ran back to the common room and fought, but it was too late."

Her shoulders slumped forward. "I was too late," she repeated, her voice breaking again. "I couldn't save them."

"That's enough of that," I said, moving close to her. "You did save them, some of them at any rate," I continued. "You shot that goblin that was on top of me. You brought down that Orc Chain with a bolt to the brain. That single action saved most of the dwarves in the common room. Who knows how many lives were preserved with that shot? Because of you, we were able to begin healing, caring for the wounded sooner than we would have otherwise."

Merin did not hear it. She turned away, angry.

I stepped forward and grabbed her firmly by the shoulders. "Look at me," I pleaded.

Merin's tear filled eyes rose off the floor to peer into mine.

"You witnessed a horrible attack where many of our kin died. Without you, things would have been much worse. Don't celebrate our victory tonight—it is tainted with the loss of our dead. But you should take solace in knowing you did everything you could to save this town from an invading force."

She stood, looking at me with sadness, nodding her head in understanding.

"You look a mess—did you know that?" she asked, running her hands along the now bloodstained and tattered fabric of the tunic she'd purchased for me only hours ago.

"I know," I sighed, stripping it off, tossing it to the floor. I reached for the bucket, but her hand on my arm stopped me.

"Let me," she insisted, picking up a linen towel from the roughhewn wooden table standing against the wall. Merin dipped the cloth in the warm water and proceeded to wipe away the trials of battle upon my body.

I had been washed like this before, of course, many times, as a matter of fact—but this time was different. Merin and I had shared more than a few intimate moments in the last two days. From our encounter in the courtroom to the life or death struggle in the common room below us, our association with one another had changed a great deal.

Surviving a battle does things to a relationship like nothing else can. The struggle against death is absolute. Those who come out alive afterward share in something intangible, a feeling that you've somehow cheated death together. I'd felt it before, and I knew Merin felt it too.

After she'd finished cleansing my body, I volunteered to do the same for her. She did not object. Instead, she allowed me to unbutton the back of her tunic. Once loose, she shrugged it off, dropping the green fabric silently to the floor. My hands were steady, and I took my time, making certain I washed her thoroughly. At some point, the princess tilted her head back toward mine as I began to clean the front of her neck. Our lips were mere inches from one another, and I found myself unable to look away.

I'm not sure who moved first, but before I knew it, the cloth had fallen from my fingers, and I was kissing her with all the passion we'd felt downstairs.

My lips moved from her face to her neck, as she moaned with pleasure in my ear. I made my way slowly downward.

"What are you doing?" she gasped, her breathing heavy.

"Just lay back," I instructed, shushing her with a kiss.

"What the hell… are you doing to me?" she moaned, her eyes rolling into the back of her head. I leaned back, taking in her beautifully formed body. She was magnificent, like a nubile goddess come to life.

"Trust me," I answered, kissing her again.

Afterwards, both of us spent, we lay, bathed in the sweat of lovemaking. I held onto Merin, my arms clasping her tightly.

"Is it always like that?" she asked when she finally found the strength to speak.

"What do you mean?" I questioned, somewhat alarmed.

"Is lovemaking always like that?" she repeated, smiling at me.

'*By Goran, she's a virgin,*' I thought to myself, realizing I'd just deflowered a princess. '*Was a virgin,*' I couldn't help but muse.

I didn't want to ruin the moment for her, but I didn't want to lie either. "I don't know," I answered with a ruefully chuckle. "I can only say that it was exquisite."

She laughed, a warm and wicked sound that was wonderful to hear. "By the Gods, that was incredible," she confessed, kissing my neck. "Can we do it again?"

I laughed softly. "Yes, though I will need a few minutes."

"How long?" she demanded, her face turning in a pout.

"Not long," I promised, kissing her ear playfully.

Chapter 9: Thorana

The princess and I slept until an hour after dawn the next morning. Gathering our things, we arrived at a very different common room than the one we'd left the night before. The dead, both dwarves and sallowskins, had been removed.

There was good news mixed with bad. Two more dwarves had slipped into death during the night, their wounds too much to overcome. Four others, however, had been saved, brought back from the brink of death by the now rejuvenated priestess. Jax had stayed up through much of the night, his magical melodies refreshing the priestess more quickly than even he could have imagined.

A counting of one hundred and fifty-three blackbloods had been slain. Their bodies were piled in a great pyre at the edge of town and burned. Of the dwarven dead, many had been laid to rest in a mass grave dug by loved ones in the night. There were tears shed and words spoken over those that had passed before their time. Sadly, there were greater challenges to be met. Further grieving of those that had fallen would have to wait.

Scouts had been out since dawn, including Ghost. There was evidence that the company that had attacked us was part of a larger force roaming the area. Tracks of more than a thousand sallowskins lay to the west of Barrel Falls, though no one could guess at their destination. With so many of the enemy close by, the residents of Barrel Falls had begun readying their defenses, preparing for battle. They would not be taken unaware again. Ghost was commissioned by the town to bring word to the dwarven king at Kazic-Thul in order to bring reinforcements.

Merin and I met Ghost in the common room, along with her proteges. Monchakka seemed recovered from the brutal thrashing he'd been through the night before. All three had re-armed themselves and looked ready to be off.

"It's about time," Ghost muttered, irritated at the delay. "I thought you might not get up until midmorning."

"It was a long night," I answered unapologetically.

"Sure sounded like it," Kora quipped, staring somewhat wistfully at Merin.

The princess's cheeks grew a touch red, and she cast her eyes to the floor.

"Let's be off," snorted Ghost, with a shake of her head.

"I need to get the ponies," I said, starting for the door.

"No," Ghost snapped, her eyes hard.

I stopped, glowering at the Engineer.

"I'm not leaving my Nel here," I argued.

"I've already spoken to Cherak," Monchakka put in, standing from his chair. "He promised to take good care of both of your mounts."

"Why do we have to leave them?" I argued, suspecting I was not going to like the answer I was about to receive.

"We're not taking the roads," Ghost explained, her tone quiet. "Too many eyes there, and we don't know who to trust."

I wanted to argue, tell her that she was being overly cautious, but then I remembered the flicker of fire I'd seen two nights ago when Merin and I had set up camp. As much as it pained me, I had to agree with the more experienced Engineer.

"Through the mountains then?" I guessed, knowing that was our best option.

"Aye," Ghost nodded, picking up her rifle. "We'll cut through the hills to the north, follow the old game trails all the way to Draymore's Outpost."

"You're hoping to find Ashten still there?" I asked.

"Yes," she answered, "he and the rest of the Gray Company. With thirty Engineers we should be able to get Merin safely to the Valley of Souls and into Kazic-Thul. Then maybe we can start sweeping these sallow skinned bastards from dwarven lands once and for all."

We left out the back entrance of the inn, keeping the hoods of our cloaks up and our heads down. Minutes later, we arrived at the eastern edge of town. There was a clear stream running north out of the eastern foothills. We walked past the white rush of the waterfall there. It carved its way into a large boulder forming the shape of a barrel the town took its name from. Walking past the waterfall, we followed Ghost into the highlands and across decidedly more rugged terrain.

"Wait," called a voice from behind us, as we approached the hills.

Turning around, we saw a dwarf dressed in heavy banded mail running toward us. I recognized her as the female Stonebreaker we had fought alongside last night.

"Been looking for you all morning," she panted, resting a heavy broadsword over her right shoulder. "Might have missed you, save for the lass with the yellow smock."

An image of a dwarf Mage from the previous evening flashed in my mind.

"What do you want with us?" Ghost asked, interrupting my thoughts.

She nodded once at Monchakka. "If you think I'll be beholden to some Stonebreaker turned Engineer, you're out of your bleeding mind," she said, looking pointedly at Ghost's nephew.

"You think you're beholden to me?" Monchakka asked, somewhat perplexed at her appearance.

"Ye saved me mate, Horath, from being crushed to death last evening," she continued, her face hardening. "I saw what you did—scooped up that Fang's shield and kept the Chains off him. Then you had the good graces to help me as well. You didn't do half bad for a bean pole, grease monkey, Engineer."

"I didn't do anything more than you last night," Monchakka protested, unsure if he'd been praised or insulted.

"Aye, that's true, the lot of you are as brave as they come," she agreed.

Like all Stonebreakers, the she-dwarf was powerfully built. Her face was handsome rather than pretty. The sides of her head had been shaved to the scalp, while on top she wore a thick mohawk that extended down behind her in a tight braid, plaited to the middle of her back. She didn't seem to me like the type that would take no for an answer.

"What is it that you want?" Ghost asked, cutting to the chase.

The Stonebreaker shifted her eyes to the older dwarf and leaned against her shield.

"I mean to go with you," she answered, almost daring Ghost to rebuke her.

"Our path is a dangerous one," Ghost replied, glancing at me. "Barrel Falls may well need warriors like you in the near future."

The Stonebreaker leaned in closer and dropped her voice. "I know what the sallowskins are after," she said. "I heard the pair of you talking last night. I doubt the town will be bothered once you leave."

Kora stepped forward. "What do you mean?" she asked. "What are the sallowskins searching for?"

"This is not the time to discuss it," Ghost said, with a furtive glance toward me.

"The hell it isn't," Monchakka snapped, his voice firm. "We are risking our lives here. I'd like to know why."

Ghost hesitated, and I came to her rescue.

"They were after me," I said, not telling the whole truth. Until we knew more, Ghost and I wanted to keep the princess and the others in the dark about the attempt on her life.

"Why?" Kora demanded.

"I have an accurate report of the invading horde to bring to King Helfer," I continued, thinking on my feet. "Also, Merin is the daughter of King Orius. She has come along to help convince the king that the attack on Lodir is true. I said as much last night, though I didn't know a mini horde of blackbloods would descend on Barrel Falls because of it."

Ghost looked at me for a moment and nodded in affirmation.

"She's a princess?" Monchakka asked, his eyes widening as he looked at Merin.

"You didn't know?" Thorana questioned.

"None of them did," Ghost answered.

"The Sallies are after you?" Kora asked, her face turning in a frown toward me.

"Aye, and the sooner we get moving, the better," I grunted, hoping the Stonebreaker hadn't heard that Merin and I were *both* targets.

"My place is with you," the Stonebreaker said firmly.

"We're going to be traveling lightly, at great pace," Ghost sighed, giving in to Stonebreaker's request. "That armor you wear will grow heavy and may give away our position."

The burly Stonebreaker snorted and gave Ghost a defiant smile. "I'll race you all wearing this," she sneered, "as quietly as any of you.

Besides, if we run across any more of those Chains, you'll be glad I'm geared for battle. I'm armed now. If I'd had my little chopper last night," she continued, patting her broadsword, "I'd have chased them all out on my own."

I smiled, taking a shine to the lasses bravado.

"We could use the muscle," I said, looking at Ghost. "We know she can handle herself. She certainly proved that last night."

Ghost looked past me, staring a moment at Merin, who had said nothing.

"Alright then," she conceded at last. "But you take your orders from me Stonebreaker...understand?"

"Aye," she nodded, picking up her shield and slinging it on her back.

"What is your name?" Merin asked politely.

The Stonebreaker smiled grimly and sheathed her sword. "It's Thorana, Stonebreaker of the Dark Anvil Clan—but my friends call me Rage."

We left Barrel Falls behind us, cutting east through the Elkdale Hills. Despite traveling on foot through rough terrain, we made better time than I would have hoped. Ghost often scouted ahead, with Monchakka left to lead the group. She would come back and speak with him every now and then, keeping contact when she could. I walked a few paces ahead of Merin, while Thorana followed close behind her. Kora brought up the rear, keeping watch on the trail we left in our wake, eradicating any sign of our passing as best she could.

It occurred to me that we had unconsciously surrounded the princess, each trying to keep her safe. This made sense to all of us, albeit for different reasons. Ghost and I knew she had been targeted for death, while the others believed she was the key to her city receiving aid in time. I could not help but wonder why anyone would have wanted her dead. She was not next in line to the throne, nor was she a political liability. Her death would be tragic but would hardly upset those already in power. Something more was at play here, but I did not have the time or the knowledge to piece it together.

I shook my head and focused on the task at hand. It didn't matter why Merin had been targeted, only that she had.

Four hours into our trek, Ghost called for a halt. We stopped at a trickle of a stream where we could refill our waterskins and enjoy a quick repast.

Ghost had taken charge for a reason. She was more than just the oldest amongst us, she was by far the most experienced. We ate in near silence, with two of our ranged members constantly on the lookout. Kora watched with Monchakka, while Ghost paired with Merin and her crossbow.

While our rest was short lived, I took advantage of it and played a rapid staccato on my drum, meant to refresh stamina. I could feel the bardic magic wash over me as I played. Though our rest was only a half turn of the hourglass, I felt as though I'd rested far longer. At a nod of thanks from Ghost, we were soon on the move again.

While she did not take watch, Thorana had proven to be a valuable member to our group. Not only did she live up to her word of moving quietly, she loped along at great speed despite wearing her heavy armor. She asked few questions, and when she did, they were succinct and to the point. On one occasion, Ghost came back, thinking we might come under attack. Without hesitation Thorana moved to the front of the line, motioning to us all to stay behind her.

"Let them show their faces," I heard her mutter. "It will take more than a few Chains to get past me."

While the attack turned out to be a wandering grizzly bear, it showed us all we could count upon the Stonebreaker to act quickly and keep her head.

We covered more than twenty miles that day as we moved through the mountains. We were lucky, as the rains from the previous day did not return. Once the sun grew close to the horizon, Ghost called for a stop. We made camp in a thick grove of trees a score of paces off the game trail that ran along the side of the mountain. Most of our gear, tents and the like, had been left behind. I wasn't overly concerned about myself, as I'd slept outdoors wrapped in my cloak more times than I could remember. I assumed the Engineers and the Stonebreaker were used to such conditions as part of their military background. To her credit, Merin had held up well, despite the journey's many hardships.

We ate a tasteless meal of salted meat, bread and cheese, and washed it down with lukewarm water. Despite our lack of comfort, I had to admit, we'd fared much better than I would have suspected that morning. We were within a day and a half of Kazic-Thul, and the security of the dwarven walls it offered. King Helfer was likely to have patrols within a half a day's ride of his city. If we could find one of those, I knew we would be safe. With any luck, we could reach the Valley of Souls by this time tomorrow.

If I'd been traveling alone, I might have loosened the reins a bit and pressed onward. Ghost wasn't about to let that happen.

"No fire tonight," she ordered, as twilight was upon us.

"Do you really think someone will see it out here?" Merin asked, looking around at the solitude of the glade.

"We're up in the hills lass," Thorana answered for Ghost, setting down her shield. "Seen at the right angle, a fire could be detected miles away—not to mention the sight and smell of the smoke."

Merin sighed and sat down with a nod, wrapping herself tightly in her cloak.

It was at that moment, the trouble began.

Kora raced into the grove, her eyes wide.

"We have a problem," she reported, licking her lips nervously.

"What is it?" Ghost asked in surprise.

Kora motioned back the way she'd come from.

"Through the trees, less than a mile away," she explained. "Both Monchakka and I saw it. A line of sallowskins, moving at speed."

"Shit," Ghost hissed, grabbing her rifle. "How the hell did they find us?"

"I covered our tracks on more than one occasion," Kora answered, her hands tightening on her own rifle. "Even an expert tracker would have had trouble following the path we took."

"This is a piss poor spot to defend," Thorana muttered, picking up her shield and drawing her sword. "How many are there?"

"A hundred, at least."

Thorana cursed under her breath. "Damn, that's a bit more than I can handle."

She looked up at Ghost, her eyes blazing. "A few of us might hold them off," she suggested, "allowing the others to escape."

"I don't want any of you to die for me," Merin said, standing up proudly. "If it's me they are after, then I will go to them and leave you all to get away safely."

"That's not an option," Ghost argued, her face set. "You, highness, are the only one of us that truly matters. Without you, no rescue can go to Lodir, and the Golden Keep will fall. If it does, the sallowskins will have a toehold here on the southern continent and it will be the beginning of the end for the eight kingdoms."

"Well, we'd better think of something," Thorana said, tightening a cinch on her shield. "Else you can get in formation behind me while I tackle them head on."

"I have an idea," I offered, looking at Ghost. "But there's no time to explain. Get Monchakka back here immediately," I ordered, tearing into my backpack.

Kora flicked her eyes to Ghost, who nodded briefly.

"All of you, gather your things," I continued. "Ghost, once they get back, sweep the area of our prints. Leave no trace we were ever here."

Less than a minute later, Kora ran back with Monchakka in tow.

"They are close," the young Engineer said, panting lightly with exertion. "Only a minute, maybe two behind us."

Thorana put an armored gauntlet upon the hilt of her sword.

"Stay your hand," I said to her, pulling my backpack over my shoulders.

"What's your plan?" Ghost asked in a growled whisper as she eradicated our footprints as best she could.

"This," I answered, giving her a smile.

In my hands I held my bamboo flute.

"Are you going to flute them to death?" Thorana asked, her face outraged.

"Trust me," I answered with a wink.

Minutes later the sallowskins entered the clearing. The Engineers had been right, there were more than one hundred orcs and goblins that swarmed forward, anxious to come face to face with their prey.

Unfortunately for them, there was no one left standing in the glade.

The blackbloods spent several moments fanning out, looking everywhere, their frustration mounting. One of the sallowskins, a well-muscled orc dressed in black leather armor, carrying a bow and a quiver of arrows, stepped forward, searching the ground meticulously. One of the others, an orc Chain, armored with two sets of black iron links, barked at the kneeling orc in obvious frustration.

The orc dressed in leather snapped back at the Chain, his eyes narrowing in anger, his hand going instinctively to the three-and-a-half-foot long machete at this side. The Chain gave a guttural command, and his company began to leave the way they had come. The orc tracker was left standing in the glade alone, trying to solve the puzzle of the missing dwarves. He sniffed at the air and cast his gaze upward, studying halfway up the trees. Seeing nothing, he snorted and left, striking out after the others.

Several minutes passed as we watched the sallowskins leave. After I deemed it safe, I changed the tune I was playing slightly, and each member of our group drifted safely to the ground.

"Where did a wandering troubadour learn to do that?" Ghost asked, her eyes filled with wonder.

I shook my head. "I keep telling you all, I'm not a troubadour, I'm a bard. That was magic, bard magic."

"I didn't know bards could work such magic," Thorana admitted, looking at me with appreciation. "Damn fine trick."

I smiled. "It's not as powerful or ostentatious as spells worked by Mages. Nor is it steeped in mystery like the incantations of the Mystics. Anyone can learn, if they have the discipline and talent to do so."

"Still, levitating us above the trees like that," Monchakka said, his admiration obvious. "That was inspired."

I laughed softly. "I've had to use it a few times in the past," I admitted, glancing at Merin. "Though never on a group as large as this one."

"Let's get some rest," Ghost suggested, stepping toward the edge of the clearing. "I'll take the first watch. Kora, I'll wake you in an hour."

Kora nodded, while I made to lay down next to Merin.

"Omens, Thorana, a word," Ghost said, halting me in my tracks.

"Back in a bit," I smiled, giving Merin a quick wink.

We followed Ghost to the outskirts of the glade, all three of us walking in silence. I did not know what Ghost wanted, but I knew it couldn't be anything good.

"What's this about?" I asked, breaking the silence.

"Thorana first," Ghost said, her eyes on the Stonebreaker.

"What is it?" Thorana asked.

"Back at Barrel Falls, explain to me how you knew where to find us."

Thorana grunted. "I answered this question already. A dwarf lass in a yellow smock told me outside the inn."

"How did you know Merin was a princess of Lodir?" Ghost pressed, her eyes hard.

The burly Stonebreaker shrugged her massive shoulders. "I saw one of the royal guards in the common room when she arrived," Thorana explained.

"Her royal guard?" I asked, suddenly confused. "Merin and I were traveling alone."

The Stonebreaker raised her left hand defensively. "It may be I was mistaken," she explained. "I did not get a good look, but I thought I saw one of those ridiculous cat tattoos on his wrist. Besides, I've seen Princess Merin in the past. I served in Lodir a few years back. Saw her a few times on occasion."

Ghost seemed appeased by Thorana's answer. "I apologize if I offended you," the Engineer managed, looking the Stonebreaker in the eye.

Thorana smiled. "Nothing wrong with being safe," she replied, clapping Ghost on the shoulder. "Your brother is known for his blunt manner. I'd expect the same from his famous sister."

"You know who I am?" Ghost asked in surprise.

Thorana smiled. "Course I do. The Engineer who was cast out of her clan, only to be accepted again. Your brother being who he is, the hard headed Supreme General of Kazic-Thul, it is the talk of the southlands."

For a moment, Ghost was silent.

"Thank you, Thorana," she managed to say, extending her hand in front of the Stonebreaker.

Thorana took it in the warriors handshake. "Honor to your clan," the burly warrior said.

"And to yours," Ghost responded proudly.

"Anything else?" Thorana asked.

"That will do," Ghost replied, giving her a smile.

With a grunt, the Stonebreaker strode back to the campsite.

As Ghost watched her walk away, I heard her sigh, as the present circumstances set her mind back on the task at hand.

"Did you see anything peculiar when we were floating above the trees?" she asked me, her voice tired.

"In case you didn't notice, I was rather occupied keeping us all in the air," I replied, sarcastically.

"Well, I did," she continued, ignoring my tone.

"What was it?"

She sighed again and scratched at her temple. "Nothing good."

Turning to me, I could make out her face in the faint light of the waxing moon. "Did you see that orc, the one in the black leather armor?"

"Not really, Ghost, I was kind of busy."

"It was a Shadow," she explained, her voice cold. "You remember them, don't you? Similar to dwarven Mountaineers, but more deadly."

I blanched. Mountaineering was the most difficult of the dwarven guilds to join. Their exploits through the centuries were legendary. Shadows, I knew, were more dangerous than most Mountaineers. We were lucky to have been rid of the one we encountered so easily.

"Well good riddance to him," I replied, spitting in the direction I'd seen him go. "Now, if that's all," I continued, turning to leave.

"Stop," she ordered, grabbing my shoulder. "There is more."

"Yes?" I asked, tired and growing annoyed.

"Orc Shadow's don't exactly grow on trees—they are rare, used only in the most important sallowskin missions."

"I know this already, Ghost, what is your point?"

"So, how the hell did we acquire one tailing us?"

I hesitated, and shrugged, unable to answer.

"I'll tell you how," she continued, sounding concerned. "When we were floating above the trees I could see over the crest of the hills. Darklight Bay is on the other side of the mountain. I made out dozens of ships sitting off the coast."

I felt my stomach tighten. "Dwarves go into the bay all the time," I reasoned, hoping that was what she'd seen. "Fishing vessels and the like."

I could make out her frown in the moonlight. "It was twilight, and they were a good distance away—but I know sallowskin warships when I see them," she answered, blasting my hopes into pieces.

"Dammit," I whispered, knowing we were in trouble. "That means someone knew we'd be here, traveling in the wilds." I paused, a thought hitting me. "Someone who saw us leave Barrel Falls."

"That's what I think too."

Looking up at her, I pressed my lips together tightly. "You think it was Thorana?" I asked.

Ghost shook her head. "No, her story checks out. I asked her downed partner all about her before we left. She is as loyal as they come."

"If not her, then who?"

Ghost let out a long breath. "I don't know Omens. The only dwarves I trust are traveling with me right now."

"Alright, so, what do we do? We have to assume someone knows where we are heading. Do we alter the plan?"

I heard Ghost inhale a deep breath and let it out slowly. "No. We need to leave before sunrise," she said. "Make for Draymore's Outpost as quickly as we can. Hopefully, Ashten and the company are still there."

"That's a long haul to make in one day," I argued, thinking of Merin.

"I know, but it cannot be helped."

I nodded in affirmation, knowing her idea would give us our best chance at success.

"One more thing," she said, her voice tightening. "If those sallowbacks catch up to us tomorrow, I want you to take the princess and run. We will hold them off, but Omens—you'll be on your own after that. A word of caution. That Shadow will skirt around us and come after you himself. They do not give up easily and are very hard to kill."

I grunted, shaking off the possibility.

"Let's see that it doesn't come to that," I said, giving her a brief smile. "One problem at a time."

I clapped her on the shoulder and took a step toward camp. Her next words stopped me in my tracks.

"Don't let your love for her get you killed."

Slowly I turned and frowned at Ghost in surprise. "You think I'm in love with Merin?"

"I know you are," she answered. "Despite your horrendous lifestyle choices and infantile resistance to authority, you are an honorable dwarf—and I know love when I see it."

She paused for a moment, before speaking one last time. "That was a good trick today, the levitating. Maybe it will come in handy again."

Ghost turned and walked away, leaving me speechless.

Most of the time I don't care what others think of the way I live. I didn't ask for my lot in life. I simply try to survive, enjoying myself as much as I can when I get the opportunity. Ghost's words made me think—both the condescending assessment of my lifestyle and her judgment of my honor. Both, I knew, were accurate.

Without another word I trudged back to camp. As I lay down next to Merin, she opened her eyes and looked at me, searching for a clue as to what my private discussion with Ghost had entailed.

"Is everything alright?" she asked, her voice thick with concern.

I gave her a smile I did not feel. "Nothing for you to worry about," I answered, reaching out, touching her face.

"Good," she replied sleepily, closing her eyes again, snuggling up next to me. I listened to her steady breathing as Merin drifted off to sleep. I lay there awake, my mind troubled. I wasn't worried about the early march the next day, nor was it the number of enemies that would be looking for us. My concern lay with something Ghost had said.

"Don't let your love for her get you killed."

Three days past I had wanted to kill Merin myself. Afterward, she became a means to an end, nothing more. Now, somewhere along the way, everything had changed.

It wasn't her beauty that had gotten to me, though that certainly was a factor. It was more than that. She was a different dwarf now than when we had set out on the road together. She had transformed from a haughty princess to a dwarven lass excited about catching a three-inch fish. Last night she had risked the furious melee of the common room, saving me not once, but twice from the sallowskin attackers. Afterwards, as she was confessing her fear, all I had wanted to do was comfort her, to make her feel safe.

I realized then that Ghost was right.

"*I'll be damned*," I whispered to myself, looking at Merin where she lay in my arms.

When sleep finally found me, my dreams were uneasy. They consisted of a dark-haired dwarf Mage, standing next to a goblin Shaman.

Little did I know that dream had already become a reality.

The Dwarves of Rahm:
Omens of War

Part III
Blood of a Shaman

Excerpt from the journal of Arch-Mage Rhiann

The most uncommon of all dwarven occupations is that of the Mage. Rare in the extreme, only one child in ten thousand will be born with the gift. Rarer still is the ability to manifest itself in a dwarf already grown to adulthood. In a land of nearly a half-million dwarves, fewer than two hundred Mages exist. One of them, an adult neophyte who manifested her magic less than a year past, is about to be swept up in an ancient war that will decide the fate of both the sallowskin continent of Garthan-Tor, and the dwarven continent of Rahm. Little does she know she has been born with a gift never before seen in one of dwarven blood.

Chapter 10: Kynnda

Two weeks ago

As Kynnda read the spidery signature on the bottom of the dusty parchment she'd been given, her heart skipped in her chest.

Arch-Mage Rhiann

It was unusual for the Arch-Mage to contact anyone other than the six masters who served directly under her. Often busy in the Tower of Storms, Rhiann was seen infrequently, and only in times of great need. Even those who had reached the coveted status of Mage did not speak to her, which is what accounted for Kynnda's shock. As a neophyte of the lowest rank, it was unheard of to receive a direct summons from *anyone*, let alone the most powerful dwarven caster in Rahm.

Kynnda looked up at Paol, a middle-aged dwarf dressed in a robe of blue cotton. Running from his shoulder to his hip was a green sash denoting his designation as one of the *Specta*—a journeyman-like rank given to those who had mastered the basic cantrips of mage training.

"What is it?" he asked in his deep voice. Clean-shaven, save for the sideburns that ran down his cheeks, Paol absently wiped bread crumbs off the front of his robes where they fell with a sprinkling of sound onto the hard stone floor. He was clearly in the dark as to the origin of the message.

"A summons," Kynnda answered absently, failing to meet his gaze through the light brown tresses that hung over her eyes.

"Best you get cleaned up," Paol grunted, his mind already on other matters. "Make it quick—the Mages don't like to be kept waiting. Whoever it is, they must be upset with you. Neophytes are never called into the Septs—not unless they are about to be disciplined."

He turned and stepped out the door of the tiny alcove that served as living quarters to the neophytes of Magehold.

Kynnda's pale gray eyes read over the message again, barely hearing the door close behind Paol.

Neophyte Kynnda,
Come to my tower with the setting of the sun. Your presence here has been called into question.

Blinking at the text, she read it a third time, wondering what she'd done to bring down the wrath of the Arch-Mage. Glancing at the lone window in the room, she saw the light of the day beginning to fade from the sky. Knowing she needed to make haste, Kynnda swept up her bright yellow smock, pulling it quickly over her white undergarments. She slipped her feet into sensible boots of soft leather and yanked open the door. The she-dwarf glanced behind her, wondering if she would ever return to the spartan room. It had not been much, but she had called it home for the past six months. Pressing her lips together in determination, the eldest Neophyte of Magehold stepped outside, closing the door to her room firmly behind her.

As always, the walk toward Magehold inspired her. Located on the outskirts of Guldor, the smallest Kingdom on the island of Rahm, Magehold was home to the majority of the spellcasters in the southlands. Magehold itself was made up of Septs, each with its own tower of magic. Numbering six in all, the Septs had been constructed in a hexagon pattern surrounding a seventh tower. The middle barbican, known simply as, 'The Seventh,' was taller than the others, constructed in the heart of the hold. It served as home to the Arch-Mage, the most powerful spell caster in the realm.

Housed on the western side of the hold, Kynnda's quarters were less than twenty yards away from flats set aside for those that had progressed to the rank of Specta. The majority of the dwarves in Stormhold, both male and female, were housed in two large buildings where they toiled daily at their studies, all to reach the much sought-after status of Mage.

Making her way past both buildings, Kynnda stepped from a path lined with stone, onto an old wooden bridge that carried her over a babbling brook. This area was foreign to Kynnda, as she had never been allowed near the Septs before, save on her first day when she'd been brought in from her home of Lodir to the north. Looking up at the Seventh Tower, Kynnda strode past the Septs located on the western side of the hold. They were dedicated to the study of necromancy and spirit. Each had an array of buildings in their midst, while their two uniquely distinctive towers jutted magnificently into the sky.

Moving quickly, Kynnda came to an open courtyard filled with the verdant green of onion grass and a smattering of ancient trees. She glanced upward, seeing both the long dark needles of evergreens swaying gently alongside trees bearing leaves that rustled with the wind. As Kynnda walked beneath them, she was inundated with the fresh smell of summer pine.

Approaching the thick oak door, the neophyte raised her hand and the entryway swung open. Kynnda hesitated, surprised at how easily she entered the most fortified bastion of dwarven magic on the continent. Shrugging, she walked through the portal, her eyes widening in wonder.

The Seventh Tower was easily the most impressive structure Kynnda had ever seen. Its main column had been crafted by powerful dwarven mages of the past. It had six different towers jutting off to the sides, one for each field of magical study. The main structure was made up of flowing, sinuous lines that soared skyward, giving the edifice a sense of balance and harmony.

Kynnda stopped short only three steps inside the room. The antechamber was austere. Its walls were plain white in color, bare, save for the iron wrought sconces that held ivory colored candles, each burning without smoke. On the dusky stone tile lay a rug of red and gold that depicted the symbol of Magehold—six perfect hexagons meeting to form a six-pointed star at their center.

Standing in the middle of the room in front of the neophyte were two figures. The first Kynnda recognized as Arch-Mage Rhiann. Standing a half-a-hand under five feet in height, Rhiann was dressed in the red and white robes of a fire mage. Earrings of polished gold and red tourmaline hung from her ears, while a matching circlet lay on hair the color of deep mahogany. In her hand, she held a scepter of polished obsidian, inset with a ruby the size of an adult male thumb on the top.

Kynnda felt her throat go dry as she remembered her manners and made a swift curtsey.

"You summoned me Arch-Mage Rhiann, I have come," the neophyte said, trying to keep her voice steady.

"Hmmphh," Rhiann frowned, glancing at the other figure in the room. "Twas not I who summoned you," she sniffed, looking back at Kynnda, her dark eyes filled with annoyance. "My…contemporary wanted to see you."

The neophyte turned her gaze to the other figure standing next to Rhiann. Smaller than the Arch-Mage, the figure was covered from head to toe in tattered robes of black and green. A gnarled staff lay in hands covered in glove-like wrappings. When the figure spoke, his voice rasped outward, infused with a harsh accent.

"I did not summon her," he growled, looking at Rhiann. "Her blood called to me."

Kynnda gave them both a look of confusion. "I...I don't understand."

The smaller figure snorted. "Nor do I—but the spirits of the five are not to be questioned, not in matters like this."

"I have sensed magic in her," Rhiann sniffed, her tone dismissive. "But there has been little proof of it since her arrival. Unless she manifests again, I fear she will never gain status here."

The figure gave a short, harsh laugh.

"Of course you sense the magic in her—it is there. It lies silent, an untapped pool of power. You simply lack the necessary means to train her. Your blood does not cry out like the blood of this young dwarf, Mage Rhiann—but to me, it howls."

"So you say," Rhiann sniffed again.

Kynnda peered closely at the diminutive figure, her gray eyes trying to penetrate the depths of the cowl. "Who are you?" she asked, feeling a sense of dread emanate from inside the hood.

The creature snorted and pulled the ivy green hood off his head. "I am Karn, Shaman of the Inner Circle, your new master," he croaked, his black eyes flashing dangerously.

Kynnda looked on in shock. Standing in front of her was one of the dwarves' ancient enemies, a goblin...its pale, yellow skin, glowing in the soft candlelight.

The neophyte flashed her eyes to Rhiann, her fear evident. "Arch-Mage... how... what is he doing here?"

Rhiann sighed, stepping forward. She placed a hand, blackened and charred by fire years ago, upon the shoulder of the neophyte.

"You are to accompany the goblin. He will see to your training from this point forward. Karn assures me of your safety and has promised no harm will come to you while under his protection."

"But Rhiann, he's... well... he's the enemy!" Kynnda gasped, forgetting to use the Arch-Mage's proper title in her surprise. She shot the shaman with a look of outrage. "You should kill him now...burn him to a crisp!"

Karn made a sound, a gurgling sort of noise that rolled over on itself through his hoarse throat and jagged teeth. Kynnda leaned back, thinking the goblin was about to be sick. As the sound continued, the neophyte realized what it was.

Laughter.

"Oh, I like this one," the shaman croaked out when he could. "She has fire in her belly. She'll do just fine, for a stump."

"I'm to go with him?" Kynnda asked, only now comprehending what she'd been told.

"Yes," Rhiann answered, understanding the lack of honorifics.

Kynnda's face grew red, her eyes narrowing in anger. "You cannot auction me off," she spat looking at the Arch-Mage. "I am not some...thing to be bought and sold. I refuse to go with him. I will return home if I must, but I won't sell out my people by conspiring with the enemy."

Rhiann looked at the neophyte, her eyes taking on a fire of their own. "You have not been bought or sold neophyte. Though he is a sallowskin, Karn has acted with honor, at great risk to his own life to come here for you. While he is my enemy, the shaman has been heard and your fate has been decided by the masters. He acts not only for the good of his own kind, but for the Dwarves of Rahm as well."

Drawing herself up to her full height, Rhiann finished. "Tomorrow, you will leave with Karn and head north. He will instruct you along the way."

"But…"

"My word is final!" the Arch-Mage snapped, ending the discussion.

Kynnda stared daggers at Rhiann, her whole body shaking in protest. "Your will, Arch-Mage," she managed to spit out, her voice shaking with anger.

"Good," sniffed Rhiann, her calm returning. "Rest tonight. A pack will be made ready for you on the morrow. You will leave before dawn."

Kynnda spun quickly in anger, and stomped out of the room, slamming the door behind her.

Alone, Rhiann and the goblin looked at one another.

"I'll have your word, no harm will come to her," the Arch-Mage warned.

Karn snorted derisively. "If she is killed, it means I'm already dead," he replied. "And saving the world will be left to you and your…Mages."

Narrowing her eyes, Rhiann smoldered. "Careful Shaman, there is only so much lip I will take from you."

He snorted in disgust. "I'll remember you said that when my people save yours."

Kynnda awoke the next morning with stars still visible in the sky. Two hours until dawn, she dressed by candlelight. Sandy eyed, she put on her traveling clothes, a gray tunic with tan trousers that went on underneath her customary yellow smock. She had been given a sturdy walking stick of holly, along with a small knife tucked neatly into her belt. A large backpack was laying on the floor inside the entrance of her room, heavily laden with the necessities for travel.

She opened the door and was met by the goblin outside.

"It's about time," he growled softly, anxious to be off.

"It's the exact time I said I'd meet you," she groused back, frustrated at this turn of events.

"We are wasting the morning hours," he snorted, waving her toward him, his fingers tipped with jagged black nails. "Let's be off."

Kynnda sighed and lifted the pack over her shoulders onto her back. She had no idea why she was leaving Magehold with this goblin, only that she had been ordered by her superiors to do so. Angry and uncertain of her fate, the neophyte followed behind the shaman, trudging every step of the way.

The pair left Magehold traveling along the worn cobbled road that led into the depths of the Brae Reach Mountains. The goblin led his shaggy haired pony by the reins. It was ladened with saddlebags filled to bursting. They were stuffed with all manner of queer items, some of which the neophyte Mage had never seen before. Vials filled with liquids of all colors, a mortar and pestle that smelled of some foul concoction. Kynnda did not know what to make of her new traveling companion.

They passed underneath the archway of the thick stone barricade that served as the hold's first line of defense. Two sentries waved them through, neither batting an eye at the odd-looking pair.

A mile outside the walls, Kynnda began to struggle. She had managed to move without difficulty in the open spaces beyond Magehold, as the waxing moon above illuminated the ghostly ribbon of road beneath her feet. However, once they'd reached the tree line at the foot of the mountains, she found herself stumbling along, barely able to see the road in front of her.

"By the Trine, why are we traveling at this ridiculous hour?" she swore, coming to a halt after she had nearly stumbled and fallen in the darkness. "I understand the need for an early start, but I can't even see my hand in front of my face."

Kynnda heard the shuffle of Karn's feet in front of her as the goblin came to a full stop and turned around. Behind him the pony made a soft braying sound in protest.

Narrowing her eyes, the neophyte mage struggled to see any part of the goblin that was leading her, cast against the darkness of the mountain as he was. Kynnda felt the hackles on the back of her neck rise when she heard Karn's voice croaking out of the darkness, less than a foot away.

"*El'dolkakaan,*" she heard him whisper in his guttural tongue.

A faint green light began to emanate from his staff, faintly illuminating the shaman's sallow colored face and bulbous nose.

"We journey in the hours before dawn, little mage, because it's less likely that we will run into other stumps at this time. How do you think I managed to find my way from beyond the Jagged Lands to your Magehold? It was not by parading throughout your city streets, I can assure you."

Kynnda leaned back a bit but was angry enough to voice her frustrations. "That's all well and good for you, blackblood," she sneered. "But I cannot see in the dark. I'm liable to wander off the road and fall over a cliff…not that you'd care."

Karn's face twisted, and he pulled his lip back in a sneer. Kynnda could see his sharp, savage teeth glowing in the green light of his staff.

"*Khrek Zer!*" he barked harshly.

Kynnda was hit by a spell from his staff and the world around her immediately changed.

The darkness of the night melted away, like a wave receding from shore. She could now see past the shadows of the trees. She had to shield her face with her hands from the faint light that was emanating from Karn's staff. It now felt as bright as the sun at high noon.

"*Tuuac,*" he growled, and the staff's light went out.

Kynnda looked around in wonder, amazed at the goblins' magic. She could see everything! The faint rays of the moon that had offered only a hint of light moments ago, now illuminated the shadows under the trees like a bonfire. The road, which had been nearly invisible to her before, spread forward beneath her feet like a royal dwarven thoroughfare. By some miracle, she could now see in the dark.

"Better?" Karn snapped, lifting his hood back over his head.

"Yes," she answered in wonder. "How did you…is this something you will teach me?"

Karn grunted and turned back to the road. "We will see."

They kept on that way, travelling up the mountain road until dawn. By the time the sun began to peak over the mountains, they had left the safety of Magehold miles behind them. Karn's spell had worn off by the time the sun was fully in the sky. Still, the pair hiked for another three hours until the goblin signaled for a stop.

"Let's step off the road," he grunted, leading his pony along a narrow path that ran adjacent to a small stream of water.

"This is a bad place to rest," Kynnda told him, a feeling of uncertainty washing over her.

"Why?" Karn asked, looking around at the surroundings. "One place up here is as good as another."

"As I recall, there is an outpost, no more than a mile or two ahead," Kynnda suggested, reluctant to leave the road. "We could stop there and rest if you'd like? We might even pick up a few supplies."

"No," Karn barked over his shoulder, continuing on his way.

Kynnda shook her head and stomped after him. "First you make me get up hours before daylight, and now you won't listen to common sense," she scolded. "There is a comfortable place to rest less than an hour away. Why are you insisting we bushwhack our way through the forest to rest on some unpleasant patch of dirt, when we could…"

"Shut up!" Karn thundered, turning around. "Use that head of yours for something besides growing an obscene amount of hair on! I am a sallowskin in dwarven lands. How many of your kin would let me walk freely upon the road? None! Why do you think we left as early as we did? To avoid other stumps!"

Kynnda stood wide eyed and speechless as realization dawned on her. She felt like a daft fool.

Without another word, the goblin strode further into the woods, his red-faced apprentice dragging her tail behind him.

He led them perhaps a quarter of a mile from the main road, deep in a wooded thicket. They could hear the songs of small game birds, but nothing that would suggest there was any dwarven presence close by. Coming to a halt, Karn unpacked his saddlebags from the back of the pony and let the four-legged animal forage for food.

"You should tether him," Kynnda warned, nodding at Karn's pony. "He's likely to wander off."

"He won't," Karn snapped, setting his staff on the ground.

Kynnda shook her head, took off her pack and sat down on the ground with a sigh, despising her companion and the situation.

"What are you doing?" Karn barked, looking at her with his black eyes.

"I'm resting," she sulked in reply, "maybe getting a bite to eat."

Karn snorted at her. "Not while there is work to be done." Reaching into one of his bags, the goblin tossed her a stiff bristled comb. "Go brush down Thistle," he said with a nod toward the pony. "Afterwards, you can fill our waterskins from that stream we passed near the road."

Kynnda hesitated, before sighing again and climbing back onto her weary feet. Walking over to the pony, the neophyte used the worn comb to brush the back and sides of the pony. As the minutes passed, the young Mage began to plan how she might make a run to the outpost on her way to fill the waterskins. She could have a sizable head start on the shaman before he discovered her disappearance. With a little luck, she could warn the dwarves at the…"

"You best forget your plan of trying and run to the outpost," Karn cut in, breaking her concentration. "Even if the sentinels there somehow manage to capture me, you'll be dragged in front of the Arch-Mage and questioned as to why you abandoned your duties at Magehold. I'll be free to go," he continued, holding forth a rolled-up parchment. "It's all here in this letter Arch-Mage Rhiann gave me."

Kynnda narrowed her eyes, wondering if this miserable creature could read her mind.

"Of course, you aren't my prisoner, only my apprentice," Karn continued, blithely. "If you think running is the best recourse, by all means, make your attempt."

Cursing under her breath, Kynnda knew the goblin was right. There was little she could do but obey the orders of her new master. With a shake of her head and a nasty look at Karn, she finished brushing his pony, snapped up the waterskins and did as she was bade.

When she returned, the two of them ate a midmorning meal of dark bread and cheese. Afterward, Kynnda cleaned up while Karn sat in a meditative-like trance, with his eyes closed. Minutes later, a swarm of yellow jackets buzzed softly over his head. He opened his eyes and beckoned to her to sit down on the ground across from him. Kynnda did so, more out of the need for rest than curiosity.

"What is a shaman?" Karn asked her, his earlier anger gone.

"Evil sallowskins bent on destroying all dwarves," Kynnda spat in answer.

Surprisingly, the goblin gave her a hideous smile. "There is that," he said, not bothering to disagree. "Perhaps I should ask it differently. What is it that gives a shaman its power?"

Knowing less about sallowskin spellcasting than she did about magic used by dwarves, Kynnda shrugged in ignorance.

"It is our connection to the world," Karn explained, his beady eyes watching her closely. "An attunement to the earth, the air, the life all around us."

He leaned in closer, staring at Kynnda intently. "Most of all, it is magic from inside our soul that can touch both the living realm and that of the dead."

"The dead?" Kynnda scoffed, her lips curled in doubt.

Sitting up straight, Karn waved his hand in front of Kynnda's face. "Observe," he said, taking a green crystal from his pocket. With a nonchalant toss, Karn threw the crystal in the air where it froze, hovering in place two feet off the ground directly in front of his new apprentice.

"Tell me what you see," the goblin croaked in his guttural voice.

"I see a floating crystal," Kynnda answered with a frown.

"Hmmph," he snorted, directing a yellowjacket towards her. The neophyte let out a yelp of pain as an insect stung her on the hand.

"What the hell?" she shrieked, unsuccessfully swatting at her attacker. "Why did you do that?"

"Focus," Karn snapped, ignoring her question. "What do you see?"

"I see a blackblooded savage who lives to torment others!" she lashed back, heat in her voice.

The goblin narrowed his eyes and directed three more yellowjackets toward his apprentice. The flying trio shot downward, angrily buzzing in the rising heat of the mid-morning air.

Kynnda's eyes flashed in anger. She raised her hand and the wasp's dive came to a halt in mid-flight. Instead of moving forward, the yellowjackets buzzed in place, frozen in the air.

Karn gave her a feral grin and focused his will further, directing the insects forward. Slowly, the wasps inched their way toward the she-dwarf.

With a snarl, Kynnda ground her teeth in fury and countered with a strength of her own.

The two stayed there, locked in a stalemate for the length of a dozen heartbeats.

"Enough," Karn said, with a wave of his hand, releasing the insects. The swarm hovering over his head dispersed, leaving the two of them alone in the clearing with only the quiet neighs of the pony as company.

"What was the point of that?" Kynnda snarled, standing up angrily. "Is this how you train your apprentices? By attacking them for no reason?"

"What did you learn?" he croaked, calmly.

"That you are an unadulterated asshole!" she huffed, dumping the cool water she'd collected in her waterskin onto her rapidly swelling hand.

"You should go and refill that," he suggested mildly. "We've a long way to walk and I don't want you dying of dehydration."

"Don't tell me what to do!" she spat back, furious with the goblin. "You are a strange, sick little creature. First you treat me like a hired hand, doing these menial chores, then you send your nasty pets after me. Now you are worried about my health? I am not your slave, blackblood. I've half a mind to turn you in at the outpost, no matter what the consequences."

Karn shrugged. "Have it your way—sit there in discomfort if you will. The cold water will help with the swelling and the pain, and you will soon be thirsty, but it's up to you."

Kynnda hesitated, and then stood stiffly. "I'm only going because I want to, not because you ordered it!" she snapped, stomping away angrily in the directions of the stream that ran adjacent to the mountain road.

"An excellent choice," Karn responded, smiling inwardly as she stormed away.

The goblin held his hand up and the green crystal floated over to him. He reached out and plucked the crystal from the air, returning it to his pocket for safekeeping. Satisfied, he shifted his weight a bit, trying to rest his back, sore from hundreds of miles of travel.

Glancing down the game trail Kynnda had taken, his thoughts turned to her.

She was stronger than he'd hoped. Despite her anger with him, the dwarven girl had managed to unconsciously tap into her own powers and thwart his will. She had a long way to go, but her potential was evident. Karn sighed. The trial of pain he'd put her through was a pittance compared to what would come. Despite his dislike of the stumps, he knew the races of the horde needed their help.

"Soon," he muttered to himself, thinking of the fiery portal located in the ruins of Ghezzdu Bhar, an ancient city located deep inside sallowskin lands. "The first of them is with me, as she has the most to learn." Satisfied he had done as much as he could for now, Karn closed his eyes and drifted off to sleep.

Had his mind not been on other matters, he may have been more aware of the golden pair of eyes that were watching him from close by.

Kynnda was frustrated. It had become a familiar feeling for the dwarven lass over the last several months. At thirty-seven winters, the she-dwarf was well past the age of any surprises. She was not comely, nor particularly well-tempered. Neither males or females were banging down her door in an effort to court her. Though annoying, she could not help but feel relieved as most of her race had proven to be oafish and slow.

This was not true of Kynnda.

She was a hard worker who strove to excel at anything she put her mind to. Long before her magic had manifested itself, Kynnda had been adept at bookkeeping and accounting. She even managed her own business as a seamstress on the side.

When her magic had manifested, Kynnda had been upset that one of the local lads, a child of no more than ten winters, had caused her to drop a new dress she'd been slaving over, in the mud. Standing barefooted in a stark wind, her feet oozing in the earth and sludge, Kynnda had lost her temper. Snatching up a hot coal with her bare hand from a nearby smithy, the dwarf maid had thrown it at the lad, wishing the coal would burn him alive.

She very nearly got her wish.

The hot coal exploded in size, ballooning into a ball of fire. It roared toward the dwarf child who had covered his head in fear. At the last moment Kynnda realized what she was doing and waved the fire aside to where it rolled harmlessly past him into a puddle of muddy water.

She had looked at her hand in shock, as the heat from the coal had not touched her at all.

Three weeks later one of the Specta had come for her. While fearful of what she'd done, Kynnda could not help but feel excited that she was going to have the chance to train at Magehold, the most mysterious city in Rahm.

It came as a great disappointment that her first months were spent in quiet study, working in the practice of learning simple cantrips, most of which eluded her. Now, with little training and no power, she was stuck in the middle of a mountain with one of her people's enemies! A goblin shaman, whom she was convinced was hell bent on killing her.

Arriving at the stream, Kynnda stretched forth her hand dipping it into the water. She sighed, letting the cold pass over it. Instantly, she felt better. The water had helped ease the sting of the yellowjacket's poison. With the lessening of pain, her anger began to dissipate. With it, came the return of Kynnda's more rational thought.

That's when it dawned on her.

She had stopped Karn from attacking her a second time!

Her eyes widened and she craned her neck back in the directions of their camp. Using nothing more than her will, the yellowjackets had stopped in mid-flight. She could feel the strength of the goblin's magic vying with her own. While she was aware he was not utilizing his full power, she too, had more in reserve.

"I did magic," she whispered to herself, unable to keep the smile off her face.

A shadow made its way along the side of the mountain, cutting through the leaves and needles of the trees above. The darkness whipped along the ground, so quickly, had she blinked, she would have missed it.

"That's a large bird," she thought, turning her eyes toward the sky. The creature, whatever it was, had disappeared. Something tickled the back of her memory, something she'd heard on her journey to Magehold.

Kynnda took her hand out of the water, replacing it with her waterskin, absently filling it within a few heartbeats.

"What was it they said?" she mumbled, searching her memories.

"We must move with caution through here," she remembered a voice say in her mind. They were the words of Lannic, the Specta who had retrieved her in Lodir.

"Why?" she'd asked, taking in the incredible view from the outpost's decking.

"There are all sorts of creatures up here that might cause us harm," Lannic replied. "Cave bears, hunting cats—I once saw a chimera off in the distance, belching fire. Most will leave you alone if they are not hungry. Still, it's best to exercise caution at all times."

There was laughter from the guards at the outpost and Lannic's face creased with annoyance.

"Did I say something funny?" he'd asked.

"Naw magekin, it's just… you've missed the worst of them," a leather clad sentinel had answered. "Bears and cats, even chimeras are scarce in these parts. Moreover, they are of no danger to anyone who respects the mountains."

"I fail to see what's so humorous," Lannic sniffed.

"That's because you don't spend any time up here," a grizzled mountaineer replied, walking in from the back of the outpost. "If you did, you know the greatest danger we face."

Kynnda had turned away from the view of the mountain valley, her eyes watching the elder dwarf address the others.

"I've told you, Torin, we don't play games at this outpost—not with folks' lives at stake," the mountaineer spat.

"Take it easy, Jediah, it was just a bit of fun," the first sentinel replied.

"Your, 'fun,' could cost them their lives," the mountaineer growled, unamused.

"We were going to tell them…" Torin argued, a bit too defensively.

"Tell us what?" Lannic demanded, cutting the sentinel off.

The mountaineer turned toward Lannic, his bushy brown eyebrows shifting over his dark eyes. "Wait until tomorrow morning to travel. It is less safe after the sun rises to its zenith as these creatures hunt in daylight."

"What creatures? What is out there?" Lannic demanded, looking toward the mountainside.

The mountaineer ran a hand through his beard and glanced at the sentinels.

"Manticores."

Kynnda's eyes widened at the memory. In the distance she heard the faint squealing of the pony.

"No," she gasped, knowing what had come. Quickly she dropped her waterskin at her side and began to sprint back toward the campsite.

Karn would have been killed in moments had it not been for his mount. Catching the scent of blood, the pony snorted softly, looking at the bushes to the left of Karn. The shaman roused himself from his dozing to peer over at his mount, aware the animal sensed danger.

From out of the bushes charged a huge creature, measuring nearly ten feet in length. It let out a bestial roar through fangs stained red with blood. It stood some seven feet high at the shoulder and had a mane of dark fur that encircled its head. Four powerful legs of a great hunting cat hurtled the beast forward, closing the distance between itself and Karn inside the length of a few heartbeats.

The pony let out a squeal of rage and charged forward, teeth bared in an equine snarl. The shaman's mount slammed into the side of the manticore, biting at the larger creature's neck. The pony found success, tearing away a piece of the manticore's flesh at the collar below the mane. The pony spat it aside, its mouth now dripping with fresh blood.

Turning, the manticore shrugged off the bite, and returned one of its own. Letting out a high-pitched neigh of terror, the pony kicked out with its hooves, trying to separate itself from the beast. With space between them, the larger creature knocked the pony to the ground, trying to savage the poor beast with its teeth. The terrified mount managed to roll away, though the manticore drew a trace amount of blood along the pony's flank with a swipe of its claws.

The delay caused by the shaman's loyal mount gave the goblin a fighting chance. Karn, his sore back forgotten, scurried to his feet and leveled his staff.

"*Dekaar ur degaan,*" he shouted, pointing his weapon at the manticore's tawny chest. A green line of fire shot from the staff, burning away at the beast's dust covered fur.

The manticore let out a roar of pain at the attack, turning away from the wounded pony in front of it. Bounding forward, the manticore leapt in the air taking flight, madly flapping its wings to gain altitude.

"Oh no, you don't," hissed Karn, raising his hand toward the monster.

"*Negin un Alaan,*" the shaman shouted, as four razor sharp blades of ice shot from his hand. The manticore banked right, dodging two of Karn's attacks. The third blade buried itself deep in the haunch of the manticore's leg, drawing another roar of pain. The last blade of ice was the most telling. It struck at the base of the left wing, causing the manticore to vacillate off balance. The monster was forced to land in the clearing only a few paces away, the wing no longer able to support its flight.

The enraged creature struck the ground heavily and dropped to all fours, raising its tail from behind it.

Karn's momentary elation vanished.

"Kruk!" the shaman swore, seeing a bevy of long spikes sticking out the end of the manticore's tail. Bunching the muscles in his legs, Karn dove to the side.

Unfortunately, he was not quite fast enough.

The manticore snapped its tail sharply and the goblin felt an explosion of pain run up the length of his leg as a jagged, foot-long spike pierced his leg.

Glancing down, Karn saw the barb had driven all the way through the muscle of his thigh. The tip of the barb was sticking out the back of his hamstring.

Karn sat up, black blood oozing from the wound. Frantically, the shaman began looking for his staff. It had tumbled out of his hands in his haste and now lay a good ten feet away. Knowing he had little time, Karn looked up to see the manticore snarling at him. Slowly it crouched forward, raising its tail, moving it hypnotically, back and forth over its head.

Karn could not dodge another volley of spikes. He knew he was about to die.

From the other side of the camp came a new sound. Across the clearing, the pony was gone. In its place was a rat-like creature, with smooth gray fur, roughly the size of Karn's missing mount. It chattered in rage, while black blood dripped from both its neck and flank. Behind its dark lips, the creature bared four-inch-long fangs.

The manticore flicked its tail at this new threat, shooting two of its spikes at the massive rodent. The rat dodged the first quill and charged at the second, angling itself so the barb bounced harmlessly to the side. In five quick strides the rat creature had leapt atop the manticore, biting and raking the monstrosity with its teeth and talons. The manticore roared in pain, fighting back with fangs and claws.

Karn, grimacing in pain, began to drag himself toward his staff. The ten feet seemed like a mile as the agony shooting up his leg nearly caused the goblin to black out. Grimly he inched closer as the melee behind him grew quiet.

Chancing a look back, he saw his mount had been thrown wide of the manticore. Its rat face was covered in blood, most of it, its own. However, despite a multitude of wounds, the shaman's mount was still alive, though its breathing was now hoarse and labored.

The manticore turned its attention back to Karn, blood dripping from a dozen new wounds raked upon its body. Helplessly, the goblin watched as the monster's tail drew back over its head.

With a snap, the manticore released three more of its spikes.

"Tek mah!" Karn gasped, desperately deflecting two of the quills with his magic. The third, however, pierced his defenses. He was struck on the shoulder and knocked flat on the ground. Lying prone, Karn had no illusions, he knew his time had come.

The shaman could hear the approaching footsteps of the manticore. Its feet were dragging, proof the goblin and his magically transformed mount had taken their toll. This Rahmish nightmare had proven more than they had bargained for. Still, Karn was not going to go down without a fight. Stubbornly he focused his magic, trying to ignore the throbbing in his leg and shoulder. A burst of flame to give this beast something to remember him by. One last...

"Hetu!" a voice screamed from behind him.

The manticore was engulfed by the biggest ball of fire Karn had ever seen. The creature was completely bowled over, its fur and flesh igniting instantly. The goblin craned his neck backward, trying to see behind him, but the movement made his head swim. The last thing the goblin saw before he passed out was Kynnda, a shocked look on her face, reaching out toward him.

Chapter11: Dwarven Honor

"You should not be here shaman, not yet," came a voice floating beside him.

Karn groaned inwardly. He recognized the speaker and knew where he was.

It would have been better if the manticore had simply killed him outright.

Opening his spirit eyes, the goblin gazed upon the swarthy features of a dwarven Rager. A shirt of chainmail hung down past the warrior's hips, while greaves of boiled leather protected his legs. He held no weapon, though there was an empty scabbard that once housed a curved blade, hanging from the belt around his waist.

The dwarf stood in an open plane of gray mist, vast and empty. Though Karn could not see more than twenty paces in the distance, he knew the plane stretched endlessly in every direction.

"I would sacrifice every one of my powers not to listen to your idealism again," Karn bristled, looking at the dwarf in disgust.

The Rager gave an amused chuckle. "And I'd double your powers just so you would abide by them," he replied with a smile.

"Kruk be damned, I hate you Ancillies," Karn spat, shaking his head.

"No," the dwarf replied, his smile fading. "You hate yourself. You shouldn't though—you are trying to atone for your mistakes."

"Bah," Karn snorted, knowing it was the truth. "I liked you better when you were alive. At least then I could loathe you in peace."

Ancillies rubbed at the scruff of dirty blonde stubble hanging from his cheeks. "Give yourself some credit Karn. Yes, you set events into motion with your actions, but you are doing what you can to rectify the situation—for both of our peoples, I might add."

"Do you know how much dwarven blood I've spilled?" the shaman asked, miserably.

"Do you know how much you could save?" the Rager countered, appraising him with a raised eyebrow.

Karn cursed under his breath, wishing he could leave. The spirit of Ancillies always made him regret the choices he'd made in his life. The dwarf was right, the shaman should not be here.

"How do I get out of this place?" the goblin asked, his eyes searching for a portal he could use to leave.

"That is up to your new apprentice," Ancillies answered, mildly. "The she-dwarf you've taken under your wing."

Karn wanted to lash out in frustration. "I didn't take her under my wing!" he argued, his voice snapping like a winter's frost. "Kruk has led me to her. I had as little choice in the matter as she did."

"Is that why you've pushed her already? The trial of pain is hardly the first test, nor is it the easiest."

"She was ready," Karn snapped, defensively.

"Ready, was she? Is that why you sent only one yellowjacket when you could have sent the swarm?"

"I don't have to listen to this."

"Is it so terrible to care for the lass?"

Karn turned around and narrowed his eyes. "I don't care a whit about her. She is a means to an end, that is all."

Ancillies looked at the goblin with empathy. "Is that why you didn't tell her all of it? Where she is going? What is being asked of her?"

"Shut up, damn you!" Karn snapped, a pang of guilt running through him. "I'll not be lectured by you. Shemak's balls, show me the way out of here!"

"I told you," Ancillies answered. "That is up to your apprentice."

"Hoar dung, I'll be stuck in here forever," Karn snarled, feeling helpless. "The female stump hates me. What reason did I give her to save a goblin?"

Ancillies looked upon Karn, a grim understanding in his eyes.

"The same reason you attacked her with only a single yellowjacket—because she cares."

Karn dropped his gaze to look at the gray mist floating above the ground.

"Even my own tribe has cast me out," he admitted. "No one cares for old Karn."

A swirling white portal appeared from the gray mist behind the goblin. Karn looked up at Ancillies, his black eyes widening in surprise.

"Someone does," the dwarf said, cocking his eyebrow knowingly. "Stay the course, shaman. The power of the five is waning. I will see you at the vortex."

In the blink of an eye, the goblin left, and the portal was gone.

"Thank the Trine, you're awake," said Kynnda, as Karn's eyes fluttered open.

It was an hour past midday, and the area stunk of burned hair and charred flesh. The sallow skinned goblin sat up with a grimace, putting a hand to his wounded shoulder. Covering the wound was a cloth bandage with a homemade herbal remedy wrapped inside.

The goblin looked at the dwarven girl, an unspoken question in his eyes.

"I made a poultice," she explained. "Linseed and wild onions—heated in clean water. I used it to take away the pain. There is one on your leg as well."

Karn nodded in understanding.

"My staff," he croaked, his throat, desert dry.

Kynnda reached across the goblin's chest and picked up the gnarled wooden staff. She placed it in his hand and stepped backward giving him space.

"*Makor Kekla*," he murmured, ripping off the poultice on his leg and placing one hand on his wound. A red glow of light pulsed from the staff, and Karn gasped in sudden pain. After a moment, his body relaxed, and he removed his hand. Underneath his torn hide leggings, the wound was healed, leaving only a faint scar in its place.

"Thank you," he said wearily, giving her a wan smile.

"Wait," she said, seeing he was about to lay back down. "Your…pet. He's still alive."

Looking across the clearing, Karn saw that his new apprentice had treated his hoargasi as well. She'd wrapped a blanket around the most serious wound located near the neck of the rat-like creature. Determined, the shaman rose to his feet, the blood rushing to his head.

"Careful," Kynnda warned, reaching out to steady him. "Maybe you should sit back down?"

"I'm alright," he said, regaining his balance. "I have enough strength for this."

Karn shuffled slowly across the clearing, making his way to his mount.

"She is my spirit animal," the shaman muttered. "A creature of the wild, one most like me."

"She is loyal and brave," Kynnda remarked, putting a hand on the goblins shoulder.

He looked at her quizzically. "Why do you say that?"

"Look at her," the dwarf girl answered, kneeling next to the hoargasi. "She took on the most vicious monster in the mountains for you. Now she lies close to death, yet I sense no regret from her."

Karn looked at her in surprise. "You can feel her emotions, can you?"

Kynnda looked at the goblin and nodded. "I don't know how, but, yes, I feel it."

"That is one of the marks of a Shaman," he grunted, kneeling next to both Kynnda and his mount. "I believe your Druids have an affinity for animals as well."

"Yes, I have heard that," Kynnda admitted. Placing a hand on the hoargasi's shoulder, the dwarf closed her eyes.

"I also feel her pain." Sighing, Kynnda glanced over at the goblin. "It might be best to end her suffering and let her go."

"No," Karn said, raising his staff.

"*Makor Kekla*," he whispered. Again, a red glow pulsed from the staff. The hoargasi twitched off the ground as it shrieked out in pain. A heartbeat later the giant rat-like creature bolted upright, rubbing its head against Karn's outstretched hand.

"Thank you, girl," the shaman said, his voice tired, but firm. "You saved my life."

The hoargasi nearly knocked him over in a show of affection.

Sniffing, the rat-like mount took notice of Kynnda. The beast rushed toward the dwarf and knocked the neophyte to the ground, licking her face with a slimy, black tongue.

"I… yes, you're… gah… you're welcome… I, Karn! Help! Get this thing off me."

"Come now girl, that is enough" the goblin ordered with a weary smile.

The hoargasi leapt away at the sound of its master's voice. With a playful nip toward Karn, the creature made its way over to the still smoking remains of the manticore and began sniffing and growling at it.

"Where did you find such a beast?" Kynnda asked, climbing back to her feet, wiping the slobber off her face.

"There are packs of them north of the Jagged Lands," Karn replied. "Thistle here was the one to answer my call when I needed a mount to come south."

"She's an ugly brute," Kynnda commented with a smile, watching the rat-like creature tear away a piece of manticore flesh.

"Yes," he snorted in amusement. "Ugly and loyal."

They sat quietly for a few moments, each lost in thought. It was Karn who broke the silence.

"Why did you save me?" he asked bluntly, his croaking voice softer than usual.

"I…" Kynnda began, tensing her shoulders. She made a face, her shoulders slumping downward. "I couldn't leave you to die," she explained.

"Last night you called me your enemy," Karn responded.

"Yes, well, that was then."

"I have been hard on you from the beginning," he continued.

"You also believed in me," she blurted, the words shooting out of her mouth, despite her reluctance to speak. "Do you know how many Mages believed in me back in Magehold? None! Not a single Mage ever spoke to me. The Sectas barely acknowledged my existence. Even the other neophytes excluded me—they wouldn't so much as share a meal."

She hesitated, looking at the shaman in front of her. "Yes, you are rude and have the manners of a Billy goat. But in less than a day, you've spoken to me more than anyone at the Seven Towers ever has. You managed to coax the magic out of me, something none of them were able to do. You spent time working with me, you've given me reason to believe I can be somebody in this world, instead of an insignificant…"

She halted, cursing herself for saying too much. "Blackblood or not, you are the only one who has believed in me in my entire life. So, I saved you, and your…pet, rat-thing," she finished, dropping her head, blushing furiously.

Karn sat for a moment, speechless. That was not what he had expected to hear. Stretching out his staff, he put the gnarled tip of the wood under Kynnda's chin and lifted it up.

"Thank you for saving me," he said earnestly. "This 'rat thing' is called a hoargasi. For what it is worth, I saw growth in you today. That ball of fire…"

"By Goran, what the hell is going on?" shouted a voice from the game trail that led into the clearing.

Turning, the pair saw a group of a half-dozen dwarves dressed in the garb of the outpost sentinels. Kynnda recognized the leader from her first trip through the mountains.

Ears flattening, Thistle bounded past the remains of the manticore and stood next to Karn, his teeth bared in warning.

"Stand ready!" the dwarven leader shouted, hoisting a spear in front of him. The other sentinels obeyed and readied their weapons.

"Thistle, no," Kynnda said, standing up, raising a hand to the hoargasi.

The leader of the dwarves hesitated, trying to read the scene in front of him. "Are you alright lass?" he asked her finally, his eyes on the goblin.

"Aye, I am Captain Jediah," Kynnda answered, knowing this would be a dangerous situation for her new master.

The Mountaineer narrowed his gaze, staring at Kynnda intently. "Do I know you?"

"Yes," she answered, "Though I doubt you'd remember me. I came through the outpost this past winter. I was with a Secta from Magehold, Lannic by name. You scolded your sentinels for not warning us about the manticores in the mountains."

Searching his memory, Jediah relaxed slightly. "I do remember that, though I'd put the instance from my mind."

Glancing at the goblin, Jediah returned to his ready position. "What are you doing out here with a sallowskin shaman and his hoargasi?"

Kynnda licked her lips absently, knowing the truth was not likely to convince the captain or his squad.

"I have betrayed my kin and come south to speak with the dwarves of Magehold," Karn said, breaking his silence. "Arch-Mage Rhiann has sent me north, on a mission of great importance."

He paused, making a quick gesture toward Kynnda. "This neophyte was selected to assist me on my journey."

"You can't expect us to believe that?" called one of the sentinels from behind the captain. The speaker had a light brown goatee, save for a line of gray hair growing from a scar on his chin.

"Captain, he's a sallowskin shaman," the sentinel continued. "My cousin was killed two weeks ago at Grimdale Ridge by just such an enemy. A gods be damned army of blackbloods attacked his company from out of nowhere. Scores of our kin were killed."

The sentinel rattled his spear against a wooden shield. "I say we slay the bastard right now, before he uses his magic against us."

"Do not," Kynnda warned, bringing her own walking stick to the fore. "He has already cleansed the mountain of its greatest threat," she continued, nodding at the dead manticore.

"What of this beast with him?" challenged the sentinel, who had not been dissuaded by her argument. "Have we replaced one monster with another?"

"This creature, a hoargasi from north of the Jagged Lands, helped us kill the manticore," Kynnda answered.

"So you say," spat the sentinel. "How are we to believe that? For all we know you are a runaway, helping one of the enemy escape. Perhaps he's a spy, sent to survey the southern lands before an all-out invasion. I've never met a sallowskin yet, who wasn't a cold-hearted killer."

Glancing at the captain, the sentinel advanced. "Give the word sir and we'll send this traitor and her blackblooded friends straight to hell."

"Over my dead body," Kynnda growled, fire in her eyes.

There was a moment of tension between the groups, as the captain weighed his options.

"Stand down," the Mountaineer muttered to the squad behind him.

"Sir?" the sentinel asked, his voice harsh with disbelief.

"I said stand down," the captain repeated, louder, with more force.

"But Captain, he's a…"

"By the Trine Uric, shut your bleating mouth!" Jediah barked, whirling on his subordinate. "Are you really so bloodthirsty you'd kill a fellow dwarf?"

Uric's face went red with fury. "I've had enough of your bullshit Captain," he spat, leveling his spear at Jediah. "You side with this traitor? With this goblin and his blackblooded monster? You are no kin of mine!"

Uric looked at the rest of the squad. "The captain's lost his nerve," he barked. "He'd rather let this rabble walk free than kill them all. Who's with me?"

The other five squad members looked to Uric, his resolve mirrored on their faces.

"You're a fool if you think you can defeat me," Jediah hissed, facing his sentinels.

"There are five of us, Captain," Uric spat, raising his shield. "You can't beat us all alone."

"He won't be alone," Kynnda said, her voice cutting through the clearing. Next to her, Thistle pulled back his lips, showing his fangs once again.

"Enough," snapped Karn, exhaustion clear in his voice. Climbing to his feet, the goblin tottered forward. "As much as it would gladden my blackblooded heart to see dwarven blood flow, I will not be party to this lunacy."

Karn reached into one of his many pockets and pulled out a piece of parchment, handing it to the captain.

Jediah took the paper from him and read through it quickly. Kynnda could not make out the words but saw it had been sealed with the insignia of a black crow. When finished, the mountaineer looked up at the goblin, a knowing look in his eyes.

"When did he give this to you?" Jediah asked.

"Ten days ago," Karn responded evenly.

Jediah nodded thoughtfully. "I didn't know you were friends."

Karn snorted. "We are not friends, Captain. I believe he'd kill you himself at the suggestion. For the time being we need one another. That is why I am here, and that is why he gave it to me."

"Then you are free to stay here and rest until you are ready to travel," the Mountaineer nodded.

"The hell they are!" Uric thundered. "If you don't do something Captain, I will!"

Jediah walked over to Uric and handed him the parchment. The rest of the squad gathered round and scanned the contents. One by one, they stepped back, surprise registering on their faces.

"This…this can't be real," stammered Uric, glancing at the shaman. "He…there's no way this piss colored goblin could know him."

"Would you like to take it up with the foremost killer in the eight kingdoms?" Jediah asked mildly. "I'm sure he'd love to hear your perspective."

Uric's face sagged in defeat. "No," he muttered, backing away.

Jediah looked at the sentinels. "Examine the corpse of the manticore," he ordered. "Let's see what we can learn and then we will leave these folks in peace."

"I appreciate that, Captain," Karn said, as the squad went to work.

"Take what's left of the day to rest," Jediah suggested. "If you come through the outpost after dark, I will have fresh food and have supplies waiting for you."

"Thank you," the Shaman said, tipping his head forward.

"I'm doing it for him, not for you," the captain said darkly.

Karn smiled. "I'd feel the same in your position, Captain. Take what you need from the manticore. He was a ferocious foe."

"How did you manage to slay the beast?" Jediah asked, looking over at the carcass.

"I didn't," the shaman answered, nodding at Kynnda. "She did."

"The neophyte Mage?" the mountaineer asked in surprise.

"I'm not a Mage anymore," Kynnda said grimly. "I'm a Shaman in training."

As she spoke, the hoargasi changed back into a pony, and nuzzled at Kynnda's ear.

After they had gone, Kynnda and Karn lay back on their blanket rolls for some much-needed rest.

"Would you really have fought your kin for me?" Karn asked, drinking deeply from his waterskin.

"Yes," she replied, her face turned in a frown. "They were wrong to have judged you so quickly."

"No," he said with a sigh. "I have killed many dwarves in my time. Truth be told, I reveled in it in my youth."

Kynnda sat up, bristling with scorn. "Are you saying I should have let them kill you?"

Karn shook his head. "No. I'm simply pointing out that I understand their motivation. I do not blame them for hating me. I have hated dwarves for most of my life."

"Then what are you doing with me?"

The goblin sighed, and bit off a piece of roasted manticore from the stick he'd cooked it on. "For the first time in millennia, our races need one another. The sallowskins cannot fight what is coming alone—nor can the stumps defeat it here in the south. Only together can this greater evil be overcome."

"What evil is that?"

Karn blinked once and turned his gaze to the ground. "Something locked away so long, even the most learned of our races have forgotten."

He looked up, grimly determined. "Best not to worry about it now, young dwarfess. We have a long way to go, and you have much to learn in that time."

She stared at him, the corner of her mouth curving into a smile.

"What?" he asked suspiciously.

"You said, 'dwarfess,' when speaking to me. Not, 'stump.'"

"By Kruk, that doesn't mean anything," he hissed. "You stumps are so sentimental. Get the notion out of your head that I care about you at all. I have killed hundreds of my own kind, that is our way. I have no time for some mawkish female dwarf."

Her smile widened. "You did it again."

"By thunder leave me alone!" he raged, railing at his own stupidity. "Get some sleep stump, we have a long way to go tonight and already I am weary."

Kynnda smiled inwardly, struggling to suppress her laugh.

She lay down, as the transformed hoargasi nuzzled at her head. Abruptly she sat up, a thought dawning on her.

"Karn?" she asked, looking over at the goblin.

"What?" he hissed, grinding his teeth together in frustration.

"Who gave you that parchment that made the sentinels leave you alone?"

Karn lay back and closed his eyes. "Never you mind," he snapped. "Get some sleep—we leave an hour before sunset."

Seeing she wasn't going to get an answer, Kynnda lay back down and closed her eyes. In her mind she saw Karn hand the parchment over to Jediah, the seal of the black crow standing out to her.

A black crow, she thought, mulling the seal over in her mind. A strange symbol to use as a...

In a flash she opened her eyes, suddenly understanding what the seal meant.

Not a black crow, she thought, bolting upright. A dark one. Darkcrow!

She looked over at Karn, a question on the tip of her tongue.

No, she thought, hearing the words of Captain Jediah once again.

"Would you like to take it up with the foremost killer in the Eight Kingdoms?"

That could only mean Karn was working with one of the most controversial dwarves in Rahm. Stories of his exploits were spoken of as things of legend. If he were involved, it meant the stakes were high. It dawned on her that Karn may well be leading her to her doom.

I could leave, she thought, glancing at her pack, still filled with her belongings. *Head back to Magehold and tell them they were duped.*

"No," she murmured, looking at the goblin. Whether he wanted to admit it or not, Karn cared about her, she was certain of it.

"I will see you through to the end," she whispered, laying down a third time. Satisfied with her decision, Kynnda closed her eyes and drifted off to sleep.

Karn, knowing the she-dwarf had deduced the identity of his compatriot, sighed in relief.

Michael K. Falciani

The Dwarves of Rahm:
Omens of War

Part IV
The Dirge of Omens

Chapter 12: The Shadow

Present time

Thorana had taken the last watch, so it was she who shook us awake. It was cool in the darkness before dawn, with a soft breeze whispering overhead through the nettles of the mountain pines. After a quick breakfast of goat cheese and dark bread, we set out, moving as quickly as we dared in the hour before sunrise.

"Why are we up so early?" Merin asked, blinking the sleep from her eyes.

"Just being cautious," I answered, evading her question as much as I could.

The path Ghost led us on took us to the high passes leading through the hills. From there we were able to get a view of Darklight Bay and see what had become of the warships below. We crested the hills only minutes prior to the sun breaching the horizon. I could see its red glow cast a growing silhouette across the waters of the bay as the sun began its daily ascent into the sky.

"That's a sight to see," I heard Monchakka murmur to Kora, as he kissed her brow.

"I never tire of watching the dawning of a new day," she agreed, smiling at him.

"Oh, right, the dawn," he quipped, giving her a look of mock surprise. "I was talking about you, lass, but the dawn's nice too."

She gave him a warm laugh and shook her head in humor. I found myself envying them both. I glanced over at Merin, and I knew she, too, had overheard the pair's conversation.

"War ships," I heard Thorana say harshly, hawking and spitting in their direction.

"Three dozen of them," Ghost agreed, looking at the bay grimly.

"What's that?" Merin asked, pointing to the beach near the ships.

"That's an armed camp," Thorana muttered, staring at sallowskins shuffling about below.

"There's six hundred Sallies down there," Kora said, looking at Ghost. "At least, with more on the way," she continued, pointing at a dozen ships sailing into the bay.

"One of them is looking at us," Merin gasped, leaning forward.

"Impossible," Monchakka responded, his eyes narrowing as he searched the beach head. "I don't see anyone."

"Not on the beach," the princess nodded off to the right of us. "On the trail, a quarter mile below us."

All our eyes moved to where we saw a lone orc dressed in leathers, carrying a bow.

A Shadow.

Even in the dark, hundreds of yards away, I could see this orc was female.

"A female Shadow?" I asked, looking at Ghost. "It can't be her."

"Do you know of another Shadow who might wish to invade the south?" Thorana asked, surprising me with her knowledge.

"How do you…" I began.

"Many dwarves have heard the tale," the Stonebreaker answered, cutting me off. "I know who you are, Omens the Bard—and you Aurora Ironhenge. Rowe was my uncle."

I stared at Thorana for a long moment and nodded slowly in remembrance.

"He was a hell of a fighter," I acknowledged, giving her a tight smile.

"Aye, he was," Thorana replied proudly.

"We need to move," Ghost insisted, setting off again, breaking our discourse.

Over the next few hours, we sped through the mountains, knowing to slow down was to risk being overtaken. Normally dwarves move faster than sallowskins through rough terrain. However, those filling up the shores of Darklight Bay did not strike any of us as sallowskin shock troops. This was an elite force, trained to move at speed. With at least one Shadow to guide them, none of us felt particularly comfortable.

We pushed hard all that morning and into the afternoon. All of us grew weary, but no one suggested we stop. Each of us had seen the orcs and goblins in the glade below the night before and no one wished to take on that many of the enemy.

Disaster struck no more than two miles from Draymore's Outpost. Kora, who had been keeping an eye on our flank, placed her foot incorrectly on the rough mountain path and twisted it painfully to the side. She let out a suppressed cry of anguish and pulled up, limping badly.

We all stopped, gathering close to look.

"How bad is it?" Thorana asked, peering back down the trail.

"I can't put much weight on it," Kora answered, wincing in pain.

"I'll carry you," Thorana said, giving the Engineer an encouraging smile.

"I'll only slow you down," Kora argued, giving us a brave smile. "Let me stay here and I'll delay them as long as I can."

"No!" hissed Monchakka, looking at her in desperation. "I'll not leave you behind."

"Kora's right," Ghost said, cutting off her nephew. "We have no choice."

"Yes, we do," I cut in, speaking quietly.

I cast my gaze to our immediate surroundings, getting a lay of the land.

"We are close to Draymore's Outpost," I reasoned, looking at our leader. "Ghost, you run ahead and see if you can get help from the Gray Company. If they have scouts out, you are most likely to run into them. Thorana, you carry Kora while Merin keeps a lookout. Monchakka and I will stay here and delay the sallowskins and meet you at the outpost."

"How?" Ghost asked, looking at me skeptically.

"There's no time to explain," I said, taking Kora's pack and handing it to Merin. "Just go, every second counts. You'll have to trust me."

Ghost hesitated only a moment and nodded, turning to the princess. "I'll blaze the trail using the standard signs. You know what to look for?"

Merin nodded, having seen Monchakka and me read Ghost's markings time and time again over the last day and a half.

Ghost exhaled slowly and gazed into the distance. "Look for my marks and follow as quickly as you can."

Turning to me, she extended her hand. "Delay them if you can, but don't be careless with your lives."

I gripped her hand tightly, and she nodded once. The elder Engineer looked at Monchakka curiously and touched him softly on the cheek. "Come back to me," she said quietly.

"I will," he answered, shooting her a smile.

In a flash, Ghost was off, racing ahead of the others.

With a grunt, Thorana hefted Kora onto her back. "Let's move," the heavily muscled Stonebreaker said, her teeth grinding together in determination.

"Don't stop for any reason," I warned, looking at Merin. "Be safe, all of you."

The remaining trio took off, lumbering along as quickly as they could.

Monchakka turned to me, his face grim. "What's the plan?"

"Do you have any explosives—grenades or the like?" I asked, hopefully.

He smiled ruefully. "Not since I used some at Grimdale Ridge. If we get out of this, I'll tell you all about it."

"No matter," I replied, taking out a small white gemstone from inside a deep pocket on my pack. Lifting it carefully, it flashed in the sunlight, spinning slowly, fastened as it was to a metal chain.

"What is that?" Monchakka asked, examining the gem closely.

"It's the throatstone of a crystal bell," I answered, hanging it around my neck. "The loudest damn bird I've ever heard. This throatstone helps amplify their mating calls. It's very rare, and only of use to a bard who knows what they're doing."

The Engineer looked at me and raised one of his bushy brown eyebrows. "Do you know what you're doing?" he asked.

"Let's hope so," I replied wryly, laughing, despite our situation. "Now," I said, becoming more serious. "This is what I want to do."

When we had stopped to examine Kora, I noted a rocky overhang looming above us. It struck me as a good place for an ambush, or at the very least, a place to delay the enemy. The trail tapered toward us down the hill, to where it was only a few feet wide at the base, marking it as a natural defensive position we could use to delay the enemy.

Or one we could block easily.

I explained my idea to Monchakka who turned his lips upward in a questioning smirk. It was dangerous and could go wrong, though he agreed it had its merits. Shooting me a tight smile, he decided we should give it a chance. With any luck, it would delay our pursuers significantly and we could make our escape.

If it worked.

If it didn't, well—things would get dangerous in a hurry.

The Engineer scampered up the side of the hill leading to the outcropping above. He sidled out near the top of the overhang, his eyes searching the path behind us. His job was to let me know when the sallowskins got close.

Not two minutes passed when Monchakka waved down to me and began his descent back to the trail. Moments later, he stood on the path, his rifle primed and ready.

"I couldn't get an accurate count, but there is a swarm of sallowskins closing fast," he told me, panting from the exertion of his climb. "They are heading right for us, following our tracks."

"Good," I answered, giving him a tight smile. "Get back on the trail behind me and stay out of sight. You've done your part, and there is no reason for both of us to be out here when they arrive."

"Alright," he agreed, somewhat reluctantly. "I won't be far away, if you need me."

I nodded and clapped him on the back. "Be ready to run," I reminded him. "Let's not be careless with our lives, like Ghost said."

"Good luck," he grinned, taking off down the trail.

I didn't have to wait long.

A few heartbeats later, the sallowskins came clamoring along the trail. I could only guess at their number, but it was more than I expected. They moved quickly, running in pairs, side by side. I stepped onto the trail, some fifty yards in front of them. The two orcs in front gave a shout of victory and began to sprint toward me.

Holding the amplification crystal up to my mouth, it slipped a bit in fingers slick with sweat, right as I bellowed as loudly as I could.

"Dek'kar!" I thundered, praying my plan would work.

I had not aimed my attack at the sallowskins, but rather at the rocky outcropping overhead. It was the loudest bellow I'd ever given, made so with the help of my crystal. There was a blast of loose rock that reverberated off the outcropping above the pursuers. A small splintering of stone could be heard, and tiny pebbles and dirt crumbled downward. Unfortunately, that little slip of the gem cost me, as nothing of real consequence happened.

"Idiot bard," I cursed inwardly, seeing my plan had backfired. It would take a few moments for my voice to recover and try again. Until then, I had to stay alive.

I dropped the gemstone, leaving it to dangle around my neck, and drew my sword, determined to stand my ground. The sallowskins in front hesitated at the reverberating blast they had heard from my voice.

Looking up, unsure of what had transpired, they recovered quickly. The first six lowered their heads and ran straight at me.

The report of a rifle came from over my shoulder, and I heard the hollow whine of a bullet whizz past my ear. One of the sallowskins, an Orc Chain carrying a spiked club, fell, his charge stopped by Monchakka's crack shot to the temple. The five remaining blackbloods scattered, ducking for cover where they could find it.

Thanks to my companion's intervention, I was given the time I needed to recover my voice. Reaching down for my amplification stone, I tried again.

"Dek'kar!" I thundered, keeping the stone squarely in front of me on my second effort.

This time the bellow worked.

Already weakened by my first vocal attack, the rocks broke apart and tumbled to the path below. As the boulders came crashing down, dozens of sallowskins were crushed underneath tons of cascading rock and the pathway was successfully blocked. Our enemies on the other side would have to find another way around.

While I was happy with the outcome, there were still five angry sallowskins close by. I made out two pairs, both orcs and goblins. A Chain and a Ravager, coupled alongside an Archer and a Fang.

Of the fifth, there was no sign.

I knew instinctively that Monchakka would target the Archer first. The last thing either of us wanted was to melee with the enemy while dodging a hailstorm of arrows. I stayed to the far left of the trail, leaving him with a clear shot at his mark.

The other three wasted no time, racing toward me, their weapons drawn.

Monchakka's second shot rang through the mountains, cutting down the Archer, who had managed to release a volley of his own. The arrow flew above me in the direction of my companion. Not having time to turn around, I engaged the enemy, full on. I heard Monchakka curse in pain from behind me, and fervently hoped he hadn't been struck with a mortal blow.

The Chain arrived first, its long legs covering the distance more quickly than his companions. He held a heavy blade, tapered narrowly at the bottom and widening at the top. The Chain drew back his blade, ready to slice my head off with a single, deadly blow.

I did the last thing he expected.

I darted forward and rolled under his swing. I could feel the wind pass above my head as his weapon missed its mark by less than an inch. I came up and parried a hasty thrust from the surprised goblin in front of me, slashing my sword across his neck. Black blood spurted out, covering my face and legs with its warmth.

I had no time to celebrate my success, as the second orc, a Ravager, attacked me ferociously. For the first few seconds it was all I could do to keep him from drawing blood.

I heard another rifle shot from behind me and sent a swift thanks to Goran that Monchakka was still alive. A quick glance told me the Engineer had fired a round at the Chain, though the big orc remained upright.

I exchanged a flurry of blows with the Ravager, who managed to cut through my defenses and score a painful hit along the side of my abdomen. Focusing, I attacked again, knowing there was a fifth sallowskin out there somewhere.

I struck low, hoping the Ravager would take the bait. He did, blocking my attack, sending a predictable counter where I knew he would. I parried quickly and my sword bit into his leg on my riposte, causing the Ravager to fall to the ground in shock. I left him there to bleed out, knowing I'd struck a mortal wound to his femoral artery. Turning, I saw Monchakka engaged with the already wounded Chain. He was fending off the creature as best he could, but his hammer and knife were no match for the Chain's wide blade.

"To me, you bastard!" I screamed, sprinting at the orc.

The Chain, already wounded, glanced back at this new threat. Monchakka, seeing the orc distracted, heaved his hammer at the creature's face, flattening the Chain's nose. As it staggered backward, I stabbed my sword deep into its side, slicing through the orc's ribcage, up into the lungs. The Chain fell to the ground and Monchakka finished it off with a merciful thrust of his knife to the neck.

I noted the Engineer had an arrow lodged between the overlapping leather pieces of armor that protected his shoulder. It was not enough to cause serious damage, but I was certain he carried a deep bruise where it had struck.

"Interesting plan of yours," he said, wincing as he bent over to retrieve his hammer.

"It…sort of worked," I panted, with a wry smile. "Are you alright?"

"What, this?" he asked, cavalierly plucking the arrow from his shoulder. "It doesn't tickle, but I'll live, though I fear Ghost and Kora will have a few unkind words for me when they find out."

"They won't hear about it from me," I joked, giving the likable young Engineer a grin.

"I'd appreciate it," he responded.

"Thanks for the assist," I said, growing more serious. "You saved me with that first shot."

"We should go," he replied modestly, rotating his shoulder gingerly under the armor. "The others will be… look out!" he shouted, rolling to the side.

Without looking, I dropped and dove to the ground on my right. Monchakka's warning had saved me again, just in the nick of time.

A pair of steel knives flashed overhead. One grazed the back of my triceps, drawing a line of blood along my arm. Whipping my head around, I caught sight of our attacker.

It was the male orc Shadow we'd seen last night.

Standing a head and a half taller than me, the leather-clad tracker drew his machete and strode forward.

I climbed to my feet and glanced back at Monchakka who'd caught the Shadow's other knife in the side, though the wound did not appear fatal.

"Ready your rifle," I shouted over my shoulder, looking back at the approaching orc. I drew my knife in my off hand, knowing I'd need every advantage I could get. I feinted with the knife and drove my sword at him, hoping to catch him unaware.

That was a mistake.

He batted my sword aside with consummate ease, and lashed out with his fist, striking me in the jaw. I tried to roll with the punch but achieved only marginal success as his blow spun me to the ground. I rolled away, narrowly avoiding a thrust that would have ended my singing career. I kicked out and landed a lucky strike to his chest. While doing little in the way of damage, it allowed me to scramble to my feet.

"Get clear when you can," Monchakka barked at me, letting me know his rifle was ready.

The Shadow was no fool and kept me between himself and the Engineer's rifle. I feinted again and dodged left, hoping to move aside fast enough for Monchakka to get a shot off. The orc wasn't having any of that, and dodged with me, mirroring my actions.

I stepped closer, determined to get behind the orc, giving my companion the spacing he needed to make the shot. Our blades rang out in a savage exchange of blows, neither of us able to gain an advantage.

He stepped back, looking at me with a grudging respect.

"How did you escape last night?" the Shadow asked, his voice friendly.

I hesitated, taken aback by his question, and that was all the time the orc needed.

He shot forward while I was distracted. Attacking quickly, he parried my sword, striking at my arm with a swift blow from his palm, knocking the blade from my hand. I managed to avoid a killing thrust, blocking his next attack with my knife, but the orc brought his knee up and drove it into my gut, driving the wind from my lungs.

I did the only thing I could think of to stay alive. I flung myself backward, finally giving Monchakka the room he needed to take a shot.

The Engineer wasted no time, firing his rifle the moment I was out of the way.

Somehow, the orc anticipated my move and rolled to his left, the opposite direction that I'd gone.

Monchakka's bullet whizzed past his head, missing by a hair's breadth.

Snarling, the Shadow raced forward, ready to finish us off once and for all.

The orc came close to success. He had accounted for my actions quite well, always one step ahead of me. However, the Shadow had not accounted for Monchakka's actions, not all of them at any rate.

The orc had dodged my companion's bullet, but he lost sight of the Engineer in the momentary cloud of smoke created by the muzzle flash. The Shadow was not expecting the butt of the rifle that came flying at his head through the smoke a moment later.

With a bruising strength, Monchakka cracked the end of his weapon against the orc's forehead. Taken by surprise, the Shadow was knocked sideways, tumbling completely off the trail. The orc slid down the steep face of the hill, his machete flying out of his grip, disappearing into the underbrush below.

Laying on the ground with the wind knocked out of me, I struggled to rise.

"Are you alright?" Monchakka asked, his breathing labored. Reaching out his hand, he hauled me to my feet.

"Yes," I managed to gasp, finally taking a breath. My ribs hurt where the Shadow had kneed me. I suspected at least one of them was cracked. For the first time in my life, I began to seriously contemplate purchasing a suit of armor if I ever returned to civilization.

Monchakka cast his eyes down the side of the hill and shook his head. "By the Trine, I hope the fall killed him," he said, pulling the steel knife out of his side with a grimace. The blade was dark and came away slick with blood, though the cut was shallower than I'd thought. "Thank the gods Ashten purchased me new armor last week."

Looking down the side of the cliff, Monchakka shook his head. "Gads, he was tough as hell."

"I'm pretty sure I injured his fist with my head," I declared, feeling the pain running along my jaw where the orc had struck.

Monchakka turned to look at me, staring for a long moment before snorting with laughter. "Come on," he said, gathering up his pack. "Let's rejoin the others. If the Gray Company is still at Draymore's Outpost, they will fix up those wounds for you. Your rockslide should keep them off us for a bit. That was some quick thinking."

"Thanks," I said, nodding at the compliment. I caught a glimpse of the knife our adversary had thrown at me laying on the trail. "It would have gone badly had you not bought me time with that rifle shot," I grunted, picking up the weapon, sliding it into my pack.

He gave me a rueful smile. "That's what friends are for."

"Are we friends now?" I asked, surprised to hear him refer to me in that way.

Monchakka shrugged. "Alright. That's what complete strangers, trying to stay ahead of hundreds of ravaging monsters intent on wiping us out are for," he said with a smile.

I guffawed at his words, which immediately hurt my ribs.

"By Goran, stop being funny," I complained, trying to keep myself from laughing.

He chuckled good naturedly, slipping the Shadow's other steel knife under his belt before starting down the trail, with me shuffling after him.

Chapter 13: Draymore's Outpost

Monchakka and I had run for more than a quarter turn of the hourglass when we caught up to our companions. Thorana had doggedly carried Kora well over a mile. I was impressed with her strength and endurance. Upon our arrival, the Stonebreaker set Kora on the ground, breathing heavily with exertion, taking a momentary respite.

We were spotted by Merin, who had dropped back on the trail to keep an eye on things behind them.

"You're alive!" she exclaimed, rushing forward, hugging me tightly.

"Easy lass," I grunted, wincing in pain.

"You're hurt," she said, looking at the swelling bruise on my face.

"I'm alright," I assured her, giving Merin a tired smile. "How's Kora?"

She turned and nodded at the female Engineer. "She's a tough one," the princess said, striding over to Kora.

"Your plan worked, did it?" Kora asked, adjusting her leg in a futile attempt to find comfort. She peered at Monchakka seeing dried blood above his hip.

"Thanks to Monchakka, yes," I answered.

"He's wounded too?" Kora questioned.

"It's just a scratch," the engineer answered with a wave.

Kora did not looked convinced.

"We should go," Thorana said, extending her hand to Kora.

"I'll carry her for a bit," I offered, shrugging off my pack.

The stalwart warrior waved me away. "I can do it," she protested, determination stamped on her face.

"I know you can," I replied, remembering how stubborn Stonebreakers could be. "That was never in question. I'll carry her for a bit, is what I meant. I don't know how much time we bought ourselves, but I'm hoping it's enough to get to Draymore's without sallowskins breathing down our necks the entire way. You'll need your strength if they come in numbers. There are two more of us to help now. Take a rest while you can."

"Omens is right," Merin said, taking off her pack. "Except there are three of us that can help. I'll carry Kora. Thorana, you are tired and both Omens and Monchakka are wounded. Let me assist her."

We all stared at the princess in shock for a moment, saying nothing. The transformation in her over the last few days was nothing short of remarkable. She had gone from a spoiled, petulant, child—angry over the misuse of her bed, to a part of our group, volunteering to do the hardest, most physically demanding of tasks.

Merin was already moving, as Monchakka helped Kora climb onto the princess's back. It was a sight to see, watching the royal princess of Lodir shuffle away carrying a simple commoner. I picked up Merin's pack and slung it over my shoulder, ignoring the pain it caused me.

The five of us started moving, each keeping an eye out for any sign that we were being followed.

It was not long after, that Draymore's Outpost came into view through the canopy of the trees overhead.

The outpost was old, having been constructed more than four centuries ago. Made of dusky granite now coated in lichen, it had been built high upon Birch Hill, its watchtower visible for miles. A long ramp, some ten feet wide at its apex, rose up from the open plateau underneath the walls for a hundred yards. The ramp ended at a heavy oak door, reinforced with a rusted iron crossbar.

The outpost had been abandoned decades ago, as no horde had ravaged this far east of Lodir in a century.

Not a month past, on the advent of spring, a horde, numbering in the tens of thousands, had won their way across the Eastgate Bridge for the first time in living memory. A large battle had been fought at this outpost not two weeks ago, the old fort playing a critical role in King Helfer's success at pushing the invaders out of dwarven lands.

Now it was under renovations, King Helfer having ordered it recommissioned in response to the incursion into the Valley of Souls.

As we moved closer, we could make out a handful of dwarves racing toward us, Ghost at the forefront.

She cast a quick look at Monchakka, frowning at his injuries. "Why is Merin the one carrying Kora?" Ghost asked, turning her gaze to me.

"It's nice to see you too," I snorted back, helping the princess lower Kora to the ground.

"It was…my idea," Merin said, laboring in the late afternoon heat. "Omens and…Monchakka are injured and…Thorana had carried her for…almost an hour…without rest."

"Let's get them inside," a tall dwarf with a short beard the color of whisky suggested, turning to the half dozen Engineers that had accompanied them. "Torgas, Verral, be good lads and get Kora to Donia. I believe there's a bit of brew left from our arrival. We'll need Kora back on her feet as soon as possible."

Two males, both Grenadiers by the look of them, nodded and lifted Kora off the ground, setting off at a good pace toward the ramp that led to the outpost looming above us.

"Ashten, this is Thorana," Monchakka said, introducing the Stonebreaker.

Ashten declined his head slightly. "I thank you for your help. Ghost told me something of your exploits in Barrel Falls."

"You're Ashten Raine," she said, her eyes hard. "Brother to the king."

"Aye, that's me," he replied, grinning at her.

Turning to Merin, Ashten bowed his head. "Princess, while I'm surprised to see you out on the road, it does my heart good to see you again."

"Highness," she responded, returning the bow.

"And you, you rapscallion," Ashten scowled, looking at me. "Where'd you get that shiner on your eye? A jealous husband?"

I gave him a wry smile. "Ghost gave it to me last night while she was climbing off of me," I joked, tossing her another grin.

Ashten gave me a hearty laugh and extended his hand. "She must have gone easy on you lad, seeing as it was your first time in her druthers."

I shook his hand warmly, and my grin became a smile. "It's good to see you again," I said, clapping him on the back.

Ghost shook her head in disapproval at her Captain. "Keep up like that, you'll be sleeping alone," she sniped. "Now, if you two dolts are done acting like fools, I'd like to hear what happened." .

On the way to the keep Monchakka and I told them of our encounter with the sallowskins. Ashten was particularly interested in the Orc Shadow, wondering at its involvement.

"You're lucky to have escaped," he said, looking at us sideways. "Most dwarves don't survive an encounter like that. I once saw a Shadow take out a whole squad—Ragers mind you, not Bolters or Engineers—but dwarves specially trained for hand-to-hand combat. You must still be in decent form Omens, to have fought him off."

"I work with my sword a few times a week," I admitted, glancing at Monchakka, realizing how fortunate we were to have escaped in one piece. "Every now and then I'll find a Rager or Stonebreaker to spar with."

"How long do you think it will be until they can find a way around?" Ghost asked, her mind on the horde.

I shrugged. "An hour or so…maybe more," I answered. "Depends on how bad they want…" I stopped, trying not to look at Merin. "…to achieve their objective," I finished.

"Well, no matter. We'll be ready in case they come," Ashten grunted, looking grim. "We should be able to handle a few hundred from behind the walls, even without siege engines. In the meantime, go to the healer's tent. It's set up in the courtyard. Have Donia or Stix see to your wounds."

"I'll see if I can hasten things along," I added, giving a nod to my lute.

Ashten snorted and sent us on our way.

Once up the ramp, we made our way through the door, into the courtyard. Towering above us was the watchtower, rising some thirty feet above the walls. Like so many dwarven creations, it proved to be more than a simple watchtower. It was made to be a piece of aesthetic architecture, both simple and beautiful at the same time. Carved on the top, southern facing wall, was the face of Draymore Ironblood, the most renowned Dwarven King in history. Flanked on either side of his likeness were the heads of two rams, the standard of his house.

Draymore's last descendent had been killed hundreds of years ago. Outposts like this one served as a reminder of both the greatness of the Ironblood line, and their fall from power.

As we walked beneath the tower, Thorana leaned in and whispered something to Merin who blushed a deep red.

We trudged along the open area behind the wall. It was mostly sweet-smelling onion grass, though there were patches of wildflowers that had not yet been cut away in the outpost's renovations. An ancient catapult sat close by, it's cup lilting to the side, a large boulder as tall as I was lying next to it. There was a dun-colored pavilion off to our left that served as the outpost's healing tent. Walking underneath the thick cotton tarp, we saw Kora sitting on a cot, her foot soaking in a bucket of cold water. In her hands was a warm mug of stout that smelled of roasted brazen nuts, a plant renowned for its healing properties.

"Glad you could make it," Kora smiled, drinking from her mug. "I feel better already."

"You should stay off it for the rest of the day luv," warned a voice from behind us.

Walking into our midst was a stern looking, blonde-haired she-dwarf, a pair of pistols at her side. In her hands she carried two more mugs of stout, their rich, nutty smell filling the immediate area.

"For you," she said, handing one of the mugs to Monchakka. "I hear you've had a rough go of it, Stony."

Monchakka shrugged, nonplussed, but took the mug with a nod of thanks.

"What's she calling you Stony for?" Thorana asked with a questioning frown.

"Because I trained as a Stonebreaker for most of my life before turning my hand to Engineering," Monchakka answered with a sigh. "I like to think they use it as a term of endearment."

"You were a Stonebreaker?" Thorana asked, her eyes widening. "I should have known after the way you handled that shield at the Toad and Peach."

"I was a poor one," he answered, giving her a self-deprecating smile. I suspected he was proud to hear such praise coming from an obvious veteran like Thorana.

"Make sure you drink it all," the elder Engineer warned, looking from Kora to Monchakka.

"We will, Donia," Kora answered, finishing her own mug.

"Stony?" Donia questioned, tapping her foot.

"I'll make sure," Ghost asked, walking up from behind us.

The she-dwarf tinker nodded once and walked away.

"Hello mother hen," Monchakka said to Ghost, as he lifted his shirt and examined the cut on his side.

"What's that you have there?" Thorana asked, pointing at the short blade tucked inside his breeches.

"One of the knives that Shadow tried to skewer us with," the Engineer muttered, wincing at the memory.

"May I?" the Stonebreaker asked, holding out her hand.

Monchakka pulled the knife from his belt and handed it over without a word.

"Goran's bollocks," Thorana swore. "This is a darksteel blade!"

"What?" I asked, peering at it closely.

"I swear by my clan," the Stonebreaker continued, a tad breathless, "look at the edges."

We all studied the knife, seeing a line of black infused into the metal.

"Darksteel is rare," Ghost breathed. "I've not seen it since…" she flicked a look at me and trailed off without finishing her thought.

"Since when?" Monchakka asked, his curiosity piqued.

"I don't remember," Ghost answered with a wave.

I stared at her, my eyes unblinking, confused at her lie.

"What is Darksteel?" Merin queried, inadvertently saving Ghost.

"The finest metal dwarves or sallowskins can make," Thorana answered, handing the knife back to Monchakka.

"The sallowskins know the secret of Darksteel?" I asked.

"Aye," Ghost grunted. "They've plenty of master crafters amongst them. Don't let their trappings fool you. The Sallies are as smart as anything walking on two legs."

"How is it done?" Monchakka asked.

Thorana shook her head. "I'm not a forge master," she explained. "My knowledge is limited. I have heard it said a master blacksmith can make a darksteel blade only with a darkstone, but that's the extent of my knowledge."

"What is a darkstone?" Kora pressed.

"No idea," Thorana admitted, leaning back in her chair.

"I thought mythic steel was the strongest metal we fashioned," Merin chimed in, surprising me with her knowledge. "My uncle Bolgir used to speak about the lost blades of the ancients. They were made of mythic steel."

Her questions hung in the air, as Ghost refused to meet my gaze.

"Mythic steel was supposedly made by the gods," I muttered, steering the conversation away from darksteel. "It is rare in the extreme. Whispers of its existence have launched legions of warriors from both Rahm and Garthon-Tor."

"Made by the gods?" Kora scoffed. "That sounds like an old wives tale."

"Met me an old wife once," Thorana joked, taking a long drink from her wineskin. "Best damn lover I've ever been with. Sweet eyed and giving. By Chara, I'd give a week of my life for another night with her."

"That seems like an old wives tale," Ghost responded, grinning at the Stonebreaker.

"Put the men folk I've known to shame," Thorana continued, laughing heartily.

With the change of subject, the mood of the group lightened considerably, and everyone began to weigh in on Thorana's words.

Without anyone noticing, I stole a careful look at the knife I'd collected from the Shadow. I saw it, too, was infused with darksteel. I searched my memories, recalling the last time I'd seen such weaponry. It had been five years since Ashten, Ghost and I…

"Hello Omens," a blonde she-dwarf purred, striding into the healing pavilion. She walked toward me, with a half grin on her pretty face and placed a mug of healing brew in my hand. She sat down in the chair next to me and leaned in close—far closer than what any decent dwarf would consider respectable.

"It's been a while," she beamed, brushing a lock of golden hair from her eyes.

"Good to see you again, Stix," I responded neutrally, sipping at the bitter brew. It was thick and creamy on my tongue, suited for the hardiest of constitutions. While not a healing draught, per se, I *could* feel its effects begin to work on me. The pain of my ribs dulled, and the cut along my triceps no longer burned.

"Wherever have you been hiding yourself?" the blonde tinker continued, leaning even closer.

"Ahem," Merin coughed, looking at the newcomer with a flash of anger. "I'm Merin, Princess of the Golden Keep."

"Highness," Stix lowered her head in greeting. "I heard you were traveling with Ghost. She said you were both beautiful and brave.

She told us you helped save her life in Barrel Falls with the finest shot she's ever seen a Bolter make. We are in your debt."

Merin took the compliment in stride. "Thank you," the princess replied, losing a bit of her starch. "How do you...how is it that you know Omens?"

Despite the shade of the pavilion, I felt my face growing hot.

Stix gave Merin a knowing laugh. "Once we get you cleaned up and rested, I'll tell you all about it," she promised.

"Ghost! Stix!" we heard Donia shout from outside the pavilion. "Captain Raine needs you!"

"I'll see you later," the tinker smiled in parting, more to me than the others. Ghost joined her and they both walked away while Kora and Monchakka beamed at me from behind their mugs. Thorana simply laughed aloud.

"Damn bard—are there any dwarf maidens you *haven't* slept with?" the Stonebreaker asked, raising a single eyebrow.

I took the lute from my pack, ignoring her question. "I think it best if we care for our wounds as much as we can before nightfall," I said, refusing to look at the princess.

Over the next half hour, Stix rejoined us, taking Ghost's old seat. We spoke to her of the day's past events. It was our first chance to relax since the attack at the Toad and Peach. Thorana voiced her praise of our defense at the inn, while Stix asked us about the path we'd taken through the hills.

All the while I played my soothing melody.

Bard healing isn't like the healing of a War Priest where one minute you're lying on the ground, bleeding to death, and the next you are sitting up, ready for battle. Bardic healing was more subtle, and it took more time. Still, a little healing was better than none. I'd say we were well on our way to good health when the camp began to stir.

"Something's happened," Thorana stated, standing quickly.

"I'll find out what it is," Stix put in, racing off.

We didn't have to wait long. The blonde tinker ran back to us a few minutes later, as my playing came to a halt.

"Scouts reported in," she said, a touch out of breath. "Sallies are incoming."

"How many?" Thorana asked, her face growing hard.

"More than a thousand," Stix answered, her eyes darting nervously toward the outpost's entrance.

"That can't be right," Monchakka murmured, thinking he'd heard her wrong. Standing up, he grabbed his rifle.

"It was Ghost that did the scouting," the blonde Engineer replied, a trill of fear in her voice. "I've never known her to be wrong."

"What are our orders?" Kora asked, rising slowly to her feet.

We all looked at her, surprised to see her standing.

"You can barely walk," Monchakka protested. "You're not going to fight."

"I don't take orders from you, Stony," Kora snapped back. "Unfortunately for us, there is nowhere else to go. A thousand sallowskins are capable of hunting us down before sunrise tomorrow, no matter where we run too. I'll not die like that. They will have to pry this rifle from my dead corpse before I flee the outpost. Besides, between the healing draught and the bard's melody, I'm feeling much better. Now, Stix, what are Captain Raine's orders?"

Thorana snorted with laughter. "By the Trine, that's what I like to hear," she grunted, nodding at Kora. "No give in you. You've the heart of a Stonebreaker, I'll attest to that before Goran himself."

Buckling on her sword, Thorana stepped toward Stix. "Point me in the direction of Captain Raine. My sword is his to command."

Turning to the rest of us, we saw Thorana wearing a fierce smile on her face. "With any luck, you'll see why they call me Rage."

Monchakka and Kora followed after the Stonebreaker, Kora moving well, albeit with a bit of a limp to her step. Merin and I went to follow, but a raised hand from Stix stopped us in our tracks.

"I've a different set of orders for you two," she said, looking toward the back of the outpost.

"What for?" Merin asked. "I can fight!"

"No one questions that, highness," I said quietly. "You've more than proven yourself on the road."

"Then why the different orders?"

Stix licked her lips. "We've added enough defenses these last few days where taking the outpost will not be easy. However, the enemy outnumbers us more than thirty-to-one. Without siege engines, we cannot hold."

"Why don't you retreat?" I asked, knowing Ashten well enough to suspect he had a plan.

Stix took in a deep breath and exhaled sharply. "General Ironhenge is leading a company of dwarves, five hundred strong, to come and man the outpost. "They could be less than a mile away. Captain Raine wants you to find the general as quickly as possible and let them know the situation here. He'd rather not give up the outpost without a fight."

"We can do that," Merin said, not understanding the catch.

"What haven't you told us?" I asked, more worldly than the princess.

Stix sighed. "It's possible the company hasn't left yet. We don't know if they marched from Kazic-Thul today or not. They could be a mile away or twenty. If that's the case, they won't arrive here in time, no matter how fast you run."

She hesitated before speaking again, looking right at me. "Even if they are far away—you must get the princess to Kazic-Thul. She is the key in persuading King Helfer to aid the Golden Keep. If she doesn't deliver her father's message, we will have tens of thousands of sallowskins roaming the countryside to go along with a full-blown war in Lodir. The fate of our race may well depend on the two of you."

That's what it came down to. This whole journey that had started with an innocent smile, had turned into this. The fate of our world riding on an untested princess and a dreg.

With an army of blackbloods at our backs and uncertainty to our front, Merin and I set off, carrying dwarven destiny with every step we took.

Chapter 14: Rage

Mering and I were only steps away from the back gate of the outpost when we heard the rapid staccato of rifles firing behind us.

"How can they hold out against so many?" Merin fretted next to me.

In truth, I didn't have the foggiest idea. If a thousand sallowskins were coming after me, I'd have run for the hills. I knew I couldn't say that to her, but I did not want the princess to abandon hope either.

"Don't you worry about The Gray Company," I said, moving quickly down the path that led to the Valley of Souls. "Ashten and his group have been through worse."

I heard more rifle shots from behind us and began to run at an accelerated pace.

"We cannot keep this up," Ghost screamed at Ashten, over the noise of gunfire. "Those Chains are halfway up the ramp already!"

"By Goran, you don't think I see that?" Ashten cursed, knowing what he'd have to do. Turning, he looked at the old catapult they'd unearthed from below the outpost. Covered with dust and time, it looked exactly like what it was; a relic from a bygone era. A half dozen of his tinkers had rolled a boulder the size of a mountain troll inside the outpost with the idea they would try launching it from the catapult to see if it was still functional. Not an hour ago the rope attached to the arm had snapped, causing the bowl-shaped bucket of the weapon to list to the right, dumping the boulder onto the ground. He'd hoped they could get it fixed in time for the attack, but the sallowskins had arrived sooner than expected.

"What I wouldn't give to lob that boulder at them," he muttered from under his breath.

"You don't need to lob it at them," Monchakka shouted, from off to Ashten's right. "We could open the doors and roll it down the ramp."

"There's no time!" Ghost cried, firing another salvo at the line of Chains making their way up the incline.

"I'll buy you time," came a voice, cutting through the sound of rifle blasts.

Thorana, dressed in her full battle gear, tossed a heavy shield at Monchakka. "Found it laying at the base of the tower," she said, giving the former Stonebreaker a broad smile.

Monchakka looked at the shield, seeing it carried the double ram emblem of the Ironblood line on the front. He looked up at Thorana and shook his head. "You're insane, you know that don't you?

Thorana laughed again. "Aye, insane enough to clear that ramp of Sallies, but—I cannot do it alone. You're the only one in this lot that's been trained as a Stonebreaker—and the only one I trust to stand with me. Are you game, lad?"

Monchakka hesitated only a moment to take a quick look at Kora. "Bazad Arum," he growled, voicing the Stonebreaker chant.

Merin and I were far enough away to where we could no longer hear the report of rifle fire coming from Draymore's Outpost. Having run more than ten minutes without stopping, I kept a sharp lookout for signs of other dwarves. We were only a mile or two from the main road that led from the Valley of Souls to the old trade route. The closer we got to it, the greater the chance we might run into a squad of dwarves running drills or practicing maneuvers.

"You alright?" I gasped, casting a quick look over my shoulder at the princess.

"Yes," she huffed in return, breathing heavily.

I came to a quick stop, narrowing my eyes on the path behind us.

"What…is it?" Merin asked, casting her eyes back on the trail, laboring for breath.

"I don't know," I muttered, breathing heavily. "I thought I saw something out of the corner of my eye."

Both of us stood there, catching our breath, searching the darkness of the forest.

"I don't see anything, and we need to move," Merin said, anxious to be away.

"Yes," I agreed, unconsciously loosening my sword in its sheath. "Keep your crossbow at the ready—and make sure it's loaded," I warned, still looking to our rear. I knew something was out there. Something moving in the darkness of the undergrowth. Something that could be seen in the daylight, while remaining hidden at night.

"The Shadow," I whispered to myself, feeling the hair on the back of my neck rise.

"Are you ready?" Thorana asked, placing a steel helm on her head.

"As I'll ever be," Monchakka answered, holding the Ironblood shield tightly against his shoulder.

"Open the gate!" the Stonebreaker roared, drawing her sword, banging it against her shield.

"Give us as long as you can," Ashten shouted from atop the battlements, with a long look at Monchakka.

The young Engineer nodded to his captain, while behind him, six Tinkers were struggling to roll the boulder into position, trying to center it at the top of the ramp. They still had a good fifty feet to go, and the process was moving slowly.

In front of the two stalwarts, lieutenant Badderson Sarl heaved back on the metal brace latched to the entrance and pushed the door open.

The two heavily armored dwarves wasted no time, knowing the further away from the door they engaged the invaders, the more time they would have to defend against them. Like missiles heaved from a trebuchet, the pair shot forward and raced down the ramp to slam, headlong, into the enemy.

Not expecting a frontal assault, the first three Chains were bodily forced off the rampart, tumbling to their deaths some eighty feet below. Thorana had taken the lead, attacking the larger sallowskins with her broadsword, while staying relatively safe behind her massive shield. Monchakka had his hammer out but knew his role was primarily to protect his partner's flank. With such a narrow ramp to defend, the pair of dwarves were able to use their smaller size as an advantage against the press of larger blackbloods in front of them. More than a minute went by and still the pair of dwarves held their ground.

"Eat this, you yellow bellied savages!" Thorana roared, thrusting her blade at the enemy, impaling a Ravager through the chest.

"Watch your left!" Monchakka shouted in warning, seeing his companion had moved too far to the right. Up until now they'd been lucky, as Thorana's attacks had kept the orcs off balance. None of their attackers had found a steady enough purchase to manage a clean blow on their shields. "Too far!" Thorana shouted back, seeing a slight gap in between their defense.

Monchakka cursed under his breath as the Chain in front of them saw it too. The big orc lowered his shoulder, ready to ram them both and swarm the two defenders underneath him. A screaming shot whistled past Monchakka's ear, slamming into the neck of the Chain. A black mist erupted from the orc's throat as he toppled to the ground.

"Thank you luv," Monchakka whispered, instinctively knowing it was Kora that had made that shot. Shields together again, Thorana went on the offensive, bullets whizzing overhead. They fought for several minutes until Monchakka could feel his shield arm beginning to ache. In the back of his mind, he began to wonder how long they could keep this up.

That was when he caught sight of the scores of goblin Archers ranging forward on the floor of the plateau beneath them. Each held a bow and a quiver full of arrows. There was no way the two could deflect that many missiles and still hold their ground.

"We're about to be in a world of hurt!" Monchakka warned, keeping his shield in line with Thorana's.

The Stonebreaker saw the threat and grunted like a bull.

"Don't worry lad, I have a plan!"

Merin and I moved quickly, though I was more wary now, half expecting an attack at every turn. Rounding the corner, I saw a wondrous sight unfold in front of us. At long last, it was the main roadway that led to the Valley of Souls. There in the valley, less than a mile away, I saw a battalion of dwarves.

Hundreds of them.

Flying proudly at the front was a banner I recognized. A white, double-bladed axe emblem swaying on an azure field.

It was the banner of the king.

"Do you see that?" I asked, glancing behind me, giving the princess a smile.

My heart jumped into my throat.

Not thirty feet away, at the edge of the forest, was the Orc Shadow, his bow knocked and drawn to where his fingers tickled the edge of his cheek.

"Down!" I shouted, tackling her to the ground. As we hit the hard packed dirt of the path, I heard the hiss of the arrow fly overhead, narrowly missing us both. Knowing I had only moments before the Shadow shot again, I rolled forward in front of Merin, and pulled my right shoulder out of the strap of my backpack, swinging the garment in front of my chest.

"Run lass!" I shouted, sprinting straight for the orc.

The Shadow never lost his cool. I saw him knock another black feathered arrow as he drew a bead on me. He loosed the shot smoothly, attacking at nearly point- blank range. I ducked low, as the iron tipped missile struck my pack, dead center in the middle of my chest. Thankfully, the pack's contents caught enough of the arrow where it stuck there harmlessly. Tossing the pack aside, I let out a furious battle cry and drew my sword, swinging it at the Shadow's lean yellow neck.

Looking at me with the utmost contempt, the orc blocked my sword with his bow and kicked out, striking me with the blade of his foot against my tender ribs. I accepted the blow as I balled my left fist and punched the Shadow in the sternum. I heard a satisfying grunt of pain from the blackblooded bastard, and I grabbed a hold of his bow. Understanding my objective, the Shadow tried to pull back on his ranged weapon, but it was too late. Using my sword, I swung the blade downward and severed the string.

Having disabled his most dangerous weapon, I stumbled backward and drew my knife.

"Get out of here Merin," I called over my shoulder, not daring to take my eyes off the Shadow. "Get to the dwarves and warn them. Leave this black hearted, son-of-a-bitch to me."

"Omens, move," she shouted, a hint of terror in her voice. "I can shoot him."

"He's too canny for that lass," I called back. "He's already dodged a bullet today. Don't you worry—I've yet to meet an orc that can best me."

There was a moment of hesitation before I heard her footsteps run off. I smiled, seeing the orc's face change from hunger to fury.

"All you've done is buy her a few extra seconds of life," he snarled in his guttural voice. He slid his machete from out of its sheath. "I will kill you first and cut her down afterwards," the Shadow continued. "Just as her father ordered."

I knew it, I thought, feeling my blood run cold. King Orius had ordered his daughter's death…buy why?

"Let me by and I will let you live," the Shadow promised, his eyes glittering with malice. "What is the she-dwarf to you?"

At that moment, I heard Ghost's words come back to me from the night before.

"Don't let your love for her get you killed."

I smiled at the orc, and my eyes went flat.

"Some things are worth dying for," I replied, knowing the Shadow was more skilled than I.

The orc snarled in frustration and moved forward, his blade leading the way.

My sword was there to meet him.

"Those Archers are getting close!" Monchakka shouted at Thorana, hoping her plan would work.

"How close?" the Stonebreaker yelled back, taking a huge hit on her shield.

"They'll be on us in seconds!"

"Give ground!" Thorana screamed, backing up slowly. "Not too fast mind you."

Glancing backward, Monchakka saw most of the company high on the walls. They were sporadically firing at the sallowskins on the ramp, but for the most part, they held their shots for later. The boulder had finally been rolled into place. The Engineer could see a half-dozen of the company's Tinkers standing behind it, ready to set the rock in motion.

Understanding Thorana's objective, Monchakka slowly retreated up the ramp, as the goblins drew near.

"Hold this spot!" she screamed, digging in her heels.

Monchakka stood next to her, his shield firmly in place. The closest of the archers drew back on their bows and let fly. Most of the arrows missed their mark, but one ricocheted off Thorana's helm and Monchakka felt another bang off his shield.

Sadly for the goblins, they had drawn within range of the rifles.

"Light them up!" Ashten roared from the ramparts above. At his command, dozens of bullets flew through the air, decimating the ranks of archers below. A handful of shrapnel grenades were cast to either side of the valley for good measure. Detonations echoed from underneath the ramp as the goblins below were torn to pieces. As quickly as their ranged offensive began, the sallowskin Archers ran screaming from below the outpost walls, running for their lives.

Before he could celebrate this minor victory, Monchakka felt a massive strike against his shield. His knees buckled and his shoulder went numb.

"Shit!" Thorana yelled, peeking over the top of her shield.

"What the hell was that?" Monchakka screamed, knowing he couldn't take another hit.

"Mauler!" Thorana shouted in reply.

Monchakka blinked in fear.

Orc Maulers were an elite group of Chains. Among the biggest, most powerful orcs known to exist on the continent. Normal Orc Chains got a single metal piece made up of black iron links to wrap around their shoulders and hips. Chains had a habit of painting a link red every time they killed a dwarf.

Maulers, though, they were different. They would challenge other Chains in single combat, often to the death. The victor took the old chain from the loser and would add it to their own collection. The more chains accrued, the more armor they wore. Once a Chain got three kills, they earned the title of a Mauler.

"How many chains is it wearing?" Monchakka shouted to Thorana.

"Four," she replied, taking the next hit on her shield. "With a dozen red links, at least."

The Stonebreaker, knowing how vulnerable the Engineer was, motioned for Monchakka to scramble behind her.

"You need me to protect your flank!" he cried in protest.

"Not for this Mauler," she yelled in answer. "He's so big, none of his fellows can get past him. Fall back lad, you leave this to me."

The Engineer turned Stonebreaker followed her orders. Monchakka fell back behind her, only a few feet from the gate.

"Come on!" thundered Thorana, smashing the shield with her sword once again. "I eat Maulers for breakfast, you yellow skinned son-of-a-whore!"

The Mauler let out a roar of its own, swinging its spiked club, trying to pummel Thorana into pulp. She accepted the hit on her shield, lashing out in return, slicing into the side of the Mauler's ribcage. Her strike glanced off his black iron chains, causing sparks to fly. The two warriors clashed again and again, neither giving an inch.

Monchakka watched, thunderstruck at the raw power of both combatants. The Mauler was huge, slamming his warclub time and time again onto the Stonebreaker's Shield in an effort to batter her from the rampway. Thorana did not finch. She stood in the middle of the ramp, defying an army for them all.

In that moment Monchakka knew the Stonebreaker was all that stood between life and death for the defenders inside the keep.

The stalemate only ended when Thorana's sword caught in one of the Maulers' chains. She tried to withdraw the weapon with a powerful yank of her shoulders and arm. Instead of coming free, the sword snapped at the hilt, leaving her with only three inches of jagged steel.

The Mauler, sensing his advantage, rained blows down upon Thorana, knowing she could not strike back.

Monchakka watched with his heart in his throat as a sudden change came over the Stonebreaker.

"Is that the best you can do?" she roared in defiance, batting aside the Mauler's attack.

The orc hesitated, shocked his enemy was still standing.

"Take this you bastard!" Thorana thundered at him, smashing her shield under the Maulers chin. Momentarily stunned, the huge orc was driven back. The Stonebreaker wasted no time, smashing the orc over and over with her shield screaming in fury.

"Take that you savage shit! I'll break every bone in your body before I'm through with you!" Come on! Bring the pain! By Goran, I'll rip your ruddy face off!"

Thorana was no longer the level headed Stonebreaker Monchakka had gotten to know on the mountain paths over the past few days. She was Rage, a warrior born, who refused to go down.

Dizzy with pain, the massive orc took the hits in stride, biding his time. In her outburst, Thorana had overextended, and the Mauler seized her shield, ripping it out of her hand.

"Eat this!" the Stonebreaker screamed, slamming what was left of her sword into the Maulers neck. The orc let out a roar of surprise. Blood spurted from its throat as the creature staggered backward. Thorana's shield rolled loose as she bore the sallowskin to the ground. Despite the wound, the Mauler managed to latch onto Thorana's arm, grappling with her fiercely. Behind the fighting pair, an Orc Chain grabbed onto the Stonebreakers leg, trying to tear her from atop the Mauler.

Knowing the position was lost, Thorana let go of her sword hilt and yanked on both the Chain and the Mauler as hard as she could, setting her legs against the edge of the ramp.

Monchakka's heart froze, as he watched her last act unfold.

"Fall back!" she thundered to him, jerking the two massive orcs over the side of the ramp.

Monchakka reached out, "No!" he gasped, helpless as he listened to her final defiant roar as they fell.

"Die! You yellow skinned sons-a…"

Just like that, she was gone.

"Monchakka, move!" the Engineer heard someone yell from behind him. It was Ghost, standing behind the boulder. In front of Monchakka were scores of orcs and goblins, charging toward the now undefended outpost gate.

"*Fall back,*" Thorana had said, issuing her last order to Monchakka. The young Engineer, tears in his eyes, swept up her shield and obeyed her final command.

"Push!" Ghost screamed, lending her strength to the four tinkers behind the boulder. Inexorably, the granite stone started to move down the ramp, gaining momentum along the way. As it picked up speed, the dwarves let go, and the boulder began to roll of its own accord. Monchakka, now near the top of the ramp, was able to squeeze to the side as the boulder rolled by.

The sallowskins at the front came to a screeching halt. Having nowhere to run, several tried to retreat, only to crash into their fellow attackers who were oblivious to what was about to hit them. The boulder slammed into the sallowskins, rolling nearly all the way down the ramp, crushing and squashing orcs and goblins alike. Scores of blackbloods died on that ramp thanks to the bravery of the Stonebreaker who held the way against all odds.

"Close the gate," Ashten shouted from above.

"Come on lad," Ghost rasped to Monchakka, grabbing his tunic, dragging him inside.

"She's gone," Monchakka whispered, pulling away from his aunt. "I...she told me to fall back."

"Aye, she did," snapped Ghost, impatiently. "She was right to do so. No one else here could have handled that Mauler. She did what she needed too—she saved your life. She saved all our lives."

"But—she's gone," Monchakka whispered, the finality of the moment hitting him.

Ghost sighed and put her hand on his shoulder. "We'll be lucky if that's the only causality we suffer. Now go lad, back up on the wall. Kora needs you and there is still fighting to be done. We will mourn our fallen later."

As she watched Monchakka mechanically climb the stairs, she fought back tears of her own. Stix, too, had fallen. The victim of a random arrow that had struck her in the throat as she ran medical supplies to others on the wall.

Ghost glanced to the east, hoping that Omens had found the help they so desperately needed.

Blood dripped from new wounds on both my shoulder and abdomen. I stood, panting in the dust our battle had kicked up. I could feel hot sweat dripping from my brow. Swiftly I wiped it away. Despite my fresh injuries, I was grimly satisfied. I had fared better than I expected against such a dangerous foe. The Shadow's machete was not the only blade wet with blood.

The orc stared at me in question, almost surprised I had not yet succumbed to his skill. Minutes had passed since the princess had made her escape, and still I stood, an obstacle between the orc and his prey.

The Shadow leapt forward once again, knowing he had to finish me quickly, or risk the princess reaching aid before he could stop her. My sword came up, defending as best I could. Twice he managed to win his way past my defenses, spilling more of my blood to the ground. I felt pain on the side of my shin and again on my shoulder as he sought to disable my ability to fight.

Still, my sword licked out, grazing his inner thigh, barely missing a killing blow. His brutish eyes narrowed in hatred as he stepped forward, attacking with blazing speed. The orc feinted low, and struck high, catching my footwork off balance. He swept his leg under mine and tripped me to the ground. I rolled right, desperate to create space enough to where I could regain my footing. Guessing at my course of action, the Shadow swung downward, his blade catching mine as I desperately parried his attack. With a quick flick of his wrist, he sent my sword spinning away. I lay on the ground disarmed, completely exhausted.

"Time to die, stump," the Shadow hissed, raising his machete.

I heard the shot before I saw it. The metallic twang of a crossbow being released, accompanied by the high-pitched whir of a bolt cutting through the air. The Shadow heard it too and threw himself backward in an attempt to dodge the attack. He was not quick enough this time, as one of Merin's black bolts struck the orc in the upper chest, impaling him to the left of his heart.

"Merin!" I cried, both in hope and despair.

The princess stood, not twenty yards away, reloading her crossbow.

"Get out of there," she yelled, her foot in the crossbow's stirrup, expertly pulling back on the cocking lever.

Ignoring her, I gathered what strength I could and scrambled to my feet.

The Shadow was already up, moving like a wraith, sprinting toward his prize. Merin's bolt hung like a macabre trophy in the orc's chest, black blood oozing from the wound.

Merin raised the crossbow quickly and pulled the trigger, scarcely taking time to aim. The Shadow spun left, the bolt speeding past his ear leaving a trail of blood along the side of his neck.

"Look out!" I shouted, racing after the Shadow.

Inside a heartbeat, the orc was on her, driving his machete toward her.

Having no time to reload, Merin used her crossbow to block the orc's attack. The Shadow's machete got tangled in the metal string of her weapon as Merin fought to tear it from his grip. Instead of resisting her, the orc let go of the blade, pivoted to his right and kicked the princess on the side of the head, dropping her to the ground in a daze.

With what remained of my strength, I sprinted toward them and launched myself at the Shadow, crashing onto his back, bearing him to the ground. A furious melee ensued where I gouged him in the eye and bit down on his neck. The salty taste of black blood filled my mouth as I tore out a chunk of his flesh with my teeth. The orc bellowed in pain, shaking me loose, catching me across the bridge of my nose with a hammer strike of his fist.

Out of the corner of my eye, I saw Merin struggling to clear her senses of the Shadow's kick. Next to her lay my pack, not three feet away.

I caught a glimpse of something that had been knocked loose in the struggle and found my inspiration.

Both the orc and I spun to our feet. He scrambled left and retrieved his machete, ripping it from the crossbow, while I reached into my old leather satchel and swept up my flute.

The Shadow stared at me, a slow smile spreading across his face.

"You going to kill me with your little instrument?" he scoffed, deftly spinning his weapon as blood poured down his neck.

"I'm going to give you…the answer…to your question," I panted in retort.

The sallowskin furrowed his brow in a momentary confusion.

"What question?" he barked.

"The one you asked me earlier, about how we eluded you last night," I answered, raising the flute to my lips.

I began to play the same song I'd played the previous evening.

The Levitating Libretto.

Slowly, the orc began to rise into the air, its eyes going wide.

"By Kruk, what the *hell* are you doing?" he screamed, his voice fearful. "Get… put me down!"

I kept playing, focusing on the magic of the song.

"You cursed, miserable stump!" the creature continued to scream, rising higher into the air. "I'll murder you and your whole clan for this!"

Once the orc had risen more than twice as high as the tallest tree in the area, I stopped playing.

"I'm sorry, I didn't quite catch that," I yelled up at him, raising my hand, cupping it around my ear.

Of course, once the music stopped, he started to fall.

The Shadow let out a bloodcurdling scream that ended abruptly as he crashed to the ground—right onto some *very* hard looking stones.

"By the way," I said, staring at his now twisted and broken body as it slowly drained of life. "I'm a dreg. I don't have a clan to murder. If you're going to hunt someone down, you should really learn their customs."

I heard Merin groan and instantly forgot about the Shadow. She was alive, though groggy from the orc's attack.

"Come on lass," I grunted, ignoring the multitude of wounds covering my body. "We're not done yet."

As quickly as we could, Merin and I stumbled our way to the company of dwarves, now only a half-mile away.

I just hoped we would reach them in time.

More than an hour had passed since Thorana's death. The sallowskins, never willing to concede defeat, renewed their attack on the gates. Bad and his squad of Grenadiers had delayed them for a while with a special concoction of combustible liquids that burned with an oily black smoke from the top of the ramp.

Not to be outdone, Rachet and his tinkers released their turrets of gunfire along with a brazen display of dwarven technology that cleared the front of the gate twice before their resources were depleted.

Ghost exhorted her squad of sharpshooters to rain hot lead on any and all yellow skinned foes below, until their supply of bullets were nearly exhausted. The ramp and valley floor were littered with more than three hundred corpses of the sallowskin horde.

Tragically, the Gray Company had taken losses as well. Bad had lost his second in command, a grizzled dwarf named Shel, a veteran of many years. Shel had volunteered to light the combustible liquid below. While successful, he'd been struck by a spear thrown by a Goblin Stick near the gate. The spear had impaled him between the gaps in his leather armor, slipping under his ribcage, piercing his lungs.

Two others, sharpshooters Torgas and Verral, were both killed by a lightning blast that come from a goblin shaman who had gotten too close.

Despite the many sacrifices of the company, the blackbloods were at the gate, pounding on it with a makeshift battering ram. It would not be long until they were through.

"Fall back," Ashten shouted, his face covered in soot, sweat streaking jagged lines down his cheeks.

The remaining members of the company abandoned the walls, running to the outpost's back entrance. Ratchet and his crew had set up their last remaining turret, a flamethrower that could be used only at close range. It was set up directly in front of the gate, ready to belch fire on the first sallowskins to break through.

Kora, limping badly now, ignored the captain and reloaded her rifle.

"Don't wait for me," she was saying to Monchakka, a steely look in her eyes.

"I'm not leaving you," he said quietly, picking up Thorana's shield. "I'll take the hits, you keep shooting."

"You're as mad as a Troll Witch-Doctor," she barked, shaking her head.

Monchakka gave her a determined look and drew his hammer once more.

Kora primed her rifle and took aim at a goblin Archer on the ramp. She fired and stopped, her eyes growing wide.

"Monchakka, look," she rasped, her voice tinged with disbelief.

Emerging from the tree line below was a much-welcomed sight to the beleaguered defenders. Dwarven cavalry, grim-faced warriors mounted on huge mountain rams and war pigs, rode from the forest and charged the enemy. The sallowskins, taken by surprise, were trampled where they stood by four score riders. The handful of blackbloods that had enough of a warning ran for the hills where they were hunted down and killed without mercy by a squad of light cavalry riding atop swift ponies.

Hearing a shout from inside the outpost, the defenders were doubly surprised to see a company of Stonebreakers rush through the back entrance, followed by a medley of Ragers, Bolters and War Priests.

Standing at the side of the dwarven commander was Princess Merin, a look of gritty determination stamped on her face. Behind her, orc blood crusted around his lips, stood Omens, bleeding from wounds all over his body.

"*Bazad Arum!*" the Stonebreakers shouted, as the black blooded invaders smashed open the gate.

Forming a dwarven wedge, the Sallies that swarmed through the entrance were killed before they knew what hit them. With no way of warning those behind, the sallowskins were cut down with consummate ease.

Caught between hammer and anvil, it took less than a quarter of an hour until the battle at Draymore's Outpost ended.

While the five hundred dwarves that accompanied Merin and I were able to savor the victory, it was bittersweet for the Gray Company and those of us who had set out together from Barrel Falls. Monchakka, Ghost and Ashten recovered the body of Thorana, refusing all help from anyone. We buried her in an ancient cairn located at the bottom of the keep. Next to her we laid the bodies of the four fallen members of the Gray Company. Ashten spoke of their valor and sacrifice—making certain to transcribe their names with honor into the archives of his company's history.

When it came time to speak about Thorana, Monchakka cleared his throat, wiped at his red eyes, and stepped forward.

"There is not a dwarf in the Gray Company that wouldn't be alive right now had it not been for you," he began, placing his hand gently on Thorana's forehead. "You took on the vanguard of the enemy— holding back a tide that would have washed over us like a storm at sea."

The young Engineer's face was bleak, wracked with sorrow.

"I am not blessed with a gift for words," he continued, "but if your spirit still resides in these walls, there is one thing I would say to you before anything else—thank you. Thank you for your bravery and belief in something greater than yourself. You represent all that is good about our race. You showed an ideal that any dwarf of honor would strive to live up to, including me, a poor Engineer, whom you deigned worthy enough to stand by your side."

As Monchakka spoke, his voice broke with emotion. "I hope, wherever you are, that you are at peace, knowing your sacrifice will be remembered."

Monchakka bowed his head and placed the shield upon the Stonebreaker's armored torso.

"Rest in peace Thorana. You are the bravest dwarf I have ever known."

I couldn't explain why, but at that exact moment, I felt the overwhelming need to play some music. Unconsciously, I pulled out my flute and the melody came to me, the notes flaring to life in my mind, etched in a golden fire. Raising the lute to my lips I played what I saw, the tune flowing out of me like a melody I'd practiced many times in the past.

It was a dirge, filled with sorrow, moving steady and slow. As I played, a faint white glow began to emanate from Thorana's body. Before I knew what had happened, a ghost-like apparition of the deceased Stonebreaker was floating above her mortal form. The other dwarves gasped in awe at the ethereal figure of our friend.

That was just the beginning, as apparitions of Stix, Shel, Torgas and Verral all rose from their bodies to hover in the air above us.

Thorana's spirit smiled down at Monchakka, who stood with tears streaming down his face. It was obvious she had felt the heartfelt sentiment flowing from those of us in the cairn. The other spirits, too, seemed very much at peace. With a last look, the newest spirits of Draymore's Outpost bowed their heads and faded away.

Chapter 15: A King's Betrayal

That night, the group that had traveled from Barrel Falls together sat down to speak to King Helfer, his brother Ashten and Monchakka's father, Arik Ironhenge, Supreme General of the king's army.

Ghost and I did most of the talking, though Merin interjected her own thoughts when needed. Helfer readily agreed to gather his forces to help Lodir against the invading horde. With that matter settled, I looked sharply at Ghost when the king asked to end our meeting. Seeing the nod of her head, I knew it was time to act.

"There is one last order of business," I interjected, as the rest of them began to rise from their seats.

"It's getting late…bard," Arik growled, looking at me with a frown. "There are wounded to tend to and preparations to make for our journey tomorrow."

"The general is right," Helfer agreed, standing from his chair, casting me with a dark look.

"It cannot wait," I said, rolling up the sleeves of my tunic.

I could tell neither of them were used to being rebuked, especially by a dreg. Still, I carried more wounds than any of them, and word of my exploits over the last few days carried weight, especially my success at almost single handedly killing the orc Shadow.

"Make it quick," Helfer grunted, returning to his seat.

"Thank you, majesty," I replied. Looking at Ghost, I nodded at her. "Show them."

The lieutenant of the Gray Company let out a deep sigh. "I found this on one of the Chains when we were attacked in Barrel Falls," she said, taking out a creased parchment. Unfolding it, she revealed the expertly drawn portrait of Merin and the rougher sketch of me on the back.

Gasps of surprise were heard around the table.

"My father had that drawn for me last year," the princess whispered, pulling it closer to her. "It was a gift to celebrate my naming day." Looking startled, she cast her eyes at Ghost. "Why would a sallowskin have it? Have they taken the city already?"

No one spoke. Slowly, each came to the same conclusion Ghost and I had reached, days ago.

"There…there has to be some mistake," Merin exclaimed, looking around the table, her eyes wide. "My father wouldn't… he loves me! There… there must be some other explanation."

"I'm sorry, Highness," I said, reaching out to touch her hand. "He ordered your death, mine too it would seem—probably long before we met."

"That's impossible!" she screeched, unable to accept the idea of her father's betrayal. "Don't touch me with those filthy hands! You… you probably planted the picture on the orc," she accused. "Stolen from my room while you were having your way with my handmaiden!"

"Merin, that's not…"

"Liar!" she shrieked, standing up, pointing her finger at me. "You are nothing but a worthless dreg. My father would never hurt me! Only one as low born as you would even suggest such a thing!"

The silence in the command tent was absolute. There wasn't a dwarf there that did not sympathize with the princess. Her outburst was to be expected.

"Do you have proof?" Arik asked in his rumbling voice.

"Yes," I answered, looking at Merin with sympathy.

"What is it?" Helfer demanded.

I cast my gaze to the king. "The Shadow confessed that he had been tasked with killing both the princess and me, just as her father ordered."

Merin shot me with a look of pure hatred. "Liar!" she screamed again. "I never heard him say that!"

"It was before you returned princess," I tried to explain. "It's not your fau…"

"I'm done listening to you sully the name of my father, dreg! Don't ever come near me again." She rose from her chair, hurling it violently to the ground and ran out of the tent.

"Merin, wait!" I shouted, making to go after her.

"Let me," Ghost said, holding her hand up, halting me in my tracks.

"But I…"

"Your heart's in the right place, Omens," she said, not unkindly. "But I know how she feels. Cut off, alone, abandoned by those she thought cared for her." She gave her brother a quick look. "I will talk to her. Go to the healing tent and have your wounds looked after by a priest."

I nodded reluctantly as the elder Engineer left the tent, trailing after the princess.

Our meeting ended shortly thereafter, with Helfer deciding to put the matter aside until the invasion was over. The others went their separate ways, most seeking their tents to get some much-deserved rest.

I headed to the healing pavilion, my heart in the pit of my stomach. It was my second time in the healing tent today, though this time there was a small fire going. After a priestess named Aishe had seen to my wounds, she wandered off, sensing I wished to be alone.

It was difficult to comprehend that I'd sat in this same spot only hours ago, talking and laughing with Thorana and Stix. Both, now, were gone, killed for some political reason I had yet to fathom.

All because of the black hearted King Orius.

As I thought back to Merin's words, I felt an anger building inside of me. A worthless dreg, she'd called me. Even after all we'd been through, it came down to that. The anger built slowly at first, like clouds before a storm. Once it forced its way past my sorrow, it spewed out of me, rising to the surface.

"The hell with this," I muttered, my anger boiling over. "I've fulfilled my end of the bargain."

I grabbed my pack, ready to light out of the camp and make my own way on the road.

"They told me I'd find you here," came a voice from behind me.

Turning, I saw an older dwarf, with streaks of gray in his coal black beard. In the light of the fire, I could see he was dressed in a chainmail tunic, its coif draped over his head. He wore greaves and armguards of hardened leather, along with a longsword of iron strapped to a walnut-colored belt. A pair of daggers hung at his waist, along with a wooden buckler. His eyes were dark, filled with intensity.

"I'm not good company right now," I muttered, only desiring to leave.

"I understand lad, and I've no wish to make a nuisance of myself," the old dwarf replied. "But they're saying you bested an orc Shadow. I had to see for myself if that was true."

I narrowed my eyes, wondering who he was.

He must have sensed my confusion because he extended his hand. "Name's Nathrak Cutter, Captain of the Deadhand Ragers serving under General Ironhenge."

Dwarven Ragers were the equivalent of Orc Ravagers. They wore less armor than the heavy infantry but were more effective with their weapons. They were the best offensive warriors we had against the sallowskin armies, save perhaps for a cadre of Mountaineers. I had seen more than one Rager offset a group of blackbloods with the ferocity and speed of their attacks.

Still, I couldn't understand why I warranted attention from their leader.

"I'm Omens," I grunted in reply, reluctantly shaking his hand.

"I hear tell you're a bard?" Nathrak asked, sitting down next to me.

"What do you want?" I grated, close to losing my temper.

Nathrak leaned forward and took out a worn brown pipe. "Tell me how you won that machete," he said, filling the bowl, packing it with a tamper.

I glanced down at the weapon I'd taken from the Shadow. It was fashioned from darksteel, and far more durable than my iron sword.

"There's not much to tell," I grumbled. "The Shadow came at me, and I fought him. He died and I'm alive."

Nathrak looked up from his pipe, raising his eyebrow. "Did you actually cross blades with him?"

I was getting annoyed. "What do you think?" I snapped. "That we danced a jig? Of course I crossed blades with him—why do you think I'm in the healing tent? We fought to a stalemate for several minutes, neither able to gain an advantage over the other."

The captain lit his pipe, puffing at the stem. "Several minutes? If you had to guess, how long would you say the fight lasted?"

"I don't know old timer," I groused, beyond annoyed. "When you're fighting for your life, you don't stop to wonder how much sand has run through the hourglass."

I turned my back on him, eyes blazing. "I've had a long day and have had enough of your questions—enjoy the rest of the evening."

I took three steps from the fire and came under attack.

A young dwarf, a male—dressed in similar fashion to Nathrak, stepped from the shadows of the pavilion and swung his blade at me. I dodged aside, cursing like a sailor and drew the machete out of its sheath.

"What the hell are you…" I began to say, when he attacked me again. I blocked his sword, countering with a riposte he knocked aside easily. Thrusting his blade forward, the Rager attacked again, as I backed out of range.

"Fight me," he snarled, his eyes wild. I caught a glimpse of a blonde beard in the light of the fire.

"I have no wish to cross blades with you, kinsman," I answered, keeping my guard up. "But I will kill you if I must."

A ghost of a smile touched his lips. "Let's see if you can," he threatened, moving forward once again.

The blonde-bearded dwarf went on an all-out offensive, attacking me from several different angles with great speed. Though I was tired from a trying day, my anger gave me strength. For more than a minute we fought, the sounds of our combat causing dwarves from all over the camp to run toward us and see what the ruckus was about.

"Ukori, that's enough," I heard Nathrak say, sounding satisfied.

"We've only just begun," the younger dwarf answered, halting his attack, breathing heavily.

"I said enough," Nathrak muttered, steel in his voice.

The younger dwarf scowled at me and sheathed his sword.

"By the hand of Andovar, what the hell was that about?" I cursed, shifting my eyes from one Rager to the other.

"We will speak more tomorrow," Nathrak said, blowing smoke through his smile.

"If I see you tomorrow, I may kill you myself," I hissed in anger.

"That was well done," another voice said from off to my right.

Arik Ironhenge.

"General?" I asked, my anger giving way to confusion.

"When I heard that a bard had fought and beaten an orc Shadow—well, I had to see your skill for myself," he explained. "I thought, the Shadow must have been wounded, or perhaps you had exaggerated your story."

"He wasn't wounded, and I didn't exaggerate anything," I spat, acid in my tone.

"No, you more than held your own against one of the best Ragers in Kazic-Thul," Arik admitted, nodding toward Ukori. "For what it's worth, I believe you now. With proper training you could be formidable."

"I don't want to be formidable; I want to be left alone."

I could hear the general chuckling to himself. "Fair enough lad. You've been through plenty today already. Go. Enjoy your night. Get some rest."

He walked away and re-entered the command tent. Seeing the action had ended, the crowd quickly dispersed, leaving me standing in the pavilion alone.

Despite the stupidity of the fight, I realized it had done me some good—it had sapped me of my anger. I no longer wanted to leave. Still, I needed to go someplace quiet, someplace where I could think.

I looked around, seeing tents all over the courtyard. It was too crowded in the outpost. The barracks had not been renovated yet, and even if they had been, this place was never meant to house more than two hundred dwarves at a time. Searching, my eyes were drawn to the watchtower. I saw nothing but darkness at the top. History had taught me it was always manned, often with four guards at a time. Two to keep watch and two to sleep. With the enemy gone, I guessed no one was at the top tonight.

It was exactly what I needed.

Picking up my pack, I strode across the courtyard grass, stepped onto the stairs, and started to climb.

Ghost found Merin standing in a corner, weeping quietly to herself.

The older dwarf knew the feeling well. She had not lied in the King's tent. To feel that alone—to be abandoned by everything and everyone you knew was difficult to bear. Ghost had been lucky in one regard, as she'd already met Ashten when Arik had exiled her from Clan Ironhenge. The young prince had railed against his family's plans, defying them all. Together the two had set out on their own, Engineers for hire, until their success had attracted others to join them.

Still, it was not an enviable feeling. To have your father order your death—worse, to have no understanding as to why.

Ghost stepped heavily behind the princess, not wishing to startle the already agitated young she-dwarf.

Hearing the step behind her, Merin glanced back and bowed her head in an effort to hide her sorrow. "I'm alright," she sniffed, trying to wipe away her tears.

"No, you are not," Ghost said kindly, taking the princess in her arms and hugging her tightly. Merin gave into the misery of the moment and sobbed into Ghost's shoulder.

For some time, they stood together, the older dwarf consoling the younger.

"Why would he do it?" Merin asked when she could speak again. "I'm his daughter. Why would he wish me dead?"

"That's what we'd all like to know," Ghost answered firmly.

"I'm not in line to inherit the throne," Merin reasoned, at a loss. "My Uncle Bolgir has a better claim."

"There is no need to try and figure it out now," Ghost replied. "As horrible as your predicament is, we have other things to worry about. Your home is under siege. We've received no news as to what has happened in Lodir. We are going to take this force of five hundred dwarves along with the Gray Company in the morning and march it to the Golden Keep. With my brother to lead us, we should be able to provide immediate relief to both Lodir and the surrounding townships. Helfer will return to Kazic-Thul and raise part of his army to send soon after. We should be able to push this horde back across the Hollowspan Bridge and free Lodir inside a tenday."

Ghost paused and wiped away what was left of Merin's tears. "You are going to accompany us, princess. You have a working knowledge of the city, and we need all the fighters we can get."

"I'm not of the warrior class," Merin said.

"Says the girl who took on a Shadow and slew the biggest Orc Chain at the Toad and Peach."

Ghost hesitated for a moment. "And, if Omens is telling the truth, you are the same lass who put a hole in the feistiest warrior trout between here and Lodir."

Merin could not help but smile at the memory. "He told you about that?"

"Oh, yes," Ghost answered, laughing softly to herself. "He gave a grand accounting of both you and the fish."

Merin looked out over the battlements. "I had been so horrible to him," she admitted. "Yet he taught me anyway."

She lowered her head in shame. "Now I've called him a liar—a worthless, lowborn dreg." She started to weep again, unable to hold back her tears. "He took on that Shadow to save me. He has protected me since the moment we left Lodir, and that's what I said to him. He will never forgive me. I don't blame him."

"Oh, he will," Ghost said knowingly. "Omens is many things, but vengeful isn't one of them."

"Why do you say that"

The older she-dwarf smiled. "I know him," she explained. "For the first time in his life, Omens has found something he cares about more than himself."

"What is that?" Merin asked.

"You," came a voice from behind them.

Both turned to see the silhouette of Omens standing at the top of the stairs.

"I should go," Ghost said, walking toward the bard. She paused, looking Omens in the eye. "We leave a half turn of the hourglass past dawn," she grunted. "Ashten and I want you to come with us and work with the Gray Company until this is over."

"I'm not sure I'm interested," he replied, glancing at Merin.

"You'll be paid handsomely."

"I'll see you at dawn," the bard agreed raffishly, not missing a beat. With a snort of laughter Ghost proceeded down the tower stairs.

As I stood at the top of the landing staring at Merin, a shooting star streaked across the night sky overhead. Merin saw the spectacle at the same time, its magnificence drawing our attention to it. As quickly as it came, the light burned out, leaving a streak of darkness in its wake.

"You don't see that every night," I said, walking carefully toward the princess, drawing to a halt only inches from her.

"It is rare," she agreed in a pensive voice, as her gaze lingered overhead.

"It's the second most beautiful thing I've seen today," I murmured, giving Merin a knowing smile.

The princess straightened her back, as the memory of her anger returned.

"Merin," I began, watching her shoulders go cold. "Are you alright?"

I saw her face twist in anger under the light of the moon. "No."

I exhaled deeply. "I don't blame you," I replied, turning back toward the stairs. "I'm sure you'd rather be alone."

"Omens," I heard Merin whisper, her voice tight with emotion.

I looked back and saw she was finally looking at me.

"I... I'm sorry," she said softly, her voice breaking. "I didn't mean what I said. I was just..."

"Hush now princess," I whispered, stepping close, touching her lips with my forefinger. "Dwarves say all kinds of things when they are scared, or angry, or upset. I'm not worth all this fuss. Don't let it concern you."

She leaned in close, and I hugged her tightly.

"You have tried to keep me safe since we started," she said quietly. "I trust you more than any of the others."

"Well, that's a—terrible idea, really," I joked, smiling at her. "I'm quite *un*trustworthy in most circumstances."

"That is not true," she said, squeezing me tightly.

After a few moments, Merin pulled away.

"Omens…what are we going to do about my father?"

I hesitated, letting out a deep breath. "One thing at a time, lass," I answered firmly. "We are about to attack a horde of thirty thousand sallowskins inside a fortified dwarven city. Let's try and get past that little obstacle first."

"Alright."

"Speaking of our enemy," I said, reaching into my pack. "I wanted to give this to you."

I pulled out the knife the Shadow had thrown at me back on the trail we'd taken through the hills. Holding it by the handle, I reversed the blade and offered it to Merin.

"It's a good knife," I said. "Made of darksteel--you earned it."

"Where did you come by a darksteel knife?"

"That Shadow tried to skewer me with it," I answered. "It is the twin to the one Monchakka carries."

Merin shook her head. "I didn't do anything to earn this," she argued. "You keep it."

I frowned at her. "I've the darksteel machete, that's enough for me—and you *did* earn it. You came back and almost killed the Shadow without me. Two inches to the left and that bolt would have struck his heart. Besides, all you have is the crossbow. You need a melee weapon, just in case."

Reluctantly, Merin took the blade, staring at it for a long moment. Shrugging, she slipped it into her pack with the rest of her belongings.

"Thank you," she said simply.

"Now," I yawned, well aware of how long I'd been awake. "I suggest we get some sleep."

"Did you set up your tent?"

I frowned at her. "No, not yet."

Merin gave me a naughty little smile. "I know for a fact there is a small alcove, cozy enough for two, right here at the top of the tower."

I raised an eyebrow at her. "How did you know that?"

"Thorana," Merin replied, growing somber. "She informed me of it when we were heading to the healing tent when we arrived."

The princess hesitated a moment and her smile disappeared. "I miss her, Stix too."

"So do I."

"I meant to ask you," she continued, her voice tinged with sadness. "How did you make their spirits return like that? That was an impressive display of bardic magic. I've never heard of it before."

I gave her a little wave. "I'll have to tell you another time. I'm exhausted."

"I understand," she acquiesced with a yawn.

As we climbed into the alcove and lay next to one another I heard the princess drift off to sleep. I rolled onto my side, thinking about her last question.

I didn't have the heart to tell her, I never heard of that bardic magic either.

Chapter 16: Ragers

We left the next day under the command of General Ironhenge. More than five hundred dwarves strode along the main road to Lodir, minus a squad of heavy cavalry that escorted Helfer back to the city. Arik sent a cadre of light cavalry and a handful of Engineers to scout ahead, making sure the way was clear. There was no report of sallowskins anywhere in the area, which led the general to believe the force that had been sent to Draymore's Outpost represented the bulk of enemy troops in the vicinity.

I spent most of my time traveling within the Gray Company, walking alongside Merin. There was little talk amongst us, as we were still dealing with the loss of Thorana and the Engineers.

It was a long, tiring day, but it passed without incident. We made camp two hours prior to sunset. The good thing about traveling with a military force is that they have their routine, and for better or for worse, they stick to it. Sentries were posted and quarters assembled in a timely manner. The evening meal was a staple of salted meat and cheese, with the always present hardtack. It proved to be tasteless, but filling. I managed to wrangle up an apple or two along with a handful of wild strawberries. I split them with Merin and the others, making a dull meal more bearable.

An hour till sunset Nathrak and his underling, along with a score of other Ragers, walked across the encampment to find me.

"Well met again, bard Omens," the elder Rager said in greeting, puffing away on his pipe. "I trust you're in better spirits this evening?"

"What do you want?" I asked warily, in no mood for this harassment.

"I'd like to cross blades with you," snapped the blonde bearded dwarf from last night.

"Easy Ukori," Nathrak cautioned. "Omens is a civilian, not of the king's army."

"He's a dreg," Ukori spat, as though that answered everything.

"A dreg who's bested a Shadow," Nathrak countered.

The stockily built Ukori hawked in his throat and spat toward me. "I'd like to see him best me before I award him the ivory axe."

I shook my head. "This blonde buffoon is right," I said, looking at Nathrak. "I'm not a sword master; I just got lucky."

Nathrak took the long stem of his pipe out of his mouth and stared at me. "I only know of one other dwarf that wears the machete of a Shadow. He's the finest blademaster I've ever seen. You say you're not a swordsman, but I watched you last night. I don't come to you now to bother you, bard, I come because I want to see you in action again. I want to learn just how good you can be."

I stared at the old Rager, long and hard. I didn't want to train, not really. I'd been through it all before, some years ago. While I was a tad rusty, I was still a more than capable swordsman and I suspected Nathrak knew it. However, I had no desire to go through the practice needed to reach the level of swordsmanship I'd achieved in the past.

I was on the cusp of walking away when I thought back to my fight with the Shadow. I remembered how close to death I had come. More importantly, I knew how close the orc had come to killing Merin. If training with these Ragers could help me, who was I to argue?

"I'll give you the next five minutes," I grunted in acquiescence, curious to see what I'd remembered from my previous trainer.

The smile on Ukori's face could only be described as hungry. Quickly the Rager shed his dark green cloak and drew out his sword. He spun the steel blade around his body in a show of speed and skill.

I yawned at him.

"If you're done making love to your sword, might we begin?" I asked, drawing my own blade.

Ukori flashed a quick look to Nathrak, who nodded in return.

The blonde bearded dwarf was a fine swordsman—of that, I had no doubt, but Ragers are a strange bunch. They're not just good with weapons, they're canny, knowing where to strike and when. In this case, they weren't interested in testing my ability with the blade— that had been done last night. Nathrak's comment about learning how good I could be was a façade. There was another game afoot, and, lucky for me, I knew how to play. They should have hidden their purpose better. The grand march through camp along with the long-winded introduction had set off alarm bells in my head. Those two things, coupled with the flashing sword display by Ukori, gave away their purpose.

They should have known better than to put on a show for a bard.

Ukori stepped forward—that's when the true test came.

From behind me, a she-dwarf Rager attacked. I'd marked her early on—hair the color of roasted chestnuts, her fingers already resting on the hilt of her sword. I heard the barest shuffling of feet in the dirt, and that's when I knew the test had come.

Spinning around, I dropped to one knee and parried her attack. My darksteel machete rang like a bell against the edge of her iron blade. She let out a gasp and her eyes widened.

The other Ragers responded in kind, while Nathrak gave me a satisfied smile.

"I knew it," I heard him say knowingly.

"Who told you about the *Corin Vie?*" my attacker demanded, her chin jutting forward in challenge.

"Exactly who you think," I answered, putting away the machete.

There was a whispered discourse among the Ragers present, ranging from mild shock to blatant outrage.

"The rest of you, go back to camp and get some rest," Nathrak stated, blowing smoke through his teeth. "Leave me to speak with the bard alone."

I was cast a few resentful looks, and my attacker glowered at me for a long moment before all twenty retreated to camp, leaving me with the captain.

"I think you've managed to upset every single dwarf under my command," he began, leaning up against a thick boughed evergreen.

"My apologies," I remarked, sarcastically.

Nathrak chuckled in amusement. "You'll have to forgive them. Every Rager feels as though *they* will be the one selected when they hear the story of the red blade.

"It's not like I volunteered," I muttered in annoyance.

"If you will forgive my curiosity—how did you come to meet him?"

I waved my hand, dismissing the question. "What do you want with me, old timer? I'm not interested in joining your squad."

"Nor would I ask you too," he replied, scratching his chin. "As for my question—I'd guess you were part of the…expedition into the Jagged Lands."

My silence spoke volumes.

"It seems I've struck a chord," he continued with a small smile.

"Best to leave it alone," I warned, having no desire to discuss the matter.

"Fair enough," he conceded, respecting my privacy.

He shuffled off toward camp, but turned, only a few steps away from me.

"A word of warning," he said, removing his pipe from his mouth. "Should the time come, you need to be ready. I offer my squad to you as a place to hone your skills. Whether you like it or not, he chose you for a reason."

With that, Nathrak left, leaving me standing there alone.

"Damn you, Gavakyn," I muttered in frustration, kicking at the rocks on the ground. "What the hell did you get me into?"

That night Ashten and the other leaders met in the command tent, while the common soldiers found ways to amuse themselves as they could. Merin was in with the commanders, and Monchakka stayed close to Kora. The two of them were cleaning their rifles and learning about some kind of technological gadget with the tinker named Ratchet. I was left alone for a good two hours and decided to make my way around the camp. The cavalry was caring for their mounts and the Stonebreakers were engaged in some kind of wrist wrestling contest. I lingered there for a bit, managing to win three silvers betting on a bull of a dwarf, nicknamed, "The Ox." I walked past a half dozen war priests, one of whom, a young she-dwarf named Aishe, had healed my wounds the previous night. I gave her a tip of my cap and flipped her one of my newly won coins. She flashed me a smile of thanks and moved back inside her tent, as the elder priests looked on in disapproval.

Finally, I came to the Ragers. Their set up was neat and tidy, with a decent sized cooking fire burning in the middle of their tents. Hanging over the flames on metal skewers were what remained of three wild turkeys, roasting. I could smell the charred flesh and my mouth began to water. Most of the squad was cleaning weapons or engaged in quiet conversations among themselves. Two, however, were sparring with one another to the occasional catcalls of the rest.

"You keep dropping your shoulder," teased Ukori, blocking the chestnut-haired female's attack.

"I'm setting you up," she snapped back, counter attacking with a dangerous thrust.

"*What do you see?*" said a rough voice in my mind, a voice I'd not heard in some time.

"They are both good," I muttered as though I was standing right next to Gavakyn. "She's overcompensating a bit, because she wants to prove herself. He's being condescending, so his defense is slightly out of balance."

"Oye," I heard a voice growl in front of me. "Who died and made you the master of the sword?"

Blinking, I saw that all twenty Ragers were staring at me, and none of them looked happy.

"Just making an observation," I said, cursing at the voice in my head.

"You think you know so much," said a well-muscled male, sporting a forked brown beard, "then show us all how you fight."

"All right," I said, drawing my machete, realizing I'd made my way here on purpose. "Let's dance."

Forked beard and I strode to an open space near their camp. The sun had set, but there was still a sliver of light under the horizon. The fire was burning brightly, and we were quickly surrounded by the rest of the squad. My opponent drew out a sturdy looking sword of tempered steel. Without preamble, the Rager and I began.

He was quick with his blade—not as fast as the Shadow had been, but dangerous none-the-less. For several seconds we gained a measure of one another, testing our defenses. I did not want to wait too long and draw this out, but I had been taught it was better to know the skills of your enemy than to guess at them. The speed of our contest increased, and I began to feel sweat running down the back of my neck. Our sparring fell into a rhythm, and I let him work his way through his attack routines. He repeated a move he'd made at the outset, though this time it was faster, and more deliberate. Remembering his sequence, I defended appropriately, and then sent a nasty counter that knocked his sword wide and left my blade at his throat.

Panting hoarsely, fork beard raised his hands in surrender.

"That was well done," he admitted, with a reluctant admiration.

"You fought well," I replied, lowering my blade. "You repeated your attack from earlier, and I took advantage."

"Hmmph," he grunted, raising an eyebrow. "So Nathrak keeps telling me." He frowned. "A lesser swordsman would not have noticed."

I had no desire to shame him, as he had been a worthy opponent. "The speed of your blade would compensate for it against most other warriors," I said. "It was a close thing."

The dwarf stepped forward and extended his hand. "Dreg or no, you've got manners," he said with a smile. "Name's Reece. Let me know when you wish to cross swords again. We'll have another go."

"Strength to your clan, brother," I replied, giving him a slight bow.

"And to you," he answered.

The Chesnutt haired she-dwarf stepped forward. "Explain what you meant when you said I was overcompensating," she said.

Just like that, I was training with the Ragers.

Alright, so maybe I'm both a lover *and* a fighter. I do enjoy a good fight from time to time, though I'd rather participate in the former.

I spent the next hour sparring with the Ragers. I didn't win every session, but I like to think the sparring helped us all. By the end of the evening, I had grown weary, and headed back to my tent. I swung by the stream that flowed nearby and washed myself in the moonlight, scraping off the rigors of the day. Dripping wet, I sat naked on the edge of the stream waiting impatiently to dry.

"What have we here?" a voice asked from out of darkness. "If I'd known you were sitting like this at the water's edge, I'd have come sooner."

I could make out Merin's smile in the pale light of the moon, her white teeth flashing.

"Hello Princess," I said, returning her smile. "Care to join me?"

She wrinkled her nose and tossed me a frown. "Aren't you worried someone will come down here?" she asked, her voice hushed.

"Unless I grow a third eye, I don't think I've got anything they haven't seen," I replied, laying back, putting my hands comfortably behind my head.

"You're incorrigible," she teased, giving me her tinkling laugh.

"I don't know the meaning of the word," I joked, biting my lip to keep from smiling. "If you are going to walk around the camp tossing out fancy turns of the tongue like that, I'll think you desire the company of a more sophisticated dwarf. What's a poor bard to do?"

She laughed again—a rich, warm sound.

"Speaking of tongues," she said, somewhat wistfully. "I was thinking about the other night...after the battle at the Toad and Peach."

"Oh, I see," I replied, my smile widening. "Would that be when you discovered your...femininity, princess?"

"Yes," she whispered, blushing in the dark.

"Will we be alone this time, or are you inviting the others?"

Her face turned in a frown. "What others?"

"Goran, Andovar, and Sapen—the three gods of the Trine."

"What are you talking about?"

"Well, I assumed they were there in the room with us that night. You kept shouting out their names."

"Oh you...beast," she crowed in embarrassment, "I did no such thing!"

"Really? Does the phrase, 'By Goran, what are you doing to me?' ring a bell? Because I heard that one quite a bit."

"Shut your clack," she scolded me, with a swipe at my head. "I didn't..."

"But you did!" I teased her, fighting against my laughter. "Then there was the, 'By the mercy of Andovar, don't stop,'" I said, mimicking her voice while moving my hips up and down in an exaggerated way. "I don't know what the God of Mischief was doing in our bed chamber, but you seemed to want him to continue...whatever it was he was doing."

"You bastard, I did *not* say that," she fumed, jumping on top of me.

"And who could forget Lady Sapen?" I asked, laughing aloud. "Surely you..."

She pressed her mouth against mine and I fell quiet. After a time, she leaned forward and whispered in my ear. "Now shut up and put that tongue to good use."

"Anything you say, Highness."

The gods of the Trine *did* visit the princess that night, right there on the edge of the stream.

They visited me as well.

Chapter 17: Lucid

The next day we moved on, making it all the way to Barrel Falls. Unlike our arrival five days past, the town was now prepared to repel an attack. Hastily raised palisades had been constructed, wrapping around much of the outer perimeter. More than six hundred wayward dwarves, both from the surrounding area and the road, had flocked to the town. Word had spread and any dwarf worth their salt knew they had a better chance of staying alive inside the defenses of Barrel Falls than they did wandering the roads alone. Between those that lived in the village and the others that had joined, Barrel Falls now numbered more than fifteen hundred defenders.

Our company made its way inside the palisade where we were given a hearty cheer upon our arrival. The field where they held their yearly summer festival was given over to Arik and his army. There was rumor of a report that had come in from Lodir, though it was unconfirmed. Arik went to the Frog and Peach to discover the truth of the rumor directly. He asked Merin and me to accompany him, to see if we could confirm its authenticity.

On our way, we had attracted the attention of an unkempt dwarven male. Dressed in a soiled brown tunic, he had a dirty yellow band of cloth tied around his head, hanging down past the side of his ear. He ran up next to Merin and began sniffing at her arm.

"What are you doing?" she exclaimed, drawing her hand back.

"You've the scent of old blood—the lions seek the doe," he gibbered, inhaling deeply.

"What do you mean?" Merin asked in confusion. "What lions?"

"The white-eyed hunter is with them," he answered, unhelpfully.

"Bah…away with you," barked Arik, waving his hand, having little patience for the unkempt dwarf. "Crazy beggar."

"Psssht," snorted the newcomer, flattening his eyes at the general. "A clansman of pitted iron, and sights unseen. Daisy would have shunned you!"

"Lucid?" I asked, looking more closely at the dwarf.

The newcomer stared at me and gave a slow smile. "Yes, the bard, he always sees, no matter where I go!" he cackled, rubbing his head on my chest. "Omens knows, as dreg sees dreg."

"What are you doing in Barrel Falls?" I asked.

"I remember a week ago," the filthy dwarf replied, ignoring my question. "You snuck out the window after a loud, long night spent with the Bronzefist wife. Fear not! I'll keep your secret for all my days."

I glanced at Merin and leaned in close to Lucid. "You keep secrets like a jealous fishwife," I muttered.

Lucid leaned in close to me and stared into my eyes. "You are changed since you were blessed by the old blood, but still, you do not see."

The unkempt dwarf began to sniff Merin's arm again.

"I take it, you know this dwarf?" Merin asked, looking in bewilderment at the mass of brown hair in front of us.

"Aye, his name's Lucid, or that is what he was called in Dregtown," I answered, tucking my thumbs under my belt. "A bit peculiar, as you can see, but harmless enough."

"He's as mad as a cut snake," Arik harrumphed, making to move away.

I glanced across the green, spying a glassblowers shop close by.

"Are you still looking for bottles?" I asked Lucid, who stopped his sniffing to glare at Arik.

The raggedly dressed dwarf's eyes lit up and he spun in a circle, cackling with glee. "The tale-teller remembers, ahh ha! I'm always looking for Daisy. By candlelight, she returns at night!"

"What the hell is he talking about?" Arik grunted.

"I have no idea," I admitted, taking out a silver coin. I handed it to him and Lucid hugged it like it was the most valuable thing in the world. "Go buy yourself the nicest bottle you can find," I said to him.

Lucid smiled at me, showing teeth stained yellow. "I'll not forget you Omens, I won't, even when the Piper comes for us all."

Looking at the princess he spoke again.

"Ware the lions in the wood, old blood, do not believe the false hopes of the heart."

Turning to Arik, Lucid narrowed his eyes. "You smell of wet cat bollocks!" he hissed, and loped off, heading toward the glassblowers.

"Barking mad," growled the general, stomping across the green. "No offense to you bard, but he's a strange one."

"He scares me," Merin admitted, drawing her hood up over her head.

I didn't respond, knowing my companions would only see things from their point of view. Yes, Lucid was odd, but to my knowledge he'd never injured anyone and often tried to help those in need, albeit in his own way.

I'd watched him once take a long stick and knock down icicles in the market square on a winter morning before sunrise. The other dregs had poked fun at him, but most left him alone. It wasn't until the butcher, tired of the noise Lucid was making, ran him off, threatening to cleave his head in two. Not long after, the local quarry workers entered the square with a massive stone they'd unearthed. It was to be the main piece used for a statue carved in the image of Goran, placed in the center of the market. When the workers dropped it, the five-ton stone shook the ground. The icicles that hung from the edges of the buildings were knocked loose and several dwarves, including the butcher, were injured.

I remember thinking afterward that Lucid might be the most brilliant dwarf I'd ever seen.

We stepped into the Toad and Peach, seeing it had returned to its normal state. Patrons were seated at tables once again, and a young female bard was on stage, practicing her skills with a lute.

In the back were four Stonebreakers dressed in the trappings of the royal guard of Lodir. Seated among them was Jax.

"Thank Goran you are alive," he said to me, standing when he saw us.

"Sit your arse down," growled one of the guards, the visor of his helmet closed, hiding his face.

"For the last time, you do not command me," Jax snarled, his face flush with anger. It was rare to see him upset. His display made me think the guards had harassed him long before our arrival.

"We're fine Jax," I responded, frowning at the guard. "Are you the scout who went to Lodir?"

"Aye," Jax replied, giving me a nod.

"Hold your tongue dreg," the first guard spat, looking at me scornfully through his pale green eyes. "We'll ask the questions round here."

"How goes the siege?" Arik asked Jax, ignoring the words of the guard.

"Who wants to know?" the leader challenged, stepping in front of Arik, his groomed red beard, inches from the general's face.

Monchakka's father gave the guard a look that could have cracked stone. "Arik Ironhenge, Supreme Commander of Kazic-Thul—I'm here to question the dwarf behind you, step aside."

The guard captain gave him a nasty smile. "I only take orders from the King of Lodir," he replied. "Not some outsider general and his dreg pet. You can wait till we are done with him."

Arik frowned and hefted his nickel plated hammer. "It has been some time since I instructed one as arrogant as you," he growled softly.

The guard snorted. "There are four of us, general. You are old, well past your prime. Your companions are a worthless dreg and a she-dwarf Bolter, you can't possibly defeat us."

"Is that right?" he said, instantly tossing his hammer to the captain who had insulted him. The guard, taken by surprise, reached out reflexively and caught the hammer. Arik stepped forward and headbutted him, crushing the dwarf's nose to a bloody pulp. The captain dropped the hammer and fell to his knees, crying out in pain.

"Would anyone else like to offer me insult?" Arik asked, his voice like a winter's frost.

The other three guards looked on in shock.

"Stand aside Regan," came the voice of the princess. Pulling off her hood, she glared at a second guard, her eyes angry.

Immediately the remaining trio dropped to one knee, bowing in acquiescence, and I realized these were the same dwarves that had been in the castle when I'd spoken to Orius.

"Highness," a dwarf with a scar over his right eye said, "you should have announced your presence."

"And you should display better manners to those who would be our allies," she grated, looking on in irritation. "Now, let the general and I question Jax, alone."

"Your will, highness," the guards responded automatically. The other two helped the captain to his feet, while the general led Jax and Merin to the back of the inn.

"Highness?" Regan asked, before she turned the corner.

"Yes?"

"I've been ordered to speak with you privately–upon your return, of course."

"By whom?"

The guard wet his lips and glanced at me. "Your father."

Merin stared at him and gave a brief nod. "Very well," she agreed, before following Arik to the back.

"Let's have a look at that," I offered, leaning close to the wounded captain.

"Piss off!" he thundered, swatting my hand away.

"Easy now," I cautioned him, knowing he was angry and humiliated. "There's no need to be like that. The generals brought healers with him. I'm sure they will…"

"The hell with the general and his healers, dreg," the captain snarled, reaching for his axe. "He isn't here to fight your battles for you now."

"Oh, I wouldn't do that," came a jovial voice from the inn's doorway.

In walked Reece, cavalierly shuffling over to my side.

"Normally, I don't mind Stonebreakers," the Rager said, walking up to them. "They are good fighters, most of them—brave to a fault and as strong as bulls. However, there is always the off chance you'll come across a few that are so full of themselves, they forget there are others that fight just as well."

"My quarrel is not with you, Rager," the captain snapped, unsuccessfully trying to wipe the blood from his nose. It's with this lowborn dreg."

Reece let out a short, barking laugh. "You misunderstand me," he drawled, drawing his sword. "I'm not here to keep *you* from thrashing *him*—it's the other way around. You see his blade?" Reece asked, pointing at my weapon belt. "That's the machete of an orc Shadow. Omens here killed him in single combat—he doesn't need my help, not for a bunch of scabs like you."

The four guards shifted their gazes to me, looking at the blade on my hip.

"I'm here to save *you*," Reece continued, absently studying the edge of his sword. "Should you attack him, well—we've enough enemies as it is. We don't need to see him wipe the floor with the four of you now, do we? It makes extra work for the healers."

The quartet looked balefully at Reece, their eyes going flat.

"Of course, if you insist on seeing this nonsense through," Reece said, smiling broadly, giving a low whistle.

Filing into the front entrance walked half of Nathrak's company, each spoiling for a fight. They shuffled close and stood in a seething mass behind Reece.

"Your choice lads," the Rager continued, patting his sword up and down rhythmically in the open palm of his left hand.

The four Stonebreakers looked nervously around, not knowing Arik's army had entered town.

"Go see to your wound," I offered, hoping my gesture of kindness would diffuse the situation.

"You won't always have your friends around, dreg," Regan hissed at me, walking out the door.

The Ragers allowed the quartet to keep what little remained of their dignity and let them leave without further incident. The last guard with sand colored stubble on his face turned his head back toward me as he made his way out the door and I felt the hair on the back of my neck rise. I had seen him before, but in the chaos of the last week, I could not place him. I blinked and he was gone, leaving me to wonder who it was.

"Never a dull moment around you, Omens," Reece said, clapping me on the back.

I relaxed, forgetting about the guard and gave Reece a smile. "Usually, I can avoid confrontations like that, but in this case, I appreciate the help.

"That's what we do for one another," he said, winking at me. "Now, let's see about getting a drink."

While we waited, I took a moment to listen to the bard on stage. With black hair and blue eyes, she was an attractive lass, cute rather than pretty. Still young, she displayed an aptitude for the lute I recognized right away. I found myself critiquing her over the passing minutes, though I kept my thoughts to myself.

It was less than a quarter turn of the hourglass later when Arik and Merin returned with Jax.

"I'll prepare my captains to be ready to move at first light," Arik was saying to the princess. "With what Jax has told us, I think we can use our cavalry units to harass the enemy enough to where we can pull them away from the keep. If we get enough of them to follow, we can whittle down their numbers and see about breaking through their lines."

"I'll leave it up to you, general," Merin said, looking at me with tired eyes.

Arik walked outside, his stentorian voice bellowing orders to the dwarves under his command.

"You should get some rest," I suggested to Merin, standing next to her, offering her a drink of my ale.

"I need to speak to the royal guards," she replied, gulping down the last of my brew. "After that, I'll find a place for our tent."

I gave her a smile. "I've already spoken to Cherak. He's agreed to let us use our old room," I pointed up the stairs.

Merin gave me a small smile and set the mug down on the table with a clunk. "I'll see you soon," she promised.

"Maybe I should go with you," I suggested, a nagging feeling in the back of my mind.

She gave me one of her smiles. "Omens, I'll be fine. The royal guards are sworn to protect my family. I've known Regan all my life—he carries a message from my father, I need to know what it is. Don't worry, I can take care of myself."

Merin leaned in and kissed me. "Get our room ready for when I get back," she teased, giving me a grin that stirred my blood, despite my weariness.

"Alright," I complied, watching her walk away. "Be safe."

"Always."

Merin walked outside onto the Barrel Falls green, as the sun was beginning to set. Absently she checked to see if her crossbow was secure, the habit becoming second nature over the last few days. Looking over the open space, Merin made out the dun-colored command marquee of the general and the neat rows of forest green tents that served as sleeping quarters to his army. Off to her left she spied the quartet of dwarves that served as her father's personal guard. Regan waved, beckoning for her to join them.

"Lieutenant," she said in greeting.

"Highness," he replied with a bow, giving her a warm smile.

"How's the nose?" she asked in concern, looking over at the captain.

"Hmmphh," the red bearded dwarf snorted, saying nothing.

"You said you had a message from my father?" Merin asked, dropping her voice.

The lieutenant nodded, scratching at his neatly trimmed brown beard. "Aye, though I think it best we discuss it away from the camp," he said softly, looking around. "We've heard the rumors from the general's soldiers," Regan continued, walking toward the eastern part of the camp. "They say your father ordered your death."

The lieutenant's face had twisted in disgust, as though the words he'd just uttered were a bitter draught he'd been forced to swallow.

Merin followed after him, her heart skipping a beat.

"It's not true?" she whispered with hope in her voice.

Regan gave her a sideways smile. "Of course not, your father adores you—he always has."

"But...Omens said..."

Regan made a sour face. "The dreg?" he asked, his voice disgusted. The lieutenant glanced around, as he and the other royal guards skirted past the squad of Bolters located on this side of the camp. "Surely you know better than to listen to that cuckold?"

Merin hesitated. "He said the orc Shadow had orders from my father to kill me," she answered, carefully.

Regan was shaking his head. "And you believed him?"

"He had no reason to lie," Merin answered, somewhat defensively.

Regan looked at the princess, with something akin to disapproval. "Highness, he is a dreg—worse a *bard* dreg, one known for carousing with dwarf maids for his own selfish pleasure."

Merin hesitated, knowing what Regan said was true.

"But he…"

"Highness, did you ever hear this orc say anything to Omens?"

"No."

Reagan raised an eyebrow. "Did it ever occur to any of you that he might be lying, to make himself look better?"

Merin looked up at Regan, feeling like a fool. "You think he made it up?"

Regan shook his head, clearly annoyed with her. "I think Omens represents the worst in our race," he explained, taking off his helmet and iron gauntlet, wiping the sweat from his brow.

By now they were at the outskirts of town, more than a quarter mile from the Toad and Peach, and a good fifty yards from any of the encamped dwarves. "By Goran it is warm tonight," Regan muttered, placing the helm back on his head.

Merin was about to speak when she saw something that made her blood run cold.

On the inside of Regan's wrist, was a small tattoo she'd never seen before. It was black, newly inked, the outline simple and easy to see.

It was in the shape of a lion.

"Omens, I have someone I want you to meet," Jax said to me, as I watched the door close behind Merin. Turning around, I looked at my old mentor and saw him beaming at the young bard who'd been playing on stage.

"This is Lyric Shadowsong, my new protégé,' he said proudly.

"It's nice to meet you," she mumbled shyly.

"It's a pleasure," I replied, giving her a small bow. "Though I have to say, I'm a little hurt. I never dreamed he'd replace me with another student."

Jax frowned. "You are well on your way already. I've taught you all I can. The road will teach you more than I ever could."

I smiled at him, my good humor returning. "I appreciate that Jax, though I daresay there are a few things I could still pick up from an old codger like you."

The elder bard pulled up a chair and sat down with a small sigh of relief. "I'm not getting any younger," he muttered, inviting me to join the pair.

He ordered ales for the three of us as I sat down.

"You went to Lodir?" I asked, keeping my voice down.

He nodded, looking thoughtful. "The day after the attack here at Barrel Falls. I knew someone needed to see how things stood at the keep. Volunteered myself and off I went. Borrowed your Nel—I hope that's alright. I needed a steady mount and she's as good as they come."

"How stands the city?" I asked, nodding at the dark eyed serving lass who thunked a mug down in front of me.

"Not good," Jax answered, taking a drink of his ale. "The walls have been breached and the sallowskins have taken the outer part of the city. No one is getting in or out, not that I could see. The invaders have been using catapults in an attempt to knock down the walls of the inner keep. They still hold, but it is only a matter of time. The gates are closed, but more and more defenders keep dying. They need help, soon, or Lodir will fall."

"Aid is on the way," I answered, looking grim. "The general has five hundred soldiers here, a balance of cavalry and infantry. He enlisted the Gray Company as well. They should make their mark before the battle's over. Two days behind us will be thousands more, as King Helfer has promised aid."

"A bit of good news then," Lyric chimed in, apparently over her shyness.

"Aye, though there's been some trouble with the princess," I said, glancing at the inn's exit once more.

"Trouble? What kind?" Jax asked.

I reached up and scratched the back of my head. "She's in danger. There has already been an attack on her life."

Quickly, I told them of the orc Shadow and what he'd told me. When finished, Jax gave me a low whistle of surprise.

"That's a bit of news," he said, his voice somber. "I'm sorry to hear about Thorana. She was a bonny fighter, and from what you tell me, a fine lass."

"Aye, she was," I agreed. "Made quite the impression on Monchakka, on all of us really. Now, I just want to keep Merin safe."

"She's in good hands with the lion guard," nodded Lyric, tipping back her mug, draining the rest of its contents."

"The lion guard?" I asked, a pang of fear echoing through me.

"Aye, the guard she addressed...Regan, I think she called him."

In a flash I replayed the scene in my head of the burly dwarf with the sand colored stubble leaving the inn. "He's the same dwarf," I muttered remembering him standing next to me in the courtroom of Lodir. A second memory hit Omens harder than the first. "Shit, he was here at Barrel Falls when we first came through," he shouted, seeing again the clean shaven dwarf spreading rumors right here in the common room. "He's the one who told the Shadow we were here! My Goran, he's one of the royal guard!"

I bolted out of my chair and ran for the door.

"Wait!" Jax called out, "what are you talking about? Where are you going?"

"Merin's in danger!" I yelled back, cursing myself for not going with her.

"Ware the lion in the wood, old blood, do not believe the false hopes of the heart."

Lucid's words came back to Merin as Regan slid his gauntlet back over his hand, covering the tattoo.

Merin's mind screamed to run, realizing she'd been led out here away from town. *No*, she thought. The princess knew she could not outpace all four of the guards. *Think*, she said to herself, a sick feeling coming over her. Merin's breath caught in her throat, as an idea came to mind.

"Ohhh," she moaned, not having to fake a queasy stomach.

"Highness, are you well?" asked Regan, looking down at her with concern.

"I've been battling something since the last time I was in Barrel Falls," Merin lied, coming to a halt. "Probably something I ingested. I need to relieve myself," she continued, managing a flush in her cheeks.

"Of course," Regan answered, turning his back to her.

"Don't look," she warned, crouching behind the underbrush a few yards shy of the woods. Moving as quietly as she could, Merin crept off, planning to enter the cover of the forest and steal her way back to the general's encampment. For a fistful of heartbeats she moved, ducking under the trees growing on the edge of the hills she'd strode earlier that week.

"Princess?" she heard Regan ask, now some thirty yards away.

Merin froze, afraid to move for fear of giving away her position.

"By the Trine, you've lost her?" she heard the captain bark, his tone accusing.

"She can't have gotten far," Regan answered, moving toward the place Merin was hidden.

"She's onto us," grumbled a third, running his hand through his sand-colored stubble.

"Impossible," scoffed the captain. "There is no way…"

"Quiet," Regan said, glaring into the forest.

Ducking behind a tree, Merin backed away from the royal guards as quietly as she could. Unfortunately, the heel of her foot caught on an old pinecone, crunching softly in the still air.

"There," shouted Regan, pointing directly at her through the trees.

Merin, knowing the game was up, ran for her life. The princess pumped her arms at her side, sprinting away as quickly as she could.

Initially she'd been able to keep ahead of her pursuers. She was lightly burdened whereas they carried the weight of full banded armor. Stonebreakers, however, were in phenomenal physical condition, and could run at speed for great distances even in full battle gear. Risking a look behind her, the princess saw they were slowly beginning to reel her in. Knowing she could not keep this pace, Merin turned west out of the trees, praying she had the energy for the mad dash back to town.

As she ran past a massive boulder, Merin caught a glimpse of a pale, sallow-skinned creature a heartbeat before its weapon struck her temple, knocking the princess from her feet. Landing heavily on her back, Merin looked up, seeing the savagely beautiful features of an orc female.

In her hands, she held a darksteel machete.

Running as quickly as I could, I rushed into the general's camp, screaming at the top of my lungs. "MERIN!"

"Gads son, what's happened?" asked a gray-haired Bolter, his nose crooked from an old break.

"The princess!" I demanded. "Have you seen her pass by with royal guards?"

"No lad. I haven't seen anyone like that—just the smelliest dwarf in all creation."

"Lucid?" I asked, daring to hope. "Which way did he go?"

The Bolter raised his finger, pointing it west toward the hills. "That way, but...I don't think he's right in the head."

"Did he speak to you?" I demanded.

"No, but I heard him...something about lions and does...it made no sense."

"Tell the general!" I shouted, racing off. "Tell him the princess is in danger!"

"Just kill her and be done with it!" Regan hissed, glaring at the female Shadow.

"Not yet," the orc replied, running a dark fingernail along Merin's bloodied temple.

"They will come for her," the captain warned, his eyes watching the trees behind them.

"They will be too late," the orc grunted. She uncorked her waterskin and poured it over Merin's face, seemingly in no hurry.

Merin sputtered back to consciousness, her eyes slowly regaining their focus.

She saw that she was in a small clearing, surrounded on all sides by trees and thick underbrush. She sat on the ground, her back up against the rough bark of a towering pine tree. Laying a few paces away was her crossbow, resting alongside a quiver containing her black iron bolts. Without making it obvious, Merin felt for the darksteel knife Omens had given her.

"Looking for this?" the orc asked, holding the blade in front of Merin's face.

The princess stared at her, saying nothing.

"Where did you come by it?" the Shadow continued, sounding quite curious. She was dressed in a black chain shirt and dark leather greaves. "I ask because it belonged to one of my brethren. What happened to him?"

"The same thing that is going to happen to you," Merin croaked, with a defiance she did not feel.

The she-orc laughed. "You have spirit, stump, I'll say that for you."

"Oganna, you are wasting time," said the dwarf with the sand-colored stubble.

"If you'd led my first company to her more quickly, she would have been captured six nights ago," the she-orc bristled, giving him a sharp look.

"I practically threw your soldiers at her on the mountain," the dwarf snarled in return. "Your vaunted Shadow underling couldn't catch them until they got to the outpost. *Your* forces are more to blame than I."

"Enough," said Regan. "This bickering is getting us nowhere."

Stepping close to the princess, Merin could smell the dank odor of stale sweat that hung on her old protector.

"I have waited long enough. Ask her your questions and kill her," Regan said, looking coolly at Merin. "We will collect her blood after, just as her father ordered."

"Why?" the princess asked, her voice breaking. "What ill have I ever done to him—or to you?"

Regan's face twisted in hate. "What ill have you done?" he hissed, his face turning red. "The four dwarves here all have their grievances against you, highness."

He nodded to the captain, whose flame colored beard matched the anger on his face. "Captain Lors should be a general by now, but one word from you kept that promotion from him."

"He was caught stealing from the royal coffers," Merin protested.

"A single coin," Lors hissed, his voice strangled in fury. "To pay for my mother's funeral."

Regan nodded at the young dwarf with the sand-colored hair.

"You insulted Keffin in front of the entire royal retinue last summer. All because he asked to accompany you to the mid-year festival."

"He demanded I go with him," Merin argued, her temper flaring. "He asked at an incredibly inappropriate time, trying to pressure me into saying yes."

Merin was angry now, looking at them all. "What of you?" she asked the third dwarf in the back who had yet to raise his visor.

Slowly the dwarf stepped forward, removing his helm. His ear had been lopped off, and there was scarring all along his neck.

"Sorran," she whispered in recognition.

"You remember me," he grated, his voice thick with hate.

"Yes," she said softly, knowing why he was here.

"I complained one time, in jest, that you cried too loudly as a baby and your bitch mother ordered my ear cut off," he snarled, pointing to the side of his head. "She's dead already, else I'd settle my account with her. Instead, I'll take it out on you—it's long past time to even the score."

"Not yet," the Shadow said, putting the point of her blade on Sorran's armored chest.

"What of you?" Merin asked Regan. "What offense have I committed that you'd have my head?"

The lieutenant looked at her, his loathing evident.

"On your word alone, I was replaced," Regan stated, stiff with anger. "I served loyally for twenty years, and you rid yourself of my presence without batting an eye."

"You were trying to control me!" Merin argued, her frustration clear. "Telling me what to eat, what to wear, whom I should talk to...it was too much!"

"I cared for you!" he hissed in disgust. "I looked after you as though you were my own child."

"You were smothering me Reagan," she argued. "I needed space to make my own choices."

"I loved you!" he shouted, his voice torn between anger and pain. "I would have done anything for you."

Merin shook her head. "No, you loved me like I was an object, one of your collection pieces. Always calling me your beautiful soul. Always trying to hold me, kiss me...You'd become obsessed! I could never love anyone so fixated on how I looked. You made me sick. I had no choice but to have you excused from my service."

Regan's face looked thunderstruck. As though his soul had been ripped out of him. Slowly, it changed, twisting malevolently in pure hatred. "Well, I hope it was worth it princess," Regan said sharply. "These transgressions against us are going to cost you your life."

"What of my father?" she asked, stalling for time. "What did I do to him that he would have me killed?"

"You were born a female," the Shadow answered. "Just as I was. A lowly bargaining chip to use as he saw fit."

Merin looked at the she-orc, staring deeply into her milky white eyes. "What was the bargain?"

"That we of the north cleanse his land of undesirables and have free reign throughout the Jagged Lands, without threat of incursion from the stumps," Oganna answered.

The female orc stopped and smiled at me. "Your blood was the price demanded by our leader for our invasion. The blood of a dwarven princess to seal the bargain and show how committed King Orius was to our cause."

Merin dropped her gaze, knowing the Shadow had not lied.

The Shadow grabbed Merin by the hair and tilted her head back, holding the darksteel knife to her neck. "Before you die, you will tell me what I want to know. Where is the one your folk call Gavakyn"

"I don't know," Merin gasped, her voice filled with pain. "I've never met him."

"You lie," the Shadow hissed, pressing the knife hard enough against Merin's neck to draw a trickle of blood.

"Oganna, someone's coming," Lors hissed over his shoulder, raising his axe.

The orc let go of the princess, turning toward the direction Lors was pointing at.

Merin looked off to the side, hope springing in her chest, thinking Omens had come for her.

There was a thrashing in the underbrush as a dwarf burst out from the bushes.

"Have you seen a hunk of goat cheese layin' about?" came a voice from the clearing. "It dropped from a hole in my britches."

Lucid.

"Deal with him," the Shadow ordered, scarcely glancing at the unkempt dwarf.

Lors snorted in contempt and rushed forward, his axe held high overhead.

An eyeblink later, the royal guard captain was dead.

Standing with a bloody knife in his hand, Lucid looked as surprised as anyone there.

"He stank of garlic and cat oil," the scraggly dwarf complained. "Daisy would not have approved."

Merin took advantage of the shock of the captain's death. She lashed out, striking the Shadow's hand, knocking the knife away from her. It skidded along the pine needles, coming to a halt a few feet away. Diving toward her crossbow, the princess grabbed hold of the handle, turned, and let fly. The bolt streaked past Regan and slammed into the back of Sorran's neck, striking the one-eared dwarf under the rim of his helm dropping him where he stood. Merin swept up the knife, knowing she didn't have time to reload the crossbow.

"Handle that dwarf!" Oganna ordered again, advancing on Merin, her machete held at the ready.

Merin knew she was outmatched. Her only chance was to fend off the Shadow long enough to hope Lucid could defeat the remaining guards and then come to her aid. The princess held the knife in front of her defensively, knowing it offered little in the way of protection.

"What do you want with Gavakyn?" Merin asked, hoping to stall the Shadow's attack.

"His heart on a stake," the Shadow snarled in reply, attacking with a thrust of her blade.

Instead of retreating, Merin blocked the attack with her knife, and rushed forward, grappling with the Shadow, trying to render the machete useless.

If the princess thought her attack would negate the she-orc's advantage, she was sorely mistaken.

A hammer strike from her enemy's hand knocked the knife back to the ground. Desperate, Merin clawed at Oganna's face, slicing open the orc's cheeks with her fingernails. The Shadow closed her hand in a fist and struck the princess several times, unsuccessfully trying to beat the she-dwarf loose. Finding a pressure point on the side of Merin's neck, Oganna grabbed on and squeezed. Howling in pain, the princess was forced to let go, kicking herself free. Rolling away from her adversary, Merin swept the ground with her hands and picked up a jagged rock, the only weapon in range.

"You're stronger than I was led to believe," the Shadow said, with a grudging respect. Oganna wiped the dark blood from her cheek, glancing down at it in surprise.

Merin waited, cocking her hand back, ready to throw when the time was right.

"Did you know your left eye is bigger than your right?" Lucid panted, sidling over to stand in front of Merin. In his hands he held a bloody long knife and an iron cast tomahawk, its triangular blade dripping with gore. Behind him were the corpses of both Regan and Keffin. The former was bleeding from a cut across the throat, while the latter was laying on the ground staring lifelessly into the sky, his head split open.

The orc Shadow looked at Lucid, and her eyes narrowed. "What are you?"

"My father once said I was an apple that didn't fall far from the tree," he chortled, nudging Merin with his elbow. "But my mother said I was a beautiful ray of sunshine."

Shooting him with a look of confusion, Oganna moved forward and attacked with several measured thrusts from her blade. Lucid blocked them all easily. The Shadow narrowed her eyes, the beginnings of frustration evident.

"What the hell?" she snapped, growing angry.

"Your ear is a bit crooked as well," Lucid remarked, tilting his head to the left. "Were you born like that?"

From the trees and underbrush behind them came the clamor of others approaching. Scores of dwarves could be heard, beating their way to the clearing.

"Merin!" they heard Omens shout, desperation in his voice.

"This isn't over," Oganna raged. "Tell Gavakyn, I'm coming for him—and for the Blood Claw."

Spinning on her heels, the Shadow ran off, her footsteps fading into the hills.

The princess dropped the rock with a thud, her head throbbing in pain.

Moments later, Omens and a dozen other dwarves flooded the clearing. Merin, still dizzy from the blow she'd taken to the head, dropped to the ground, fighting against a wave of dizziness, before blacking out.

"Princess!" I shouted, reaching her side at the same moment that she fell. Carefully I laid her on the ground. "Merin, can you hear me?" I asked, trying to remain calm.

A half-dozen heart beats went by, and I saw her eyes flutter open.

"Hi there," I said, relief filling me. "You've had quite a day."

Merin looked around and gave me a weak smile. "Is it morning?" she asked.

"It's nearly nightfall," Lucid claimed, sitting next to her, taking her hand. Looking over at me, his scraggly face showed confusion. "She seems a wee bit mad."

I couldn't suppress a smile at the irony of his comment.

"Drink this," I said to her, lifting my waterskin to her lips. Merin drank slowly, a trickle of water dribbling down the side of her face.

"Let me see her," a voice said from behind me. It was the young War Priestess, Aishe, I'd seen yesterday at the camp.

I nodded and stepped backward, closely followed by Lucid. He bent down, calmly wiping the blood off his weapons on the clothing of the four dead dwarves.

"Lucid, what happened here?"

"The lions came," he muttered. "I tried to warn her."

"How did... did you kill these dwarves?"

"Only three," he responded. "Old blood shot one in the back of the neck," he continued, nodding at one of the corpses. "All that armor and still he's dead," he continued, musing to himself aloud. "Stonebreakers, they never know their own weaknesses."

I paused, giving him a long stare. It was the first time I'd heard him speak plainly since I'd known him.

"Lucid," I began carefully, "how did you kill three Stonebreakers?"

"With these," he answered, holding up his knife and tomahawk proudly.

Narrowing my eyes at the weapons, a memory from long ago entered my mind.

"May I?" I asked, pointing at the axe-like weapon.

He passed the tomahawk over to me with a grunt. I looked at it, seeing a familiar marking etched on the bottom of the steelhead. A gray diamond with a pair of emerald green spears crossed, one over the other.

"You're a Mountaineer?" I asked in shock.

He frowned at me. "Not since Daisy," he snapped, taking his weapon back.

I let out a long breath. There was more to Lucid than I knew, but this was not the time to ask. "Who did these dwarves...,"

"Lions," he corrected, slipping his long knife back into its sheath.

"Lions," I agreed, holding my hands up deferentially. "Who did they meet with here?"

Lucid flared his nostrils and looked to the hills behind us. "The whited-eyed Shadow. She cared naught for the old blood—but she hungers for the blood of the Darkcrow, and what he took."

"Darkcrow?" I asked, feeling uneasy in the pit of my stomach.

Lucid smiled. "You know of whom I speak. Storm Sorrow, who took the Blood Claw. She wants it back."

I blanched, as the former Mountaineer confirmed my suspicions.

Oganna had come at last to wreak her revenge upon the greatest dwarven warrior seen in a generation.

"Gavakyn," I muttered to myself.

Chapter 18: The Handmaiden

I spent that night in our room holding Merin in my arms. It wasn't the attempt on her life that troubled her the most, as that had become commonplace in the last week. It wasn't even the thought of her father betraying her and wishing her dead that kept the princess awake. Though troubling, she had decided to push it aside until after Lodir was no longer under siege.

It was the idea that four dwarves, each sworn to protect her, had turned their backs so easily on their duty. The princess spent a restless night in bed, my arms offering little in the way of comfort.

The next morning, I listened to Ghost report under the darkness of a threatening sky. The Shadow's tracks headed north toward Darklight Bay. Neither of us were surprised, as we'd already seen warships of the enemy docked off the coast. Ghost had lost the trail less than half a mile from where we'd found Merin, as the female Shadow had moved to solid rock, leaving no trace of her footsteps behind.

"Oganna's canny, there's no denying that," Ghost said, drinking deeply from her waterskin. "She always has been. Even as she moved through the hills, she was careful not to break branches or leaves off the underbrush."

I was more concerned with what she wanted with Storm Sorrow, but that was a riddle I'd have to solve at another time.

There had been some amusement the previous night as Lucid's action's demanded attention. General Ironhenge wanted to reward him for saving the princess's life. Arik and his officers had come across Lucid down by the stream, drinking deeply of its dark waters.

They had procured a suit of studded leather armor, the same kind used by the Mountaineers of Monza.

One of Arik's aides made some quip about how Lucid smelled, and the disheveled hero took offense. Lucid picked the reprobate over his head and, quite bodily, tossed him into the stream. A furious melee ensued and by the end, the five Stonebreakers, their general included, ended up in the stream along with the bedraggled former Mountaineer. My understanding is when they came ashore the quintet of Stonebreakers were covered in all manner of bruises and abrasions. Hell, Arik had *teeth* marks on his arm.

Even with everything that had happened, I wish I had been around to see it.

The War Priest who had healed Merin came across the waterlogged group and took Lucid aside, asking him sweetly if he'd like to come with her. He spent the rest of the evening under the ministrations of the half-dozen healers of the dwarven trinity.

When we came across Lucid that morning, he looked like a completely different dwarf.

"This tunic is itchy," he complained, scratching vigorously at his armpit. His hair had been combed and was bound behind his head with a now clean yellow band. His beard had been trimmed neatly, with a trio of braids hanging in the front. His clothing was new, a dull olive tunic, along with sturdy breeches, the color of tea leaves.

"You look handsome," Merin said, leaning over to Lucid, kissing him on the forehead. "Thank you for rescuing me last night."

"They tried to give me a bath," Lucid grumbled, not hearing anything she said. "I fought against it, but there were too many. The General doesn't taste very good. Like meat that's been hung out in the sun too long."

"Did you actually *bite* him?" I asked, failing to hide my smile.

"Aye and he was as tough as rat leather stew," Lucid complained.

"I like that armor," Merin said with a laugh, admiring the suit.

It was well crafted. I knew it came from the town leather worker, as I'd seen similar suits in his shop in the past.

"You can have it," he said, looking at her hopefully. "It chafes my bollocks something fierce."

I could hear Merin giggling next to me.

The princess and I were reunited with our mounts, and I could tell Nel was happy to see me. Though Jax had taken her to Lodir and back in the past four days, she was fit and ready to travel. Merin's mount had recovered from its exhaustion and was pawing at the ground in anticipation.

The army moved out an hour past dawn and made good time. We stopped once at noon to feed and water our mounts and give the infantry a chance to eat with a brief rest.

Say what you will about dwarven shock troops, but they can move with speed when they need to. General Ironhenge understood the necessity of getting to Lodir soon and knew the mettle of his army. However, the dwarves under his command had to be fit enough to fight when they arrived. That wasn't easy to do after a long day's march under the heat of the summer sun. Arik knew we were less than two days away. The General was pushing his troops today, trying to cover as much ground as he could. On the morrow, his soldiers would have less distance to travel and would arrive in good condition.

We stopped for an hour and then pressed onward once more. We covered a good twelve leagues that day, leaving us with roughly four to go. As we set up camp, a squad of Arik's light cavalry rode in on a score of dust covered ponies.

They were not alone.

"Rhosyn?" Merin asked, surprised to see her handmaiden.

"Princess!" the blonde she-dwarf cried, running forward.

The two embraced, holding one another tightly.

"It's good to see you," Rhosyn said, holding Merin's head between her hands.

"And you, my love," the princess replied, her face turning with confusion. "Why are you here? What news from Lodir?"

Rhosyn blinked back tears, shaking her head. "Nothing good, I'm afraid," she stammered, looking around at Arik's army. "This will not be enough to free the Golden Keep, that is, if it still stands tomorrow."

"Go get Nathrak," I said, nodding at Reece, who was standing next to me. "Better inform the General too."

"Right," he nodded, throwing me a half salute. Without another word, the veteran Rager loped off to the back of the column.

"Omens?" Rhosyn asked, looking at me in wonder.

"Hello lass," I said, giving her a tight smile.

"How did you… I've never seen a dreg order about a clansdwarf before." Her eyes watched the departing Rager. "Reece is pricklier than most. What have you done?"

I opened my mouth, but my flippant response died on my tongue. What had I done? She was right. More and more, the dwarves of Arik's army were listening to me—treating me with respect. I'd been traveling with Ghost and her company for so long, I didn't even realize their open attitude toward me had diffused to the rest of the troops.

"That's what happens when you've saved lives," Merin answered for me. "Omens has earned the respect he's been given."

"I thought you wanted to string him up for…" Rhosyn glanced at me as her voice trailed off.

Merin was able to repress the momentary irritation I know she felt.

"Much has happened since we last spoke," the princess answered, barely managing to keep the blush from her cheeks.

"We'd best make for the general's pavilion," I suggested, wanting nothing more than to diffuse any discomfort in either of them. "He will want to hear whatever news you carry."

"Does Lodir still stand?" Merin asked, her face falling in concern. "Does… does my father still live?"

Rhosyn's face drooped with sadness. "I think it best to tell all of you at once," she muttered grimly.

I felt my heart sink in my chest.

"What do you know lass?" Arik asked, his gravelly voice rumbling in his pavilion. "How do things stand in Lodir?"

Rhosyn sat with the General, along with the leaders of each faction of his army. The princess sat on one side of her, while I was on the other.

"The first day, everything proceeded as planned," Rhosyn began, with an encouraging nod from Merin. "The armies of King Orius secured the gates, while runners were sent to summon aid to both the south and west."

"None to the east?" asked a long-legged dwarf named Caballa. Dressed in a black, studded leather tunic given to the Captain of the Bolters, she had long ebony hair braided in more than a dozen locks behind her. She had fierce green eyes and spoke in a clear, intelligent voice.

"No," Rhosyn answered, glancing at me. "Omens and the princess were to be the messengers...or so I was told."

Caballa grunted and gestured at Rhosyn to continue.

"The sallowskins surrounded the keep, though they kept their distance that first night. General Bolgir managed to destroy one of the enemies' catapults with a war cannon, but the rest of the sallowskins stayed out of range. By morning, everything changed. Most of the horde had moved into an attack position. Our scouts reported a small force of a few hundred moving east at dusk, but there was little that could be done to stop them or discover their purpose."

"I think we met them," Ghost stated from her place next to Ashten. "Some of them at any rate. That was likely the force we encountered in Barrel Falls. They were searching for something."

Her eyes came to rest on Merin a moment, before taking in the rest of the dwarves in the room. "I tracked them the next morning. They had come from the west. I suspect those that survived the attack on Barrel Falls joined the group we dealt with at Draymore's Outpost."

"Almost certainly," Ashten agreed, chiming in his support.

"They must have been moving at speed," grunted Caballa.

"Aye," Arik agreed. "They can cover fifteen leagues a day given the right motivation."

"By the second day, the King began acting out of character," Rhosyn continued. "He called a meeting with his seneschal, Thalmok, to discuss his options."

"What about his brother?" a swarthy dwarf asked, her lips turned in a frown. This was Lorric, the leader of the cavalry. "Bolgir is the Supreme General of Lodir and should have been the first one called in."

"Prince Bolgir felt as you did, Captain," Rhosyn agreed. "He demanded an audience but was turned away."

The military officers at the table looked troubled. Orius might have been despotic, but he was not thought to be stupid or ignorant.

"He called in his head of household?" an older dwarf dressed in banded armor named Armon asked, sounding dubious. "What was the topic of their conversation?" As he spoke, he rubbed at his bushy sideburns that ran all the way down his cheeks, past his face.

Rhosyn looked at the leader of the priests, growing tense. "No one knew, as they talked long into the night. I was close by and heard Thalmok pleading with the King through the door, but I was chased away by his royal guards.

Merin's handmaiden took a drink of honeyed wine, wetting a throat parched from the dust of the road. Her thirst satiated; she continued her tale.

"The next morning Thalmok pulled me aside. He took great pains to make certain we were not followed. We met for only a few moments, but in that time, he revealed to me the King's words."

She hesitated a few moments, looking directly at the general. "Orius ordered the army to fall back from the outskirts of Dregtown. He wanted the sallowskins to enter the ghettos there without resistance."

"Did he wish to draw them in?" Arik asked. "Execute some ploy to…"

"No General," she answered, cutting him off. "He told Thalmok he wanted to cleanse Lodir of the dregs once and for all. Those without a clan would no longer be a burden carried by the city."

A stunned silence followed her words.

"What?" I asked when I found my voice, feeling a jolt of anger.

"For the last twenty years he has blamed the dregs for the death of his son," she explained, her voice hard. "The king has nursed his hate, letting it smolder in private."

There was a murmuring of anger that ran through the dwarves in the pavilion.

"Prince Othar was cut down, disobeying orders," Arik snapped, his voice cutting through the noise. "Bolgir told me of the act years ago. Prince Othar was with the dreg volunteers, who had, by all reports, given a good accounting of themselves, when he ran off. At least one dreg was killed trying to save him."

I felt a pang of loss at the memory.

"That is the report I heard as well," Merin agreed. "I spoke with several of the soldiers who were there. My brother was a tyrant who enjoyed inflicting pain on others. He used to torment me, even as a babe. I was not surprised at the manner of his death, nor that he wished to continue the slaughter of an enemy beaten."

"So, Orius wanted to let the sallowskins inside Dregtown without a fight?" Nathrak asked, his eyes narrowing. "That's treason."

"It is worse than that captain," Rhosyn said gravely, her voice tight with anger. "King Orius admitted to Thalmok that he'd brokered a deal with the enemy. He'd let them wipe out the dregs and give them access to the Hollowspan Bridge. Even now, thousands more sallowskins are massing in the Jagged Lands, bent on conquering the south."

A ripple of shock hit everyone in the tent.

"By the Trine, what is he *thinking*?" Caballa hissed, rising from her seat. "What the hell does he have to gain from this?"

The others in the tent began shouting, and the order that was usually apparent evaporated in outrage.

As I looked around, I found myself staring at Merin. She had gone pale, and I knew she had something to share.

She just needed those in the tent to listen.

"*Quiet!*" I thundered, roaring above the noise.

Every dwarf inside curtailed their outrage, staring at me in surprise.

I let a handful of heartbeats pass.

"My apologies," I said, "but I believe the princess has something to say."

All eyes turned to Merin, who licked her lips nervously.

"Princess, can you offer some reason for your father's slip into madness?" Arik asked, his fists clenched tightly on the table in front of him.

Merin took a deep breath and let it out slowly.

"He's dying," she answered.

Another round of surprise hit us.

"What do you mean, he's dying?" Ghost asked, looking concerned.

"He has a sickness, a tumor in his brain," Merin continued, her green eyes misting with tears.

"There are priests aplenty in Lodir," groused Armon, his voice patronizing. "Surely one of them…"

"Don't you think he tried?" Merin snapped, exasperated. "The high priest of Goran prayed to the gods for his salvation. It did not work. He tried every priest in the temple, all to no avail."

Armon froze, puffing thoughtfully on the stem of his pipe, his wizened face furrowed in contemplation. "There is only one reason the healing would not have worked," he surmised, taking the pipe from his mouth.

"The gods have abandoned him," I reasoned aloud.

"Yes," Armon nodded with a frown. "If they have forsaken him…" he left his words hanging in the air.

"Still, why not die in peace?" Nathrak asked. "Let Lodir pass to his brother, or to Merin."

Ashten cleared his throat. "I may be able to shed some light on this."

The eyes of all turned to the prince of Kazic-Thul.

"It is common knowledge that Orius is despised as a king," he began. "However, his grip over the Golden Keep is absolute. As long as he protected the Hollowspan Bridge and kept the sallowskins on the other side of the Braenwater Gorge, the other monarchs of the eight kingdoms were content to levy their soldiers to Lodir in exchange for that protection."

"What has changed?" Lorric asked, her intelligent eyes watching him closely.

Ashten sighed. "A month ago, my brother, King Helfer, received a letter, sealed by the southern rulers. All five, along with the king of Durn Buldor, requested he join them in convincing Orius to renounce the crown in favor of his brother. The soldiers they levied to Lodir have complained of his barbaric treatment of the dwarves who hail from anyplace other than the Golden Keep. It has become bad enough to where the other monarchs are considering whether or not they should pull their forces from Lodir and let Orius fend for himself."

A bubbling current of surprise made its way around the tent at this news.

"They are willing to reconsider," continued Ashten, "but only if he agrees to step down. I was to carry the message to Orius a month ago, when Kazic-Thul was invaded from the north."

Ashten looked at Merin and shook his head. "I was at Barrel Falls last week on other business and I suspect word of the letter got to him. Though he has the heart of a weasel, I never believed Orius would act the way he has. However, in light of the gods forsaking him in his hour of need coupled with the possible loss of his kingdom, well…it may have pushed him over the edge."

The tent became quiet for the length of a heartbeat.

"He knew," Merin muttered.

"What do you mean?" I asked, flicking my eyes to her. "He knew what?"

She looked at me, and I saw a tired resignation sink in. "He knew that he would not see me again," she breathed. "When we parted, the day you and I left—he told me I'd never live to see the day Lodir would fall. I thought he was being brave, showing me his resolve to fight. Now I see—he never expected me to return."

A silence descended upon us all as we looked at Merin with sympathy.

"If you're all done scratching each other's arses, you've got visitors."

Standing at the tent entrance was Lucid, a dark silhouette looming behind him. As he moved aside, the figure behind Lucid entered the tent. Each of us looked on in surprise.

In walked a male warrior, broad of shoulder and lean of hip. Dressed in black chain mail, he carried an assortment of weapons. A six bladed mace hung at his side along with a brace filled with knives.

A pistol was tucked under his belt alongside an ivory powder horn fashioned from the tusk of some huge creature.

He was known among the dwarves by many names, though the most common was the one he'd been given at birth—Gavakyn Darkcrow. In his youth he had been called the Warden of Rahm. The sallowskins knew him differently. To them, he was Storm Sorrow or the War Mage.

Though I had met him before, it had been many years. I looked on in awe. Strong and fast, Gavakyn was the most potent warrior our people had ever known. Combined with his vast experience and training as a Mage, no one had ever seen him lose a fight. On his back in a simple black scabbard was a red steel machete. A weapon that once belonged to the deadliest Orc Shadow the dwarves had ever known.

It was the legendary blade, Blood Claw.

Though hale, Gavakyn looked weary, as if he had traveled a long road. There was mud and dust caked on his arms and legs, evidence that he'd traveled a long way to get here.

"Darkcrow," Ashten said, rising to his feet, giving his old comrade a smile. "It has been too long."

"Prince Raine," the newcomer replied, his face softening a fraction.

"Begging your pardon, *Gavakyn*," Arik said bluntly. "But what brings your traitorous arse out of your hole?"

The two glared at one another. I could tell right away there was no love lost between them.

"They do," Gavakyn growled, jerking his thumb behind him.

"Who?" Arik demanded.

Looking over his shoulder, Gavakyn motioned to the darkness outside the tent. "Best you get in here," he said softly, "and bring the rest with you."

Entering the pavilion, we bore witness to a rare sight. Two she-dwarves, one dressed in the trappings of a Shaman, the other wearing the garb of a Mage, walked inside the tent. Both were older than I, by a decade at least. To see a Mage this far away from their academy in the south was rare enough—but the sight of a *dwarf* dressed in the trappings of a Shaman, well, such a thing was unheard of. I found myself staring at her closely. There was something familiar about her…like I'd seen her before, quite recently, but I could not place her. I shook my head, realizing this was not the time to dwell on it.

Normally the two spellcasters alone would have been enough to surprise us all. In this instance, their arrival was the least remarkable thing we saw. It was the other trio of travelers that captured our immediate attention.

One, Merin recognized right away.

"Oganna!" she gasped, placing her hand to the hilt of her knife.

The orc Shadow narrowed her eyes in anger, glaring at us all.

"Easy lass," came a deep voice from behind her. Ducking his head under the entrance to the tent, a massive, seven-foot-tall creature with bark like skin entered.

"Troll!" shouted Nathrak, drawing his sword.

"Stay your hand, all of you," barked Gavakyn, his words carrying instant authority.

"You are not in command here," snapped Arik, his voice, glacier cold.

"I do not answer to a bigot like you," snarled Gavakyn, his temper flaring.

"Enough," came the croaking voice from the entrance of the tent.

It came from the throat of a goblin Shaman.

"By Goran, what are you playing at?" shouted Arik, raising his axe, ready to attack.

"Standfast," Gavakyn barked, his dark eyes on the general.

"The hell I will," the general roared, moving forward.

The Shaman raised his hand, a green light emanating from its palm. Arik swore, dropping his axe on the ground, as he rubbed at his hands in pain.

"What did you do?" the general asked, staring daggers at the Shaman.

The goblin ignored him, looking instead at me. "Hello Omens," he said in greeting. "Are you ready to help save my people?"

"Why would I do that?" I challenged, staring at the Shadow that had threatened Merin. "I remember the last time I followed you to the Jagged Lands. It ended in nothing but blood and death."

The Shaman smiled, a greasy smirk that slithered across his face. "Because if you don't, every dwarf in the southlands will die."

Looking back at Arik, the shaman twitched his hand and sighed deeply. "Now, let us see what we can do about this mess in Lodir." As he spoke, the green glow coming from the general's axe faded.

"You...you are going to help us?" Arik balked, stunned at the goblin's words.

"Yes, stump, I am," the goblin replied, bitterly. "In return, you and the other stumps are going to help me save the world."

"What, by the Trine, are you talking about?" asked Ashten.

Gavakyn snorted and pulled up a chair. "We have much to discuss, old friend, none of it good."

The Dwarves of Rahm:
Omens of War

Part V
The Blood Claw

Chapter 19: Gavakyn

One week ago

The dwarven warrior looked down at the dark obsidian ground around him, eyes wide with shock. It was littered with corpses of the dead. A squad of Ragers, a dozen of the finest warriors the King of Kazic-Thul could send, had been cut down with consummate ease by an Orc Shadow. The savage creature stood in the midst of the dead, lording over his kills like a macabre god of war. In the blackblood's hands was a blade, forged from red steel. It was newly wet, slick with dwarven blood.

"You think yourself worthy of the Blood Claw?" the Shadow sneered at his adversary. "Come Darkcrow! Try and take it! You will suffer the same fate as your kin."

Bleeding from a wound on both his hand and scalp, the dwarven warrior wiped a trickle of blood from his brow. Knowing the eyes of his lover watched, he hefted his steel blade and stepped forward, accepting the challenge.

Gavakyn opened his eyes with the dawning of a new day. Sighing, he rolled over in his bed trying to ignore the ghosts of his past—the same ghosts that had haunted him for the last five years. There was no escaping his destiny, he knew, but he was not ready to deal with it yet this morning.

Outside his bedchamber there came the clanking of a pan being placed on a metal grill. In the room that served as his kitchen,

Gavakyn could hear the padded feet of someone puttering about. The sound of eggs shells cracking on the lip of his old iron pan were quickly followed by the soft bubbling of eggs cooking in oil. A small grin worked its way onto his face. He breathed deeply at the aroma. The thought of crispy bacon and sausage sizzling together in the same pan made his stomach grumble.

A seam of light wriggled its way into the room as someone cracked open the door.

"Gavakyn?" came the rasping voice of Viir. "Breakfast will be ready in a few minutes."

The warrior grunted from his bed.

The old troll sighed in warning, his seven-foot frame taking up the entire doorway. "You might be the master of this outpost, but if I were you, I'd find your way to the practice yard."

"I need to feed the livestock," Gavakyn groaned, with a yawn.

"Holden's already done it," Viir answered, an edge in his voice. "She wants…well you'd better get up before she is finished."

"Have you seen some vision of her yelling at me with your magical powers," Gavakyn muttered, still laying on the bed.

"I don't need a vision to see she's in a foul mood," tsked Viir. "Don't say I didn't warn you."

With a click, the door was pulled shut leaving the room dark once more.

Gavakyn groaned inwardly and closed his eyes, his thoughts turning to the great love of his life. Eyes opened or closed, Gavakyn could still see her face. A face he'd not laid eyes on for five years.

"The others, my brother—they will not understand," Gavakyn heard her say.

"We will make them see," he promised, kissing his lover's dark hair, leaning forward from his place behind her.

"How did this happen?" she asked, with both surprise and joy in her voice.

"The gods only know," Gavakyn answered. Wrapping his powerful arms around the female's bare shoulders, he embraced her lovingly. "I'm glad it did."

She looked up, her white eyes staring into his dark ones. "I am too," she answered, leaning back to kiss him.

"By the Trine, get your lazy ass out of that bed or I'll burn it to cinders while you sleep in it!" screamed a voice Gavakyn knew well.

The door had been kicked open and light from the kitchen poured in.

"Holden, give it a rest," the warrior groaned, shielding his eyes against the brightness of the sun.

"I woke up early to feed your stupid goats and chickens," the slightly built dwarfess spat, ignoring him. "The goats, at least, were docile, but that clucker with the black spotted feathers damn near took my hand off! That little bitch is going to be served up for tonight's meal if she keeps that up!"

Gavakyn snorted at the thought of the encounter. "That's Morning Glory, and I find it best to feed her first. She won't be served up anytime soon, Holden. She produces the best eggs in the roost."

"I don't care if that squawker shits silver ingots—one more peck from her and she's laid her last egg! Now get up. I need to learn and by some sick act of the gods, you have been chosen as my mentor!"

"Just give me a minute," Gavakyn muttered, his voice annoyed, "and take it easy on the door as you leave."

Without another word, the she-dwarf slammed the door hard enough that it shook the walls.

"By Goran," Gavakyn cursed loudly, his frustration boiling over. "I'm a dwarven hero you know!"

"Get up hero!" Holden raged back. "Your breakfast is getting cold! Try to find a clean tunic for once! You smell like goat dung!"

Sitting up, Gavakyn placed his bare feet on the stone floor and put his hands onto his now throbbing forehead.

"How in the hell did this become my life?" he wondered to the darkness.

"How many today?" Gavakyn asked, a half turn of the hourglass later.

"Five," answered Holden. She looked at the figures in front of her, studying them with eyes of a rich, earthly hue. Hardened with disdain, they were set with an intensity that could penetrate one's soul.

The sun was only an hour past dawn and the midday heat had yet to arrive. They stood in the courtyard of a long-abandoned post Gavakyn had taken to calling his home. In the last few years, the solitary warrior had fixed the place up, adding improvements and modifications where he could. The old barracks was now home to his herd of goats and a surprisingly large roost of chickens. The officer's quarters had housed many visitors through the years, including Holden the Mage and Viir the Seer, who represented two thirds of his guests currently staying at the outpost. The last was emerging from the kitchen, eating her breakfast from a large wooden bowl.

"Draega, we're waiting on you," Holden hissed impatiently.

The huge orc Mauler grunted and handed her bowl to Viir. "Thank you for making breakfast," she said politely, her voice deep and rumbling.

"You are most welcome," the troll replied, declining his head slightly.

"Now," the Mauler growled, looking at the five warriors in front of her. "Which is mine?" Draega did not wear her customary chains, but she picked up a wicked looking spiked club along with a well-made wooden shield that was leaning against the outpost wall.

"In a moment," Gavakyn said, stepping forward.

Clearing his throat, the well-muscled dwarf spoke, his voice touched with a hint of steel.

"Some of you," he nodded to the pair of goblins in front of him, "have been here in the past and already know my rules. For those of you that are new," he continued, looking at two orcs and a solitary dwarf, "one hour of training equals two hours of work. If you want a second hour of training, you will be here all afternoon. You will have the opportunity to spar with each of my guests as well as with myself. We will discuss tactics, group attacks, and the strengths and weaknesses of both you and your adversary. Questions?"

"What are *they* doing here?" the newly arrived dwarf asked, looking sullenly at the sallowskins next to him. He had a barrel chest and a mane of red hair cut in the style of a spiked mohawk.

"There is a truce here, youngster," Viir explained, his leather skinned face the picture of a grandfather's serenity. "Gavakyn provides his neighbors with food stuffs and training—in return they let him live here in peace."

"How do you think you passed through this part of the Jagged Lands unmolested?" Draega growled.

The newcomer looked at the Mauler and narrowed his eyes. Seeing she would not be cowed, he turned back to Gavakyn. "You would train the enemy?"

"What is your name?" Gavakyn asked firmly.

"Zaor, of Clan Ice," the dwarf answered proudly.

"There are no enemies here, Zaor," Gavakyn explained. "Only prejudice and ignorance, often found by those who carry it with them."

The dwarf stared, unblinking at the older warrior and nodded gruffly, though he looked unconvinced.

"Even odds," Gavakyn heard Holden whisper to Viir. "*If* you haven't already seen the outcome."

"Being a Seer doesn't mean I see everything that's going to happen," muttered Viir. "Curse you and your dwarven luck, I'll take the bet."

"Have you ever been beaten?" asked one of the orcs, a wide shouldered youth with deep sallow skin and black markings over his left eye.

"Everyone loses from time to time," Gavakyn answered truthfully. "The idea is to train and make that as difficult as possible. Now," he continued, picking up a wooden practice lathe the length of a longsword. "I think it's time we begin. Goblins, face off against the Mage and the Seer. Remember, they are casters, your best chance at success is to close quickly before they have a chance to use their spells."

"But... I'm trained as an Archer," protested the first, a female goblin carrying a short bow and arrows.

"Yes," Gavakyn answered, nodding at Holden. "However, you have a pair of knives as well. In battle, anything can happen. If you are engaged elsewhere, or out of arrows, you would have no choice but to use your secondary weapons. Face off against the casters, sharpen your melee skills against them."

After a moment's pause, the goblin nodded and faced off against Holden, who was whirling her staff with a practiced ease.

The rest squared off, with Zaor facing Gavakyn and the orcs taking turns against Draega. Each of the combatants had picked up the practice weapons where they could. Gavakyn's adversary held a wooden axe, lined with lead, but it had been blunted to prevent risk of serious injury.

Time passed by, with the more experienced group defeating the newcomers every time but giving out sound advice on each pass. They fought bouts in groups and alone. After only a few minutes, each combatant began to sweat with exertion. The clack of wood striking against wood filled the courtyard.

Into the morning the training went on, each newcomer working to strengthen their skills. After nearly an hour, they faced off against their last opponent. Trouble began almost immediately, as Zaor was sparring with Draega.

"By Goran, that's not fair you blackblooded bitch!" hissed the dwarf, rubbing at his shoulder. "Are you trying to kill me?"

The orc Mauler stood across from him leaning on her club. Her face was relaxed.

"Of course not," Draega answered, mildly. "Your shoulder was at the wrong angle."

Zaor's face turned red. "I have been trained by the Stonebreakers of Clan Ice!" he spat in response. "I watched you earlier as you took it easy on your kin! Now that you have one of your ancient enemies in front of you, you go for the kill!"

"Enough," Gavakyn growled, striding over. "No one is trying to kill you boy."

"What would you know of it?" Zaor snarled back. "You live among these creatures. There is talk that you have a soft spot for the blackbloo…"

Faster than he could see, Zaor was struck by Gavakyn's backhand. A meaty slap to the face sent the younger dwarf sprawling to the ground.

"I told you," Holden snickered to Viir, "pay up."

"Later," the Seer answered, helping the red-faced dwarf to his feet.

"You sallowskin loving son-of-a…" the young dwarf began, before Viir cut him off.

"Enough of that," the troll chided, placing a restraining hand on Zaor's shoulder. "Any one of us could kill you if we wanted. Don't let your pride cause you more trouble than you can handle."

The young Stonebreaker glared at Viir, slapping away the troll's hand. "Don't touch me!" Zaor barked, his eyes angry.

"Watch and learn, all of you," Gavakyn said, ignoring his kin. He walked over to the wall and picked up his metal shield. The powerful warrior strode back until he stood across from the Mauler.

"How hard are we fighting?" inquired Draega, her tone still mild.

"As hard as you can," Gavakyn answered, his voice cool. "I want to set an example for this child."

The Orc Mauler smiled and raised her shield to a ready position. Without warning, she exploded forward and attacked.

"Sallowskins," Gavakyn bellowed, blocking the Mauler's first strike with his shield, "tend to be overly aggressive," he continued, countering with a thrust from his practice sword. "However, most are bigger than we are, and oftentimes have a height and reach superiority."

Gavakyn blocked another blow, the club slamming off his shield with a loud bang. Everyone, including Zaor, could see just how hard Draega could hit when she wanted too.

"A good warrior can take advantage of that aggression," Gavakyn continued, striking at the Mauler with a series of lightning attacks. "Given enough time, you will find a weakness."

Draega blocked a thrust of Gavakyn's sword and moved her shield downward quickly, disarming her opponent. Gavakyn's lathe instantly fell to the ground with a metallic clang. The dwarf raised his shield, knowing Draega's club was descending fast. He angled his shield away from him and deflected the powerful blow to the outside of his body. Reacting swiftly, he launched himself forward, moving inside the orc's defenses, and placed the tip of a wooden dirk up under Draega's chin.

The Mauler snorted and pushed the dirk away. "Almost had you that time," she growled, picking up his practice sword, handing it back to him.

"That was a good move with your shield," Gavakyn said with a humorless smile. "I will remember it."

Turning away from Draega, Gavakyn looked over to Zaor. "Your clan has taught you well, Stonebreaker. You fight with balance and precision. However, you have not learned everything they have to teach. When fighting a bigger, stronger opponent, very few dwarves, no matter their strength, can absorb more than a few hits from a Mauler like Draega. You have to think on your feet—angle that strike away from you, so you don't lose feeling in your shoulder."

He turned and looked over to the sallowskin trainees who were watching, their jaws open in wonder. "As for you goblins, the same message applies. Dwarves are, in general, bigger and stronger than you. Be wary of that but know when to take advantage. You orcs," he continued, looking at the last two trainees, "when fighting dwarves, remember you have superior reach, and they will have to attack from a position beneath you. Guard against such an attack. Draega made a brilliant move in disarming me, but in her haste for the kill, she allowed me to slip under her guard. Don't make that same mistake."

He leaned his practice sword and shield up against the wall and cupped his hands full of cool water from a nearby basin. "Enough lessons for today," he said. "Two hours of labor, if you please. The goats need to be milked and the eggs gathered from the chickens. Afterwards, you can share in a brief meal and be on your way. Same time again tomorrow if you are so inclined. Viir, if you would show them the way?"

The Seer straightened his blue robes and nodded in affirmation. "Follow me," he said, moving toward the goat pens. He took two steps forward and then staggered to his left, bracing himself against the wall with his hand.

"Are you alright?" asked Draega, moving over to him in a flash, a look of concern in her eyes.

Viir shook his head, as if to clear it of some hidden pain. The troll flashed the orc with a brief smile. "Yes, I just got dizzy for a moment—I must have moved too quickly."

Draega laughed softly. "You are getting old, troll. Best get some sleep when you can."

"I will," the Seer replied, and began moving again.

The five trainees were still looking at Gavakyn and missed most of the exchange between the pair.

"Did you see them move?" asked the orc to his sister. "I've never seen such speed and power."

"In which?" Zaor grunted, reluctant awe in his voice. "The Mauler was impressive."

Their excited conversation faded as they followed after Viir.

Draega joined Gavakyn at the basin, her large hands scooping up water to splash on her face.

"I've been here for two months now," the orc stated, running her fingers through her dark hair, now slick with sweat. "I have yet to understand your motives."

Gavakyn grunted, pretending not to know what the orc was hinting at.

"You had me," she said, frowning at him. "At least twice in the bout early on. I exposed my chest, just a fraction, I know, but you usually take advantage of those mistakes."

"Maybe I'm getting old?" the dwarf suggested, shaking his hands dry.

"No," she breathed, her eyes hard. "You could be in your dotage and still whip most of us."

Gavakyn grunted in amusement but said nothing.

"You know what I think?" the orc offered, drying her face on a linen made of worn cotton. "I think you are trying to get the races to stop hating each other."

Gavakyn said nothing. He just looked off to the north, his face expressionless.

"For two months I've watched you, Gavakyn the Slayer, the Butcher, or whatever other titles have been thrown on your shoulders. Not once in that time have I seen you lose your temper toward a blackblood. If rumors are to be believed, it is said you never turned away a single sallowskin, especially orcs."

"What is your point, Draega?" the dwarf asked, a tinge of annoyance in his deep voice.

"Why are you doing this?" she snapped back. "Dwarves and Sallowskins despise one another, they always have. You are wise enough to know this. Why waste your time trying to bring about something that will never happen?"

"You don't like me?"

Draega snorted. "I respect you, dwarf. You are the finest warrior I've ever seen. It's not the same."

"You wish to leave?" Gavakyn countered, looking up at her.

Draega narrowed her eyes. "No, I have been ordered here by my War chief and his Shaman. They have yet to tell me why—though I suspect you know the answer."

"I do," Gavakyn responded, turning away.

Holden walked over, her usual sour expression on her face. "If you two meatheads are done holding hands, we have training to get to."

"You are right," Gavakyn said, moving to the stairs that led to the upper part of the outpost.

"You never answered my question," Draega growled at the retreating figure.

"You're not ready to hear it," Gavakyn tossed over his shoulder, and turned his mind once more, to the past.

"How many are there?" Ashten asked, his face beaded with perspiration.

"Near a hundred," Ghost reported, her eyes steely and focused.

Tucked in a cave on the side of a rocky plateau, a group of both sallowskins and dwarves finalized their plans outside a place called Mott-Godaan.

"The storm will break in an hour," rumbled the voice of a huge orc Chain from his place near the entrance.

"Gron is right," a goblin snapped. "We can use that if we are patient."

"Karn, I told you," an old bard chimed in. "Omens and I will keep us hidden."

"Are you certain, Jax?" asked Viir. "I have not foreseen this. I only know that we must go inside."

"I have been practicing," said Omens, a determined expression on his clean-shaven face. In his hands was a simple reed flute, fashioned from bamboo. "We can do it if you all stay close together."

"We still need to clear the guards at the front," rumbled an Ogre, dressed in the trappings of a Mage. "Else there will be no entering Mott-Godaan."

"Leave that to me," came the voice of an orc female, staring at Gavakyn fiercely.

"It will be a risk, Oganna," Gavakyn said, knowing they had no other choice.

"I am ready," she answered, looking back at him, her white eyes unblinking.

The upper section of the dwarven outpost had been smoothed out centuries ago by stonemasons. Walls six feet in height had been built in a circular pattern on the outer rim. This upper part of the outpost once housed machines of war, as bits and pieces of cannon and catapult lay strewn upon the dirt covered floor. Now it lay empty, save for a few chunks of rock that had been knocked loose from the mortar over time. Gavakyn had made it into a practice area for any spell crafter who wished to train.

"I'm going to make lightning today," Holden announced from her place at the top of the stairs, her face set in determination. She looked behind her at Gavakyn who said nothing. "Storm Sorrow, did you hear what I said?"

"Yes," the older dwarf answered.

"Well, show me how!"

Gavakyn took a pipe from his pocket and tapped it on the side of the wall to loosen the remains of any old tobacco.

"Gavakyn!" snapped Holden, obvious frustration on her face.

"What?"

"By the Trine, tell me what I need to do to make a bolt of lightning!"

The dwarven warrior pulled a small pouch of southern leaf from another pocket of his tunic and began to fill the barrel with pipe weed.

"You know everything you need already."

"You've been saying that for days," she barked. "Still, the best I can muster is a single spark of energy."

Gavakyn tucked the unused leaf away and placed the pipe in his mouth. "Have I ever…"

"No, no more of these stupid riddles of yours about balancing the magic or, forgetting what I know. That's hogswallop! For once in your god's be damned life, speak plainly and tell me what I need to do!"

Gavakyn frowned at her and began packing down the leaves in his pipe with a tamper.

Holden's face grew red, and she lost what little was left of her temper. "You don't even know, do you?" she accused. "Gavakyn the Great, who rose to Mage status in just three years. What a joke. It was a mistake to come here. All that talk about how you're gifted…"

Moving like an adder, Gavakyn took two steps forward and extended his hand. In a single expulsion of breath, he bellowed out words of power.

"*Nahel Dahn!*"

Shooting forth from his hand was a bolt of lightning, cutting through the air past Holden's ear. The bolt struck the far wall, leaving a black scorch mark on its dusky surface. Pieces of the wall crumbled to the ground where the lightning had hit, each glowing white with heat.

A moment later, Gavakyn was back to packing his pipe while Holden stared at the wall in shock.

"What the…how did you…are you trying to kill me?" she shrieked, her emotions jumbled together.

Gavakyn listened calmly to her tirade, waiting patiently. He focused his will for a moment, lighting his pipe with a sliver of magical fire. Drawing the smoke into his mouth, he smiled in delight as Holden pulled herself together.

"Have I ever told you about the time I made my first cake?" he asked.

"Wha…what?" she sputtered. "What in the hell does…"

"I was terrible at it," he continued with a soft chuckle, ignoring her interruption. "Oh, I mixed the ingredients correctly—had to fish a bit of eggshell from the batter as I recall, but still, everything looked the way it was supposed to."

He took another puff on the stem of his pipe and nodded in satisfaction. "That is good," he murmured, blowing a smoke ring upward watching it drift away over the course of several heartbeats. "I can almost taste the flavor of the leaf. Last season was a fine year for growing, don't you think?"

"I don't care," the Mage growled, retaining a tenuous grip on her temper.

'Where was I?" Gavakyn asked mildly.

"You were talking about cake," Holden answered in a strangled voice, her annoyance, colossal.

"Ahh yes," Gavakyn continued, regaining his train of thought. "I had mixed the ingredients correctly and popped the whole thing into a brick oven. By Goran, the smell was heavenly. I often wonder if I should have been a baker if I had to live my life over again? However, that is by the by. When I took the cake out, I let it cool for a sufficient amount of time and dug in. I remember my mouth was watering with anticipation."

Gavakyn stopped and sighed, leaning back against the wall. "Sadly, I had made a mistake. In my excitement, I had measured the proportion of the ingredients incorrectly. The wrong amount of leavening agent is crucial. When I took my first bite, well, it was a blow to my ego I can tell you."

"So what?" snapped Holden, near the end of her patience. "You're not a baker, who cares about…"

"Oh, I've gotten better since then," Gavakyn replied affably. "It wasn't my skill at baking that failed me. I simply needed to get things *in the right proportions.*"

Holden made to say something, but stopped.

She gave him a curious look, turned around and extended her hand.

"*Nahel Dahn!*" she shouted again, aiming at the far wall.

A bolt of lightning, less impressive than Gavakyn's perhaps, but remarkable nonetheless, shot from her hands and struck the top of the wall.

The silence between them was deafening.

"I...I did it," she whispered finally, gaping at her hand. "Did you see that?" the Mage exclaimed, looking over at Gavakyn.

"Not bad," he replied, giving her a fatherly smile.

"You...fah, for the love of the gods, why didn't you just tell me?" she asked, a ghost of her anger returning.

Gavakyn scratched at his cheek. "The Mages at Stormhold, they are an...interesting bunch. They preach about following rules, having strict discipline...some of that is necessary and true. However, they are so caught up in study and lore, they sometimes forget the power of thinking for themselves."

The elder dwarf stepped forward, looking at her with his deep brown eyes. "You left Magehold for the same reason I did. It was too confining of an environment for you. Luckily, you had already gained Mage status, else they may have thrown you out for your beliefs. When Viir and I heard about a spellcaster who told Arch-Mage Rhiann to, 'stuff it in her ear,' well, I had to meet you myself."

"So, this was a test?" Holden asked, her voice a bit hollow.

"More like an audition."

"Did I make it?"

He put the stem of the pipe back in his mouth and gave her a reassuring smile. "It looks favorable so far. Now, keep practicing. Don't wear yourself out, but try and play with the proportions a bit. Fire and air are important, but water is the key—just like the leavening agent in my cake. Too much or too little and you have a disaster."

The older dwarf left Holden on the upper part of the outpost and made his way back down the stairs. Behind him, he could hear her shouting words of power as bolts of lightning cut through the air.

"*Did I make it?*" He heard Holden's words again.

"Sadly, yes," he said to himself, feeling his heart sink in his chest.

They crept close as the clouds overhead unleashed their downpour. Jogging ahead of them, Oganna came to a halt in front of the sallowskins standing guard at the entrance to Mott-Godaan. There was an eclectic mix of goblins and orcs, with a troll Lizard Rider thrown in to boot.

"By the Trine, she can't outrun the troll cavalry, can she?" cursed Ghost, glancing at Gavakyn.

"She's the fastest thing I've ever seen on two legs," quipped a dwarf from next to her, holding a tomahawk in his hands.

"Quiet Roe," warned a goblin named Karn from beside him. "Leave it to Oganna, she knows what she's doing."

The female orc strode up to her kin, speaking with them briefly. She seemed to be arguing with the orc Chain who advanced to the front of the defenders. Without warning the Chain stepped forward, taking a wild swing with his fist. Oganna swayed to the side, lashing out with her machete, stabbing him in the heart. The other sallowskins looked on in surprise, hesitating for only a moment before howling after her. Oganna took off like a missile fired from a dwarven cannon and made tracks in the opposite direction of the raiding party.

"Damn me," whispered Orvin, Captain of the squad of Ragers sent by Kazic-Thul. "She did it!"

"We're not done yet," warned the Ogre, clutching his staff tightly. "There are still a half dozen left."

"Let's move," barked Karn, nodding to Jax and Omens.

The two bards placed themselves in the middle of the group and began to play their lutes.

"Stay safe," Gavakyn thought, with a last look in the direction Oganna had run before fading from view.

"We need to talk."

Gavakyn looked up at Viir and nodded slowly.

The two of them were standing a quarter mile from the bottom of the keep an hour till dusk. Their eyes watched a herd of goats' grazing on tufts of grass and flowers growing here and there on the small, fertile patches of the rocky plateau.

"What's on your mind?" the dwarf asked.

"Your dreams are getting more frequent," the Seer said.

Gavakyn did not reply.

"Time is starting to run short," Viir continued, seeing the dwarf wasn't about to speak.

"Why do you say that?" Gavakyn asked, glancing at the troll.

Viir shook his head. "I may be getting old, but I still see."

"What do you see?"

"Those orcs this morning—they were of the Ebon-Eye tribe. That is a clan that lives to the north of the Jagged Lands."

"You noticed that, did you?"

Viir hmmphed loudly. "Yes, that little nugget failed to elude me, just as I know it failed to elude you."

"So, one of the northern tribes is moving," Gavakyn said with a shrug. "It happens all the time."

"Don't play coy with me Gavakyn, I know you've seen the fires dotting the landscape these past weeks. Something is happening. If I didn't know better, I'd say it was another invasion, bigger than the one sent against Kazic-Thul."

"I am not blind Viir, I know what's coming."

"It's time to tell them," the Seer insisted. "They need to know."

"The way I knew last time?" Gavakyn argued, picking up a stone, tossing it from hand to hand. "I don't remember that helping any. I will tell them when they are ready."

Viir looked at Gavakyn and spoke softly. "It is time."

The younger warrior looked sharply at the Seer.

"What do you mean?"

"I mean, it is time. I have seen it."

Gavakyn stared at his old acquaintance, unwilling to accept his words. "You've had a premonition?"

The troll nodded. "This morning, after your bout with Draega. It came to me as I led the trainees to feed the goats."

Gavakyn narrowed his eyes, remembering the troll's stumble. "I thought you moved too quickly?"

Viir gave him a smile that spread slowly across his pale-yellow face. "I lied."

Gavakyn looked off in the distance, imagining an army of sallowskins marching south. "Where are we going?"

"We need to cross the East Gate Bridge into Kazic-Thul," Viir answered, focusing his vision to the south.

"Doesn't sound too bad," Gavakyn hoped.

"From there we need to move east and make a stop at Draymore's old outpost. After that we will move to a place called Barrel Falls."

There was a catch in his voice that Gavakyn might not have detected if he didn't know the Seer so well.

"What aren't you saying?"

The troll let out a deep breath. "She will be there Storm Sorrow— and she will try to kill you."

The dwarven warrior blinked once, nodding in affirmation.

"Best we prepare," he muttered, throwing the rock at what was left of an old tree. The stone hit the bark, lodging itself deep in the punky soft trunk.

"Did you hear what I said?" demanded the Seer. "She *will* kill you."

"I heard you," Gavakyn answered. "She can kill me if she wants, but I won't raise a finger against her."

"You great, honorable fool!" Viir shouted, growing angry. "She doesn't care about you anymore, don't you know that?"

"Yes, I do," Gavakyn replied, his voice soft. "I do not blame her. I broke my promise, her ire is what I deserve."

Turning around, the dwarf strode back to the outpost. "We've much to accomplish in little time. I want the four of us ready to leave at dawn."

Viir began to mutter to himself. How was it that the greatest dwarven hero in generations had fallen in love with one of his mortal enemies?

Their raid group had made it inside the cavernous entrance moving carefully past the guards. The group of twenty-two remained unseen, hidden as they were behind the magic of the two bards. Once inside, they made straight for the portal, hoping to catch the inhabitants unaware.

"Have a care," Karn croaked, his voice ragged with exertion. "There is a bend ahead perfect for…"

They turned the corner and ran smack dab into the middle of a company of sallowskin warriors.

"Shit!" cursed Gavakyn, racing forward. "Gron, next to me," he shouted, positioning the Chain to his left.

The orc did not hesitate, stepping into place on the front line, his black iron chain wrapped around him from shoulder to waist.

"Omens, get next to me, Roe, flank Gron," Gavakyn ordered, drawing his sword. "Orvin, ready your Ragers to fill the gaps."

The red-haired captain nodded, and a dozen swords slid from their sheaths.

"By the Trine, there are more than a hundred," Ghost hissed, looking on in surprise.

"Stay on the casters and the archers," Ashten answered, hefting a grenade. "If our front line goes down, we all die."

Jax stepped between the Ogre Mage and Karn.

"Stay with us bard," the troll Seer muttered from his place behind them all. "We will need you before it's done."

With a blood curdling yell, a wall of sallowskins rushed forward, slamming into the front line of raiders.

"No, no, no," hissed Gavakyn, looking at Draega. "Stop rushing forward—let them come to us."

"It's not in my nature, dwarf," the Mauler spat, grinding her teeth in frustration. "In the lands to the north it is kill or be killed. We don't have time to play this defensive game of yours."

"You're going to get us both killed if you don't start listening," Gavakyn answered, shaking his head.

"Enough for today," Viir cut in, lowering his staff from his position opposite the two warriors.

"We need more work," Gavakyn argued.

"No," the Seer replied, his voice firm. "There will be time on the road, and the two of you have been at it for weeks now."

Gavakyn looked to argue further, but Draega dropped her club and shield, storming off to the kitchen.

The dwarven warrior watched her leave, his dark eyes set in a frown. With a sigh he leaned his practice shield and lathe up against the wall. He reached down, uncorked his waterskin and took a long drink.

Holden strode over, her eyes still alight with excitement at her earlier success. "Where are we going tomorrow?" she inquired, placing the end of her staff on the ground.

"South, across the East Gate Bridge," Viir answered.

"Back to Rahm?" the Mage questioned, looking puzzled. "I thought we needed to go north?"

"We do," Gavakyn said, his voice weary. "But first, we have to go south."

He put the cork back on his waterskin and wiped the sweat from his brow. "Let's eat within the hour. Afterwards, we will pack and get some rest. I want to start early tomorrow. Holden, make sure the ponies are fed and ready. Check on Draega's boar as well."

"That thing is as foul tempered as she is," the Mage muttered, walking toward the area of the barracks that served as a stable.

"Why don't you give her a hand?" Gavakyn suggested to Viir. "Check on that reptile of yours, while you are at it."

The Seer raised an eyebrow and glanced at the entrance to the kitchen. "So, you're finally going to talk to her?"

"Best give us a few minutes alone. There's no telling how she's going to take it," Gavakyn said.

Viir nodded thoughtfully, scratching at his beard. "I suppose you want me to inform Holden?"

Gavakyn shook his head. "No, I won't put that on you…"

"Lad," Viir interrupted gently. "You are not alone in this. I recruited her—I will tell her."

The dwarf paused a moment before giving the Seer a grim nod and walked toward the kitchen. The entrance was only a few steps away, but the memory that flashed in his mind made those steps seem like miles.

"Give ground slowly!" shouted Gavakyn, absorbing another hit on his shield. His armor and shield were covered in black blood. The rough granite in front of him was littered with dead sallowskins, though the front line of the raiders had been pushed steadily backward.

"Get ready," hissed Viir to Jax, the troll watching the rear line of attackers intently. "I see their casters moving in range."

Jax set aside his staff and took hold of a drum made of dark wood. The leathery skin of a shark was stretched over the top.

"You're certain you can do this?" Karn asked, a bead of sweat running down the side of his face.

"I guess we're going to find out," the bard quipped back, with a nervous laugh.

"Hold the line!" Gavakyn barked, still giving ground.

"There are too many," shouted Ghost, the report of her rifle echoing throughout the chamber.

"Stick to the plan," Ashten roared, heaving his last grenade over the top of his allies. The grenade exploded in a burst of fire, igniting a half score of sallowskins on the other side of the shield wall.

At that moment, the sallowskin casters, eight in all, moved close enough and began to work their magic.

"Now!" hissed Viir, looking at Jax in desperation.

The bard, as cool as an autumn morning, began to pound on his drum, its music rising above the clamor of battle. His rich baritone began to sing out, and a wave of magic energy emanated from both him and his instrument.

"It's not going to work," muttered Karn, leveling his staff at his own kin.

"Yes it will!" thundered Viir, raising a knotted cane of hickory above his head.

"*Gorkuth Thoral,*" he shouted, waving his outstretched leathery hand from shoulder to shoulder.

His spell, timed perfectly with Jax's enchantment, formed a wall of magic that extended from one side of the cave to the other. It dropped in front of the front line of raiders just as the sallowskin casters unleashed spells of their own. Fire, ice, lightning, and an acid like mist of green, all were stopped by the Seer's wall of impenetrable magic.

The sallowskin casters looked on, dumbfounded that their attack had been neutralized.

"Enough running," roared Gron, snorting at his kin. The orc Chain barreled ahead, slamming his shield into any defender in his path.

"No! Not yet," shouted Gavakyn, looking on in dismay at the orc's suicidal charge.

Dropping his shield to the ground, Gavakyn raised a hand, his fingers outstretched in front of him.

"*Nahel Dahn!*"

A bolt of lightning, as thick as his hand was wide, cut a swath through the sallowskins in front of him. A dozen orcs and goblins fell, their bodies scorched black from the power of the blast.

It was not enough. Gron ran forward, directly into an Earthshaker, an ogre warrior of extreme size and strength. It was flanked on either side by a pair of orc Ravagers. Running headlong into this larger foe, Gron was down inside the blink of an eye.

"Orvin, go!" Gavakyn ordered, his voice hollow. The captain of the Ragers led his squad past Gavakyn and ripped apart the ranks of sallowskins in front of them.

"Do we follow?" panted Omens, blood dripping from a cut on his arm.

"Yes," cackled Roe, with a glance toward Gavakyn. "Leave those casters to Omens and me. You take down that Earthshaking son-of-a-bitch."

"Now," Gavakyn ordered, his eyes narrowing on the ogre that had slain Gron.

"Stay on those archers," he shouted over his shoulder to the pair of Engineers still firing away.

As he ran toward his foe, Gavakyn glanced down at the still form of his frontline mate.

"You should have waited," he whispered to himself.

Gavakyn was tired. More tired than he had been in a long while. It wasn't a physical exhaustion that plagued him. Indeed, he was the most fit dwarf on either continent. His muscles were as hard as iron, his stamina prodigious. No, it was an emotional exhaustion, one that had been a drain on him for a long time.

He entered his room once again and closed the door behind him. His talk with Draega had gone better than he'd hoped. The orc was more intelligent than her uncle Gron had been. More astute as to why she had been selected from the thousands of orc warriors that may have fit the bill. Like Gron, she did not care for Gavakyn, but she did respect him, just as her uncle had.

The dwarven warrior had packed his belongings for this trip months ago. Gavakyn knew the day would come when he would leave this place, likely never to return. Looking at the old brass sconce still attached to the wall, Gavakyn focused his will.

"*Hetu*," he uttered under his breath.

The white candle held inside the sconce sprang to life, the light of its flames casting ominous shadows that flickered about the room. Gavakyn busied himself, setting out his clothing for the following day. He also inspected his suit of black chain mail, which he'd kept in good order. Opening a drawer located at the bottom of an old cabinet, he took out a plethora of weapons. A brace of knives, along with a pistol, complete with an ivory powder horn and bandolier. He set these on the ground in front of him. Last was a mace, its steel head sporting six blades, it had been fixed expertly atop a haft of black oak.

Satisfied his weapons were in order, Gavakyn returned them to the drawer. He climbed to his feet and sat on the bed, knowing he had one last item to check. It had been years since he'd seen it. He hated the artifact. It served only as a reminder of how much he had lost.

With a sigh, Gavakyn stood, pacing over to the closet located on the far end of the room. Dragging a chair from under the desk, the dwarven warrior placed it at the front of the closet and climbed onto the seat. Deep in the recesses of the top shelf, Gavakyn patted around blindly until his fingers tickled the side of an old wooden box. Quickly he grasped onto it and climbed back down to the floor.

Moving back to his bed, he placed the box on the top of his wool bedding. Hesitantly, he unlatched the hook on the lid, and memory filled him.

Moving further inside, the raid company knew they were getting close. They made their way quickly through the roughhewn hallway of an old keep, the depths of its roof soaring far overhead. They climbed up a flight of stairs, once a silvery white, now dulled to a dark gray.

"Careful now," Karn warned, his voice cautious. "The spirits of the dead are close."

"Hold," Viir ordered, peering into the chamber ahead of them. He extended his hand and bowed his head, searching the room in front of them with his powers.

"Something has gotten through the portal," he warned, his green eyes narrowing.

"We are ready, Seer," Captain Orvin barked in reply, scraping dried blood from his gauntlets.

"He comes," the troll hissed, nodding toward the top of the stairs.

Everyone looked up to see a powerful orc step to the front of the landing.

No one spoke it aloud, but a name flashed through their minds.

Vey'rok, the Kinslayer.

Standing a hand over six feet, Vey'rok was the epitome of an orc warrior. With the strength of a Mauler, and the swiftness of a Ravager, Vey'rok was the greatest orc champion alive. He wore six, black iron chains wrapped tightly across his chest, three draped over each broad shoulder. A dozen of the links had been stained red, with twice that number colored yellow. Underneath the armor were rippling muscles that spoke of speed and power. In his hands was the reason they had come all this way.

The red blade forged from mythic steel known as Blood Claw.

Vey'rok held tightly to the weapon, its blade curved like a machete along one side.

"I will feast on your flesh," he promised in a deep growl, his white eyes blazing with an inner fire.

"You are done here Kinslayer," Captain Orvin shouted, drawing his weapon from beside Gavakyn. Behind him, the rest of the Ragers prepared to attack.

Vey'rok smiled.

"Do you hear that, pet?" he asked, glancing behind him. "They have come to play."

A shrill, monstrous scream blasted from the darkness behind him.

"Whatever comes out of that chamber, you must kill it," Viir said, looking at Gavakyn. "If it wins its way past us, it will ravage the continents. Leave Vey'rok to Captain Orvin, that's why he is here."

"The hell I will," muttered Gavakyn, wetting his lips.

"You must trust him," Karn barked, readying his staff.

Gavakyn's reply stuck in his throat as a massive creature of nightmare, larger and more savage looking than a cave bear, launched itself from the darkness, bearing down on them all.

The dwarven warrior placed his hand on the top of the box but did not open it.

"Bugger this," he muttered, not yet willing to experience the heartbreak that came with the artifact. Instead, he refastened the hook and placed the box on top of the old pine desk shoved up against the stone wall of his room. Laying back in his bed Gavakyn closed his eyes. It was a wonder to him how the happiest time of his life could be so closely related to the most heartbreaking. Most days Gavakyn fared well, keeping his mind occupied with training and discipline. Tonight, however, on the cusp of a long-awaited journey, the demons of the past closed in around him.

"The others, my brother—they will not understand," he heard her voice say once again in his head, some five years past.

"We will make them see," Gavakyn had promised, kissing Oganna's dark hair, leaning forward from his place behind her.

"How did this happen?" she had asked, with both surprise and joy in her voice.

"The gods only know," he had answered. Wrapping his arms around her waist, he embraced her lovingly. "I'm glad it did."

She looked up, her white eyes staring into his dark ones. "I am too," she replied, leaning back to kiss him.

In the minutes after their lovemaking, Oganna had turned to Gavakyn, her eyes intent upon his.

"You must promise me something love," she'd said.

"Anything," he'd replied, giving her a smile.

"You must spare my brother's life. Vey'rok is not himself, he—I can bring him back, given the opportunity."

Gavakyn had looked at her, supremely confident in his own prowess and gave her the answer she desired to hear.

"I promise, my love. I will not kill him."

Gavakyn opened his eyes, cursing his ignorance for the thousandth time. *How could I have been so stupid*, he thought, balling his fists in frustration, slamming them against the bed. He had never been impulsive, nearly everything he did was carefully planned—from the way he made his bed in the morning to the way he studied his opponents in battle. When he met Oganna, he had felt something new, something foreign to him. He realized now he had been infatuated with the orc female. Her savage beauty stirred a fire in his blood unlike any feeling he had never known. Because of that, because of his fear of losing her, he had made his promise. A promise he could not keep.

Unbidden, the memories of his duel against Vey'rok came flooding back to him, as sharp as the day the two had fought.

The creature that attacked from the darkness was a demon, borne of both fire and earth. Viir named it a Murag in the aftermath of its attack upon their force. It scattered both dwarves and sallowskins alike. Only a combination of Karn's ice magic, coupled with Gavakyn's spell of frost, lead to the creature's eventual defeat. Less than a minute had passed, but Omens and Ashten were down, both badly wounded, Ghost standing over the two of them protectively. In front of her, Rowe and the Ogre Mage lay dead.

"Go," Karn panted, much of his energy spent in his fight with the creature. "I did not realize how powerful Vey'rok has become. Only you have the skill to beat him dwarf. For the sake of both our races, do not fail."

Gavakyn turned to see the last of the Ragers fall to the orc Shadow. At the bottom of the stairs, he caught sight of Oganna, who had finally returned. She had a jagged wound on her left leg and bled freely from her shoulder and cheek. He nodded once at her and turned around.

Gavakyn looked down at the dark obsidian ground all around him, eyes wide with shock. It was littered with dead. An entire squad of Ragers, a dozen of the finest warriors the King of Kazic-Thul could send, had been cut down with consummate ease by the orc Shadow. The savage creature stood in the midst of the dead, lording over his kills like some macabre god of war. Gavakyn could make out the severed head of Captain Orvin, his open eyes staring into the black void of death. In Vey'rok hands was a curved blade, forged from red steel. It was newly wet, slick with dwarven blood.

"You want the Blood Claw?" the orc sneered at Gavakyn, his voice deep and hollow. "Come," he beckoned at the dwarf, curling his fingers, prompting him forward. "Try and take it! You'll suffer the same fate as your kin."

Bleeding from a wound on both his hand and scalp, the dwarven warrior wiped a trickle of blood from his brow. Knowing the eyes of his lover watched, he hefted his own steel blade and stepped forward, accepting the challenge.

He drew up short of the orc, the pair taking a measure of the other.

"I promised your sister I would not kill you," Gavakyn said, breaking the silence.

"A pox on you dwarf," the orc spat, his eyes narrowing in hate. "If she has chosen to side with our enemy, I will kill her too."

Gavakyn's lip curled in anger as he felt a drop of blood run past his eye.

"You will not touch her," Gavakyn snarled, hefting his sword.

"Come then, hero—I'll gut you before I cut her throat."

Gavakyn's world disappeared in a red haze as he launched himself forward to fulfill his destiny.

Chapter 20: The Promise Broken

They left at dawn the next day.

Gavakyn took the lead, riding quietly on his shaggy brown pony. Next to him rode Draega, her eyes fixed on the horizon in front of them. Holden and Viir were at the rear of the quartet, each carrying saddle bags full of gear. The two ponies had shared a stable long enough where neither balked at the massive boar that served as Draega's mount, or the twelve-foot-long reptile that Viir was riding.

As the group rode away, Gavakyn looked back at his outpost. He had lived there for the last five years, but it never felt like home. He'd spoken to the village chieftain the night before, a wise goblin named Skor, and left the place in his possession until Gavakyn's return.

"When might that be?" the wizened voice of the goblin asked, showing the dwarf a grudging respect.

"A month? A year? It could be that I never return," Gavakyn had answered. "If that is the case, the outpost is yours."

Skor snorted and shook his head. "You have been a good neighbor these past years…for a stump," he added quickly.

"So have you," Gavakyn replied with a chuckle. "I thank you for keeping up your end of our bargain."

"Ahh, well, after seeing you fight, no one wanted to tangle with you," the goblin admitted.

Gavakyn had laughed aloud. "Fair enough. Now, I best get back, as I have my things to pack."

"Good luck to you," Skor said, haltingly. "Should you return…well, the village would be happy to have you stay on again. As long as our agreement holds."

"I hope for that very thing," Gavakyn had replied.

Skor turned to go, but stopped, a curious look in his yellow eyes. "Do you really have it? Is there such a blade as the Blood Claw? Did you truly best the Shadow to win it?"

Gavakyn gave him a sad look. "Stay safe Skor," he said, trudging away, leaving the goblin's question unanswered.

"No one believes you beat him," the goblin called after, "or that you have the artifact!"

The dwarven warrior kept going, wishing the goblin was right.

Gavakyn stood over his foe, the light of rage fading from his eyes.

"What have you done?" gasped Oganna, rushing to her brother's side.

"He gave me no choice," Gavakyn stated, unapologetic.

"How could you? You swore to me you'd leave him alive!"

Gavakyn reached down to touch her hair and she slapped his hand away.

"Get away from me, murderer! You are nothing but a bloodthirsty Oathbreaker."

"Oganna, I had no choice. He was going to kill…"

"Leave me alone! How could I have trusted a redblood like you? "She reached out and picked up the Blood Claw hurling it at him. "Take your prize and go! Don't ever return. Should I see you again, I will kill you myself!"

"Oganna, please…"

"Go," she hissed, backhanding him across the face.

"Come with me," Karn had said to Gavakyn, from his vantage point a few paces away. "She's in no place to listen to reason."

Gavakyn had walked away, holding the Blood Claw in his hand. It was the last thing she'd ever given him. That, coupled with her death threat, made him wish he'd never heard of the Blood Claw.

Now, the weapon of the ancients hung on his back, it's red steel blade hidden inside the confines of the scabbard he'd fashioned years ago. When he'd finally found the courage to look upon the weapon, Gavakyn felt a wave of emptiness and sorrow. It was the same feeling that had threatened to engulf him over the last five years. Even after all that time, this artifact still filled him with dread. Now, he and his companions had set out on a journey to complete what had been started so long ago.

They traveled the twenty leagues to Eastbridge in two days' time. The dwarves of Kazic-Thul were on high alert after the invasion that had taken place only weeks ago. They groused a bit at the sight of Draega and Viir but let them by with a word from Storm Sorrow.

They passed through the Mountains of Mist and descended into Kazic-Thul. The dwarven army was on high alert. Rumor of a great horde, one larger than its predecessor, had reached the ears of the city. It was enough to where General Ironhenge had left along with King Helfer earlier that day. They were heading to Draymore's Outpost, site of the deciding battle between the invading sallowskins and the dwarven defenders ten days ago.

The group stuck to the city's outskirts, laying low at an old friend of Gavakyn's, who lent them his barn to sleep in. The next day the trio left before sunrise, making good time around the outer walls of the city and onto the old trade road. By the time the sun set, they had made it to their first destination.

"Well, they've fixed the place up, haven't they?" Holden offered, looking at the northeastern gate. "Came through here a piece back. It wasn't fit enough for a troll's nursery, no offense," the mage added hastily, shooting a look at Viir.

"Hmmpht," the Seer snorted, heading through the gate.

Upon entry they were stopped by a dwarven Stonebreaker named Kell. He had a golden beard, neatly braided in the front, that hung down to his chest. There was a spark of humor in his hazel eyes.

"Storm Sorrow," he said, giving Gavakyn a formal bow. "It's good to see you again."

Gavakyn peered at the Stonebreaker intently. "You do look familiar—remind me where we've met."

Kell's eyes brightened a bit more. "I wouldn't expect you to remember me, but my uncle, Orvin, traveled with you into the Jagged Lands years ago. I met you briefly at his funeral. My father said you spoke well of him."

A vision of Orvin's severed head flashed in Gavakyn's mind. He forced his face to relax and gave the Stonebreaker an easy smile. "That's it," he rumbled. "You favor Orvin a bit, especially around the eyes. He was a bonny fighter–I think of him often."

"Kind of you to say," Kell smiled, beaming.

"Stonebreaker," asked Viir, moving his lizard mount forward. "Was there a battle here recently?"

"Aye, less than a day ago," Kell answered, frowning at the troll. "Two thousand sallowskins attacked up the ramp. Would have lost the outpost had it not been for the Stonebreaker that was here."

His face lost some of its glow. "Alas, she was killed in the fighting, though her sacrifice will be remembered long after we are gone."

"She's buried in the cairn," Viir said, moving forward. "We must go there."

"Woah there, old timer," Kell said, raising his hand. "I can't just let you…"

"It's alright lad," Gavakyn said wearily. "I will stay with him."

"What of this one?" Kell scoffed, looking at Draega.

The big orc smiled, dismounting from her boar. "There is nothing to fear from me, Stonebreaker. Honor to your clan."

Kell gave Gavakyn a sidelong look and exhaled slowly. "If it were anyone else, I'd say no. But you are with Storm Sorrow. Come, I'll let the captain know you are here with your…friends."

"Good of you," Gavakyn said, thanking him.

"We traveled all this way to see a tomb?" Holden mumbled in question, staring at Gavakyn.

"Apparently," he said with a shrug, following after the Seer.

The foursome walked down the steps into the cairn, their footfalls echoing on the stone beneath their feet. Holden cast a spell of pale green light that illuminated the chamber better than any lantern ever could. Most of the coffins were old, covered in dust. However, five were new, clear of debris. Four were draped with the clothing the deceased wore in life—Engineers by the look of their gear. Rifles and hammers lay alongside suits of hardened leather armor. The coffins had been covered with heavy stone slabs.

Upon the top of the last of the coffins was the shield of a Stonebreaker. Laying across the emblem of a dark colored anvil was a broadsword, three feet in length.

"I can sense her presence," Viir whispered, looking reverently upon the tomb. "It has been held in place by magic. A type of magic I have never seen."

"What is he talking about?" murmured Holden, casting a sidelong look at Gavakyn.

The dwarven warrior shrugged his broad shoulders, just as bewildered as the Mage.

"Quickly, while there is still time," continued Viir, his voice excited.

The Seer took out a crystal vial from under his robes and placed it atop the shield. Stepping away from the coffin, the troll set his staff firmly on the ground in front of him and extended it away from his body.

"Eonitu Nehu Ashta!" he whispered, looking intently at the vial.

They could detect the faint movement of air in the still chamber.

"Eonitu Nehu Ashta!" the troll said again, louder than the first time.

A breeze began to waft into the room, strong enough to rattle the vial where it stood.

"What is happening?" Holden asked, her eyes darting around the room.

Underneath the lid of the coffin, a blue light flared to life.

Gavakyn watched in fascination as the Seer shouted the words of power one last time.

"Eonitu Nehu Ashta!"

The breeze became a wind, strong enough to lift the vial off the coffin, where it hovered in place, floating in the air.

"By Kruk, what are you about, Mucklander?" bellowed Draega. The normally stalwart Mauler had raised her eyes in alarm.

The blue glow from inside the coffin seeped out of the cracks and occupied the space above the vial. Viir motioned with his hand and the mist began to fill the container.

"Do not let it hit the floor!" roared Viir, struggling to contain the magical essence.

No sooner had he said those words than the blue mist was gone, every bit of it inside the vial. Still several feet away, Viir staggered backward where Draega scrambled to catch him.

"The vial!" the Seer croaked, seeing it fall to the ground.

Gavakyn, viper quick, dove forward and caught the crystal container inches from the floor. He held it tentatively in his hands, still trying to decipher what had just happened.

"Are you alright?" Draega asked, setting the troll on the ground.

"Yes," Viir said weakly, looking up at Gavakyn. "Thank you, lad. You have done well."

"What, in the name of the gods, was that all about?" hissed Holden, her brown eyes blazing with heat.

"It was a necessity," Viir answered, waving his hand at the mage.

"What the hell did you accomplish?" Holden demanded, unwilling to accept his answer.

The Seer reached out and took the vial from Gavakyn. "She is part of it. She needs to go with us."

"Who?" Draega asked, looking around.

Viir looked reverently at the vial and smiled.

"Thorana."

They spent the night camped out in the forest just outside the outpost. Kell had spoken to his captain, and they had been invited to stay. However, Draega pointed out the invitation might cause an incident considering an invading force of sallowskins had attacked only a day ago. Agreeing with her wisdom, Gavakyn led them to the bottom of the ramp and set up a camp near the tree line, in clear sight of the outpost.

The next day they made their way through the mountain paths, hoping to arrive at the town of Barrel Falls by dusk.

The group made good time, as the weather stayed fair. A half hour until dusk they came upon a clearing and Gavakyn raised his hand, calling for a halt.

"There is a fire ahead," the dwarf warrior said softly, glancing at the troll. "It's her, isn't it?"

"Watch yourself," Viir said evenly, with a small nod of acknowledgement.

Gavakyn glanced back at him, a faraway look in his eyes. "Stay here while I take a look." Pulling out his six bladed mace, the dwarven warrior stepped forward.

"Shouldn't we go with him?" Holden asked.

"Not for this," was all the Seer would say.

Gavakyn moved forward, creeping as quietly as he could to the clearing.

He stepped out of the shadows of the trees, the sun shining on his black armor. He glanced around the clearing, his eyes everywhere but on the fire burning brightly at the center. She was nearby, he knew, but would likely attack when he was…

A fraction of a second was all the warning he received. A knife, thrown with incredible accuracy, flew at him from the darkness of the trees off to his left. Gavakyn heard the whirring of air and dropped to the ground, rolling quickly to his right. He sprang back to his feet just in time to intercept an attack aimed at his head.

His assailant pulled back on her machete, malice etched on her pale-yellow features.

"I told you I would kill you when I saw you again," Oganna spat, her voice dripping with hatred.

The dwarf said nothing, taking in the sight of her.

She looks the same, he thought, with her long black hair pulled back in a braid, her body covered in dark chain armor. She stared back at him, her pale eyes taking him in.

"There is no need to fight," he said softly from behind his mace. "I'm not here to kill you."

"You broke your word," she hissed, drawing a knife with her other hand. "I have taken a blood oath to remove your head!"

She stepped forward and attacked again. Gavakyn parried her machete and knocked a swipe of her knife away easily.

"Do you still think of me, Oganna?" he asked, his tone soft. "I think of you every day."

She sneered at him, flashing teeth through her beautiful face. "I dream of killing you!" she answered, attacking again.

The she-orc had the reach, but Gavakyn was both quicker and stronger. Like so many of her kind, Oganna was too aggressive, especially when outmatched. The dwarven warrior, seeing his opening, knocked the knife from her hand. Now enraged, Oganna made a furious attack that was off balance and poorly timed. Gavakyn grabbed her wrist and wrenched the machete from it. The blade fell in the dirt, and he kicked it away.

"Enough," he bellowed, letting her go. "I love you Oganna, and you loved me once. Don't let your brother's warmongering separate us further. I have been lost without you all these years."

He dropped his mace to the ground and drew forth the Blood Claw. "Take it," he said, tossing her the blade. "I both bless and curse the day I heard about that thing. The journey led me to you, and for that, I will forever be grateful. But it also led to losing you and betraying your trust. I will not fight you for it, nor will I stop you from killing me."

Gavakyn stepped forward, mere inches away from her. "Every day my heart weeps in sadness as I fall asleep without you by my side. Every day I wake and die a new death, knowing I won't see you."

She stared at him; her eyes full of anger.

"You killed Vey'rok," she accused, her voice shaking with emotion.

"I did," Gavakyn admitted, "because he threatened to kill *you*." The dwarf sighed deeply. "I wish I had not made that promise to you. I was a fool to think I could keep it. I could not bear the thought of losing you, not for any reason."

His expression turned fierce and his eyes radiated power. "But I would do it again to keep you safe, Oganna. Should I die here and now, I will not regret taking his life over saving yours."

The Shadow looked at him, a titanic battle of emotions warring inside of her.

"But you are right," he continued, placing his hands to his sides. "I broke my word to you. If you wish to kill me, I will not stop you. My life is a wasteland without you anyway. Part of me wants you to take it. Better the void of death than spending a moment more without you in my life."

Oganna stared at him, her face contorted with uncertainty. She glanced down to the red blade in her hands, knowing it had ruined the life of her brother. Looking back up, she saw the face of the dwarf that had taken him from her and narrowed her gaze.

Seeing her anger rise, Gavakyn closed his eyes, accepting his fate.

In that moment, time froze for Oganna. Gavakyn had meant what he said. He stood at ease in front of her, with no semblance of defense. Oganna looked down at the Blood Claw. A magical artifact that had consumed her brother.

"No," she said, casting the blade to the ground.

Gavakyn opened his eyes.

"I will not let the Blood Claw ruin my life as it did Vey'rok's," Oganna said with conviction, looking at Gavakyn. "I have been blind all these years. Blinded by anger and sorrow."

Looking at her former lover, Oganna's visage changed. From savage and proud, she now showed a sensitivity rarely seen in an orc.

"I am... sorry, Gavakyn. Sorrier than you will ever know. I... I was wrong to blame you. The power of that blade ended my brother's life long before you did. I heard the truth of *Vey'rok's* words long ago. I just... I just could not accept them."

She looked down at him and dropped her eyes to the ground. "I don't expect you'll ever forgive me. I would not blame you if..."

Gavakyn stepped forward, sweeping up the orc female into his arms and kissed her, the aching bitterness that had plagued him, lifting from his heart as if it had never been. The feeling was replaced with a soaring spirit, as the two souls found peace at long last with their haunting past.

"It's about time," grunted Viir from his place at the edge of the clearing.

"What is this?" snorted Draega, looking on in shock. "A dwarf with an orc? It goes against the laws of natur..."

A knife sped toward the Mauler, who swore and scrambled to block the throw with her shield.

"Where did you hide that?" Gavakyn asked, arching his eyebrow.

"I'll show you later," she promised, kissing him again.

A rustling in the bushes put them all on alert as Gavakyn and Oganna both dropped into a fighting crouch. Emerging from the underbrush came two riders, each appearing dirty and tired.

"Karn?" asked Oganna, her voice surprised. "How are you here?"

"I see you two idiots have decided to grow the hell up," the goblin croaked, his voice dripping with sarcasm.

"Good to see you, Shaman," Viir smiled, with a nod to his old compatriot.

"Hmmph," snorted Karn, turning to his companion. "Kynnda this is Viir, Seer of the troll marshes. The two milksops in front of you are Gavakyn and Oganna."

"Gavakyn," said Holden, looking at Karn skeptically, "who is this?"

"You are going to find out Mage," Karn answered, barking with laughter. "We'll see if you do better than the ogre we brought last time."

Holden glanced at Gavakyn and frowned. "What is he talking about? What ogre? What happened to him?"

"He was killed by a demon of earth and fire," Gavakyn answered, slipping his hand back into Oganna's.

"What the hell is he talking about?" Draega asked, her face twisted in confusion.

"I don't mean to be rude," said the dwarf Karn had named as Kynnda, "but I'm hungry. Let's eat and afterward these elders can answer our questions."

"You're from Magehold," Holden said, looking closely at the she-dwarf.

"I was," she replied, studying Holden just as closely. "You must be the renegade, Holden."

The Mage snorted and shook her head. "I see they're still making the neophytes learn about the 'wild mages,' that left?"

"Yes, though I am no longer a neophyte."

"What are you?" Holden asked.

"I'm a Shaman," Kynnda answered, giving her counterpart a satisfactory smile.

"Dwarves have shamans now?" Oganna asked, speaking everyone's thoughts.

Kynnda snapped her fingers, and the pony Karn was riding transformed into a *hoargasi*, eyeing them all viciously.

"You bet your ass they do."

Michael K. Falciani

The Dwarves of Rahm:
Omens of War

Part VI
Blood of the Ancients

Chapter 21: Old Blood

Present time

"Say your peace," Arik grunted, his eyes never leaving the sallowskins standing in his tent. "Though it will avail you nothing."

Tensions were high, as there was little trust to be found on either side. Besides myself, only Ashten, Ghost and Jax had accompanied Gavakyn and his companions to the Jagged Lands five years ago. Even we, who had witnessed the horrors of *Mott-Godaan*, did not know what to expect from him.

"I think it best we hear from Karn," Gavakyn reasoned, his eyes shifting to the goblin. "He has the most experience in what we are dealing with."

"A goblin Shaman," hissed Arik, his voice thick with hate. "By all reports it was *he* and his raiding party that caused the calamity in the first place."

"This is true," the old goblin croaked in response. "Our expedition did set these events into motion. I do not ask, nor expect forgiveness from any of you. However, we are past that now. If we do not come together…"

"You think I would trust you?" Arik asked, his voice harsh. "Karn the Killer—a sallowskin with more dwarven blood on his hands than any other spell caster in the northlands!"

Arik leaned forward in his chair, his eyes filling with rage. "I should butcher you right now for the savage monster you are. Instead, I am forced to sit here and bandy words with one who has waged war upon my kind his entire life!"

"General," Gavakyn cut in, his eyes hard, "while I understand your perspective, we are past that. A larger issue has come forth and we must deal with it, *together*."

"You sully thousands of years of dwarven bloodshed and suffering to even *consider* an alliance with this scum," Arik shot back, disgust filling his voice. "Dwarves and Blackbloods have only known war with one another. I will not rest until these piss-colored savages have been eradicated from Garthan-Tor."

Most of the dwarves seated near Arik, captains of their respective squads, rumbled in agreement. Lorric had not taken her eyes off of Viir since he had entered.

"While it's true our races have not gotten on well through the years," said the troll quietly. "There *are* instances of peaceful—even friendly exchanges between the Redbloods and those of us who reside in the north."

Most of the dwarves at the table scoffed at the words of the massive Seer.

"Take Gavakyn here," the troll continued, unfazed in the face of dwarven anger. "He is called, 'Storm Sorrow,' despised by my kind. He has spilled more sallowskin blood than any of you—yet somehow he has managed to co-exist peacefully with a tribe of goblins and orcs for years."

"'Storm Sorrow' or not, Gavakyn has developed a soft spot in his heart for *your* kind," Arik spat. "He doesn't speak for me. As far as I'm concerned, he can go straight to hell with the rest of you."

"You arrogant bastard," Gavakyn snarled, rising to his feet. "Can't you see these sallowskins have risked everything to come here! They did not travel hundreds of miles out of spite for you. They are here to help save us all! You are too ignorant to see their sacrifice, blinded as you are by hatred!"

"I'll not be hounded by one who has betrayed the principles of his people," Arik thundered back, leaping to his feet. "All because of some orc whore!"

A pall of silence fell over the room, as the two mighty warriors glared at one another. Gavakyn's face began to redden, and his hand twitched for the Blood Claw strapped on his back.

There was a blur of movement from across the room, which stayed his hand. A high-pitched whirring cut through the air. Two knives, thrown with incredible accuracy, flew past the head of Arik Ironhenge, narrowly missing his ears. With a *thuuck*, they thudded into the two-inch wide beam that was part of the tent frame located behind the general.

All eyes turned to Oganna, the orc Shadow, who was staring at Arik, a sickening malevolence in her white eyes. "I have trained my whole life to kill stumps," she began, her voice quiet, dripping with venom. "You redbloods have slain thousands of my people. I made it my mission in life to hunt down the stumps, wherever I could find them, and kill them all without mercy."

She turned to Karn, who was watching her closely. "Five years ago, this goblin," she continued, pointing at the shaman, "tells me he has discovered an artifact, one that will help defeat the stumps to the south. My brother and I, wishing for that very thing, volunteered our services. Many of the four races of the horde went with us. When we arrived at *Mott-Godaan*, my brother was able to win the artifact, wresting it away from its champion."

The she-orc paused, taking in the dwarves at the head of the table.

"But he changed," she continued. "Possession of that weapon consumed him. It twisted his soul until he became evil, bent only on serving those beyond the gate. Many of my kin that traveled with us fell under the influence of the Blood Claw. It was only by some lucky act of the gods that Karn and I escaped."

Walking around the perimeter of the tent, Oganna circled toward the general. "We retreated back to the northlands, lost and uncertain."

She paused, placing her hand on the shoulder of Viir. "Then the Seer came. He spoke to us of many things. An ancient enemy, one that united the stumps and the sallowskins ages ago. He says if we do not unite once again, all of us will be killed."

Moving once more, Oganna slid behind the general. Reaching out, the orc pulled her knives from the wooden beam with a grunt. "When the Seer told me we must bury our enmity with the stumps, I felt the same as you, general. I hated you and your kind. I wanted all of you to die."

Moving again, Oganna completed her circle, coming to rest next to Gavakyn, who was looking at her with an implacable expression. "But I cared for my people, I cared for my brother. So, I decided to go with the Seer, to meet these stumps we are forced to fight beside."

Oganna's voice was firm, matter of fact. Everyone in the room was riveted by her words.

"I traveled south through the Jagged Lands and met these stumps. Many were familiar to me, their names spoken as curses among my people."

She paused, pointing at Ashten.

"The leader of the Gray Company, Ashten, who we call, 'Flame Hand.'"

She moved her finger to the dwarves next to him. "Ghost, nicknamed, 'The White Death.' They were my enemies, slayers of my people."

She looked at both Ashten and Ghost, and her expression changed, softening. It was a subtle difference at best, but a change nonetheless.

"After spending days on the road with them, I discovered they were not what I thought them to be. They were strong, disciplined, and just—even to me, one of their mortal enemies."

Oganna narrowed her eyes and glared once again at Arik. "One day, as we headed north, we ran into a stump leader. He wished to kill me, to bury his axe in my head. Ashten and Ghost stepped forward, they told the leader to sod off."

This drew a chuckle from Monchakka and Kora, but Arik hardened his glare.

"This leader, he did not heed their warning and moved to attack," the orc continued, her eyes burrowing into those of the general.

Oganna placed her hand firmly on Gavakyn's. "That's when The Butcher of the North stepped forward."

The Shadow sneered at the general, reliving the scene. "This stump," she said, moving her hands to rest on Gavakyn's shoulders, "who has killed more of the four races of the horde than any southlander I've ever heard of, came to my defense. He, who would become Storm Sorrow, fought, and beat the stump leader, forcing him to choose between life and death. The stump leader cursed us both, telling me he would have his vengeance."

The tent grew quiet as her story came to a close.

"Now we stand here today, General, plagued by the same horror we faced five years ago. Gavakyn and I have not changed our minds. I will go with him to the gates of *Mott-Godaan* and once again try to save our peoples. Will you allow this to happen?"

She paused, and leaned forward, her voice a sibilant hiss. "Or do you need to be humbled again, like you were five years ago?"

A momentary silence descended upon the tent, as those inside realized it was Arik who had been defeated by Gavakyn on that bygone day.

The General's face reddened as he remained unconvinced. "You would have me believe you have changed, Oganna?" he gritted out between clenched teeth, his eyes narrowing. "It was only yesterday that you were part of the group that tried to kill Princess Merin."

A dark rumbling of protest began again as the dwarves looked back to the orc.

"No," she said, defiance in her voice. "I did what I could to *save* the princess. The Lion Guard of Orius were supposed to dispatch Merin when they could and collect her blood. Had I not stepped in, they would have completed their task."

"But I heard you tell Regan you sent the sallowskins after us in the mountains," Merin accused.

"I had to," the she-orc answered, without regret. "The other Shadow would have been wise to my true reason for heading south had I not done so. He was assigned to travel with me by my superiors. He was sent to observe my actions, as much as to hunt down the princess, along with the bard who accompanied you."

I had almost forgotten. Almost.

"What of your blood oath to slay Gavakyn?" challenged Nathrak.

Oganna lifted her chin proudly, looking squarely at the Rager. "I was wrong," she stated. "I admit this to you all, freely. Storm Shadow showed me he was as good as his word—even after I had sworn to kill him. Any creature, stump or sallowskin, who would sacrifice themselves for the greater good deserves my respect. It is because of the bravery of Storm Sorrow I have come to see my mistake."

She looked from Nathrak to Arik and gave a sniff of indifference. "If I, a piss-colored savage, can see the error of my ways, then you can too, General. If not, that makes me, an orc whore, far better than the likes of you."

There was silence once again in the tent.

"She is right," said a voice from off to the side. I turned and saw it was Monchakka. The young Engineer looked at the General.

"The old ways are changing, father—it is time we change with them. These sallowskins from the north show great courage in coming here. They sit in the heart of your army to ask us for our help."

"You are young lad, you don't know what you're asking me to do," Arik replied, his voice fighting the outrage he felt.

"He is asking you to give them a chance," Kora chimed in from her place next to Monchakka. "Lodir is in trouble. They may be able to aid us."

"When was the last time a blackblood helped a dwarf?" Nathrak asked, looking unconvinced.

I glanced at Karn and his dwarven apprentice, and a vision hit me. In a flash, I saw myself lying prone once again on the floor less than a week ago at the Toad and Peach.

"Damn it, that's where I saw you!" I exclaimed, looking at Kynnda.

All eyes in the tent turn to me.

"What are you saying, bard?" Arik asked.

"During the battle at the Toad and Peach," I explained, the memory fresh in my mind. "I had been knocked to the ground, my weapon flying from my grasp. I was completely at the mercy of the sallowskin invaders."

I paused, looking Nathrak squarely in the eye. "That goblin," I said, pointing at Karn, "along with his dwarven protégé, cast their magic, saving us all. It happened quickly—I doubt anyone saw it but me."

"A ghostly wolf," Kora said, confirming my words with a nod of her head. "I did not see who cast the spell, but it saved Monchakka's life as well."

I pointed over toward Karn and Kynnda. "Without their intervention many of the dwarves standing before you, including me, would not be here today."

Turning to face Karn I gave him a rueful grin. "I did not realize it was you, though I should have suspected. Why did you not reveal yourself to me?"

The shaman shook his head. "In the middle of a battle started by the horde? No. Kynnda and I did our part and left, seeing things were under control."

Nathrak looked from Karn to the dwarfess next to him. "You can attest to this goblin's actions?" he asked Kynnda, giving the she-dwarf his attention.

"Yes," she replied simply. "He helped kill one of his own kind to save the lives of at least a half-dozen of the dwarves in this tent, your kin included."

Nathrak sniffed at the girl in appraisal, pursing his lips. Looking back at his general, the Captain of the Ragers gave Arik a grim look. "I trust in Omens," he said flatly. "With the Engineers' confirmation paired with Kynnda, it may well be that the goblin speaks the truth. I've no love for the blackbloods, General, you know that—but it might be best to hear what they have to say. Kora is right. Lodir is still under siege. We could use all the help we can get."

"This is outrageous!" hissed High Priest Armon, standing in anger. "They are *blackbloods!* Certain to betray us once they get what they want. How can you even consider such a course of action?"

Arik glanced at the priest, then over to Ghost. She gave her brother a slight nod. The General released a frustrated breath and sat back down. "We will hear them out," he growled, looking at Armon.

"But General…" Armon began to protest.

Arik furrowed his brow in anger. "I have spoken, priest—either sit down or leave."

Armon looked ready to burst but managed to find his way back into his seat, though his face was still flush with anger.

"Speak your peace, Shaman," said Arik. "I don't know what will come of listening to you, but," he glanced at me, pressing his lips together firmly. "If Omens and Kora will vouch for you, then I will listen."

The attention in the room turned back to Karn, who leaned lightly on his staff. "I appreciate that General. For what it is worth, I come to you filled with only the best of intentions, for both of our peoples. If we somehow survive what is to come, we can happily go back to hating one another in peace."

Arik stared at the goblin for a long moment and snorted with a burst of laughter. "A goblin with a sense of humor, next it will be a musical orc!"

There was a general lightening of the mood in the room at Karn's quip and the tensions eased.

"I am going to speak of events of the ancient past," the shaman began, taking a long drink from a clay flask.

"What is that?" I asked, nodding at his container.

"Goblin Lort," Karn answered, making a face, wiping his lips clean. "Very strong, an acquired taste for certain."

I saw one side of his lips curl, as the memory I hoped for stirred.

"Too potent for dwarven bellies," he continued, with an offhand wave.

I hid my smile behind a hand raised under the pretense of itching my face.

He'd remembered.

"Oye, just a minute you," Cabella called, rising to her feet. "Are you saying you can outdrink a dwarf?"

"Not at all," Karn said mildly. "Goblin Lort is simply…difficult on the constitution of any creature but a goblin."

"I wouldn't argue the point," Oganna chimed in, her voice calm. "I tried it once—my insides were on fire for a week."

There was a challenging murmur that carried throughout the tent.

It was a well-known secret. Dwarves are a ridiculously proud race. They know what they excel at, and they revel in it. We compete in everything from hammer throwing to beard growing. When it comes to the making, barreling, and consuming of alcohol, well, that's a source of pride for our race as well. Whether it's our golden ales or stout beers, we take our drinking seriously.

A few of us got to talking with Karn one night while sitting around the campfire some five years ago and it was suggested that instead of killing one another, the races should offer up drinking champions. The winners would get the proceeds for their race while the losers forfeited whatever was at stake, be it land, food or a good old-fashioned ass whooping. Of course, we were caught up in retrieving the Blood Claw at the time, so that talk became just another campfire tale, subject to be lost in the annals of history. However, the idea always held merit with me, and I tucked it away in the back of my mind. After the way this meeting had started, I couldn't resist the idea of breathing a little life into our old fireside chat.

"Let me explain something to you two gits," Armon, the warrior priest said archly, taking the bait. "There's not a brew in the world that a dwarf can't handle. Our folk have stomachs of iron."

Karn smiled. "You haven't tried the drink of my people," he responded. "It will turn your belly to fire."

"Is that what you think?" Cabella chimed in, her face red with challenge. "After you finish tonight, you'll come to my tent, and we will see if your gut can back up your mouth."

"You won't be alone," Lorric cut in, her eyes flashing.

"I accept your offer," Karn answered, tipping the flask in the direction of both dwarves, while giving me a sidelong look of approval.

I know it wasn't much, but the races had to start *somewhere*.

The moment subsided quickly as Karn got back on track. "As I was saying, more than a thousand years ago, our races came together. The sallowskins and dwarves united as one in the face of a common enemy."

There was a general murmur of voices grumbling under their breaths.

"What enemy was that?" Arik asked.

Karn fell silent and looked to Viir. The big troll sighed, his rumbling voice rolling throughout the tent. "The old tomes of our ancestors call them *Valkir*, spirits of earth and fire. They come from a different plane than our own."

"What plane?" asked Nathrak. "What are you talking about?"

"There are places that exist all around us," explained Holden, speaking for the first time. "For example, the gods of the Trine, and those of the Sallowskins, exist on a plane we call Yewlysian, known more commonly as Haven's Mists in the layman's tongue. When we die, our spirits travel there, if they are allowed. If not, they exist in the plane of Formar, the Gray, waiting for salvation."

"This plane you speak of, is it different from Yewlysian?" asked Arik.

Holden looked to Armon who shook his head. "I have read there are other planes, though I do not know how to access them," the War Priest admitted.

"But you *have* heard of them, priest," the troll said gently. "One at least. The ancient grimoires call the plane of the *Valkir*, Iridyes. You know it as Hell."

Whispered murmurs made their way through the tent.

"It is a place of molten fire and rock," Viir continued, the tent quieting again. "Much like the volcanoes here on Rahm and Garthan-Tor. In truth, little is known about Iridyes, or those that call it home. Five years past, when we last traveled to *Mott-Godaan*, several of the people in this room fought against one of the denizens of that plane."

Those in the tent looked at the handful of us that had been part of the raiding party.

"What was it?" asked Rhosyn, her voice soft.

It was Ghost who answered. "I've been to all corners of Rahm and covered a fair amount of ground in the Jagged Lands to the north," she said quietly. "I've fought against all manner of creatures. Manticores, Chimeras, even an armored Hela Lizard ridden by a Troll Juggernaut of the Taymir Swamp. Let me tell you all right now, none of those monsters could hold a candle to that hound of hell."

Those in the tent sat rapt with attention, listening to the veteran Engineer.

"It shot out of the darkness, moving with the speed and agility of the great mountain cats of the Brae Crags," she continued. "It was big, larger than the Cave bears ridden by the Ogre cavalry to the north. Its bulk was all sinewy muscle, with jaws that could rip a Chain in half."

She paused, gazing at Arik, a haunted look on her face.

"Its initial charge scattered our forces," she continued, speaking faster. "Gavakyn and Omens were thrown aside like scraps of cloth in the wind. The Ogre Mage that was with us launched a devastating bolt of lightning, driving the hound back. Ashten and I..."

She trailed off, still scarred by the memory. "At the end of the battle the hound lay dead—but we had lost the Ogre, a Mage of incredible power, and a Mountaineer named Rowe, a bonny warrior who was brave and strong."

Ghost paused, looking over at Ashten. "Of the rest of us, only Gavakyn and I were left fit enough to fight. Should a second beast have emerged..."

Ghost trailed off to silence, casting her eyes to the ground.

"I did not know," Arik said softly, turning sympathetic eyes upon his sister.

"There are few that do," Karn croaked, his voice grim.

"What can we do to stop this?" Nathrak asked, leaning forward in his seat.

"First, we must help you liberate Lodir," Viir answered, rubbing his chin absently. "There is a sallowskin inside who we need for the journey north."

"Who?" asked Caballa.

Viir hesitated, looking over at Oganna.

The Shadow pressed her full lips together in a frown. "He is an orc warrior named Bardok."

The dwarves in the tent showed little reaction upon hearing her words.

Oganna tensed her shoulders, "You may know him by a different name," she said softly.

"What name is that?" Nathrak asked, his tone suspicious.

She looked at him and spoke, her voice cold.

"Rehgur, the Darksoul."

"By the Trine, no!" bellowed Nathrak, his outrage echoed by many of the dwarves in the tent. "You get me anywhere near the Black Shredder and I'll kill him where he stands!"

Calls for Rehgur's head among the dwarves were loud. Even those with more sympathetic tendencies toward the sallowskins were up in arms.

"You can't expect us to work side by side with Darksoul," Ashten was yelling. "He's killed more dwarves in the last five years than any sallowskin on the continent!"

The fervor in the tent had become angry, bordering on violence. I did not know what to do, and I looked at Merin who glanced toward me in dismay.

"*Dreka-Karr*," shouted a voice, bringing the cacophony of the tent to a halt.

One could have heard a pin drop as Jax stepped forward.

"I have kept my silence long enough," he shouted, his green eyes blazing. "I, too, was there at *Mott-Godaan*. I fought the sallowskins who had fallen under the sway of the Blood Claw. I tested my skills against the hound of hell as well. I, along with Viir and Karn, have spoken to the guardians of the portal between our world and that of the *Valkir*. Believe me when I say this, we need one another, now more than ever, else every soul on Quasa will die."

He stopped and moved within inches of Nathrak's face.

"You hate this Darksoul do you?" he asked, his voice like stone. "You've every right to. However, when that hound of hell attacked, I stood alongside six of the greatest heroes on the continents. One, just one of those *Valkir* nearly killed us all! Had it not been for the mystical powers of Karn, Viir and a now deceased Ogre Mage, along with the fortitude and strength of Gavakyn, that portal would already be open and all of us lost. Hear me and know the truth, whether you want to admit it or not. Every dwarf in Rahm, every creature in Garthon-Tor, owes their lives to those brave sallowskins who fought against the *Valkir*. Yes, there were dwarves who fought too, but alone we would have failed. Only together will we stand a chance."

He glared at every one of us in the tent. "If this, Rehgur the Darksoul, is the most competent warrior in the sallowskin horde, then we will need him should any more of those *Valkir* break through."

Jax leveled his gaze at everyone in the tent, dwarves and sallowskins alike. "The time for bad blood and petty grudges has passed. The ancient guardians of the waygate have called upon the heroes of all the races. That is all any of you need to know."

Those in the tent were left speechless. Jax was more than just a bard. He was more well-traveled than any of us, even Gavakyn, who had lived in Sallowskin lands. No one in that tent had his experience, not even Karn. When he spoke, all of us, the sallowskins included, listened.

It was the troll, Viir, who broke the silence. "Bard Jax speaks the truth."

He looked over at Nathrak, who was slumped in his chair. "It is unfair of us, Captain, to ask the dwarves to put aside an enmity that most of you have known your entire life. I do not expect you to trust any of the sallowskins. A horde of them currently occupy one of your cities, threatening your very way of life. I can only ask that you give those of us in this tent a chance to prove ourselves to you. That chance means we help you retake your city. It means we will have to fight against and kill our own kind. I do not enjoy death, nor spilling blood of any color. But tomorrow, I will do so in an effort to save us all."

Arik leaned back in his chair and glanced at his captains.

"I will follow your lead, general," said Caballa, folding her arms over her chest.

"I vote against this alliance," Armon hissed, his eyes boring holes into Karn. "I trust no sallowskins, General. To do so would lead to certain doom."

Nathrak remained still, his face torn by indecision. "Darksoul killed three of my company, sir," he said, his words slow, deliberate. "Good dwarves, who fought to keep our lands safe."

He sighed, reaching a decision. "I cannot promise I won't try and kill him if I get the chance, Arik, but I will do as you command."

"As will I," echoed Lorric, her dark eyes flashing.

General Ironhenge nodded at his captains, appreciating their candor. He looked to his sister, the one dwarf he felt he could trust more than any other. "You would trust your own blood," he said, nodding to Monchakka, "on the word of these…northerners?"

Ghost glanced to Ashten, who nodded firmly.

"I would," she answered, looking over at her nephew. "Karn, Viir and Oganna, they were boon companions once—I see no reason to doubt them now. Gavakyn believes in them…their actions tomorrow will far outweigh any words spoken in this tent. I say we give them a chance."

Arik stared at his sister for a long moment and nodded. "So be it," he said, turning his gaze to Viir. "I accept your offer of aid. What do you propose we do?"

Viir looked back to Karn, who cleared his throat. "Let us speak to anyone familiar with the defenses of Lodir," he said. "Gavakyn has told us what he remembers, but I'd like to hear from you and your captains, General, to see what we can come up with…together."

As we sat down in the tent planning our strategy, I couldn't help but wonder. It may well have been the first time the Dwarves of Rahm and the Sallowskins of Garthan-Tor had planned an offensive with the purpose of *saving* as many lives as they could rather than killing one another. As I sat back and listened to the General and his captains, it struck me as a watershed moment. There was a long way to go of course, but for the first time in millennia, there was a real chance for peace between our people.

Chapter 22: The Raid

The next morning dawned to gray skies and a threatening storm. Sadly, I was on the move before sunrise. An hour before dawn the raiding groups were already on the outskirts of Lodir.

Arik had set up camp more than two miles away from the city. It was far enough from the thick walls of the Golden Keep to where his army was out of sight from any casual observer who might be looking out from atop the battlements. Since our offensive was based on speed of movement and surprise, it was in Arik's best interests to keep out of sight for as long as possible.

The council of war the previous evening had been an interesting one as Ashten and Ghost had taken the lead in the planning. Arik, more used to fighting out in the open, deferred to their greater expertise. Karn and Oganna had been helpful as well, especially when it came to advising us on how the sallowskin troops were most likely deployed.

Somewhat unexpectedly, it was Rhosyn and Merin who had offered them the most useful information when it came to planning the attack. In retrospect, I guess I should have been less surprised. Merin had spent much of her life training with her uncle, listening to him issue orders to soldiers in the keep. Over the years, she had become well versed in his battle tactics. It was Rhosyn who had the most recent intelligence on the deployment of the sallowskin horde inside the walls, as she had escaped the previous day using the sewer tunnels that ran underneath the city. Merin's handmaiden seemed highly motivated to help us sneak into the city.

Those tunnels, we decided, would be central to our plan.

Our strategy hinged on the retaking of the southernmost gate. The problem was, there were Sallowskins crawling all over the outermost defenses of the city. Any number of them would be able to see Arik's army massing on the outside getting ready to launch an offensive. What we needed was a diversion on the *inside* of the city, one that would give the Sallowskins reason to think they were under siege in another part of the keep. While distracted, a small band would attack and retake the gate, opening it for Arik and his soldiers to come through.

Such an undertaking was difficult, needing at least three moving parts. A primary group would have to cause a distraction on the inside near the center of the city, kicking up as much of a ruckus as possible. The second group would have to retake the gate as quickly and as quietly as they could manage. The last group would be the General's, which would move the moment the gate was seized. The army would then rush from their place of concealment and enter the city just as the gate was opened.

Timing would be critical for any chance of success. Gavakyn was chosen to lead the group causing the distraction. Much to my dismay, I was assigned to him. It was determined our group would attack the marketplace. It needed to be a loud attack, offering enough of a threat to turn the gaze of the sallowskins leaders to it.

No one said anything to me directly, but I think we all understood being assigned to this group was a huge risk. Attacking the blackbloods in the middle of the marketplace was dangerous in the extreme. Because of this, the General assigned members strong enough to withstand an assault against a massive force of sallowskins for as long as they could. I was none too pleased to hear Gavakyn, Oganna and I would act as the front line, each of us wearing chain armor and holding broad shields. Banded armor might have been thicker than chain, but none of us wanted the added weight if we had to beat a hasty retreat out of there.

While our trio fought to keep the attackers at bay, Holden, Karn and Kynnda would use their magic, cutting a fiery swath into the ranks of the enemy. Arik hoped their pyrotechnics would cause enough bedlam to grab the invaders' attention. Ashten volunteered the Gray Company to add some much-appreciated firepower. Besides, if it came to fighting in the tunnels, I relished the idea of a few well-placed grenades and the occasional piece of dwarven technology hidden in just the right spot. I was thrilled to have Monchakka and Kora with us again, as I had fought with them before and knew they would stay cool under pressure.

Surprisingly, Merin insisted that she go with us. She argued that she had been sneaking out of the palace since she was five years old. Few knew the city better than she did. I was shocked that Arik agreed to this, though the princess, being the ranking member of our force, had no one to challenge her authority.

The gate group would enter the sewers with us but break off shy of the market. In an absolutely stunning move, Jax was placed in charge of that unit. He immediately chose Draega and Viir as his lieutenants along with Rhosyn who, like the princess, knew the city well. As sallowskins, our orc, troll and goblin allies would be able to move easily inside the city unchallenged. Caballa and a dozen of her Bolters were selected to accompany them, along with a crack squad of Ragers under the command of Captain Nathrak.

The last selection was a strange one, as Armon, the only dwarf to have voted against joining the sallowskins, volunteered to go. His face was a thundercloud of anger, but he said little while listening to the others prepare.

The Gate group was ordered not to engage the enemy in a long-drawn-out fight, but rather strike hard and fast, holding the gate open long enough for Arik and the rest of his army to get through. It was the General's belief that the three companies of Stonebreakers he'd brought with him would be able to push back the invaders once inside the narrow city streets. If Bolgir saw this, he'd be free to unleash his soldiers as well and, together, we could drive the sallowskins out of Lodir.

Of course, this was all conjecture, as any number of things could go wrong. The sallowskins might see our party of raiders sneaking into the sewers. They might not fall for our distraction, or the gate squad could fail in capturing their objective. Most concerning was that Bolgir would not see our attack as an opening, or worse, had been killed in the earlier fighting and Orius had taken command. All of this had been considered the night before. If things went to hell, Lorric's cavalry was going to be held at the ready. They would hold back outside the city gates. If things turned bad, they were in position to fight a rear action as the Stonebreakers and the rest of us retreated. Should things go as planned, her force would enter the city and help where they could, acting as scouts and the like.

Marching under the cover of darkness, the raiding parties, made up of more than fifty dwarves and sallowskins, reached the rusted gate that led to the sewers underneath the city. To our surprise, the hinge had been unlocked already, and we were greeted by a familiar face none of us had expected to see.

"I see you're all dressed for a party," Lucid commented, looking at Gavakyn, his face twisted in a buffoonish smile.

"Lucid," Jax said, looking at the badly dressed dwarf warily. "What are you doing here?"

"I had to check on Daisy," the unkempt dwarf replied, shaking his head as though the answer was obvious.

"You went inside?" I asked, stunned at the revelation.

"Course I did," the former mountaineer muttered in reply. "A good thing too—there were blackbloods in the way, but I chased them off."

"Damn it Lucid, now they will know we are here!" Nathrak whispered harshly.

"No," Merin said, looking at the unkempt dwarf. "He wouldn't do that, would you?"

"No," Lucid answered, mimicking Merin's voice perfectly, "he wouldn't do that, would you?"

We all stared at him wondering what to do.

Lucid threw back his head and cackled with glee. "Come on, I'll take you to Daisy!"

Turning around, Lucid bolted into the sewers with nary a glance behind him.

"By Goran, he'll get us all killed," grumbled Nathrak, taking off after him. "Let's go, all of you, before it's too late."

I followed after Merin, ducking my head, dropping down into the tunnels underneath the city.

As a dreg, I've had to stay in my share of...how best to say this— *unsavory* places. As a lad I had to sleep under any number of rusted tin roofs crammed against the wall of a side alley in Dregtown. Once I slept behind the butcher's shed, which reeked of rotting meat. My point is, I was hardly sensitive to malodorous conditions—but by the gods, that sewer was the worst smelling place I'd ever been. I'd hidden in outhouses that were more pleasant. I found myself breathing through my mouth from the get-go. Even then, the stench of empty bladders and loose bowels was nearly enough to overwhelm me. Twice I had to stop, choking back bile as the smell worsened. I could hear others behind me retching their guts out, not that I blamed them.

We walked, nearly half a mile before coming to a branch in the tunnels. Water ran more freely from the right side, which is where we saw the brightly smiling Lucid standing.

"Not far now," the unkempt dwarf said, motioning us forward. "The gate is to the right; the marketplace is to the left."

"He's right," Merin mumbled, wiping at her lips, still struggling with the smell. "This is where we split up."

"Wait until you hear our attack," Gavakyn warned Jax, firmly taking the old Bard's hand in his.

"How will we know?" asked Nathrak from next to him.

"You'll know," Holden said, giving him a grim smile.

Nathrak stared at the Mage and grunted, tossing her a solitary nod.

"Lucid, where are you going?" asked Merin.

A dark look came over his face. "I need to find the Piper, he's sure to put up a fight."

Merin glanced over at me in confusion. I shrugged, having no idea what he was talking about.

"Stay safe lad," Jax said, clapping me on the back. "Don't forget, you're not just an ordinary warrior with a sword, you're a bard."

"That's not helpful at all," I replied, raising my eyebrow.

He smiled at me and followed after the gate unit, leaving the rest of us to go to the left.

"Let's go stir up the hornet's nest," Gavakyn muttered.

"This should be fun," Holden quipped, her eyes alight with excitement.

A quarter of an hour later we were standing underneath the grate that led up into the middle of the market square. The stink of the sewer pipes had lessened to the point where it was merely bad rather than unbearable. Even before we reached the grate, we could hear the army of sallowskins stirring above us.

"By Goran I'm a fool," I heard Gavakyn mutter from his place next to me.

"What's the problem?" I heard Ashten ask from his spot in line behind us.

That's when Gavakyn's thought became apparent to me.

The grate *did* lead to the market, however, it led upward to the busiest, most open part of the square, something none of us had considered. There was no way for us to start our attack without the sallowskins seeing us climb out of the grate—even if it was possible, there was no defensive position for us to move to that was close by. Ashten was cursing softly under his breath as he realized our plight at the same moment I did.

"Dammit, we were so busy trying to get here, we didn't consider the dynamics of the square," Karn whispered from behind us. "We can't just pop up from under them—we need to know the layout of the place."

"I know the layout," said a voice from the shadows.

A young she-dwarf, no more than fourteen winters old, eased out of the darkness. Her sandy blonde hair hung in dirty strands, her long bangs covered a pair of azure eyes. She was dressed in a ragged tunic the color of soured ale. Pants, once a dull orange in color, were tattered at the bottom, caked in the dried crust of the sewer tunnels.

"Who are you?" snapped Kora, raising her rifle to eye level.

"Put that away," Ghost chided, pushing the barrel of the weapon down with her hand. "She's naught but a wee lass."

"What are you doing down here?" asked Gavakyn, looking at the darkness behind her. "Are you alone?"

"I am now," she sniffed, giving Kora a hard look.

"What's your name?" Ghost asked, her voice friendly.

The young she-dwarf glanced over at the Engineer and her bearing relaxed a fraction. "I'm Cotton, formerly of Dregtown. She turned her eyes to me and gave a faint smile. "And you're Omens, the Bard," she said, a twinkle in her eyes.

I frowned at the lass. "You know me?" I asked.

"Everyone in Dregtown knows you," she answered, with a quiet little laugh. "The males either hate you or want to be you, and the females, well…" she trailed off without completing her thought.

"Well, what?" Merin demanded from behind us, eyeing me coolly.

"It's really not impor…" I started to say before Cotton cut me off.

"Mostly they want to sleep with him," she answered happily. "A few of the males do too."

Even in the dim light of the sewers surrounded by stench, I could *feel* the rest of them staring at me in disapproval.

"I think we are getting off track here," I said, rather defensively.

"I agree," Gavakyn growled, focusing on the moment. "What can you tell us about the marketplace above?"

"I can tell you whatever you want to know…for the right price."

We all stared at her in a stunned silence.

"Why you little…" Kora began, stopping when Ghost shook her head.

"Surely you want the city liberated?" Gavakyn asked, his face hardening.

"I don't really care," Cotton replied. "Dwarves or Blackbloods, it's all the same to me."

"How can you say that?" Monchakka barked, somewhat harshly. "The dwarves are your people, the blackbloods are cold killers, bent on destruction," he glanced quickly at Karn and hesitated. "Present company excluded," he added hastily, glancing from Karn to Oganna.

"Hmmph," the goblin grunted, shaking his head.

"Why should I want the city liberated?" Cotton challenged. "So the dwarves that live in the city proper can spit on me every time I leave Dregtown? The same dwarves that turn their noses up as I beg for food on the street? The same bloody dwarves that use my body as they choose whenever they want too?"

Cotton hawked and spat on the ground. "At least with the blackbloods, I know my enemy. With the dwarves, I haven't a clue."

A harsh rasping laugh cut through the darkness and the stench.

"Finally, a Redblood I can relate too," Karn rasped.

"Look kid," Gavakyn growled, his voice strained, "we need your help, and you are going to tell us what we want to know."

"No, I'm not," she countered, her voice set. "Not until we negotiate."

It was hard to tell in the dim light, but I could imagine the legendary Storm Sorrow's face was mottled red with frustration.

"What is it that you want?" asked Merin, easing herself up to the front of our group.

Cotton stared at her, momentarily dumbfounded.

"You… you're the princess," the urchin managed to stammer out.

"Yes… how did you know?" Merin asked.

The young dwarfess grinned, glancing at me. "Just like Omens, you are one of the most…desired dwarves in Lodir."

"Desired? By whom?" the princess asked, forgetting where she was.

"Oh, by everybody!" Cotton gushed. "All the males talk about is what they'd do if they had you to themselves. Melosh, the baker's apprentice, said he'd kiss every inch of your body! Then there was Vianna, the apprentice to the seamstress down by the market, she said she'd bathe you with her tongue—and there was Jori the barrel maker's son, he once said he'd bend you over his pap's barrel and…"

"Stop right there," I heard Merin say, putting both her hands up in an effort to keep Cotton from continuing with her narrative. I was absolutely certain she was standing in the faint light of the sewers, blushing furiously. "I get the idea."

It occurred to me that the success of our entire mission here, and possibly the fate of the world, was now resting on the shoulders of this impudent young she-dwarf. I decided I should take a hand in the conversation.

"Cotton," I began, stepping next to Merin. "Do you know why we are here?"

The young urchin shrugged her shoulders with indifference.

"It's not just to liberate the city," I continued. "We also want to change things. If we can successfully drive the sallowskins out of Lodir, the princess is going to make certain that dregs like us are treated more fairly."

"I've heard that before," she sniffed, glancing at Merin. "The King has said the same, many times. It won't happen. Did you know he let the horde into the city to wipe out the dwarves of Dregtown?"

"Yes, we are aware of that," Merin answered. "The King will not rule for much longer. He has committed treason against us all."

"So? Whoever the next ruler is won't change anything," Cotton grumbled.

"That's not true," Merin argued. "There is a chance I, or my uncle Bolgir will rule. He has often argued that the dregs of Lodir deserve better than they have been given. After spending the last week with Omens, I am in wholehearted agreement. Both my uncle and I understand the importance of the clanless in Lodir. It is time for things to change."

The princess stopped and looked at me, her eyes narrowed in thought. "Omens has taught me how much we owe those without clans. A dwarf's worth should be measured by the quality of their deeds, not predetermined on whether or not they were born into the right family."

Merin paused as all of us listened to the sincerity of her words. "Omens has shown himself to be a dwarf of the highest quality. Like him, many of the clanless have modeled the same kind of character through the years. My father wrongly blamed them for many of his sorrows. Foolishly, I went along with those beliefs, ignorant to the truth. I see things more clearly now. The dwarves of Dregtown are an important part of our society. It is time the leaders of the Eight Kingdoms recognized it. I am ready to see those without clans in Lodir are given a chance at a better life."

Merin stepped closer and looked the young dwarfess directly in the eyes. "But none of that can happen without your help. If we cannot retake the city, nothing in Lodir can change. Will you help us, Cotton? Everything relies on you."

The dwarf lass blinked at Merin for a long moment, weighing her words. Finally, she looked over to me. "Did you sleep with her?"

I froze, surprised at her question. "I don't think that's relevant to the task…"

"Did you?" Cotton pressed, leaning closer to me.

I looked over at Merin who raised her eyebrow, her face hard.

"Yes," I replied, glancing at the others, "not that it's anyone's business."

I could make out the corners of Cotton's mouth curling upward in a smile. "At least you're honest," she said with a giggle.

"Omens!" hissed Ashten from behind me, his voice filled with disapproval. "Tell me you did not!"

"He did," Merin interjected, taking my hand in hers. "I care for him, and he cares for me."

The leader of the Gray Company did not look convinced. "Omens, I have known you for years. This would be the first time…"

"I'm in love with her," I blurted, shocked at my own admission.

Everyone standing nearby looked on, stunned. Everyone except Ghost, who already knew.

"You love me?" Merin asked, her voice quiet.

I saw Monchakka standing in the background. He gave me an encouraging smile. "I do," I answered, feeling my heart beating like mad inside my chest.

"I love you too," Merin said, stepping forward, taking my hands in hers.

"By *Kruk*, is this how you stumps prepare for battle?" snorted Karn in disgust. "How we have not conquered the entire southlands by now is beyond me."

The goblin looked over at Cotton who was watching Merin and me in fascination. "Go ahead and ask him, little she-stump, I can see the question lingering in your eyes."

Cotton flicked her gaze over to the goblin and nodded once. "Do you believe her?" she asked me. "Do you believe the princess thinks our deeds are more important than whether or not we are born into a clan?" Cotton continued, refocusing on our discussion. "Will she make the changes she spoke of, or is this another lie by the nobility? I trust you Omens because you are a dreg like me."

I looked at the beautiful dwarf in front of me. I could feel the steady beat of her pulse running from her hands to mine. I knew it was stupid—insane really. She was a princess, and I was a dreg, but I felt deep down in my heart I could trust her.

Turning to look at Cotton, I kept my voice even. "Yes, I would trust Merin with my life. If you help us here, she will do what she can to fulfill her promise."

Cotton pursed her lips in thought a moment before nodding curtly. "Follow me," she said, turning east, back the way we came.

We all stood there staring at one another, uncertain of what to do.

"She has nice feet," came the voice of Lucid from behind Gavakyn. "Daisy would trust her."

"You're barking mad, the lot of you," Karn grumbled, looking at Gavakyn.

The leader of our group sighed, moving to follow Cotton. "What choice do we have?" he countered, drudging after her.

"You're going to attack the Sallowskin army going off the word of this little she-stump?" the Shaman asked, his eyes wide.

"Lucid trusts her," Monchakka answered, falling in behind Gavakyn.

"The insane stump?" snapped Karn. "I saw him chewing on a tent pole last night! That's not exactly a ringing endorsement!" The goblin was left standing alone in the sewers as the rest of us filed past him. "Bunch of idiots," he grumbled as he trudged along behind us. "I should have sliced my throat open this morning instead of risking this venture."

"This is the place," Rhosyn whispered, pointing at the opening above them.

Nathrak looked uneasily at the orc Mauler next to him. The two were standing in the sewer tunnel looking up into the privy. These were the gatehouse barracks, a place that usually housed dozens of dwarven soldiers. It was currently filled with orcs and goblins, most of whom were asleep.

"You sure you can do this?" Nathrak asked, still skeptical of the orc's loyalties.

Draega snorted but said nothing.

"Assuage your fears, Captain," Viir whispered from his place next to him. "Draega knows what she is doing."

The captain of the Ragers watched as the Mauler, more deftly than he would have suspected, climbed up through the hole that served as a privy at the end of the building. Before he could blink, the orc had moved out from the jakes and into the main chamber. Nathrak waited with Caballa and Viir in silence for several minutes as they listened for Draega's return.

"You really think she'll kill her own kind?" Nathrak whispered to Caballa.

The leader of the Bolters snorted softly. "The four races of the horde live violent lives. They kill one another for status all the time."

"Even so," Nathrak continued, undeterred, "she's an orc."

"If this goes bad, we are going to be swimming in blackbloods," Caballa warned.

"Orcs live harder than most," Viir cut in. "But they have an honor of their own. Draega is as good as her word."

"Coming from another sallowskin, that is hardly reassuring," murmured Armon from behind them.

They heard footsteps approaching from overhead and ceased their discussion. Nathrak quietly slid his sword from his scabbard, unable to see who was approaching.

"Come on, quickly now," came the soft whisper of Draega's deep voice from above.

"The deed is done?" asked Nathrak skeptically, as he climbed through the filth covered hole.

"See for yourself," the orc grunted, nodding behind her.

As the rest of the gate company climbed through, Nathrak examined more than a score of goblins and orcs that lay on the cold stone of the barracks floor. Each had been killed, their lives snuffed out by the Mauler as they slept.

"Believe me now?" asked Viir, who had walked over to join him.

"That was well done," Nathrak admitted, his voice flat. "But we are not there yet."

"I remain unconvinced," Armon rumbled, his deep tone like a distant thunder.

"We can bicker among ourselves later," Jax growled from behind them, his voice filled with authority. "Nathrak has the right of it. The deed was well done. We still have the gatehouse to take, and we need the Mauler and the Seer to gain access. Enough talk, priest. We have work to do."

"Ware yourself Jax—you are not in command," Armon hissed, narrowing his eyes.

"Yes, he is," Nathrak cut in. "The General put Jax and Gavakyn in charge of each raid force, remember?"

"Arik has lost his mind," the priest muttered looking at the Bard in disgust. "Gavakyn isn't even in the army—and the Bard is…"

"The most experienced dwarf among us," Nathrak said, his words biting. "No one here, me included, outranks him."

"He's only just joined our force," Armon argued, gesturing to Jax. "He has no idea how to deploy our troops, nor does he have any experience in leading our forces."

A spark of light flashed from behind them as Reece scraped his knife along the edge of his sword. In that moment, those at the front of the column could see the hint of anger growing in the Rager's dark eyes.

"Beggin' your pardon Jax, but if this priestly sod says one more thing against ye, I'll cut his ruddy balls off," Reese spat, his voice low and dangerous.

There was a momentary silence before Jax responded. "That won't be necessary," he said with a wave. "Better that he got it off his chest before the attack."

"As you say Cap'n," came Reece's rasping voice, now hidden in the darkness.

Armon glanced at the Rager, his face wrinkled in anger. "I hope you don't fall in battle today," he spat through clenched teeth. "As I'm the only healer *Captain* Jax brought."

They could hear Reece give a snort of laughter from the shadow where he stood. "Worry bout your own arse curmudgeon, else I'll chop it off."

The tension between the two was thick enough to where one could cut it with a knife. A deep chuckle broke the silence as they all looked at its source.

"What's so funny?" Armon asked, looking at Draega.

"You are," the Mauler answered, her voice melodic. "All this time I thought you redbloods were an implacable enemy, united as one. But you bicker as much as the orcs—and for more foolish reasons."

Draega moved to the head of the group, beckoning for Viir to join her. "Come Seer, time is short. Gavakyn will attack soon, and we must be in position."

"The Mauler speaks sense," Viir said mildly. "Let's go."

"Move out," Jax ordered, turning to follow the Sallowskins.

The rest of the raiding company shuffled along, creeping quietly in the darkness. Unseen were the eyes of Armon, whose glare was fixed on the Sallowskins leading them.

Had anyone chosen to look they might have noticed another pressing detail.

Their guide, Rhosyn, was gone.

"This is a hell of a way to start an attack," I heard Ghost mutter to Gavakyn, as she stared out into the marketplace in the faint light of the dawn. The group was standing inside the wall of a tiny alcove that sold some kind of sweetmeats judging by the smell emanating from the wooden stand.

"I know," Gavakyn agreed, seeing hundreds of sallowskin warriors milling about, shaking sleep from their eyes.

"I always eat fresh caught trout before going to market," Lucid said, a silly smile on his face. "I could go get some if you like?"

"That...won't be necessary," I told him, with a little shake of my head. "Best you stay behind us until we need you."

"A fine idea," he whispered in a conspiratorial tone, squeezing behind Gavakyn, so close his fingers rubbed up against the big warrior's back. Turning, he made his way past Ashten's Engineers humming a little tune.

"We should hit soon," Oganna suggested, returning our attention to the task at hand. "They aren't awake enough yet to be aware of what's about to happen."

"By the Trine there are enough of them," muttered Merin, looking out the entrance.

"If you get in trouble you can hide in the tunnels to the east of here," chimed Cotton with a giggle. "Plenty of places to get lost in there."

"Thank you, lass, for helping us," Merin said, tearing her eyes away from the sallowskins outside. "I will not forget this."

"You are welcome," she said simply, glancing at me. "Tell me princess—is he as good as they say?"

I could hear Oganna's snort of laughter as I suppressed my urge to strangle Cotton.

Merin leaned in close to Cotton and wrinkled her nose playfully. "I'll tell you after," she promised. "Now go, stay safe."

"Alright," she said, sounding a bit disappointed. Quickly she made off back the way we had come.

"Yours is a strange race," Karn muttered, watching her leave.

"We have other concerns at the moment," growled Gavakyn, motioning for Oganna and me to move closer. "The three of us will slip out into the main square as swiftly and as quietly as we can. Make a shield wall fifty feet from where the street meets the square. We will hold for as long as we can. Casters," he continued, looking at the trio of Karn, Kynnda and Holden. "You will unleash almighty bedlam. I want it as loud as possible. Afterwards, fall back.

Intersperse yourselves between Ashten and his Company. Prince Raine, you direct your people as you see fit. Make it loud and costly. Jax and his group will need every second. When things start to turn, we fall back into the sewers and fight a steady retreat from there. I want to hit them as hard as we can, but with as little risk as necessary."

"You realize we are about to attack a sallowskin horde," Monchakka said dubiously. "It's somewhat risky."

"I know lad," Gavakyn admitted grimly. "But they will be focused on me." He reached around for his sword. "They have been obsessed with getting this back for the last five…"

His voice trailed off.

"What the hell?" he asked, looking over his shoulder. "Where is it?"

"Where's what?" Ghost asked, peering at him curiously.

"The Blood Claw!" he snapped, his voice panicked.

My eyes jumped to his back. There, hanging high on his broad shoulders was his homemade scabbard of fine stitched leather.

It lay hollow and empty.

"That makes no sense," I said, looking at the ground at his feet. "I just saw it on your back."

"When?" Gavakyn demanded, his eyes everywhere.

"Only a minute ago, right when Lucid…" I trailed off, my heart turning to frost. I replayed the event in my head, seeing what had occurred. "He took it," I mumbled to myself.

"What?" demanded Oganna. "Speak up!"

Wincing at her tone, I stared at Gavakyn. "Lucid—he placed his hands right on the hilt when he made his way past you. I had no idea he'd take the blade."

Storm Sorrow, usually as unshakable as a mountain, let out a string of curses, hot enough to fry the morning air. "That crazy, twisted, son-of-bitch!" he hissed in fury. "What the hell was he thinking? We need to find him, immediately! By the Trine, where has he run off to?"

At that moment, from inside the marketplace, we heard the high-pitched call of a rooster sound out the dawning of the new day. Looking out through the crack in the doorway, my heart froze. There was Lucid, standing atop an overturned peddler's cart, crowing like the cock of the walk.

"Oh shit," Monchakka hissed, giving a voice to everyone's thoughts.

"He's madder than a pox-ridden, goblin whore," Karn wheezed in absolute shock.

"Wake up, you yellow bellied bastards!" Lucid roared, his voice booming through the market square. "I hear you piss colored varmints are in search of this!" he howled at the top of his lungs. Punching his fist over his head, Lucid brandished a blade of red steel.

The Blood Claw.

Scores of sallowskins nearby could not help but take notice. I think they were more surprised to see a dwarf in their midst than the weapon he carried.

"If you want it, you'll have to catch me," Lucid screamed in delight. Turning on his heels, the mad dwarf leapt from the cart and sped off as fast as he could, heading down the street that led right past where we were hiding.

Howling in rage, scores of sallowskins tore after him, screaming for dwarven blood. As Lucid huffed his way past, I heard him cry out in excitement.

"I forgot to get the trout!"

With a flick of his wrist, the deranged Mountaineer cast the Blood Claw toward us. It skipped along the cobblestone road with a metallic scraping sound that was lost in the uproar of the sallowskin battle cries. It continued on its path, slipping through the hidden doorway and skidded to a halt at Gavakyn's feet. At that moment, hundreds of Sallies came tearing around the corner in hot pursuit of the dwarf who had shown them their prize.

Inside a dozen heartbeats, the orcs and goblins that had been in the market square had sped past our place of concealment, without a single glance behind them.

"Well, that cleared some of them out," I heard Monchakka say, his eyes wide.

"By Uthel, it did," Oganna agreed, peering at Gavakyn. "We should be able to hold the marketplace a bit longer now that so many of its forces left."

Gavakyn blinked in surprise and shook his head in bewilderment. "He could have told me what the hell he was planning," he muttered to himself. "Alright," he continued, once again cool and ready. "Let's go!"

We slipped out the hidden doorway and set up our defenses. Even with Lucid's hairbrained scheme, time was not on our side, and I knew we'd be in for a furious fight.

"Attack!" roared Gavakyn, as battle exploded inside the market square.

Chapter 23: The Attack

"I think it has begun," hissed Draega, peering out the doorway from her place inside the barracks. "I heard the sound of sallowskin screams coming from the center of the city."

"Gavakyn said we would know for certain," Nathrak warned, doubt in his voice. "I heard little that would signify anything out of the..."

His voice faded at the sound of several explosions, followed closely by cries of distant pain to the north. The thrum of feet moving on the battlements above told them that the sallowskins on the wall had heard it too.

"Viir, with me," Draega commanded. "The rest of you, wait here." Without bothering to see if anyone had followed her instructions, the orc Mauler ducked out the door and started climbing the ramp up to the top of the wall.

"Keep out of sight," Viir hissed, taking Draega's place at the doorway. "Don't make a sound."

Hearts in their throats, the group in the barracks listened as Draega's heavy footsteps came to a halt above them.

"Who's in command here?" she bellowed, her voice carrying instant authority.

"I am," came a deep, guttural response.

"What is your name, Chain?" Draega asked sharply.

"Ravor, of the Daur Sun," the orc's voice snapped. "Who are you?"

"Bardan-Sur, Mauler of the White Sands," Draega lied.

There was a pause and then a harsh laugh. "I didn't know the Orcs of the White Sands had joined with us," came a response. "What do you want?"

"The market in the center of the city has come under attack," Draega answered. "I have been ordered to pull your unit to help suppress the uprising."

"Piss off," the Chain snapped, his voice carrying down to them. "My orders are to hold the gate until told otherwise."

"I am here to relieve you," Draega continued. "You are needed…"

Another explosion rocked the marketplace, the sound cutting Draega's words short.

"What the hell is happening?" Ravor asked, his voice more hesitant than before.

"By Kruk," Draega cursed. "I don't have time to explain everything! The stumps have counter-attacked—they are trying to break out of the western postern. We need more soldiers to pin them in the marketplace."

"But what about the gate…"

"Shemak's balls, there is no time to argue about this!" Draega thundered. "Take two of your squads to the marketplace and I will take command of those still asleep! We'll keep an eye on things here until your return. Those are my orders—unless you want to take up the matter with Darksoul?"

There was another pause as the Chain mulled it over. "What if I refuse?" he asked, his voice becoming hard.

There came a sound of a meaty smack followed by a grunt, and the crunch of bones breaking. This was followed by the metallic rattling of chain links rubbing together, one next to another. A heartbeat later, the body of a now dead Chain rolled down the ramp and came to a halt at the doorway in front of Viir.

"Now, which one of you sorry scalawags is second in command?" they heard Draega bellow in challenge.

"I will lead the squads to the marketplace," came a new voice, brutish, but more cowed than the last.

"Do so with haste," barked Draega, her voice carrying over the rattle of a new chain passing over her shoulder. "Else Darksoul will hear of this insubordination."

"Let's go," ordered the brutish voice, leading two squads down the stairs. Running past Viir, two score sallowskins descended from atop the battlements, taking care not to step on the sprawling body of their previous commander.

"Come on," hissed Viir, the troll beckoning the dwarves inside the barracks to climb up the ramp leading to the battlements. The troll grabbed the shoulders of the dead orc, dragging it inside the sleeping quarters.

"Damn fine work," Caballa muttered, more than impressed.

"Don't celebrate yet," Jax warned softly. "Nathrak, get your squad on that gate, now. Leave me Reece, and two others. Caballa, send the signal to Arik. After that, position your soldiers along the battlements and get ready to defend. At two miles out, it will take at least a quarter turn of the hourglass for the General's army to get here. We need to hold the gate until they do. Reece, you and your fellow Ragers stay inside. Make preparations in case we get company. You know what to do. Armon, find a spot on the battlements that is sheltered. We will use that as a place to work with anyone who becomes wounded.

"How long till the ruse is up?" the priest asked, his eyes turning north toward the marketplace.

A flash of green fire burst out of the marketplace, shining brightly in the last moments before dawn. Cries of pain echoed throughout the city's streets.

"I have no idea," Jax answered, "if we're lucky, a few minutes, no more than ten."

"If we're unlucky?" Armon grunted.

"Then we'll need to be ready," the Bard answered simply.

Behind them, Caballa fired a torch, which flared to life with a bright yellow flame. Quickly she dipped it under the battlement wall, waving it to the south where Arik and his army were sure to see it, even at this distance.

More than a minute passed as each member of the raiding party got into a defensive position while listening intently for any sound of approach from below. Another explosion rocked the market square, followed shortly by a plume of black smoke billowing upward.

"I see the General," hissed Caballa, her voice carrying to the rest. "The Stonebreakers are on the way!"

Glancing at Jax, the Bolter Captain shot the Bard a tight smile. "We may pull this off yet."

In the streets to the east of their position, there was a stirring.

"Movement from inside the city," Armon reported, his face grim. "Looks like you spoke too soon Captain. Our luck won't hold."

"Viir, that's your cue," Jax commanded, squatting down behind the walls atop the battlements.

"I know," the troll said with a nod. "Draega, be ready to join me from inside the barracks."

"Aye," the Mauler nodded, racing down the steps and ducking out of sight.

"Get here fast, General," whispered Jax, looking to the south.

A company of sallowskins, easily numbering in the hundreds, came running into the courtyard below. "Stay out of sight and be ready to defend," Jax hissed, nodding to Nathrak. "How many of your soldiers are needed to pull open the gate?"

"Four at least," he answered. "The damn Sallies jammed it up good—almost like they knew we'd try something like this."

"Stay out of sight for now," Jax responded. "As soon as you see the General is close, get it open."

"Aye Captain."

Jax heard more screaming in the distance and prayed Gavakyn and his group were still alive.

"It's on you now General," he whispered, thinking of Arik.

"There it is!" shouted one of Lorric's scouts, his keen eyes seeing the torch waving from the battlements. "There's the signal!"

"Stonebreakers, advance!" Arik bellowed, running at the head of his battalion.

"Bazad arum!" the army echoed, moving forward.

Like a rolling wave of the ocean, more than three hundred armored dwarves began to jog at a steady pace from their position behind the hill, some two miles away.

"Steady," Arik shouted, knowing his soldiers might be tempted to push their speed and break ranks. The key was to arrive quickly and together, without being too winded to fight effectively. All his troops had trained for this kind of battle many times. He knew they could be counted on.

Flanking both sides of his companies rode Lorric's cavalry. The lighter armored scouts were riding tough, short-legged ponies. There were twenty of them ranging ahead on their swift moving steeds, each equipped with shortbows, arrows and an assortment of light melee weapons.

Behind them came her regular cavalry. Sixty dwarves, mounted on specially trained war boars, each bred for their size and strength. Both mounts and riders sported intricate chain armor, with each of the latter carrying a javelin and pistol, along with a range of other weapons used for hand-to-hand combat.

Bringing up the rear was Lorric herself. She was surrounded by twenty riders of the heavy cavalry. Each rode upon the back of a powerful mountain ram, barded in armor of sturdy iron plate. In their hands they carried short, sturdy lances, each tipped with steel. Longswords and battle-axes adorned their sides as they readied themselves for battle.

One hundred members of the king's cavalry, their task, to keep an eye out for any force that might intercept Arik's before the Stonebreakers could arrive at the gate.

The army ran for the first quarter of a mile without incident, their pace steady and measured. The gate was still closed, and they were too far away to see if Jax's raiders had come under attack. Off to the west, Arik saw something else come into view, something he knew could disrupt their plan.

"General," warned his lieutenant, a powerful dwarf with short, dark hair named Skurn.

"I see them," Arik nodded, knowing Lorric would have to deal with this new threat.

Racing toward his army was a force of enemy cavalry numbering three times as many riders, racing across the plain to cut them off. Arik glanced to his left, seeing Lorric and her hundred veer east to intercept the sallowskin riders.

"May the gods be with you," he whispered, knowing the odds were against her. Steeling himself, Arik turned his attention back to the gate.

"There looks to be three hundred, at least," shouted a young rider named Mraz from in front of the captain.

"Closer to four," Lorric shouted back, knowing her force would be overwhelmed in a head-to-head fight, outnumbered as they were.

Calculating quickly, she waved her hand toward the company's horn blower to issue the signal for her lighter units to fall back behind the heavy cavalry.

Two blasts on his brass horn and the other units slowed, drifting professionally into place behind her squad.

Lorric narrowed her gaze as the sallowskin troops came closer into view.

"Shit," she cursed, seeing their leader.

Riding at the front of the horde's cavalry was a huge Ogre, sitting atop a massive cave bear.

"Talon Rider," she murmured to herself, tightening the grip on her lance.

She kicked at the sides of her mount increasing the battle ram's pace. "When the time comes, leave the Ogre to me!" she roared, the wind causing the hair to fly wildly from under her helm. "For Rahm and the eight kingdoms!" she shouted, charging forward.

"Dol Gol Rahm!" echoed the hundred, racing behind her.

"Hold the damn line!" Gavakyn hollered at Oganna and I, his voice growing hoarse.

"I'm trying," the she-orc answered, sweat glistening from her forehead. "It's tough to focus when our magickers are insane!"

"Try having the Engineers on your ass!" I shouted back at her, batting away a stray arrow.

We had started our attack only minutes ago, but I felt like I'd been in the marketplace for hours. Holden had struck first, casting a sizzling bolt of lightning aimed at a pocket of casters she'd spotted in the distance. Four of them had been killed, knocked from their feet by the magical blast of energy. More importantly, the attack had been loud, cutting through the air, giving off a sound like thunder that reverberated through the market.

Not to be outdone, Karn melded his power with that of his apprentice. The Shaman cast a second spell, a green wall of fire that burst outward from his staff, screaming over the head of Gavakyn. The flame passed close enough to where it actually singed the top of Gavakyn's helmet. The fire rolled forward, striking a mass of sallowskins who were still trying to see what the commotion was about.

Needless to say, in those first seconds there was mass confusion among the ranks of our foes. After a few minutes, enough time had passed, where things were slowly getting organized.

That's when the Gray Company went to work.

Rifles belched hot lead, raining it upon the enemy ranks. Grenades, both incendiary and shrapnel, burst outward, engulfing the sallowskins' forces, burning into their flesh, ripping it to shreds.

All the while, Oganna, Gavakyn and I lashed out at any attacker who got close enough, killing them as quickly as we could.

"Ghost, what do you see?" barked Gavakyn, his eyes scanning the marketplace from behind his shield.

"Nothing yet," she yelled, firing another shot. "I'm guessing it won't be long. We are making enough noise to wake the dead!"

"Lieutenant!" shouted Kora, glancing behind us. "We've got company!"

"How many?" Ghost snarled in question.

"A score at least!" Kora answered, reloading her rifle.

"Omens, go!" Gavakyn ordered, ducking behind his shield as an arrow shattered against it.

Without a word, I moved away from his flank and ran to the rear of our group, preparing to defend the narrow alleyway.

"Not yet," a tiny dwarf named Ratchet said, holding up his hand.

"They're…almost on us," I warned, breathing heavily from exertion.

"I need them closer," Ratchet muttered, his eyes focused on a tiny metal box in his hands.

"Closer?" I stammered, looking up at the rapidly approaching group. Hefting my shield, I knocked aside a heavy throwing axe an orc had flung in our direction.

"Whatever you're going to do, you better do it fast!" I yelled, catching a stone tipped spear that followed immediately after the axe.

I heard a succession of tiny clicks, as Ratchet turned the dial on his box. Without warning, no fewer than a half dozen explosions went off from concussive mines hidden along the street where Ratchet and his squad had placed them. Sallowskin bodies were torn apart by the blast. Two, an orc Ravager and a goblin Stick were heaved forward and slammed into my shield, knocking me backward. Luckily, my shield was in position, else I might have been bowled over by their gunpowder propelled bodies. When the dust cleared, there was dirt and soot all along the sides of the buildings, along with spattering of black blood splashed everywhere.

"How about a word of warning next time?" I rumbled, surveying the damage.

"I thought the walls would collapse as well," Ratchet mused to the dwarfess next to him, ignoring me completely.

"Looks like a few didn't go off," she answered, twisting her head to the side.

"I think it did the trick," I muttered, shaking my head.

"Omens!" I heard Gavakyn shout. "Is it clear?"

"For now!" I shouted back, seeing nothing moving on the rubble-filled street.

"Get your ass back up here, we've got hundreds more pouring in from the south!"

Cursing under my breath, I raced back to the front, as the report of rifle fire increased in tempo.

"A dozen rounds left," I heard Kora mutter to Monchakka.

"I've got more than twenty," he answered, ruefully. "When you are out, I'll give you mine and go melee."

"Fair enough," she answered, wiping the sweat from her brow.

"Fire storm is ready Cap'n," I heard the sour faced Bad say as I ran past him. He was holding a circular glass bottle, filled with a crystal clear liquid.

"Hold it for now," Ashten replied, lighting a small wooden brand from a flickering clump of fire smoldering on the side of the street.

"Wait till we get a cluster that is close," he continued, smiling in satisfaction as the brand flared to life. Let's be smart with our resources."

I don't know how they can manage to be so calm in the middle of a battle, I thought to myself as I rejoined Gavakyn and Oganna.

"Get ready," I heard Oganna say, her voice grim. "They brought in a pair of Juggernauts."

From out of the entryway to the south strode two massive trolls, each fully armored in heavy iron breastplate.

"That's your target," I heard Ashten say to Bad, his voice cool.

Three heartbeats passed when I heard the grizzled Grenadier grunt with effort. He heaved his container directly at the trolls. The bottle landed a pace or two in front of them, shattering on impact. Immediately after, Ashten tossed the flaming brand he'd been holding. It landed in the middle of Bad's concoction, igniting the clear liquid at the exact moment the trolls stepped into the area.

With a massive *WHOOM*, the liquid ignited, flaring up from underneath the two Juggernauts in a plume of black smoke. The first let out a cry of pain as his hide boots caught on fire. Desperately, the Juggernaut flung himself forward, blind and burning. The other staggered through the fire struggling to breath, engulfed as it was in oily black fumes.

Oganna shot forward, her sword a blur. A moment later, the first troll was down, clutching at a terrible wound in his neck. The second Gavakyn killed with a quick thrust to the inside of the troll's thigh, which severed the artery. Warm, black blood spilled down the Juggernaut's leg. A moment later, the troll crashed to the ground, quickly bleeding out.

"Back in formation," Gavakyn panted, falling into position once more.

"We cannot keep this up," Oganna shouted, slipping in line next to him.

"It hasn't been long enough," Gavakyn shouted, looking for the next attack. Turning his head, he barked a new order out over his shoulder.

"Holden, get up here. It's time for you to cast with me."

"Finally," Holden shouted, moving forward, standing behind Gavakyn's shield.

"They are charging, en masse," I shouted, trying to keep the quiver from my voice.

"Go on my command," Gavakyn said to Holden, ignoring my words.

"This is going to be close," Oganna screamed, licking her lips, glancing at the pair of spellcasters next to her.

"Now!" Gavakyn shouted, dropping his shield to the side and pointing the Blood Claw at the approaching horde.

"*Thoe Nothnel!*" they roared in unison.

Bolts of blue lightning shot from their hands, ricocheting from one sallowskin to another. Scores of the enemy dropped in their tracks, electrocuted by the magical outburst.

"By the Trine, he's gotten better," Ashten muttered, looking at the wall of devastation the pair had caused.

"It is a lull only," Monchakka said from behind them, surveying the scene. "More are coming in."

"We have to fall back," Kora said, raising her rifle to her shoulder once again.

"Not yet," Karn rasped, moving forward. "Kynnda," he barked, looking at his apprentice. "It's our turn."

"Ring of fire?" she questioned, raising her eyebrow.

Karn gave her a death's head grin. "*Rain* of fire," he corrected, raising his staff.

The Gate group remained hidden, crouched down behind the corners and crenulations of the battlements as best they could. On the street below, a company of sallowskins led by an Orc Ravager moved in front of Viir. The orc was tall, the same height as Draega, though not as broad of shoulder. His dark hair had been shaved on the sides and cut into a long mohawk. He had a silver ring through his nose and held intelligent eyes that studied Draega with suspicion.

"Where's Ravor?" he asked, eyeing the Seer skeptically.

"He and his squad were moved to the marketplace," the troll answered.

The orc curled his lip in a sneer. "On whose authority?"

"Mine," growled Draega, exiting from the barracks doorway.

The Ravager did not look convinced. Instead, he moved forward, looking Draega straight in the eye. "I don't know you, Mauler," he spat, looking at her suspiciously. "Where do you hail from?"

Draega moved close, aggressively butting her head against his in challenge. "I don't answer to you, Ravager. I take my orders from Darksoul, no other."

The Ravager furrowed his brow. "Interesting," he growled, his eyes darting toward the empty battlements.

"What's that?" Draega asked, knowing he suspected something was wrong.

"I just came from Darksoul," the male orc said quietly. "He told me to reinforce Ravor's company and kill anyone who stood in the way."

Draega snorted with a hard laugh. "There must be some mistake."

"I agree," the Ravager hissed, drawing his sword. "They are imposters!" he roared to his troops. "Kill her and the Seer!"

Without hesitation the company of sallowskins drew their weapons and surged forward.

Viir wasted no time. With one hand he grabbed hold of Draega's collar and yanked her back toward him. With the other, he raised his staff and brought it down sharply on the heavy stones of the courtyard.

"*Ollinor Martog!*" he shouted, letting go of Draega, pointing his hand at the force of sallowskins in front of him.

Upon the release of his magic, a rumbling shook the ground beneath them. The solid stone in front of the Seer rose in undulation. Like a wave crashing into shore, the stones rose up sharply, knocking every enemy in the courtyard from their feet.

"Attack!" Viir thundered, backing up to the landing that led to the barracks.

Bounding from the entrance of the sleeping quarters, Reece and his squad rushed past Jax and fell upon the prone sallowskins in front of them before they had a chance to recover. A score of the enemy never rose from where they had fallen.

The Ravager with the mohawk was the first to his feet. Picking up his sword, the orc attacked with a vicious savagery, locking blades with Reece.

Atop the battlements, a dozen Bolters rose from their places of hiding and shot iron bolts at the confused enemy. Dozens of the attackers went down, killed by the withering assault from above.

Bounding down the stairs came all but four of Nathrak's remaining Ragers, each intent on killing as many sallowskins as possible.

"Form on me," Draega cried out, drawing her sword and defending the rampart on the right side of the gate. Working as one, the Mauler and the Ragers ground their way through the ranks of Sallowskins in front of them. Draega was careful never to overextend herself as Gavakyn had taught.

Atop the battlements, Captain Caballa chanced a quick look behind her. In the distance was Arik and his battalion, only a mile away now, maybe less.

"Be ready on that gate!" she shouted, looking at the four burly Ragers standing nearby. "Opening it at the right time is everything!"

"On your command, Captain," said one of the Ragers. She was young, with a full head of dark red hair. Her voice was calm, almost bored.

Caballa snatched a second bolt from her quiver and set it to string. Smoothly she placed a foot in the cocking stirrup and grunted as she pulled the bolt into place. Raising the crossbow to eye level, she let out her breath, aimed and let fly. She saw her bolt fly true, knocking a goblin Archer from its feet. She grinned with momentary satisfaction, but her lips froze, just short of a smile. From her vantage point on the battlements, she could see a larger force of sallowskins only seconds behind the one already in the courtyard.

"Jax!" she screamed in warning. "There are more on the way!"

"How many?" the bard panted from his position next to the Ragers in the courtyard below.

"Hundreds!"

"Fall back," he commanded Nathrak and his squad.

In a flash, his Ragers disengaged the enemy, leaving the sallowskins in the courtyard dying or in retreat. All save one.

Reece broke off his attack on the Mohawk haired Ravager, respect clear in his eyes. "Who are you?" the dwarf asked, knowing this was no ordinary warrior.

"Karthac, Scourge of the North," the orc spat, still spoiling for a fight.

"I'll see you again," Reece promised, retreating up into the battlements.

"You can count on it," the Ravager barked, glancing at what little remained of his force.

Atop the wall, Caballa chanced another look out on the planes. Arik was closer now, only three, maybe four minutes away. Looking back to the courtyard, a full division of the sallowskins were pouring in.

"Focus on those archers and casters," she ordered, putting another bolt to string.

Off to her left on the far side of the wall, Caballa caught her first glimpse of a new problem. There were hundreds of blackblooded cavalry making straight for the gate. She saw Captain Lorric's force drawing close and knew they were doomed.

"We must hold the gate!" Caballa screamed, launching a new attack. She saw her bolt slam into the chest of an orc Witchdoctor and quickly loaded another.

Three minutes, she thought to herself. *We must hold for the next three minutes.* There was a cry from next to her as one of the Bolters, a heavy-set dwarf with pale green eyes named Ionus, was struck with an arrow in the shoulder.

"Armon!" she screamed, seeing the wound was serious.

"I'm here," the priest called out, moving over in a flash.

Caballa chanced a quick look over the crenulation and loosed a bolt at another target. Her shot was rushed, and it ricocheted off the stone in front of the Shaman she'd been aiming at.

"Bollocks!" she cursed, grabbing at another shaft. A second of her Bolters fell back, struck in the throat by a stone tipped arrow.

"Is it time?" the red haired Rager asked, her voice still bored.

Caballa looked down to the plain and calculated the distance. A bit more than a quarter mile.

"Yes," she said, wiping sweat from her brow. "Open the gate!"

The quartet of Ragers swarmed into action. All four grabbed onto the thick ropes they had rigged to the gate doors, a pair on each side. They began to pull with all their strength. Slowly, ever so slowly, the gate began to open.

Looking back down upon the plain, the general and his forces did not appear any closer.

"*Dammit Arik*," Caballa thought, "*run!*"

"Is it time sir?" puffed Skurn, his face red with effort. Arik could see the heavy wooden doors of the southern gate begin to swing open. Looking past that, he saw the portcullis was still down.

"Maintain our current pace!" he shouted, knowing they had to hit the opening at the right speed. They could not afford to get there too soon and lose their momentum.

"The portcullis is still down, General," fumed Skurn, glancing at Arik.

"They will raise it," Arik replied, sounding far more confident than he felt. At this distance, he could see there was a flurry of action atop the battlements. Jax's forces were split on both sides of the gate, trying to fight on two fronts. Off to the west, he caught a glimpse of Lorric's cavalry closing the distance to the enemy riders. He knew they had to push now if there was any chance of saving his people.

"Battalion," he bellowed in his deep, stentorian voice. "Double time!"

With a roar, the three hundred Stonebreakers shot forward, keeping a tight formation while racing toward the gate.

Timing was everything, Lorric knew. Too soon, and her company would be out of range. Too late, and they would suffer atrocious casualties. The cavalry commander was close enough now where she could see the majority of the enemy's forces. Most of the orcs rode upon the backs of the most common horde mounts; bristle backed hyenas that were savage and fierce. There were some that rode on the backs of the huge wild boars that roamed the northlands, but those were few and far between. The goblins shrieked their war cries from the backs of *hoargasi*, giant, rat-like creatures that scoured the Jagged Lands in hunting packs. She made out a handful of trolls mounted on *varanos*, large lizard-like creatures that were bred in the swamps they called home.

She knew her force was the swifter, but the enemies' mounts held more stamina.

"Ready!" she shouted, raising her hand high in the air as her company bore down on the enemy. The gap between them closed rapidly as she analyzed the distance.

"Now!" she called, pointing sharply to both the left and right.

Swiftly, her forces divided in two, one breaking to each side of the enemy. The heavy cavalry was in the front, leading away from the blackblood forces. The light cavalry was next, firing a volley of arrows from their short bows. A few of the more skilled riders actually spun fully around on their saddles to fire a second arrow at the sallowskins. They had to face away from where their mounts were running, trusting the animals to keep their footing among the chaos. Adroitly, the dwarves of the light cavalry spun back around in their saddles and continued right, riding back to their rally point.

Several of the enemy cavalry fell out of their saddles, wounded or slain by the arrows. Of those who managed to survive falling from their mounts, a handful were trampled by their own forces, ground into the dirt underneath the weight of churning hooves and claws.

The last riders of the dwarven company were the medium cavalry. They were close enough to the sallowskin riders that they could smell the sweat running off the flanks of the enemy mounts. The dwarves let loose their javelins, the sharp metal weapons slamming into the sallowskins with deadly force. Dozens of blackbloods fell, many sporting mortal wounds.

Lorric looked back over her shoulder, praying she had measured correctly.

The dwarves of these last squads were the most vulnerable in this attack. They would be closest to the enemy and were the most likely to be killed in the charge. Lorric saw that the riders that had veered left were a hair further from the oncoming horde. While those dwarves had done less damage, that squad had escaped without casualties. Those who had gone right were not as fortunate.

Three of her medium cavalry strayed too close to the horde. One managed to break through to safety, though he was now galloping west instead of east, the opposite of the rest of Lorric's group. There was a pack of blackbloods on his tail and it was almost certain they would ride him down.

The last two riders managed to throw their javelins with great effect, but were caught by a trio of snarling *hoargasi*. The rat-like predators swarmed the pair, hamstringing the boars that gave out a deep squeal of fear. Knocked from their feet, the dwarves were swallowed up by a rush of sallowskins, never to ride again.

Lorric clenched her teeth in a mixture of grief and rage.

"Reform for a second pass," she bellowed, coming together once again with her entire company. She knew they could only afford one more attack. They were dangerously close to the General's forces and most of her mounts would be nearing exhaustion, galloping as they had been for the last few minutes.

The ground behind them was littered with the enemy dead. She calculated at least thirty of the blackbloods were down. In the center, she saw the massive cave bear rushing forward, his lust for blood readily apparent. The Talon Rider urged his mount onward, knowing if they could get close enough, the dwarves were done.

"On my lead," Lorric hissed, shouting out to her horn bearer. A long blast of the bugle summoned her troops to her, as they galloped forward again.

Kynnda stood behind Oganna and focused her power as Karn had instructed. The dwarven shaman could feel the goblin tap into her magical strength until he was filled with all he could hold.

"Kac ur degaan!" Karn roared, pointing his staff skyward.

A yellowish mist shot from the end of his mahogany staff and formed a cloud thirty feet above the sallowskins in the center of the market. With a flick of his wrist, Karn unleashed his spell and thumb sized droplets of fire began to fall from the cloudlike apparition he had summoned. The orcs and goblins caught underneath the cloud began to scream in pain, running blindly for cover. The magical assault did something the other attacks had not. It cleared the immediate area of the enemy.

"That should buy us a bit of time," Karn said, his face grim.

"That's a hell of a spell," muttered Gavakyn, mopping sweat from his face taking a much-needed breather. "I've not seen it before."

"That's because it is one of my own make," Karn replied, breathing heavily, stepping away from Gavakyn.

"How long will it last?" Omens asked, watching with fascination.

"A minute, maybe two," Karn grunted in answer. "Now, let's plan our retreat..."

The goblin stopped and spun around, his eyes looking at the expanse of the marketplace in surprise.

The magical mist he had summoned dissipated right in front of their eyes.

"What devilry is this?" Oganna asked, her white eyes trying to pierce the ranks of the enemy.

"Kruk," the shaman swore. "Darksoul is nearby."

"How do you know?" Gavakyn demanded, fingering the hilt of Blood Claw.

"He's brought the *Shekun*," the goblin answered, his eyes narrowing dangerously.

"The what?" I asked in confusion.

"The five most powerful casters in the northlands," Oganna answered. "Mordun is sure to be with them."

Karn's eyes flattened in hate, as he searched the marketplace for his rival.

"Get everyone into the alley behind us," the goblin ordered. "If the *Shekun* are here, I will have to shield us the best I can."

"No one Shaman can handle all five," Oganna said, concern thick in her voice.

"Not alone I can't," Karn agreed, looking to Kynnda. "I need your strength lass, if we have any chance of victory. I will need you to meld with me once more."

The wrinkled goblin looked at Gavakyn, determination stamped on his face. "Kynnda and I will defend as long as we can. The moment our defenses fall, we need to leave. Do you understand?"

"I do," Gavakyn answered, raising the Blood Claw once more.

"Is there nothing we can do?" asked Holden, listening intently.

"Kill as many of the *Shekun* as possible," Karn barked, giving a sharp laugh. "If you see one, hit it with everything you've got."

"What about Mordun?" Oganna asked, surveying the landscape.

"Leave him to me," Karn snarled, moving to the edge of the alleyway, dragging Kynnda along with him. The yellow-skinned goblin sat next to his apprentice, closed his eyes and entered a trance-like state.

"You heard him," Gavakyn said gruffly, eyeing Ashten. "Fall back to the alley and keep the blackbloods off our backs."

"What about you?" Merin asked, from her place near the marketplace stall.

"The same as before," I said to her. "We hold the line for as long as we can. Arik has to be close to the gate by now. We just need to give him time to win his way through."

"Here they come again," Ghost warned, setting up against the wall of a merchant stand on the perimeter of the marketplace. "We've got Sallies coming in from behind us too."

"I'm on it," I said, dropping back into the alley once again.

"I wish we had our turrets," I heard Ashten mutter to Ghost.

"We'll give them plenty to think about," she answered, priming her rifle once again.

"Don't shoot me," I snapped sarcastically as I moved as far down the alley as I dared. Dozens of Sallies were heading towards us, stepping more cautiously than before, seeing the bodies of so many of their comrades lying dead in the rubble. I noted the western wall was barely standing after Ratchet's earlier detonations.

"Slide right," I heard a voice say as a figure moved beside me, interrupting my musings.

Glancing over, I saw Monchakka holding a thick round shield made from heavy wood one of the Chains had dropped earlier in the battle.

"What are you doing?" I asked, surprised at his temerity.

"I'll hold the line with you," he answered, gripping an iron mace he had picked up.

Monchakka gave me a rueful grin. "I'm nearly out of ammo anyway. Best if I help you back here."

"Just like in the mountains with that Shadow, ehh?" I asked, giving him a grim smile.

The sound of a rifle exploded behind us. I could hear the high-pitched whine of lead zip past my ear. The bullet slammed into the closest sallowskin, a goblin Stick who had been preparing to throw its two-pronged spear at us.

"At least we aren't alone this time," Monchakka answered, focusing on the blackbloods in front of us.

Realizing there were no more traps left in the alley, the horde surged forward.

Monchakka and I rose to meet them.

"*Ool ei hon lait,*" Armon murmured, sending his healing magic through the Bolter who had been struck by a crude spear in the chest.

The dwarf's eyes fluttered open, and he sat up, clutching gingerly at the wound above his heart.

"If I had time, I'd heal you properly," the priest said, helping the Bolter to his feet. "The ministrations of Goran will hold you together for now."

"What of them?" the Bolter asked, looking at three of his fellows sprawled out on the battlements.

"Those I could not save," Armon answered in frustration. "Go, extract a heavy toll. The General draws close."

"I will," the Bolter growled in determination. He stood and took two steps away from Armon when a goblin arrow slammed into his throat, killing him instantly.

"Son-of-a-*bitch*!" Armon roared in frustration, kneeling next to the dwarf he had just healed, knowing there was nothing he could do.

Quickly the war priest stood, craning his neck around the backside of a crenulation, looking at the battle raging beneath him. Draega and Jax were doing their best to hold the line on the far side of the gate, with Reece and a trio of Ragers fighting alongside the big Mauler and Bard. So far, they were holding their own defending the narrow ramp, but the priest knew it was only a matter of time.

The greater concern was the other ramp closer to the barracks. Nathrak and his Ragers were fighting like mad, but none of them was equipped for defense the way Draega was. They had been forced to fall back to the steps, and two of his Ragers were down, laying in pools of blood at the bottom of the landing. The only thing keeping them from being overrun was the presence of the Seer.

Armon hated the sallowskins, he always had. They had killed so many dwarves in his lifetime, he knew he could never truly trust any of them. However, the sight of the great troll using his magic to defend the Ragers as best he could gave the priest reason to pause. Should Viir fall, the mission would fail. As a fellow caster, Armon could see the troll was tiring. Soon the blackbloods would overwhelm Nathrak and his Ragers. If that happened, they would be free to stop the quartet pulling at the gate in their efforts to get it open.

Armon knew Arik needed another minute, maybe more to reach the entrance and swarm the courtyard.

What the gate force required was a defensive warrior to hold the line.

Armon snorted into his beard and gave a swift prayer to his gods. "May the Trine be with me," he whispered, knowing what he must do.

Standing up, Armon rushed across the battlements, arrows flying past him, several clanging off his shield. He tore past the Bolters on the wall and ran until he was only a step behind the Ragers near the barracks.

"*Shakka Kor!*" he screamed, leaping like a dwarven God of War, landing directly in the front line of blackbloods battling Nathrak and his squad. When he landed, a magical force of white energy pulsed from him, knocking down a dozen sallowskins where he landed.

"Form a fighting wedge on me!" Armon shouted, slamming his hammer downward, crushing the skull of a Goblin Stick. "Viir, get your ass atop the battlements and protect my people!"

The troll, stunned by what he had just seen, knew the sacrifice the priest was making for him. Taking a deep breath, the Seer raced up the ramp to the top of the battlements and cast a spell of warding on the nine Bolters who remained.

The incessant volley of arrows that had pinned them down began to strike an invisible barrier. The rain of goblin shafts, so deadly a moment ago, dropped harmlessly to the ramp below. A flash of green fire burst from deep in the ranks of sallowskins as a shaman cast a spell. Viir narrowed his gaze as a cloud of acid began to fly toward the Bolters on the wall. Viir focused his will and thwarted that attack as well, dispelling the shaman's magical attack. Free from danger for the moment, Caballa shot and ended the threat as the shaman dropped to the ground, an iron bolt through its chest.

Viir staggered in exhaustion, needing to steady himself against the crenellations he was standing next to. Glancing outside the walls, the troll could see Arik had drawn near. Less than two hundred paces away, Viir knew they were close to success.

The Seer moved his gaze to the Ragers straining for all they were worth against the ropes that would open the gate. The huge wooden doors creaked to a halt, and the quartet dropped the ropes they had been pulling. The gate was now open, and Viir began to feel hope swell in his chest.

"The portcullis," a female with blazing red hair panted, knowing they were not done yet.

The four dwarves grabbed onto a large wheel that was attached to a pulley system that would raise the heavy iron grating. Red faced and weary, the quartet pushed as hard as they could.

The portcullis groaned but did not budge.

"*Move Viir*," the troll thought to himself. "*You have the strength for this.*"

Stumbling toward the gatehouse, the Seer extended his hand.

"*Hahkim bakam*," the troll whispered.

Slowly, the portcullis began to inch upward.

His focus elsewhere, his spell of warding faded. Arrows began to whistle past him and the Bolters once again.

Still, he kept his focus.

"Push!" screamed the female Rager, knowing this was their only chance. The portcullis continued to rise, more than a foot off the ground now.

An arrow struck Viir in the shoulder, but he gave no mind to the numbing pain that flashed down his arm.

"Almost there!" the Rager shouted, her voice shrill.

"BAZAD ARUM!" The battle cry of the Stonebreakers resounded from outside the gate, only yards away.

A second arrow sliced past the Seer's cheek, leaving a burning wound along the side of the troll's face.

Implacable, the Seer dug deep into his magic reserves, moving his hand upward as beads of perspiration dripped from his neck. He felt something strike his side, but ignored it, focused as he was on the task at hand.

With a sudden lurch, the wheel gave a full turn and slammed into place. The portcullis was now raised, a good eight feet off the ground. At that exact moment, Arik's force swarmed through the gate and rolled over every sallowskin in their path.

"We did it," the female Rager panted, leaning against the wheel in exhaustion. She looked up and smiled at Viir, who was gazing at them all, triumph in his eyes.

"Thank you for your…" her words trailed off as the smile froze on her lips.

The Seer looked down and saw the black feathered shaft of a goblin archer sticking out from under his armpit, perpendicular to his lungs.

Viir looked back at the Ragers, his eyes filled with confusion. The last thing he saw was the dwarven female take a hesitant step toward him before he collapsed on top of the battlements.

When Arik saw the portcullis begin to rise, he lowered the visor of his helmet and roared at the top of his lungs. "Stonebreakers, charge!"

"BAZAD ARRUM!" more than three hundred voices thundered in reply.

A split second before they arrived, the portcullis lurched a foot or more above them. With General Ironhenge leading the way, the three companies of Stonebreakers flooded the entryway, cutting down the unsuspecting Sallowskins like a scythe reaping wheat.

A few of the braver blackbloods tried to stand and fight but were crushed under the weight of the dwarven heavy infantry. Those who could, fled, sprinting north along the main avenues that led to the city market. Others tried to retreat the way they had come, but many were run down until Arik called for a halt.

"Nathrak," Arik barked, seeing the Captain of the Ragers leaning on his sword. "Well done lad. I see the blackbloods didn't make it easy."

"They never do, sir," Nathrak answered, still breathing heavily from exertion.

"Tell me," the General said, his voice quiet, glancing at Draega. "How did they fare?"

Nathrak wiped a trickle of blood from his forearm. "Admirably General," he answered, honestly. "Truth be told, we'd not have held without them. Draega and Viir, both performed as well as any in our army, better even."

The Captain of the Ragers nodded toward Draega. "The Mauler still stands, the Seer...I don't know."

"We need a priest up here!" came the frantic shout from the battlements. "Our troll ally is down!"

A momentary silence fell on the dwarven army, as those words hung in the air.

"I'm on my way," Armon volunteered, wiping black blood from his hammer. "That Seer saved us all, it's time I returned the favor."

It took all of Arik's willpower not to blanch in front of his soldiers. Armon, who hated the blackbloods more than any dwarf he'd ever known, was volunteering to save one.

"General!" came a second call from atop the battlements, breaking Arik's thoughts. It was Captain Cabella.

"What is it, Captain?" Arik shouted back.

"It's Captain Lorric, sir. She's in trouble."

Arik cursed under his breath, knowing he could do nothing to help. "Do what you can to assist her," he called out.

Caballa stared at him a long moment, before nodding in understanding. Turning, the bolter captain began issuing fresh orders to her remaining soldiers.

"I will stay with them," came a voice from near the gate. Arik looked over to see the young priestess, Aishe, start moving up the ramp.

Arik nodded his consent and turned his gaze to Jax, who was tending to a wounded Rager.

"You did well, bard," the general said, walking over to him.

"We did our best," Jax replied, looking up from the Rager who was bleeding from an arrow in the thigh. "Your orders sir?" the bard asked, his face tired, but determined.

"I'll take the Stonebreakers and the rest of the healers. We will push toward the inner keep, see if we can entice Bolgir to join us."

Jax furrowed his brow in concern. "What of Gavakyn? He and his squad still fight in the market."

Arik sighed. "I know—but without the forces of Lodir, we cannot push the Sallowskins from the city. We need Bolgir's army. The only way to do that is to free them from the keep."

"We're with you sir," Nathrak said, walking up from behind them, gripping his sword.

"No Captain, you and your squad have done enough. I need you to stay here, keep a lookout and let me know if the sallowskins attack us from behind. That is your place in the battle now."

Nathrak gave his commander a crisp salute. "Yes, General," he said, looking at his Ragers.

Arik spun around and addressed his army. "Eight ranks abreast!" he thundered. "We move to the keep to free the army of Lodir. We fight or we die!"

"BAZAD ARRUM!" thundered the Stonebreakers.

Arik and his three companies marched east down the main avenue that led into the heart of the city keep.

Draega moved over alongside Reece and Jax who were drinking deeply from their waterskins.

"You are a hell of a fighter," the Rager said, offering his skin to the Mauler.

"Thank you," she answered in her deep voice, taking the proffered skin in hands coated with the black blood of her kin. "I would say the same of you, holding your own against Karthac. He's one of Darksoul's doughtiest brawlers."

"Reece," they heard Nathrak call from across the courtyard. "I want you to head to the market with Ukori. Keep me posted on what is happening. You know the drill."

"Yes sir," Reece answered, taking back his water skin. The pair of Ragers left, moving as swiftly and silently as they could.

Nathrak glanced at Jax, a half apology on his face. "Gads, I'm sorry Jax. I'm just used to giving the orders."

The bard gave a small laugh. "No need. This is your company, you know their skills better than I. Do as you see fit."

Nathrak gave Jax a smile along with a half salute and turned around. He stopped as a call came from behind them.

"Lower the portcullis!" came a shout from high above them. Caballa was screaming at the Ragers still standing atop the gate house above.

"Damn," Nathrak swore, running up the ramp. "Now what?"

Draega was about to follow when Jax grabbed her shoulder. He pointed at the portcullis, which was shaking in place, but would not move from its position. Try as they might, the dwarves above could not get the grating to budge. Without hesitation, the orc Mauler ran to the gate and peered outside.

"By the balls of Kruk," she whispered in shock. The orc immediately ran back inside and grabbed onto the bottom of the portcullis, throwing her weight and strength into closing the gate.

Less than one hundred yards away the two armies of cavalry were galloping like the wind, each seeking to gain entrance to the keep.

"It's jammed," Jax yelled, his eyes looking through the gateway. "Find a way to fix it!" he continued, racing outside, his eyes gleaming in determination.

Draega's eyes darted behind her, frantically searching the courtyard. There! She saw a spiked hammer laying in the lifeless hand of one of her kin. Racing over to it, she heard a thunderous bellow, filled with magical power, followed by shrieks of pain and fear from outside the gate.

Sprinting back, the Mauler swung her hammer as hard as she could. The chain that had been jammed snapped, coming loose in an instant. The portcullis, fashioned from thousands of pounds of wrought iron, began to descend quickly.

"Not yet!" Draega bellowed, catching the gate on her shoulders, struggling to keep it open. "Get the cavalry inside!"

The dwarves atop the gatehouse, seeing the approach of the dwarven riders, threw themselves against the wheel above, straining to keep the portcullis open long enough to save their people.

"Get inside, now!" thundered Jax, waving at his kinfolk.

Draega could feel the weight of the portcullis dropping. Without the help of the pulleys, she and the four dwarves above were all that stood between saving the dwarven cavalry and leaving them to the sallowskin horde.

Lorric's second pass through the hordes' cavalry had been more damaging, but also more costly, especially to her heavy mounts. Six of her twenty rams and their riders had fallen, though they had taken their share of blackbloods with them. Lorric had repeated the earlier flanking tactic with one difference. This time she and the heavy cavalry ran right through the middle of the blackblood force. Lorric had slain three of the enemy. One, a troll lizard rider, had been gutted through the chest with her lance. Two others, a goblin mounted on a *hoargasi* and an orc riding a warthog, had been run over by her more powerful battle ram. When she turned around, Lorric saw only a baker's dozen of her allies still with her.

Scores of blackbloods lay dead, their bodies riddled with both arrows and hot lead, fired at close range from her cavalry's pistols.

In the midst of the horde was chaos. Enough to where Lorric and what was left of her heavy cavalry were able to make a successful dash back to their rally point. A quick glance told her nearly thirty of her company had fallen. A steep price she knew, but one they all had been willing to pay. Both armies came to a halt, gathering in the confusing aftermath of the attack. The two groups stood less than three hundred yards from one another. The ogre, still astride his cave bear, stepped to the forefront, the bloody-toothed creature roaring out to the dwarves in an obvious challenge.

Narrowing her eyes, Lorric's moved her mount to the front of the company. "Once I make my charge, ride hard for the gate," she commanded, her eyes never leaving the Talon Rider.

"Captain, don't do it," cautioned her second, a lean female with blue-black hair named Charr.

"I have no choice," Lorric answered. "The keep offers the only safety we will find. Out here, they will ride us down."

"Lorric, I saw the ogre kill two of our kin on the last pass," warned another member of her squad. He was a young, steady eyed dwarf mounted on a ram of black and gray. "He is not just a brute. That ogre is cunning and swift."

"You make a run for the gate the moment I reach half the distance to the horde," Lorric ordered, ignoring his warning.

"The enemy is closer to the gate than we are," Charr argued, seeing she would not convince the captain.

"Your mounts are swifter over the short distance," Lorric reasoned, adjusting the shield on her off hand. "You best pray the enemy is too busy watching me to notice your movement."

She clapped her metal visor down over her face with a steely snap. "Don't worry about me Lieutenant; you get the company to safety."

Without another word, Lorric dug her heels into the sides of her mount and took off.

Across the way, the cave bear reared on its back legs and shambled forward, faster than any beast that size should move. The black-eyed ogre raised his own lance in challenge as he and his mount bore down on the advancing dwarf.

Lorric knew the Talon Rider had the advantage of reach on her. Her enemy's mount was bigger, stronger and far more deadly. If she got too close to its claws or fangs the fight would be over before it began. However, the dwarven mount was quicker than the bear and more nimble at close quarters.

She needed to take full advantage.

The distance between the two combatants closed. Lorric was halfway and knew her company would be breaking for the gate. At fifty yards, she gave her mount a verbal command.

"*Tak-un!*" she shouted in ancient dwarven, her voice carrying above the sound of the hooves racing on the ground.

Lorric felt a subtle shift in the ram's stride.

"*Roc-Thay!*" she shouted again, now only twenty yards away.

She could feel the ram gather its strength.

The Talon Rider had lowered his lance, knowing this joust could end in only one way.

"*Bay-nah!*" Lorric screamed, dropping the point of her lance parallel to the ground at the last possible moment.

Lorric's mount bunched the muscles in its legs and leaped, a full eight feet into the air. Timing it perfectly, the ogre's weapon passed less than an inch underneath the soaring form of the battle ram. Completely airborne, Lorric drove her lance dead center into the chest of the Talon Rider, driving the huge ogre off his mount. The jolt of hitting a foe of that size nearly caused Lorric and her mount to tumble to the ground. Landing heavily, the two skidded to a halt. Quickly the ram righted itself and continued on its run, aiming right for the rest of the horde. Having lost her lance, Lorric drew her saber and raced toward the first enemy she could find. It was an orc, so engrossed in the duel, he did not see his own danger until it was too late. Riding past, Lorric swung her blade, slicing the creature's head from its shoulders. Knowing she could never defeat so many, the dwarven captain guided her mount toward the walls of the castle, hoping her company had obeyed her last order.

Looking back, she saw more than thirty of the enemy trailing after her, howling for blood. In the distance, she could make out her company, riding hard for the gate.

The sallowskins, now recovered from their shock, saw the dwarves making for safety and sprang forward to cut them off. The dwarves were now ahead of the horde, but their mounts were tiring. They had been ridden at a gallop through two attacks over the last quarter of an hour. Such tactics leached the stamina from their steeds, and many had not had sufficient time to recover.

Fear of failure touched Lorric for the first time, knowing her company was in danger of being overtaken. She noticed movement along the top of the battlements in front of her. It was Caballa and what was left of her squad.

Inspiration gripped Lorric at the sight of her friend, and she decided upon a desperate plan. Turning her mount, Lorric made for the gate, hoping the Bolters hadn't used all their shafts. Riding hard, she and her pursuers drew within range.

"Don't let me down Caballa," she thought, seeing the sallowskin cavalry had nearly caught up to hers. As she had hoped, the Bolters atop the walls loosed a round of iron shafts, striking a handful of the blackbloods racing behind her.

While the quarrels did little in the way of damage, it forced the sallowskins to steer away from the walls to try and avoid this new plight.

Seeing how close the horde's cavalry was to her own, Lorric knew she had to act now. Tugging on the reins, her mount veered sharply to the right. In doing so, the dwarven captain cut in front of the riders of the horde pursuing her company, narrowly avoiding what would have been a bone-jarring collision.

The blackbloods trailing behind her were not so lucky. So focused on capturing Lorric and avoiding the Bolters on the wall, they too cut hard to the right, blindly pursuing their prey. Before they knew what had happened, Lorric's pursuers slammed sideways, crashing into the riders of the larger force that was chasing the rest of the dwarven cavalry. The chattering squeals of *hoargasi* and high-pitched screams of hyenas echoed off the walls of the city as the smaller group folded under the head of the larger. Such a collision caused the riders directly in the front to veer off to the sides or simply crash into the mass of bodies that appeared unexpectedly in front of them. Dozens of the horde were pitched from their mounts, some trampled to death only feet away from the gate. Still atop the battlements, the Bolters fired at will, wreaking havoc among what was left of the sallowskin cavalry.

Lorric turned sharply to the right, watching as the pandemonium unfolded. Only a handful of yards from the gate now, she could see a dwarf, Jax, standing near the entrance, beckoning to her cavalry to get inside. Cursing, Lorric realized her momentum had carried her too far away from the entrance. Even with the confusion, she knew her force was outnumbered here, and she would not make it to the gate. Helplessly she watched as scores of sallowskins recovered and shot toward the gateway.

"*Dek'kar!*" Jax bellowed, blasting the sallowskins with a thunderous bellow.

Seeing how close the blackbloods were, those of the light cavalry who were close fit arrows to string and let fly. Four more of the sallowskins fell, adding to the confusion.

"Get inside, now!" roared Jax, waving frantically at the dwarven riders.

Seeing her company enter the city, thanks in part to a herculean effort by Draega keeping the portcullis up, was all Lorric needed. Knowing there was no more she could do, the captain of the cavalry circled back to the scene of her joust. Along the way, she sheathed her sword and swept up her lance, still impaled through the chest of the eight-foot-tall ogre. The cave bear had strayed, ambling south, away from the city. If she had time, Lorric would have hunted it down and killed it. Knowing the city was not yet won, she stayed her hand and continued on her path around the mass of screaming sallowskins, her mount bounding at a canter along the city wall.

Her enemies had to have come out from some place nearby, most likely a postern, well hidden, but close.

Lorric was determined to find out where.

Chapter 24: The Captain of the Gray Company

The smell of naphtha and smoke was thick in my nostrils. I could feel the weight of the shield on my arm dragging me down. I don't know how long we had fought against the Sallies, all I knew was falling meant death. To his credit, Monchakka held his own next to me. His shield had taken a beating and I could see at least two arrows and a hatchet embedded in the wood. Still, we'd managed to hold the blackbloods off so far. Behind us, I could hear the Engineers frantically loading their rifles, firing and dropping back in an organized fashion, never at ease or at rest. Initially several grenades had been tossed over our heads, extracting a heavy toll in the narrow quarters of the alleyway. Such projectiles had ceased coming, as the Engineers had depleted their supply.

The blackbloods did not give up. On they came, their fallen quickly replaced by fresh warriors of every caste. I stabbed out with my machete, taking the Chain in front of me down with a quick thrust to his unarmored legs. You would think they would have figured out to wear some kind of leg protection in all the years they'd been fighting us, but few ever did. I sliced his artery and warm blood spilled down the inside of his thigh. Showing no mercy, an orc Ravager kicked his comrade aside and renewed the attack, pushing me backward a few inches. A heartbeat later, a black iron bolt slammed into his eye, evidence Merin was still very much in the fight.

Monchakka and I had been pushed back a good twenty feet from where we had begun our defense. Even with the support of the Gray Company, neither of us were true front line warriors. Soon we would be forced to retreat, unable to hold the square long enough for Arik to come to our aid.

"You're not just a sword," I heard Jax's voice say. "You're a bard."

A wild idea came to me, one that might buy us some time.

"Monchakka!" I called, knowing I would need him. "I'm going to step back for a few seconds. You'll have to hold the line alone." I blocked a clumsy swipe of a goblin Fang aside and missed on my counter as the creature skipped backward out of harm's way.

"I'll do my best!" he shouted back, swinging his mace wildly, where it clanged off a Chains shield.

"He'll not be alone!" shouted a voice from behind us.

Ashten stepped forward and fired his pistols, killing both the orc and the goblin in front of us. "Go!" he shouted, shouldering his way past me, sweeping up a broken sallowskin shield.

The deaths of the two blackbloods gave us only a moment's pause, but it was enough to let me back away to relative safety.

"Alright Jax," I whispered to myself, letting my shield drop to the ground. "Let's see if I learned this properly." From around my neck, I took out the amplification crystal and held it in front of my face. Inhaling deeply several times, I prepared my voice for what was to come.

Glancing behind him, Gavakyn saw Karn and his dwarven apprentice enter into some kind of trance. Knowing a thing or two about magic, he suspected the pair could not be disrupted. To do so would break their concentration and doom them all. He glanced at Oganna who gave him a wry look and snorted in humor.

"You better live through this," she growled, with the light of mirth in her eyes. "I'm not scouring the southlands for another dwarf to give a damn about. You're too much trouble, the lot of you."

Gavakyn gave her a fierce smile and clamped his shield down next to hers, ready to defend once again.

A harsh cry came from the hundreds of sallowskins in front of them. Rows of orcs and goblins parted ranks as five casters stepped forward.

Two were goblins, a male and a female, each dressed in trappings similar to those worn by Karn. They were Shamans of the Basalt Moon, a particularly fierce tribe of goblins living on the northern borders of the Jagged Lands.

To their right stood a troll, tall like Viir, but far more savage looking.

"That's a Totem," Oganna hissed, her eyes narrowing in hate. "Similar to Shamans, but more steeped in nature's spirits."

"Dangerous?" Gavakyn asked.

"I've seen one create a storm that could tear down an ancient roanwood tree," she answered, fingering her machete.

On the left of the Shamans was an Ogress, dressed in animal hide and leather skins. In her hand, she held a jagged spear, tipped with obsidian.

"By the fires of hell," Oganna whispered, her eyes growing wide.

"What, in the name of the gods, is that?" Holden asked, her voice fearful for the first time.

"That's an Ogre Mage," Oganna answered, blinking in surprise. "I didn't think any would crawl out of the safety of their mountains."

She turned and flashed Holden with a quick look. "Ware her magic dwarf, she will be powerful."

Stepping into the middle came the final caster. A yellow eyed orc dressed in a bear skin cape. On its head it wore a helm fashioned from the skull of an ox. A black jade circlet jutted from the top of the orc's staff, which emanated with a dull green light.

"Morag," Oganna snarled, crouching low, waiting for his attack.

"Shaman?" Gavakyn asked.

"Witch Doctor," she corrected, eyeing them all warily.

"I don't see Darksoul anywhere," Gavakyn muttered, searching the ranks in front of them.

"He's out there," Oganna responded, knowing the leader of the horde was close.

Morag stepped forward, glaring at the dwarves tucked into the alley in front of him. "Why do you hide, traitor?" he roared, his voice magically amplified, enough where it filled the marketplace. "To think, the great Karn would betray his own kind."

Karn gave no response.

"He's too clever to expend his magic bothering with you," Oganna snarled back, her voice calm, despite the danger.

The Witch Doctor glanced at Oganna, contempt clear on his face. "Yet another turncoat, one who has forsaken her people to fight alongside the same dwarf who killed her brother."

Oganna snorted and spat in his direction. "You know nothing of our plight," she fired back. "Stand down, else you, and the rest of the horde will die here today."

In answer, Morag leveled his staff and shouted a single word. "*Shaz!*"

A green bolt of fire, smoke trailing behind it, shot forward, heading directly for Oganna's chest.

"Sorcerer!" I heard Ghost yell, her eyes searching the alley.

"Hurry Omens!" Monchakka screamed, knowing a single bolt of lightning from an orc Sorcerer would be enough to kill us all.

Inhaling one last breath, I focused my voice.

"Brak'dur!"

I didn't aim my bellow at the sallowskins in the alley, though several of them fell to their knees from the sheer force of the sound. Instead, I aimed it at the lower part of the western wall that had been weakened by Ratchet's earlier explosions. The stone and mortar, already brittle, shattered from the power of my magic and the wall toppled, crushing several of the sallowskins in the alley. The weight of the wall was strong enough to where the one on the opposite side collapsed as well, effectively blocking the way between us and the blackbloods further down the alley. There were a few sallowskins on our side of the debris, now cut off from their support. We made quick work of them, the last falling to a harsh blow from Monchakka's mace.

Ghost looked at me and shook her head. "That was good thinking Bard. It should buy us some time."

"Well done," Ashten echoed, tossing me a weary nod.

Turning, he looked at Monchakka, who was laboring with exhaustion. "Proud of you boy," the Captain of the Gray Company said, clapping the younger dwarf on the shoulder.

"Let's get back to…"

Ashten stopped, seeing movement on the rubble behind them.

The orc Sorcerer had climbed atop what was left of the wall and pointed its hand at Monchakka.

"Move!" Ashten shouted, grabbing the younger dwarf protectively, shielding the Engineer with his own body.

"Kora!" Ghost screamed, desperately loading her own rifle.

The young female Engineer raised her weapon at the same time Merin loosed a quarrel at the Sorcerer.

It seemed to me that time slowed in that moment.

The orc did not hesitate.

"*Arduk ro Vayel*" it screamed, unleashing its spell.

Five steel shards, each several inches in length, shot from the Sorcerer's hands, whistling through the air. All five struck Ashten, each making a wet sound upon impact. At the same time, Merin's bolt slammed into the orc's throat and Kora's twin shot split the orc's temple. The Sorcerer fell back, tumbling down the backside of the rubble, dead.

Ashten gasped once, loudly in Monchakka's ear, his eyes wide in surprise. The Captain of the Gray Company sagged forward, and the young dwarf caught him. Gently, Monchakka eased him to the ground.

"Ashten!" Monchakka shouted, removing his leather helm.

"Keep fighting lad," Ashten gasped, blood bubbling from his lips. "The battle's not won." He reached up with his hand and touched the young dwarf's cheek. A peaceful smile appeared across his face. "Remember me, my boy, it was an…honor to know you."

He coughed once, blood staining his lips and lay very still.

Ashten Raine, leader of the Gray Company, was dead.

The small knot of dwarves did not move, the suddenness of his death shocking them into silence.

The quiet was broken by the sound of metal scraping along stone.

I glanced down. On the ground, skidding to a stop at my feet, was the Blood Claw, somehow no longer in Gavakyn's hands.

Shocked again, I looked up. Our leader, Gavakyn, was sprawled out on the cobblestone of the marketplace trying to clear his head from some unseen attack.

This was a double blow. Of all the dwarves among us, we had just lost our two finest leaders.

"Omens!" came a call, hollow and filled with despair.

It was Oganna, entrenched in an all-out fight for her life against the biggest, most deadly orc warrior I'd ever seen.

Darksoul.

Without thinking, I leaned down and picked up the Blood Claw, feeling a jolt of power run though my arm.

Behind me, I heard Ghost choking back tears, pleading with Monchakka. "We will mourn him later, for now, we must continue the fight."

In her words, I found my purpose.

Running forward, I charged toward the orc commander, rage lending my tired body strength.

Morag's bolt of fire exploded in front of Oganna, striking an invisible barrier not two feet away from her. The Witch Doctor narrowed his eyes in hate, staring balefully at the alley behind Gavakyn. "You can't resist us all!" the Witch Doctor shouted.

Looking at his four companions, Morag screamed his orders. "Destroy them!"

Each caster pointed hands and weapons at Gavakyn and Oganna, unleashing their magic.

"Thurinmar ashturat!"

"Drear garlun!"

"Utor en graad!"

"Cor du thal!"

Four attacks, each different from the others, came shooting at the defenders. The magic raced across the space between the two groups inside a length of a heartbeat. All four were deflected by the magical barrier that Karn had constructed in front of Gavakyn and Oganna.

"Again," Morag shouted, his anger rising.

"Holden!" hissed Gavakyn, hoping she could respond in kind.

That was all the prompting the Mage needed.

Moving with purpose, Holden strode between her defenders and extended her hand toward the *Shekun.*

"Nel daan!" she shouted, shooting a blue bolt of lightning towards the sallowskin casters. Taken by surprise, Morag was able to partially deflect the attack, saving himself and the goblins. The Totem was struck by a glancing blow and fell to one knee, fighting to stay upright.

The Ogre, deep in the throes of her own spell, released a blast of fire right as the lighting struck. The mage's body shook with a jolt of electrical energy before falling backward, toppling to the ground, senseless or dead.

Morag was the first to recover and responded in the blink of an eye. Before Holden could retreat to cover, the orc cast another spell.

"Aluur Harth!" he screamed.

A black hand made of a shadowy mist shot forward. It dissipated a fraction as it struck Karn's magical shield. The Shaman, however, was tiring. Enough of the spectral hand got through to reach into Holden's chest and grasp at her heart.

"Ohhh!" she cried out, shuddering in pain. Twitching sharply, the Mage collapsed on the blood slick cobblestone of the marketplace. While alive, her breathing was hoarse and shallow.

"Our magic has been depleted," croaked Karn, his voice drooping with exhaustion.

"Get back inside the water pipes!" Gavakyn ordered, gathering his strength. "You've done enough."

The dwarven leader dropped his shield slightly and pointed a fist filled with red steel at the four remaining casters.

"*Ryute Osyn!*" he bellowed, unleashing a spell of his own.

Enhanced by the Blood Claw, a wave of power surged forth, smashing into the four remaining members of the *Shekun*. Both goblins went flying, knocked backward like pods of dust in the wind. The troll, too, was knocked from his feet. Rolling away, it smashed with a bone jarring crash into a stone building that served as the community privy in the market. Black blood seeped from a cracked skull, slowly pooling outward from the dead troll.

Only Morag kept his feet, though he was hard pressed to do so under the strength of such an attack. The Witch Doctor cursed at Gavakyn and retreated further back into the marketplace.

Before Gavakyn could enjoy an iota of success, he was struck hard in the chest by a kick delivered with incredible power.

Darksoul.

The dwarven warrior grunted in pain, falling hard to the ground, the Blood Claw flying from his grip. It hit the cobblestone with a sharp clang and skidded into the alley behind them.

Oganna saved Gavakyn's life, as she desperately swung her machete at their attacker, forcing the most feared orc in the horde to focus on her.

"Traitor," the big orc hissed, his red eyes blazing in anger. "You've sold your soul for this stump?"

"Do not test me *Kajin*," she panted, with a confidence she did not feel. "You have never bested me."

The powerful orc sneered at her in contempt, his face twisted in rage. "Much has changed since you left the Northlands, Oganna," he snarled. "Your time has passed."

As he bit off the end of his sentence, Darksoul attacked. He was bigger, stronger and faster than Oganna. Only her years of experience saved her from his initial onslaught. Had she been fresher, she may have made a fight of it. Tired and wounded as she was, Oganna knew she was in trouble.

"Omens!" she called out, her voice shrill with desperation.

"The stumps won't save you!" Darksoul snarled, pressing his attack. Like a great hunting cat of the northern crags, he swarmed his opponent, overwhelming her in moments. She felt a blow land on her elbow, followed quickly by a knee to the stomach that knocked the wind from her lungs. A third strike smashed against her face, knocking her to the ground. Lying on the flat of her back, Oganna knew her time had come.

"Kill them all," Darksoul ordered a squad of Ravagers behind him. "Let no stump escape from Lodir alive!"

Two of the orcs launched themselves at Omens, who fought like mad to win his way to Oganna's side.

"Time to die," Darksoul hissed, raising his sword over his head. Like a thunderbolt from the clouds he struck, driving his sword toward Oganna's heart.

An iron cast tomahawk blocked his strike at the last possible moment as a foot covered in sewer muck kicked outward, driving the orc back.

"You've a little dimple on your right cheek when you yell," Lucid remarked, as though they were calmly strolling down a sunny lane at mid-morning.

Darksoul's face turned black as his cheeks flushed with rage. With a snarl he attacked, his serrated blade moving like a viper.

Lucid, however, was up to the task, blocking every blow aimed at him. The orc halted his offensive, his eyes wide in bewilderment.

"Who are you?" Darksoul asked.

"That's not the question that should be asking, Piper," Lucid answered. "The real question is, who... are... you?"

A pistol blast from behind them caused the orc to glance over his shoulder. The Ravagers fighting Omens were down, one bleeding from a gash across his neck, the other had blood pumping from a hole in his chest made by the point-blank shot of a pistol.

His chest heaving in pain and exhaustion, Omens tossed the Blood Claw to his right where it was caught by Gavakyn. The older dwarf's eyes were burning with fury as they came to rest on the foremost warrior in the Sallowskin horde.

"Time to die, blackblood," he spat, his voice dripping with hate. He tucked his pistol back into his belt and drew his six bladed mace. "Let's see if the *great* Raegar can handle me one-on-one, when I'm not distracted casting spells."

Darksoul spat to the side and raised his sword in challenge. In his offhand, he drew a long hunting knife.

"My horde will raze this city to the ground," he promised, glancing at his advancing ranks. "I'll start with you, Storm Sorrow, while my kin flay what's left of your allies."

From behind Darksoul strode a pair of massive trolls—Barkskins. The heaviest infantry in the troll ranks. Scrambling from behind them were hundreds of warriors of the horde, each ready to rend the dwarves limb from limb. In the distance thousands more waited in the streets and alleys on the north side of Lodir, anxious to push forward.

Darksoul shot forward, his sword a blur.

The Blood Claw rose to meet it, the two weapons clanging together, showering both combatants in sparks.

I watched in awe, not feeling the wounds in my left leg or ribs.

Never had I witnessed such a battle. Darksoul and Gavakyn, possibly the greatest warriors alive, had squared off on the streets of Lodir.

Wearily I scrambled to my feet watching as the pair circled one another. Darksoul had the reach, but Gavakyn was by far more experienced. The orc lashed out with his knife, and Gavakyn blocked it with the haft of his mace. Darksoul thrust with his sword missing as Gavakyn dodged under it.

"You cannot win," the orc snarled, as more of his soldiers filled the marketplace.

Storm Sorrow did not reply.

"Too tired to talk?" Darksoul teased, lashing out again.

Gavakyn countered and stabbed with the Blood Claw, narrowly missing the orc's leg.

"You should fall back," I said to Gavakyn, still panting from my efforts. "We have fought them as long as we could."

"Not yet," Gavakyn ordered, a knowing smile moving across his face.

From the northwest came a faint pattering of sound. Closer it drew, until the earth began to tremble under the weight of an approaching form. Louder it grew, until, bursting out of a side alley came a battle ram, its iron shod hooves clattering along the cobblestoned street. On its back was a rider, Lorric, her flaming red hair streaming behind her. In the blink of an eye, her lance slammed into the chest of the closest Barkskin, the troll helpless to stop her unexpected attack. The dwarf released her hold on the lance and drew her saber as the troll clutched at its chest and fell to the ground. The captain's mount reared on its hind legs, driving its hooves into the chest of the second troll. Dwarven steel flashed in the light of the morning sun, as Lorric swept her blade in a wide arc slashing the bark-like skin of the troll's throat, spilling dark blood all down its front. With a muted roar, the Barkskin toppled to the ground, choking to death on its own blood.

"I am with you, Storm Sorrow!" Lorric called defiantly, riding her mount toward us both.

"Bah, what matter a few trolls," Darksoul roared, waving the rest of his army forward. "You are outnumbered a thousand to one."

From the south side of the city came a rumbling, growing louder with each passing moment.

For the second time in as many minutes, Gavakyn smiled fiercely. "You sure about that?" he asked, pointing his mace toward the noise.

Craning our necks, we saw a handful of terrified sallowskins enter the marketplace, running for their lives. Belching from the streets behind them came Arik and his three hundred, along with thousands of dwarves flying under the banner of Bolgir Shadowbane. Like an iron wave, the dwarves of Rahm slammed into the ranks of sallowskins, driving them bodily out of the marketplace.

Darksoul was stunned. In a matter of moments, his force was on the run, routed from their occupation in Lodir.

"Morag!" he bellowed, searching for his Witch Doctor.

"He's gone," said Oganna, climbing to her feet. "Run off, like the coward he is."

"Lay down your weapons and you will be spared," Gavakyn added, his eyes fixed on his enemy. "There is nothing left to fight for."

"There is vengeance," Darksoul hissed, taking up his fighting stance once again.

"Raegar, enough," came a deep voice from behind them. Shuffling down the street was Viir. The troll was being supported on either side by two dwarven priests, Armon and Aishe.

Stunned at the sight, Darksoul's face twisted in a sneer. "I never thought you would betray the races of Garthon-Tor," the orc spat in disgust.

"Karn tried to tell you, child," the Seer continued, unaffected by Darksoul's anger. "You chose to follow Morag on his path of blood instead."

"Karn gave me no choice!" the orc raged. "What would you have me do? Join forces with the stumps? I'd rather be dead."

"That can be arranged," Gavakyn muttered darkly. "Order your horde to retreat and the dwarves of Lodir will spill no more black blood."

"You think I'd trust the word of you, Storm Sorrow? "He tilted his head toward Oganna and snorted. "She trusted you once as well. You killed her brother, my clan leader. I will never trust a stump, not while blood runs in my veins."

"Raegar, enough," Oganna said, lowering her weapons. "When it came to *Vey'rok,* Storm Sorrow had no choice."

Darksoul stared at Oganna, his eyes boring into hers. I watched as his shoulders slumped ever so slightly.

"I need more than the word of this stump," he said finally. "Where is the king, or his brother?"

"The king's whereabouts are unknown," I said, my voice weary. "His daughter, the princess, will give you her word."

I turned around, looking for Merin.

"Highness," I shouted, searching the dust filled rubble behind me. More than twenty members of the Gray Company cast their eyes about, looking for the dwarfess, stunned at their inability to locate her.

"She was right here a moment ago," said Bad, lifting his goggles.

"She's off to see the sick blood," said Lucid, happily, putting away his tomahawk.

"Lucid, what do you mean?" I asked, beginning to panic.

"Come, we'll go see Daisy," was all he said in answer. The filthy dwarf began to whistle a happy tune and strolled into the alleyway merchant's stand that led to the underground tunnels.

"I'll come with you," Kora said, wiping tears from her eyes.

"So will I," echoed Monchakka, but Ghost stopped him. "No lad...you. . . have to remain here. I have much to tell you."

"Merin is missing," he argued, his voice hardening. He hesitated, fighting down a well of emotion. "I'll not lose another friend," he continued, a catch in his voice. "Not today."

Ghost paused and handed him Ashten's pistol. "Rifles won't be much good in the tunnels," she said, priming it for him. "Keep your knife and hammer handy."

He nodded once and entered the sewers, trailing closely behind Lucid, Kora and me.

Chapter 25: Betrayal

The shock of Ashten's death had brought tears to Merin's eyes. Seeing him fall into Monchakka's arms had nearly broken her heart. Only Oganna's call for aid had forced her to look away. She watched, her heart in her mouth, as Omens lifted the Blood Claw from the cobblestone streets and ran forward into battle. Wiping away her tears, the princess drew another bolt, preparing to load it to her crossbow.

"Merin!" came a quiet call from the market stall behind her.

Turning around, the princess saw a familiar silhouette in the gloom of the shadows.

"Rhosyn?" she asked, surprised to see her handmaiden. "What happened? Did they take the gate? "She realized as she said it, if the gate mission had failed, then Ashten had died for nothing.

"In truth, I do not know," Rhosyn confessed, waving her friend forward. "But I have other news to tell."

"It must wait," the princess muttered, turning back toward the battle. Omens was entrenched in a fight for his life with two Ravagers.

"It's your father," the handmaiden blurted out, unable to contain her excitement.

Merin hesitated, looking back to Rhosyn. "My father? You've seen him?"

"Yes, my love—he's close by. I've just spoken to him," she continued, eagerly. "I can take you to him, it's not far."

For a moment, Merin felt an inkling of hope. She took three steps forward and stopped. Something did not feel right about this. "You saw him down here in the sewers?" she asked, slowly reaching for the darksteel knife at her belt.

Rhosyn stepped out of the gloom and into the light, her blue eyes like ice.

"Take her," she commanded, spinning around.

A moment of panic hit and Merin turned to run back out to the alley. A Stonebreaker, one with a lion tattoo on his arm, stood in her way.

She opened her mouth to scream when a coarse hand from behind clapped over her mouth, muffling her shriek. She knew the rest of the raiding party was engaged in battle and were unlikely to notice her disappearance. Struggling, Merin dropped her crossbow as her kidnapper grabbed her around the waist and began dragging the princess away from the market.

"Gag her," she heard Rhosyn say from the darkness ahead of her. "We don't need the others rushing to her aid. He prefers her alive to complete the ritual."

Swifty, her hands were bound tightly behind her with a stiff chord of rope. A ragged cloth was stuffed in her mouth, a gag tied roughly over it, keeping her quiet.

Rhosyn appeared suddenly, directly in front of her, and kissed Merin lightly on the cheek. "I'm so sorry, highness, but this moment has been a long time coming." Rearing back, the handmaiden struck Merin a jarring slap across the face. Turning around, Rhosyn moved further down the underground tunnel. Stunned, the princess had to be half-carried by the dwarves of the Lion guard as they followed after Merin's handmaiden.

"Her crossbow," I said, seeing the princess's weapon lying on the ground only minutes later. "She'd not leave it behind willingly."

Lucid sniffed once and kept on going. "Daisy is waiting—so is the old blood."

"Why do you keep calling Merin, 'Old blood," Monchakka asked, following after.

"She has the blood of Varna and Carnak, first rulers of Lodir." Lucid answered, sniffing the air. "I can smell it as easily as you can wiggle your fingers, even in the midst of so many royals, her blood stands out."

"Is that why we are going this way?" Kora asked, looking unconvinced. "Can you smell her blood in the air?"

Lucid spun around and gave Kora a quizzical look. "I'm following the footsteps," he said simply, pointing at the ground. "You can't smell blood inside a body—not unless they've eaten garlic."

We followed Lucid for a good ten minutes until we came to a ramp heading upward on the outskirts of Dregtown. Already the horde had been driven from here. Despite Darksoul's surrender, there were scores of dead sallowskins laying throughout the area. A few dwarven corpses, several days old, were scattered about on the city streets. Clear evidence that, despite the warning given to Bolgir, not everyone in Dregtown had escaped in time.

Once atop the ramp we immediately entered a small ramshackle building tucked into the corner at the furthest edge of town. Lucid lifted his finger to his lips, warning us to stay quiet.

"Daisy is in there," he said, lifting a trapdoor in the floor I never would have seen. A wooden ladder led downward and west, underneath the walls, leading outside of the city. The three of us followed after him, not knowing what to expect.

"Wake up!" a harsh voice barked, followed by a splash of cold water to Merin's face. The gag had been removed, though now she had been tied to a rickety chair in a room someplace beneath the city. The room itself was dark, save for the faint light of a single candle that burned from an old sconce hanging crookedly on the wall. In front of her were a pair of dwarves, her father's personal defenders, the last two members of the lion guard. Standing between them was Rhosyn holding an empty clay pot, wearing a cold look of superiority.

The princess felt her haughtiness of old return and stared defiantly at her handmaiden. "Rhosyn, you have lost your mind! Release me at once!"

"Pretty princess gets her way all the time, doesn't she," Rhosyn mocked, stepping close to Merin. "Not today," she spat, her voice turning harsh. "Today I get what I want, you pox ridden slag."

Merin saw the twisted look on Rhosyn's face turn her pretty countenance into a feral visage of fury.

"What is it that you want?" Merin asked, confusion filling her. "What have I done that you would betray me like this?"

Rhosyn's fury increased its intensity, and she struck the princess another blow, a hard slap that sent Merin reeling once more.

"Betray you?" Rhosyn whispered with a barely suppressed fury. "You betrayed me from the moment we met, you arrogant bitch! Always so superior to the rest of us. I, too, am a princess of the blood, or have you forgotten? I came to Lodir years ago on the promise of becoming its queen."

"You are a princess?" Merin stammered, her ears ringing. "From where? What house?"

Rhosyn's face grew red, as rage threatened to overwhelm her. "I am the third born daughter to King Keymic of house Granitestone," she raged. "I was to be married to your brother!"

Merin thought back through the fog on time and the dizziness from being struck. There had been many suitors once, each vying for her brother's hand in marriage. One by one, they left, having seen the monster her brother could be.

Save one.

"You are the Spider," she whispered, her voice wilting in fear. "The lady of Modru."

Merin narrowed her eyes. "You were even crazier than my brother."

"That's going a bit too far, don't you think?" said a voice from the darkness.

Stepping into the candle light was Orius, King of Lodir.

"Father!" Merin gasped, shocked to see him here.

"Hello child," he responded, his voice weakened with disease. "It's nice to see you again, alive."

Merin's face soured as she glared at her father. "How could you have been party to such treachery?" she snapped, shaking her head. "I am your daughter! Why have you done this?"

Orius moved closer. As he did, Merin could, for the first time, see the madness in his eyes. "What would you have me do?" he asked.

"You are not fit to rule—your brother is dead, and Lodir needs strong leadership."

"So, you decided to betray every dwarf in Rahm?" she stammered.

"They have betrayed me!" he rasped, as loudly as he could. "I have ruled this city for more than five decades. I have given my blood for the Golden Keep. Many of the inhabitants have prospered under my reign. Now, those imbeciles to the south, dwarves who are hundreds of miles from the front lines of battle I deal with daily—they have chosen to vote *me* out of my rightful position!"

His face was red with anger, and his hands shook with rage.

"No daughter, I was not about to stand idly by when everything I have worked for was taken from me."

Merin's heart sank. Some of what he said was true. Merin could even understand why he felt as he did. But, to betray the entire south like this. It was more malicious than she thought him capable of.

"You could have petitioned the rulers of the other seven kingdoms," she argued. "By Goran, why would you betray…"

"Goran?" he thundered. Even in his weakened state his voice echoed throughout the room. "Don't speak to me of the high god! He, who has cursed me with this sickness. He who has abandoned me to my fate? We are here today *because* Goran would not answer the call from his priests. I have had to find alternate means of healing to cure me of this affliction."

Merin hesitated, taking in his words. If the mightiest healers among the dwarves could not cure her father, then he would have had to turn to other ways of restoring his health. That meant…"

"We must hurry," came a crisp voice, accented in the sallowskin tongue. "My brethren have been pushed from the city. It won't be long until we are discovered."

Stepping into the light was an orc, dressed in the clothes of a Witch Doctor.

Morag.

"What have you done?" Merin whispered, her voice tight with fear. "You have sold your soul to the enemy—all to prolong your miserable life?"

"No," Rhosyn hissed, a rapturous smile on her face. "He hasn't sold his soul, he's sold yours."

"Get her on the table," the orc muttered, taking out a knife crafted from black steel. "We need to do this quickly. I fear Bolgir has come out of his hiding place inside the keep and counter-attacked our forces. Hundreds, if not thousands of sallowskin lives will be lost."

"Perhaps if you hadn't broken your word in the first place, there would be less loss of life," Orius snorted, glaring at the orc.

"That was Darksoul's decision, not mine," Morag muttered, as he began to prepare.

"Wait, what are you doing?" Merin asked, seeing the orc draw out a second knife, very thin, specifically made for bloodletting.

"It's your time princess," Rhosyn said, crowing with victory. "In a ritual such as this, your father can only be healed by one who shares his blood. Bolgir was far too well protected, surrounded as he is with Lodir's army. I suggested we use you."

"What?" Merin shrieked, her heart hammering in her chest.

"Oh, did you think it was an accident we chose Omens that night?" Rhosyn quipped. "A dreg Bard of no renown, whose father failed to protect your brother, *my* fiancé, in the attack twenty years ago?"

The handmaiden cackled in true happiness. "No, my love. We couldn't have you die here in the palace—that would be too suspicious. I had your father orchestrate a sallowskin attack on Lodir—one bent on wiping out the dregs once and for all. We would kill two birds with one stone you see. I would help save his life and extract revenge for a wrong done to us both. Omens was our patsy the entire time."

Her face turned angry again, as her voice went cold. "If he'd had the decency to die in the mountains to that Shadow, all of this could have been avoided. We would have brought you here, quickly and quietly—you'd already be dead."

Her smile returned. "No matter, now. You will die and your father has promised to take me as his bride. I will be queen of Lodir! The first order I'll give is to dump your corpse in the market square privy, where every dwarf in the Golden Keep can shit on your bones for all eternity!" She laughed at Merin, purposefully walking behind her.

Merin's eyes followed Rhosyn with a mixture of horror and disgust. "Father," she pleaded, turning to look at the dwarf that raised her. "Don't do this. Killing me will avail you nothing. The others, Gavakyn, Arik, they know the truth…"

A rag, still damp with her saliva, was crammed in her mouth from behind. Rhosyn tied a strip of cloth over the gag, holding it tightly in place.

"No more talking for you dear," she mocked. "There's not a soul in this room who cares what you have to say."

". . . No more talking for you dear," Rhosyn mocked. "There's not a soul in this room who cares what you have to say."

"The hell there isn't," I hissed, emerging from the shadows.

All of them turned and looked on as my companions and I fanned out from the corridor behind us. Without hesitation, we dove forward to engage our enemy. I leapt toward Morag, knowing he was the most deadly adversary in the room. Taken by surprise, the orc had little chance as my machete took off his head with a sickening crunch of bone. His severed head rolled to the wooden floor with a sick clacking sound. Beside me, Lucid ran forward, screaming at the top of his lungs.

"You'll not defile Daisy!"

Lucid's tomahawk flew from his hand, hurled with incredible accuracy. With a *thuuk*, its cast iron blade buried itself in the face of the first dwarven lion. The king's guard fell back to the ground, twitching in the throes of death.

The second lion barely got his sword up to deflect Lucid's longknife. A heartbeat later the two were locked in combat, the Lion guard falling back under the ferocity of Lucid's offensive.

Kora, her face stern and unyielding, sprinted into the room and tackled Rhosyn to the ground. The two she-dwarves fought tooth and nail for several heartbeats until Kora elbow smashed the handmaiden in the face, knocking her senseless.

Monchakka, still reeling from Ashten's death, launched himself at King Orius, who did little to defend himself. The Engineer did not bother with his weapons, content to drive the older dwarf to the ground with a barrage of heavy blows to the face and torso.

"Enough!" I shouted, moving over to Merin. "We need him alive. I want that coward to answer for his crimes." Quickly I removed her gag and the rope binding Merin to the chair.

When loose, she stood and embraced me tightly.

"Are you alright?" I asked, breaking away, looking at her face.

"Yes," she answered, her voice thick, struggling to hold back tears. "They were going to kill me," she continued, her eyes glistening.

"I know," was all I could say, holding her tightly to me once more.

A cry of pain broke our embrace, as Lucid buried his knife in the neck of the last of the lion guards.

Panting, the former Mountaineer kicked at the dead dwarf, his anger evident.

"You think to defile my Daisy," he snarled, through teeth clenched in rage. "Not today you bastards!"

"Easy Lucid," I said, breaking away from Merin. "He won't bother you or Daisy."

I looked around, my eyes taking in the rest of the room. It was filled with old crates and boxes, with a bevy of metal plates and wires strewn all over the place. More prevalent were the colored bottles used to hold candles. Dozens littered the area, each with an ivory white candle jammed in the bottle's openings.

All of us looked over to Monchakka who held his knife at Orius's throat.

The King was beaten and bloody. Weakly, he held up his hands in a gesture for mercy. "Please, don't kill me," he begged in a ragged voice. "I'm the king of Lodir!"

"You are a worthless piece of shit," Monchakka hissed, his face mottled with rage.

"I am a noble," the King scolded, finding some inkling of courage. "Of a line that dates all the way back to the first kings of Rahm."

Monchakka's face darkened further. "I know goblins with more nobility than you, you son-of-a-bitch!"

In a rage, the Engineer heaved the King to his feet and slammed him on the table meant for his daughter. "What kind of king chooses himself over the good of his people?" Monchakka snarled, grasping the front of Orius's robes. "What kind of father sacrifices his child over himself?" Monchakka drew back his fist and slammed it into the King's gut, knocking the wind out of him. "What kind of dwarf slaughters his own people for the price of personal vengeance?"

Monchakka drew his hammer and held it in front of Orius, who began weeping in agony. "Because of you, Ashten Raine, the first dwarf who ever believed in me, lies dead. All because of your cowardice and fear."

"Please," coughed Orius, trying to draw breath. "I demand justice, and a fair trial."

Monchakka narrowed his eyes in hate as he leaned in close to the King. "This is the only justice you will get from me," he roared, swinging his hammer over his head.

"Monchakka, no!" came a voice from behind us.

Ghost and her squad of sharpshooters had made their way into the room. Carefully she stepped forward, her hand outstretched toward the infuriated engineer.

"This is not our way," she said, her voice gentle and sad. "I would not have you become a murderer because of him. Let go of your hate. Orius will go down in history as the worst king Rahm has ever seen. Do not darken your soul on account of him."

Stepping closer, she reached out and lay her hand on his shoulder. "Ashten would agree with me."

Monchakka stared at her, his eyes slowly returning from their madness. Carefully, he put his hammer away and buried his head on Ghost's shoulder, weeping at the loss of his mentor.

"Take him," Ghost said, motioning toward Orius. Quickly the members of her squad secured the King and led him away. Rhosyn too, was removed from the room, still unconscious. Monchakka and

Kora left with Ghost and her Engineers, leaving Merin and me alone, with Lucid.

"Not used to so many people, are we Daisy?" Lucid said, seeming to mutter to himself.

"Who is the Daisy you keep talking about?" Merin asked gently, coming over to embrace me again.

With a grunt, the unkempt dwarf made his way over to one of the crates leaning against an old shelf and righted it, placing it close to the wall. He made sure to step on both lion guard corpses, in a petty act of defiance toward the two.

"Daisy is my best mate," he said, lighting a candle held in the neck of a bottle. Looking closely I saw it was the bottle he had purchased days ago back in Barrel Falls. Carefully he lit the wick using the still flickering candle burning in the sconce. Once alight, he shuffled over toward the crate he had turned upright and reached down, picking up a metal sheet filled with tiny holes. He placed the sheet gently on the crate, using the seams in the wood to hold it securely in place. Carefully, his hands steady, Lucid held the candle behind the metal, where it cast its light on the wall.

There, in that dark room at the edge of the city, I saw a beautifully detailed outline of a dog seated on its haunches. Merin and I looked on in wonder, as Lucid replaced the metal sheet with another. This time it showed the outline of a dog at a full run.

"That's Daisy?" I asked, shocked at what I saw.

"Aye," Lucid said, his voice filled with a bittersweet sadness. "She was my best mate when I served with the Mountaineers. Went with me everywhere. She was our squad's good luck charm on more than one occasion."

His voice sounded normal, without its customary madness.

"We walked point together so often—I've lost count of the number of times she saved my life. A few years ago, we had a mission here, near the Golden Keep. Daisy and I stumbled across Orius conspiring with the Sallowskins, even back then. One of the guards had seen Daisy as she'd sniffed them out. The bastard Lion guard shot her in the neck with a crossbow bolt. There was nothing I could do to stop him."

He stopped and sighed, staring up at the golden outline on the wall. "I managed to escape the guards who chased after me and brought my girl down here. Try as I might, I couldn't save her. She died right here in this room, her head in my lap."

Lucid sat in front of the silhouette of Daisy as a single tear ran down his face. "She was the only friend I ever had."

We sat quietly, for a moment, not knowing what to say.

Merin placed her hand on his shoulder. "I am sorry to hear about Daisy," she whispered, giving him a little smile. "But you are wrong. You have friends, right here in this room. I will never forget what you have done to help me."

"I didn't do anything," he whispered, wiping his tears away.

"You've saved me, twice now," she answered, making him look at her. "Once in the woods near Barrel Falls and once today."

"You also led the orcs away when you stole the Blood Claw," I said, giving him a smile. "You also saved Oganna from Darksoul," I continued. "Even before that, I've always admired you Lucid. Remember that time in the marketplace with the icicles? I saw what you were doing. You tried to save everyone. You are a good person, better than most I've known."

He was looking at us both, his eyes unblinking.

"I'm a wee bit mad, you know?" he said, scratching at his head. "Not as mad as you, Omens, but I'm a bit unstable."

"You think I'm madder than you are?" I asked with a laugh.

"Aye, I do," he beamed. "You remember when you seduced the baker's wife and daughter on the same day?"

My eyes widened, and I gave a slight shake of my head trying to tell him to stop talking. "I don't know what you're…"

"Don't shake your head at me," he continued, oblivious to my discomfort. "I saw you that morning. The baker left for his shop at sunrise, and you climbed up that cedar barrel outside his bedroom window. I could hear the cries coming from inside shortly after. I always meant to ask you, was there a dog in there, because something was howling like I've never heard."

I let out a nervous little laugh and held my hands up defensively. "I don't remember any of that happening…"

"Sure you do," he said, clipping me on the back of the neck in comradery. "Because an hour after the howling stopped, I heard it again, but this time from the other side of the house. I watched you climb out of the daughter's room soon after. Your tunic was on backwards and you saw me looking at you when you hit the ground."

I began to rub at my temple, refusing to look at Merin who was staring at me with what I could only guess was a withering frown.

"I'm sure you are mistaken," I mumbled, shaking my head.

"There's no mistake," he said, giving me a conspiratorial smile. "You looked at me and winked, saying, 'It'll be our little secret,' before you headed off to market. I always meant to ask, afterwards, did you go and buy bread from the baker? It only seems right, since he was the only one in the family you didn't visit that day."

I knew this was going to be funny to me later, but right then, I wanted a hole to open up under my feet and swallow me.

Chapter 26: Ironblood

Three days passed before things truly settled down. The other Sallowskin leaders wanted to continue their offensive as it was the first time any of their hordes had breached the walls of a dwarf kingdom. Darksoul, as good as his word, did what he could to convince them otherwise. However, it wasn't until the armies from Kazic-Thul and Durn Buldor arrived that they were finally dissuaded.

I can't really blame the sallowskins. They had a massive army, tens of thousands strong and, besides killing a few hundred dwarves, had little to show for it. I'm sure a few of them had looted what they could from Dregtown and the surrounding areas, but the real treasures lay in the palace, which had held strong under the steady hand of Bolgir.

Rhosyn confessed to the entire affair, especially since she knew Orius was not long for this world. Her cooperation was paramount, not in condemning the King, for he had done that himself while speaking to his daughter—but in finding his place in history as the traitorous and weakest king Rahm had ever known.

I, along with Monchakka and Kora, had heard much of his confession as well. Rhosyn bargained with Bolgir to spare her life and spend the rest of her days in a prison in Lodir. As other details began to emerge, we found out that Orius had brokered a deal some time ago to find out where Gavakyn and the Blood Claw had been hiding.

There were a few other, more personal matters to attend to. Both revealed secrets I would never have dreamed possible.

The first and most important was the funeral for Ashten. It was a private ceremony attended by the survivors of Gray Company, along with those of us who had fought beside him. For perhaps the first time in history, sallowskins were in attendance for the funeral of a dwarven royal. Draega, Oganna, Karn and Viir all were invited to join us. With them came Darksoul. No one wished to see him, but Viir said it was necessary, without giving an explanation.

King Helfer was there, and spoke well of his brother, citing his many victories in battle throughout the lands of both Rahm and Garthon-Tor. Ghost delivered an emotional speech. She spoke more of the private moments the two of them had shared, revealing the depths of the dwarf he had become over the years.

Afterwards, Jax and I were asked to play a song in his memory. Jax smiled and played a fiery tune on his mandolin that Ashten had been fond of hearing. When it came to be my turn, I planned on playing something a bit slower in the hope of conjuring up images of his life. However, like when I had been near Thorana's corpse, I felt an overwhelming urge to play something, the same dirge I had conjured in the cairn at Draymore's Outpost.

As I set the flute to my lips, I could feel the music flowing from me. The melody, filled with sorrow, brought a tear to many an eye. Once again, a glow began to emanate from Ashten's body, until his spectral figure rose in front of us. The ghostly apparition did not look at Ghost or Monchakka as I thought it might. Instead, it gazed in the distance over my head, at someone behind me.

I heard a second melody, this one coming from a high-pitched reed instrument. At first, I thought Jax had taken out his flute and began to play with me. When I glanced over at him, he was staring behind me, wearing an awestruck look on his face.

I heard footsteps draw next to me as this new melody synchronized perfectly with my own. As it grew louder, I noticed Ashten's corporal form grow more solid, less like an apparition. The form stepped lightly to the ground and reached out to Ghost, who stood, unmoving, with tears streaming down her face.

Ashten's hand moved to touch her cheek. "I love you," he whispered, giving her a knowing smile. The corners of Ghost's lips turned upward for just a moment, her heart beating with a bittersweet joy that could not possibly last.

Looking away from Ghost, Ashten's spirit took in the sight of Monchakka. "It breaks my heart to leave you, now of all times," he said, placing a hand on his shoulder. "But there is no one I'd rather have by Ghost's side than you."

He gave Monchakka a warm smile. "Take care of them lad. I will love you, always."

Looking up at Viir, he nodded and spoke one last time.

"I am ready, Seer."

With those words, the old troll stepped forward and took out a crystal vial from under his robes placing it atop Ashten's chest. Stepping away from the body, the troll set his staff firmly on the ground in front of him and extended it outward.

"Eonitu Nehu Ashta!" he whispered, looking intently at the vial.

"What are you doing?" Monchakka asked, glancing at Ghost in alarm.

"What is necessary," she answered, staring up at the apparition.

A slight breeze was felt by all those present.

"Eonitu Nehu Ashta!" Viir said again, louder than the first time.

The air grew stronger, making the vial vibrate in place.

"What is…" Kora began to ask, when Gavakyn cut her off.

"It will be alright lass," he said, holding his cloak tightly to keep it from billowing in the breeze.

From underneath the vial, a blue light began to glow from Ashten's chest.

All watched in fascination as the Seer shouted the words of power again.

"*Eonitu Nehu Ashta!*"

The breeze became a wind, strong enough to raise the vial in the air, where it hovered over the still form of the leader of the Gray Company.

Everyone at the funeral had to raise their hands in order to shield their eyes from particles of dust that whirled around them.

The blue glow from inside Ashten was drawn out of his body and took up the space above the vial. Viir motioned with his hand and the mist began to fill the container.

"Gavakyn!" the Seer shouted, visibly trying to contain the magical essence of the Engineer.

Storm Shadow was already moving. Quickly he stepped forward as the blue mist entered the top of the vial. Once full, the Seer ceased his magic, dropping to his knees. Inside the length of a heartbeat, Armon and Nathrak were next to him, their eyes filled with concern.

Gavakyn had grabbed the vial, holding it reverently in front of him.

"What was that?" Monchakka demanded, his voice filled with anguish. "Is this some sallowskin ritual?"

"Easy lad," Gavakyn said, handing the vial to Viir. "Ashten made his decision years ago. I assure you, this is what he wanted, for you most of all."

"I don't understand," Monchakka continued, looking at me in confusion.

"We will discuss it soon," Ghost said, walking over, putting a comforting arm on his shoulder.

Monchakka made as if to argue further, but nodded at Ghost, trusting that she knew what had happened.

I went to put my flute away and looked at the person standing at my side, wishing to thank them for their assistance.

My heart froze in my chest.

There, standing next to me, holding a well-made syrinx, was Darksoul, the orc.

"The Piper," said Lucid from his place next to Jax.

I watched as the old Bard glanced down to Lucid and he whispered something I could just make out.

"We need to talk."

I walked away from that funeral with many questions racing through my mind. What had happened to Ashten? Why had Darksoul joined me? What did the elders of our races know that I did not? Heavy were my thoughts as Merin and I walked away.

"What do you suppose he meant?" Merin mused, clenching my hand tightly.

"Who?" I asked, not really listening, caught up as I was in my own thoughts.

"Ashten," she answered, looking up at me wistfully. "Didn't you hear what he said to Monchakka?"

"I don't remember, exactly," I confessed. "I was concentrating on the music."

"He said, 'Take care of them lad. I will love you, always,'" Merin answered, repeating Ashten's words.

"I don't know what you're getting at," I said, looking at her in confusion.

"'Take care of *them*,' she replied, rolling her eyes at me. "Who is, *them*? Ghost? That's just one person. Who else was he referring to?" Who indeed.

As surprising as the funeral turned out to be, nothing was more shocking than what was revealed to Monchakka and me at dusk on the next day.

The trio from clan Ironhenge had invited Kora, Merin and me to their private quarters an hour after sundown. I invited Lucid along, almost as an afterthought. The four of us entered the chambers reserved for visiting nobility. Ashten's brother Helfer was busy working with Bolgir who, it was decided, would be the next ruler of Lodir.

Merin had confided in me that this was the best-case scenario for the Golden Keep. Many of the other nobles and clan leaders were set against the daughter of Orius becoming the new queen. Not only was she his offspring, but she was deemed too young for such responsibility.

We filed in, exchanging pleasantries with one another, and sat down. On the table in front of us was a large assortment of salted meats and cheeses, with a carafe of red wine sitting next to a small keg of stout.

Arik cleared his throat and looked at his sister who nodded briefly.

"Before we begin," he said, his gruff voice quiet. "I wanted to thank you all. According to my sister and Gavakyn, each of you performed admirably in the battle three days ago. Had it not been for those of you in this room, along with the other members of your raiding parties, there is no way we would have taken back the city in such a timely manner. You have been called here because Aurora and I trust each of you."

When he said this, he kept a lingering eye on me, as if to convince himself of his last statement.

"I ask that you take care whom you tell about what you hear in this room tonight. I know it will come as a shock to all of you."

"You can trust us," Monchakka said, glancing at Kora, squeezing her hand.

"That's good," Arik replied, firmly pressing his lips together. "Because this might not be easy for you to hear."

"What's happened?" Merin asked. She had been a bit distant these last few days—not that I blamed her. Between her father's betrayal and the loss of her best friend, trust was in short supply for her. I think the bonds she'd formed with the rest of us was the only thing keeping her sane.

"Nothing to alarm you about," Arik said, not wishing to rile up any fears. "However, Aurora and I wanted to speak to you all, in particular about Ashten. For this news has to do with him."

I could feel Ghost, of all people, tense up at her brother's words. I studied her face carefully. She was looking directly at Monchakka. The others, I knew, did not see it yet, but I could. There was a world of emotion behind that look she gave him. More prevalent than any other, was fear.

"What is it you have to tell us, father?" Monchakka asked, sensing something was not right.

"Well...," Arik began, before Ghost cut him off.

"I will tell him."

Arik frowned. "No sister, it was I who..."

"We all made the decision," she snapped, more forcefully than she needed too. Knowing she had been too hard on him, Ghost dropped her voice. "Please, let me do this. I have wanted to tell him for a long time."

Arik scratched at his graying whiskers before relenting with a nod.

Ghost took a deep breath and looked directly at Monchakka.

"Ashten and I met many years ago," she began. "Arik and Helfer were boon companions when they were young, and it was only natural that our families intermingled from time to time. Ashten and I grew up together, and before long, fell in love. While Clan Ironhenge was allied with Clan Raine, ours was not of the noble class. Any union between Ashten and me, we knew, would be looked down upon."

She paused and took a drink of red wine from a flagon on the table in front of her.

"I tried to stay away from him, for the sake of both of our families' honor—but Ashten simply would not relent."

She smiled, despite her discomfort. "He used to tell me he loved me so much, he would defy the world for me."

Her smile faded and she continued. "In the spring of my twentieth year, I discovered that I had become pregnant with his child."

I sat back, shocked to hear this news.

"I wanted to keep the pregnancy hidden and move away from Kazic-Thul, but Ashten wouldn't allow it. He marched into the throne room and demanded his father, the former king, recognize our child as a legitimate heir to the throne."

She sighed and shook her head. "He was so brave and foolish at the same time. He was convinced his father, old king Dousin, would accept the child. Unfortunately, Ashten was wrong."

She stopped again, looking at Monchakka with tears in her eyes.

"Ashten and I would not give up the child, and we were forced into exile—to live outside Kazic-Thul."

"Yes," interrupted Merin, her voice clear. "But you'd be able to raise the child as your own. Away from the politics of the city and the king."

Ghost shook her head. "It was not so simple," she replied. "Ashten and I were given nothing to start with. His family abandoned him. Arik had disowned me as well."

"I should not have done that," Arik admitted, his face dropping in shame. "It was a mistake. I was so young then, and unforgiving."

"You did what you thought was right," Ghost said, nodding at him.

She turned back to the rest of us and continued with her tale. "With little money and no support, I knew we would not be able to raise the child on our own."

Ghost's voice slowed and I could almost taste the guilt she felt.

"What happened to the child?" Monchakka asked, still unable to see what was right in front of him.

Ghost made to speak, but her words froze in her mouth.

"Please sister," Arik said, placing a hand on her back. "I will tell…"

"No," she hissed, finding her courage. Looking at Monchakka she forced herself to continue.

"I gave care of my child into the hands of the only person I trusted, even though he'd cast me out of my clan."

Monchakka blinked as her words sank in.

"You mean…" he faltered, looking from Ghost to Arik, "you are not my father?"

"No lad," Arik confessed. "I am your uncle. Ashten Raine was your father. He was as fine a dwarf as I've ever known."

His eyes widened in absolute shock, turning toward Ghost. "That means that you are…"

"Your mother," Ghost finished, staring at Monchakka. "I'm sorry, my son," she said, her voice breaking. "I wanted to tell you so many times, but...I have no excuse. I should have never let you go."

Monchakka was staring at both of them in surprise. He sat speechless for several heartbeats, trying to make sense of the news he had just received.

"If he's the son of Ashten Raine, then he's the heir to the Granite Throne," Merin stammered, giving Monchakka a wide-eyed look.

"Aye, he is," Arik said, looking at the dwarf he had raised. "I'm sorry you had to find out like this lad. Ashten and I discussed the possibility of telling you before the raid. We agreed it might be a distraction and decided to wait until after."

Monchakka sat back in his chair, stunned by the news. He looked down at his hand as he felt a squeeze from Kora.

"You're my mother," he said at last, looking back up at Ghost.

"Aye," she said, barely able to breathe.

Slowly Monchakka stood and looked her squarely in the eyes. "I've never had a mother before," he said, his voice steady, considering the news. "Tell me, do you love me?"

Ghost stood up, her face tight with emotion. "I have always loved you son," she answered, her voice trembling. "I'm so sorry I have not been in your life."

Monchakka smiled bravely at her, as tears filled his eyes. "I hope you can tell me of my father's life. I would very much like to know more about him...and you."

He extended his arms toward Ghost who engulfed him in a bear hug as sobs wracked her body. Merin looked on and I saw her wipe tears from her own eyes, as Kora and Arik joined them. I slipped behind Merin and hugged her tightly.

"Was that the big secret you needed to tell us?" Lucid chimed in, popping a piece of roasted pork in his mouth, "or is there more?"

I laughed and pulled him close to Merin and me, and the three of us watched the family reunion.

"Your father was so proud to have you join our Company," Ghost said, when they finally broke away from one another. "We both marveled at how quickly you picked things up. It was our dream that you become Captain one day. I hope it is something you will consider."

"Maybe," he answered, glancing next to him. "If Kora doesn't take it from me first."

As the four of them shared in the closeness of familial bonds, Merin and I made to leave. However, at that moment the door opened. In walked Gavakyn, followed closely by Karn and Viir.

"I ask that you excuse this interruption," Gavakyn said, his face serious. "But something has come to my attention."

Arik looked up and snorted derisively. "This is a family and friend affair, Storm Sorrow. Whatever you have to say can wait."

Gavakyn and Arik stared darkly at one another, neither looking like they were about to back down.

"By Kruk," Karn croaked, shaking his head. "You dwarves are the most pigheaded lot I've ever seen. Not even the Ogres of Clan Crabvine are as stubborn as you."

Arik made to retort, but Ghost placed a hand on his shoulder and stopped him. "You have proven to be an honorable ally, Karn. So, too, has Viir. While it's true my family and I have much to discuss, those issues can wait. What is it that you need to tell us?"

Gavakyn nodded to Ghost and then looked over his shoulder at Viir.

"Say your piece," he grunted at the troll, moving next to Merin and me.

Viir bent his tall frame and ducked beneath the doorway, entering the private quarters.

"May I?" he asked, motioning to a cushioned divan located on the southern part of the room.

"Of course," Ghost said, giving him a quick smile. "Would you care for some refreshments?"

"Perhaps in a bit," he answered, sliding his considerable bulk into the comfort of the divan. He leaned back and sighed deeply. The troll had mostly recovered from his ordeal on the battlements near the gate. Armon, to everyone's surprise, had healed him to almost perfect health. However, I could tell there was still some lingering pain that Viir was going through, and he still had a ways to go.

"I want to apologize ahead of time," he began, looking at each of us. "I am given signs to read—flashes really, but often their meaning is unclear, or open to interpretation."

He turned his attention to Gavakyn, who reached forward and poured himself a flagon of wine. "For example, I knew Gavakyn was fated to win back the Blood Claw, though I did not know what the circumstances would entail. I only knew he had to travel to the Jagged Lands and do his best to retrieve the artifact."

Viir paused a moment and shifted his bulk forward. "I will take some wine, if you would?" he asked Gavakyn, who obliged, pouring him a flagon.

"What is it you are apologizing for?" Kora asked, somewhat skeptical of the Seer.

Viir drank from his flagon and set it back down with a small sound of glass striking wood.

"Because I know, now, what needs to be done," he answered. "It was not made clear to me until my recent stint with death."

He motioned to the goblin next to him. "Karn and I have both been in contact with the spirits that rest near *Mott-Godaan*. After much speculation with the five, I was finally told what must transpire."

He paused again and looked closely at Monchakka.

"It will affect you, Prince Raine," he said, pressing his lips together firmly.

"Wha…what?" he stammered in surprise. "How did you…I only found out minutes ago. How did you know?"

Viir said nothing. He only moved his head slightly to the left. All of our eyes turned to look upon the only person sitting on that side of the room.

"Are you going to eat that?" Lucid said, stabbing at a roasted squab sitting on a platter in front of Arik.

"Lucid," I asked, motioning to the unkempt dwarf. "Did you know Monchakka was a prince?"

"Course I did," he answered, his lips smacking together. "I could smell the old blood in him the moment we met."

We all muttered to ourselves, shocked at his admission.

"Twasn't the only one here with old blood," Lucid sniffed, gulping down another flagon of wine. "Merin has it, of course," he continued, taking a large bite of squab. "She has a bit in her too," he finished, pointing casually at Ghost.

"Me?" she asked, stunned. "I'm not of the old blood. My line is far more recent. You must be mistaken."

"Nah," he answered, wiping grease from his mouth. "You don't have the old blood. What's growing inside you does."

Each of us took a moment to understand the implications of his words.

Arik's eyes flew wide open, and he looked in surprise at this sister. "Are you with child?" he asked.

"I...I don't know," she answered, honestly. "It's been..." she narrowed her eyes counting days inside her head. "It's possible," she admitted, a stunned look on her face. "I am...late."

"You are pregnant," Lucid said nonchalantly. "I knew it the moment I saw you at Barrel Falls. Hell, your husband's specter said as much yesterday."

"Take care of *them*," murmured Merin, looking at me with satisfaction. "That's what he meant!"

"I offer you my congratulations Ghost—but the question remains," Kora said, unrelenting. "What does any of this have to do with Monchakka?" she asked again, still waiting for an answer. "How is he to be affected by any of this?"

"Because, he has been chosen as one who must go to *Mott-Godaan*, just as his father did before him," answered Viir.

"I will not be ordered about by you," Monchakka said, his voice soft. "I have done my part and then some in this war. I will not abandon my mother when I've only just discovered her existence— especially if she is with Ashten's child. . . my little brother, or sister!"

"You will go," Karn barked, his eyes flat. "None of us wants this. However, our personal desires are outweighed by what is best for our people."

"You do not command here," Arik shouted, his voice hard.

"Neither do you," Gavakyn retorted, staring daggers at the General.

Lucid began to laugh, a rolling sound that made them all take notice.

"What the hell is so funny?" Arik snapped, his face twisting in a sneer.

"You are all funny," Lucid cackled, sinking his teeth into a piece of marbled cheese. "There is only one person in this room that has the authority you all strive for."

"Who would that be?" Arik asked, clearly unamused. "Monchakka is a fine lad, brave and strong, but he does not possess the experience needed to undertake leadership in such an expedition."

Arik stopped and glanced at Merin. "The princess is brave and true, but she is even less prepared to lead such an undertaking."

"Old blood, both of them," the former Mountaineer sniffed, nodding at each. "Brave and strong, but no, they are not of whom I speak."

"Then what do you mean?" asked Ghost, peering at him intently. "Speak plainly."

"One of the ancient blood," Lucid answered, his voice even and somber.

"Ancient blood?" scoffed Arik, his face souring in confusion. "Whose blood would that be?"

The room grew quiet as Lucid looked slowly around the room.

"The blood I have sensed since first coming to Lodir," he answered quietly. "The blood of the most ancient dwarven king. The greatest ruler in the history of Rahm. I speak of the Ironblood line."

There was a dead silence in the room for the span of several heartbeats.

"Draymore?" said Ghost, her voice a whisper. "But…his line died out long ago."

"His official line did," said Karn in agreement. "However, he had a child, a daughter, out of wedlock. She and her descendants have lived in Lodir for the last ten centuries."

"Impossible," Arik said, disbelief in his voice. "There would have been records of such a dwarf…"

"The records were wiped clean," Viir added from his place beside Karn.

"How could you possibly know that?" Merin asked, looking at him with suspicion.

Viir glanced at the Shaman, who gave him an encouraging nod.

"Draymore's son, or the spirit of his son, told me," he answered with a shrug.

"I don't believe you," Arik snapped, leaning forward angrily.

"You should," Lucid said, eyeballing the General with disapproval. "For his ancestor sits with us here in this room."

All eyes turned to Gavakyn who snorted with disdain. "It is not I who carries the blood of the king of king's."

"Then who?" demanded Kora, glancing at Monchakka.

"He does," Lucid answered, lifting his hand and pointing his finger.

"That's not possible," I said, my voice suddenly dry.

"It's true lad," Viir said, his face tight with anxiety.

Slowly, I sat back in my chair, incredulous.

The person Lucid had pointed at was me.

Here ends book 1 in the Dwarves of Rahm Series. The story continues in book 2, The Dwarves of Rahm: Gates of Hell.

If you enjoyed The Dwarves of Rahm: Omens of War, then check out <u>The Raven and the Crow series</u> or other works by <u>Michael K. Falciani</u>

The Raven and the Crow series: https://www.amazon.com/gp/product/B0971MB8BL

Michael K. Falciani: https://www.amazon.com/stores/Michael-K.-Falciani/author/B087WM4PN7

Or find other great titles from Three Ravens Publishing on our main web site at https://threeravenspublishing.com/impressions/

Omens of War

You can also keep up to date with our latest release announcements on Scifi.radio and get some of the best fandom programing on the planet.

Scifi for your Wifi